SANCTION FOUR

KURT WINANS

SANCTION FOUR

A NOVEL

bhc
press™

Livonia, Michigan

Editor: Rebecca Rue
Proofreader: Amanda Lewis

SANCTION FOUR

Published by BHC Press

Library of Congress Control Number: 2020934449

ISBN: 978-1-64397-166-7 (Hardcover)
ISBN: 978-1-64397-167-4 (Softcover)
ISBN: 978-1-64397-168-1 (Ebook)

For information, write:
BHC Press
885 Penniman #5505
Plymouth, MI 48170

Visit the publisher:
www.bhcpress.com

SANCTION FOUR

SANCTION FOUR

Preamble

FOLLOWING DIRECT INSTRUCTIONS from earlier that evening, Secret Service Agent Heath Bishop knocked on the bedroom door of President Jordan Harwell at precisely their agreed upon time. For Heath it was not the first instance of standing outside that specific door in the upstairs residence portion of the White House, as in the past he had been posted there for protective duty status on numerous occasions. However, what made this occurrence different from any other was his advance knowledge that he would be invited inside the room for a private conversation. That upcoming action would go against established protocol, but the president had expressed a desire to converse with Heath in a location that he believed would be more secure than the Oval Office.

After hearing verbal instructions from beyond the door to enter, Heath did so and moved toward the twin couches where the president was seated.

From a respectable distance of roughly ten feet, he asked with dutiful professionalism, "You wanted to see me, sir?"

With a confirming nod and an extended arm motion toward the adjacent couch, Jordan Harwell, in a volume of speech roughly half that of his normal level, replied, "Indeed I do, Heath, please sit down."

Immediately heeding to the hospitable offer as if receiving a direct order, Heath moved to sit while responding, "Yes, sir."

Leaning forward toward his guest, the president then began by stating, "Heath, I think you know that there is no one whom I trust with my safety, or that of my legacy, more than you. Based on the two bullets you once took while protecting me, it would be difficult for anyone to argue against my viewpoint on the matter as being rightly justified. That being said, I have asked you to the residence this evening so that we may discuss something of tremendous importance that is rather delicate. I believe this private location for such a meeting is necessary to ensure that the content of our upcoming discussion remains both uninterrupted and kept off any official record. Now is that clearly understood?"

"Yes, sir, I understand."

"That's good, Heath. Now I'm sure that as I explain what must be done, you will have several questions. Please feel free to ask them at any time but do so quietly."

Then in matching the soft tone of the president to express not only his grasp of the given instruction but the potential gravity of the upcoming topic, Heath replied, "Yes, sir, I understand. Anything you need, sir."

"Thank you, Heath. I knew that I could count on you."

Throughout the next several minutes the president explained his position and what he hoped Heath would do to help resolve the situation. As Heath listened intently to the plan, he realized that as with most of what the president conveyed throughout the time they had known each other, it was both sound and well thought out. However, in this instance there were some obvious gaps in the complete picture that would need to be addressed. With that impression came the added comprehension that in the modern world no individual could achieve the lofty position of President of the United States, no matter how well intended, without striking a deal with some adversary along the way. In the case of Jordan Harwell, the forming of a certain agreement with a few individuals during his political rise in his home state of Washington—and then on the various campaign trails for national office—had been made long before he took an oath as the nation's chief executive. That agreement would lead to what could be viewed as an inevitable byproduct, an insurance policy that would silence a few key voices until the days after his presidency if it became necessary.

While continuing to listen, Heath became aware that the president had no desire for the public to learn of certain aspects or of the indiscretions of his actions back then, nor did the man want them to surface in the future. Therefore, the president had come up with a plan that could pressure any of his potential enemies into maintaining their silence after his second term in office concluded. Although that task would be impossible to achieve without trusted help, those who possessed the damaging information, and thus leverage over Jordan Harwell, would need to receive a message of serious deterrence before any of them considered going public with what they knew. In addition, each family would be made to realize that their newfound suffering could be amplified in the future should the need ever arise.

Based on what had been brought forth by the president, Heath knew that the overall scope of the intended plan would not be easy to accomplish. As instructed, he freely voiced his opinion that although the end game objective was perhaps justified, the plan to achieve it could take months or even a few years to see it through with no guarantee of successful completion. Heath expressed that, as the first point of many factors to consider, the most reliable intelligence on several fronts would be essential. To that end, said action would require that those providing the intelligence must never know the reasoning behind why it was being delivered. Other variables, such as the necessity for cautious and meticulous planning, a bit of luck during the execution to keep security risks at a minimum, and the correct person to handle the multilevel task would also be a must. Each of those elements, and surely others that had not yet been factored into the equation, would in their own way be paramount to success.

In closing, he added, "Sir, I believe we will need to address and clarify several issues before we put this plan in motion to enhance the chance of its success. Beyond that, the overall process will require a collective patience by all the players, from you on down through me to the selected operative. But I do believe that it can be done."

"I'm glad that you see it all so clearly, Heath, and yes, I agree with your assessment. Patience will be essential."

"Yes, sir. And thank you."

"Now, I would like this matter addressed sooner as opposed to later, which is why I have brought it to your attention presently."

"I understand, sir."

"All right, so you mentioned that it could take months or years to complete. Although I can certainly be accepting of the former, the latter would in time become an issue."

"Very well, sir. May I ask what you see as the top end of allowable time for this plan to be completed?"

President Harwell spoke to what he viewed as an easily defined timetable. The nation had just cast votes for the midterm elections in the most recent of days, and although members of his party would soon enjoy a majority in both the house and senate as a result of those tallies, he as the president was now in a lame-duck position. In slightly less than two years someone else would be elected to follow in his footsteps, with that individual then assuming the mantle of high office in January of 2033. That inescapable fact, as defined by the constitution, would leave Jordan Harwell in a virtually powerless position to do much of anything other than author a book and go on a lecture tour. But he also expressed that until such a time came, he possessed a certain amount of power and leverage that could be beneficial. As president the man could call upon various resources when needed, especially with a now more favorable legislative branch of the government to work with, and in the extreme, perhaps an executive order could be issued.

As Heath nodded in agreement, the president concluded with his belief that they had a finite amount of time to get this done. Give or take a few weeks, the window of opportunity was roughly two years. If success was not achieved, the president felt that the American people would remember him as a less than favorable member of society, and the history books could cast an even darker view. In turn, such an impression upon his legacy could damage positive legislation that came about during his administration.

Aware that many things in life can take more time to accomplish than originally planned, the president wanted to account for that probability by creating a cushion. He proposed completion of his plan by the 2032 national election, as such a date would allow for a fallback position of roughly seven weeks until Christmas. Then if for some reason it was required, there would also be an emergency buffer of four additional weeks before the newly elected president was sworn in.

Heath agreed that such a timeframe sounded doable, and that building in the cushion of extra weeks would be a prudent move in the event unexpected snags were encountered.

In response, President Harwell said, "Very well then, it's decided. Now do you have any areas of concern that need to be discussed before we begin?"

"Yes, sir, I do. But I prefer not to comment on specifics at this moment. This matter will require some additional thought regarding logistics, so with your permission, I would like to mull this over for a little while to develop a clearer picture."

After a few seconds of quiet contemplation, the president nodded positively as he rose from the couch and stated, "Very well, Heath. Let's meet here at the same time tomorrow evening to discuss any thoughts you may have on the matter."

Standing at nearly the same instant, Heath replied, "Yes, sir, until tomorrow evening then. And thank you."

Throughout much of the night, and portions of the following day when his duty would allow, Heath mulled over troublesome aspects as well as how the plan could be successfully carried out. Several items had occurred to him, and now he would present his thoughts to the president on how to circumvent many potential obstacles.

Once again knocking on the residence door at the agreed upon time, Heath entered when instructed.

Then while seated in the same location as the previous evening, the president motioned toward the opposite couch and said softly, "Good evening, Heath, please sit down."

A reply of "Yes, sir, thank you" was projected in a matching tone.

Not wasting time with any idle chitchat as Heath took a seat, the president asked him bluntly, "So then. With regard to our discussion last evening, what questions or concerns have you come up with?"

"Well, sir. There are several points that I would like you to consider."

"All right, I'm listening. And don't be afraid to speak candidly."

Following the given latitude, Heath began with his opinion of how vital it would be throughout the entire endeavor to keep the president in a position of plausible deniability as much as possible. Therefore, a need existed to go outside the recognized norm by selecting an operative who had no affiliation with any federal agency or law enforcement group. That same mindset would also include any state or local law enforcement officers, and Heath believed that the use of military personnel should also be eliminated from consideration. He stressed that in his position as the current commander in chief, the president should not employ the use of anyone from the armed services to do his personal bidding. If such an act were to be discovered, it could be interpreted as a blatant abuse of presidential power.

After assessing Heath's prudent logic, the president asked, "What else?"

Heath added that for additional security levels the entire project should be privately funded by the president so that there could be absolutely no link to any use of federal funding or taxpayer dollars. He also stated that no aspect of the operation should involve electronic transmissions of any kind, and nothing between the two of them should ever be discussed on any cell phone, as all of those communication methods could be easily traced. Taking it further, Heath stated that any interaction involving the president would need to be either face-to-face verbal or by concise, handwritten coded notes. In short, it was strongly urged by Heath that they go old school throughout the length of the operation to avoid even the slightest possibility of a future subpoena.

After voicing his appreciation of Heath's recommended security measures, including the exclusive use of private funds and how they would create distance between him and any wrongdoing, the president asked how the handwritten notes that Heath spoke of could be handled.

Based upon the large volume of correspondence that the president received on a daily basis, and the accompanying security measures that included a team of staffers who sorted through it all, there was too much risk involved with sending them through standard White House mail. As for outgoing messages, those, like everything else from the Oval Office, would be typed on official letterhead with the autoclave signature added before being sent. Keeping this in mind, Heath suggested an alternative to get around those issues.

Although a very tight circle must be maintained, someone on the inside that was trusted implicitly would need to act as the required go-between. Without ever knowing the scope of the plan, or the content of an envelope, that person could use their personal residence as the mailing point for two-way coded messages from the president to a P.O. Box on the other end.

The president pondered that thought for a moment, and upon realizing that Heath was probably correct, he nodded in agreement and said, "Well, other than you, my most trusted confidante would be Mrs. Dawson."

"That was who I had in mind as well, sir."

"All right, Heath, I will make that happen. Now what else do you have?"

In conjunction with the previously mentioned protective measures, Heath wanted to establish multiple false Canadian identities for the selected operative. His conviction in that stance was based upon the rationale that an operative using a Canadian identity could move on the targets sanctioned by the president either in the United States or on foreign soil without reprisal. Should the operative be caught, the tactic would eliminate any connection to the United States, which would in turn protect the current administration from any connected allegations that could arise.

Intrigued by the thought process, and believing that such a safeguard would be wise, the president inquired as to why Heath mentioned that a target could be on foreign soil. He was quickly reminded of what he had conveyed the previous evening, as according to what the president remembered from his long-term relationship with each family, they all possessed an adventurous spirit that included travel to foreign lands. When coupling that tendency with difficulties that could be encountered while attempting to hit each sanctioned target in or near their residence, it seemed logical that the best chance to strike could be during a vacation. Amplifying his bluntness on the subject, Heath felt that the best-case scenario would be to kill each target on foreign soil if the opportunity was there, and in closing, he added that each sanction should be carried out in such a way that it favored the appearance of an accidental death.

Conceding to the well-argued point, the president asked, "So then what is your plan if a target does leave the country?"

"My thought for such an instance is to first legally move our operative into Canada via a United States passport. Once there, the use of a Canadian identity would be employed to fly into whatever foreign nation was necessary for an attempt on the target. Then whether the attempt is successful or not, the operative would return to Canada before reversing the identity process and entering the United States."

"That sounds nice, Heath. It's easy and clean with no trace back to me."

"Yes, sir."

"All right, so let's go with that. Now please continue."

Heath once again delved into what he believed would be an astute and concise course of action and stated that he would like to be personally involved in the selection process of the operative. He also recommended that he take full responsibility for the supervision of any training and briefings of the individual, while also traveling with the operative using his own false identities. He detailed that if all was executed properly, then the selected operative, and any intelligence-gathering personnel, would never know that the orders came directly from the president. By acting as the only liaison between President Harwell and those various players, Heath believed that the anonymity of the president would remain secure. However, in order to proceed with those proposed aspects, Heath would also need to be placed on special assignment by the president as had been done in the past.

The president nodded positively while stating that Heath should consider his requests to be approved, as everything he presented seemed practical. As for the private funding, the president would contact a business associate in Seattle later that night to have him launder some funds from a portfolio into a bank of Heath's choosing. Once that was taken care of, the same fast-working associate would provide an account number and the access code for an ATM card. Barring any snags, Heath would have the information he needed by the following day.

Hearing that news, Heath replied, "That should work nicely, sir. Thank you."

"No problem. Now, is that all we need to cover?"

"Not quite, sir. If I may, there are a few more items."

"All right, let's move on then."

Although hesitant to broach the subject, Heath felt it was imperative to do so. For the sake of self-preservation, he needed to know with certainty what his level of authority was within the process and how that would pertain to the operative. Before each sanction was given to move forward, what exactly were the parameters of his role? He believed that the operative would need to study each target and their respective tendencies well in advance. That would be the best way to increase the chance of success, and a preliminary file on each could be developed easily. But if the primary target from each family was not obtainable during the actual mission, how much latitude with regard to any satellite targets was the president willing to provide? Would he, through Heath, sanction the operative to move on a secondary target?

Upon hearing those questions, the president leaned in closer with a resolute look and stated, "No, Heath, I absolutely will not! I understand the reasoning behind what you are asking, but I feel that each primary is the most effective way of sending my message."

There could be no doubt of the sincerity with which the president spoke, so Heath nodded while responding, "Very well, sir. I understand."

The president then reiterated his complete trust in Heath, and that it stood without waver. But he also made certain that his protectorate fully comprehended a vital point. In moving forward Heath would be free to inform the operative of whatever was necessary regarding backgrounds and tendencies to assist in the success of each sanctioned kill. But under no circumstance would that operative be allowed to move on any target other than the one specified.

Then, to ensure compliance, he asked firmly, "Now is that clearly understood?"

"Yes, sir. I understand completely. And the operative will be fully aware of it as well."

"That's good, Heath. Now what else do you have?"

"There's just one more item, sir. How do you intend to make it known to each family that the message of deterrence came from you?"

"What do you mean?"

Heath detailed his complete understanding that there would be no latitude in moving to a secondary target, as well as the common desire of both men to make each sanction appear as an accidental death. Although those issues were clear, he pointed out that the problematic issue of how each family would confirm without any doubt that the president was behind the death had not yet been addressed. Heath believed that a method that allowed the operative to leave behind an appropriate, yet unmistakable, message must be devised, and for that to transpire, logic dictated that a close-range kill would be required.

The president thought for a moment before stating, "All right, I can see where you are going with this. So, do you have any suggestions?"

Assuming that a kill could be made at close range, and that the operative would have a few seconds or longer before needing to flee, Heath expressed that the time could be used to plant a coded message on the body. When asked what type of coded message, he replied that only the president could make that decision. The code or phrase should be something that only his adversaries would understand, while also seeming to be nothing of importance to anyone who could be investigating the accident.

The president pondered in silence for a moment before admitting that he liked the thought process, but he did not have anything to offer at the moment. Then he added that he would give it some thought and hopefully come up with something useful. In the meantime, the president suggested that they talk again privately the following evening. By then he would be able to provide Heath with an account number and the mailing address for Mrs. Dawson.

After a moment of silence that implied there were no other matters to discuss, the president stood from the couch and reached out a hand of thanks.

Then he stated, "This has been most educational, Heath, and I appreciate your insight on certain matters that I did not consider. Now, I will contact your superiors immediately to have you placed on special assignment for me again, and then I will inform Mrs. Dawson that I would like to see her right away. As for you, please get started on your preliminary work as soon as you can."

As with every other instance during their history except when he was in recovery from having the two bullets surgically removed, Heath stood when the president rose.

Clasping the hand of Jordan Harwell, he replied, "Yes, sir. That will not be a problem. In fact, I can begin the process for the recruitment of our operative tonight."

"Tonight, you say. Well, that sounds as if you may already have someone in mind for the job."

"Yes, sir, I do."

"Well, that is outstanding, Heath. And you believe that this individual can be properly motivated to attempt the task without knowing the reason behind it?"

With an affirmative nod Heath replied, "Yes, sir, most definitely. And I also believe you will be satisfied with my choice of operative. She is perfect for the job."

ADVANCE PREP

1

Ellsworth, Kansas

THE WOMAN KNOWN by the previous identity of Kristen Royce was aware that thirty-one months had passed since she became an inmate within the maximum-security facility in Ellsworth, Kansas. As a consequence, she also knew that her twenty-year sentence had only just begun. Her long fall from grace and that of the existence as a navy lieutenant with a comfortable Pentagon posting had been humbling, but her numerous crimes of high treason and conspiracy against the United States could have, and should have, warranted a more severe penalty.

A correct accounting of how slowly the calendar turned had not been a challenging task for her, as there were ways of learning about the outside world even when certain guards were not in the mood to provide meaningful information. Therefore, based on a simple count since receiving her most recent update, she understood that this particular mid-November morning was only nine days after the national midterm elections of 2030.

Kristen had been given the false identity of Susan Greer by Agent Bishop before being transferred to Ellsworth, and even though the moniker was not one she would have chosen, she had no choice. In her eyes the name was absent of even a hint of flair, and therefore she was not particularly fond of it. Nevertheless, she was grateful to have use of such an identity, as the fabricated history and accompanying criminal conviction behind it had been provided by the Secret Service as insurance to keep her safe from harm.

Throughout the time of her incarceration, the guards and administrative personnel knew Susan Greer as a convicted murderer of three individuals and had accordingly treated her with due caution. However, inside the facility she had stayed out of trouble and had always demonstrated what was necessary to be labeled as a model prisoner who obeyed the restrictive guidelines. The bulk of inmates knew her as someone who was generally quiet and that she tended to mind her own business, so in time she gained much-needed respect from several of them. Susan was not certain if their respect was based upon her reputation since arriving or the cover story of why she was there, but she was not going to risk questioning why it came about. She developed a few friendships with other women who shared in her current plight and began to receive offers for favors from many within her cellblock.

As a result of abiding by the established rules of the prison without question or rebellion, Susan had also earned certain privilege opportunities from various guards. The majority of those privileges could only be obtained from certain female guards in exchange for companionship and physical liberties; however, they were of no real interest to her as they would not provide anything she craved. Regardless of that fact, it was nice to know privileges could be negotiated for if the desire ever struck her. In time, Susan had learned to filter the various offers with prudent caution, while also bending to a point in cases where the favor or privilege was important enough to her. However, in cases where an opportunity was passed up, she always took care in showing proper respect toward the offering soul while turning them down.

Although she had a personal history of good health, physical fitness became a higher priority for Susan while in prison than it had ever been during her entire life as Kristen. The reality was that she had become an addict of sorts with daily pushups, crunches, and stretching, but that was not enough to satisfy the drive within her. In spite of the quarter-mile track in the exercise yard being surrounded by high fences and a tight security perimeter, running at a fast clip around it as often as possible was how she felt most free. She believed that there was not a more productive nor more enjoyable way to spend what little time she had while out of the cellblock, so there was one offer of privilege that was never passed up. Susan had realized early on that she would gladly exchange whatever was necessary for any extra time on the track.

Beyond the established norm of armed security in the adjacent towers, as a standard practice there were also guards posted at each corner of the track while inmates jogged or walked. Six days a week Susan could run during the midmorning yard time until her desire faded. In addition, her record of good behavior, as well as an occasional, secretive fondling embrace with a high-ranking female guard, earned her the right to complete another lap while other inmates were required to return to the cellblock. Susan believed that such an embrace of a few seconds with someone in power was a worthwhile sacrifice for an additional minute of fresh air against her face.

On the current mid-November morning, after the normal breakfast routine and time spent in the common area with other inmates, Susan returned to her cell and completed her morning stretching ritual. Then when fully prepared to run at her typical fast clip, she waited patiently for yard time to commence. A few moments later, she lined up in single file with the other inmates and marched through the door to the exercise yard where she was met harshly by the discomfort of a sharp drop in temperature. In her cell or the common area chamber, she had no advance warning that this day dawned to an overcast sky with a steady wind from the north and had reasonably gambled that the weather would be moderate. Although dressed in standard issue sweatpants and a T-shirt, Susan had left the added warmth of her sweatshirt in her cell. A cold rush of air bit into her bare forearms and through the thin T-shirt as she made her way toward the dirt track, but she knew that her discomfort would be short-lived. The intense movement of running would soon warm her body enough to fend off any sting.

Near the completion of yard time, Susan rounded a corner with a forward-driving lean to her brisk pace. She was running at a good clip and could really feel the adrenaline kick in to create what some referred to as a "runner's high." Then when refocusing on the track ahead to see if other inmates might be walking or jogging directly in front of her, Susan could see four people of more official dress standing at the end of the straightaway. Drawing closer, she recognized that the three women were the warden and two of her senior guards positioned as sentinels beside her, while the fourth person was a man in a dark business suit and sunglasses.

Slowing her gait as she approached, Susan came to a halt roughly twenty feet from the warden. She instantly recognized one of the guards as someone who had been physically forward with her on several occasions in exchange for liberties, and her immediate fear was that the warden had learned of that breach in security. Harsh penalties could ensue for Susan if that were the case, but then again, the guard may have preferred to keep their arrangement unknown. In either case, Susan did not want to risk any potential misstep, as she had no desire to be manhandled and punished by either guard if perceived as a current threat to the warden. To avoid that possibility, she extended her arms with open palms in a gesture of submission.

Most people running at her speed for an extended length of time would have been quite winded, but Susan's chest did not heave one bit from exertion. In fact, her body showed no sign that she had ever been in motion except for her sweaty and clinging thin T-shirt.

Looking directly at the warden, then the man beside her, and back at the warden again, Susan said, "Good morning, ma'am."

"Good morning, Ms. Greer. How is your run today?"

"It's been good, ma'am, and thank you for asking. But with your permission, ma'am, I would like to get in another few laps before my allotted yard time expires."

"I understand your desire, Ms. Greer, but I'm afraid that won't be possible today." Then with a hand gesture to the side she added, "As I'm sure you can see, we have a visitor."

"Yes, ma'am, I can see that."

"Good. Now, this visitor has been cleared for entry into this facility by a power higher than mine in order to pass along some vital information. He and I had a lengthy discussion in my office with regard to that information, and at the conclusion of our meeting, he asked if he could speak with you directly. I have willingly granted him that request, so you will show our guest the respect that is due by providing him with the opportunity he seeks. Do you understand what I'm saying, Ms. Greer?"

"Yes, ma'am, that's perfectly clear." Then after relaxing her arms, Susan proceeded to tug her clinging T-shirt away from her body and added, "I'm just not sure this would be the best time to speak with him."

As a woman the warden understood the subtle message that inmate Greer was putting forward. At the moment, she did not look her best and was dripping with perspiration.

However, that was her own doing, so the warden showed little sympathy by replying, "Well that may be, Ms. Greer. But since he has made this effort to see you personally, you should treat him with some courtesy."

"Is that an order, ma'am?"

"Yes, it is, Ms. Greer. And believe me, you will want to hear what this man has to say."

Susan nodded in compliance and let her T-shirt fall back against her body. Then she shifted her gaze toward the well-dressed man, and said, "Good morning, sir. How can I help you?"

Removing his sunglasses and shoving them into the breast pocket of his suit, the man gave a faint smile and replied, "Good morning, Ms. Greer. My name is Agent Bishop."

2

Unexpected News

SUSAN WAS KEENLY in tune with the fact that she had to continue the elaborate ruse. It was vital for her cover to maintain a cool demeanor in front of the warden and her two guards, even though she already knew exactly who the man was. She shared a past with Agent Heath Bishop during the later stages of her true identity as Lieutenant Kristen Royce, and she knew within her heart that except for the one incident, their past relationship had been more good than bad. However, the warden did not need to be made aware of that, as she, along with every guard or inmate in the prison, had known Kristen only as Susan Greer.

After the warden gave a nod of approval along with an encouraging motion of her hand, inmate Greer cautiously advanced toward her and the others. Agent Bishop responded by stepping forward to meet the inmate halfway, while one of the guards followed close behind. That guard had done so on her own accord without instruction, but the warden did not curb her instinctive movements. The woman in uniform had not been privy to what the warden and Agent Bishop had discussed previously, so she still maintained a belief that Susan was a convicted three-time murderer. Therefore, her repositioning was done in order to protect not only the warden, but their guest from possible harm.

Agent Bishop was unaware that a secondary cause for the guard to move forward also existed. However, the warden was, as with most things inside the prison, keenly aware of the reasoning behind it. Inmate Greer was an attractive and physically fit young woman who had caught the eye of many, and as this particular guard preferred women over men, she was one such admirer. The warden knew of their supposedly secretive liaisons and had willingly turned a blind eye to them and other such actions within the prison. She believed that if there was the slightest possibility of acquiring any valuable intelligence about inmate plans or happenings in exchange for the allowance of some indiscretions, then it was well worth it.

Throughout the brief chat with the warden and her supposed first-time introduction to Agent Bishop, Susan had begun to cool down from her run after standing in the chilling wind for a few minutes. Triggered by the rapid drop in her body temperature and accelerated further by the dampness of her sweaty and clinging T-shirt, an obvious physiological change with regard to her nipples became quite apparent. The warden noticed what was occurring, and that also to his credit, Agent Bishop did not alter his gaze downward to look upon them as he approached the inmate. As a sign of true professionalism, he maintained eye contact with Ms. Greer the entire time. However, that same measure of respect could not be said for the woman who stood at his right flank. That high-ranking guard was a proud lesbian who made no secret about it, so without hesitation she took the opportunity to gaze upon an object of her desire who was experiencing a vulnerable moment.

Now standing closer to each other than either would have recently imagined, Agent Bishop reached out with an open hand of friendship and said, "It's nice to meet you, Ms. Greer. May I call you Susan?"

With a glare that could bore through his skull, Susan took several seconds in an attempt to size up what the intentions of Heath could be. She left his empty hand waiting in front of her until hearing the warden clear her throat as an obvious sign of disapproval.

In response, she quickly clasped his hand firmly and replied, "It's nice to meet you as well, Agent Bishop. And yes, you can call me Susan."

Heath could sense the mistrust in her words and the insincerity in the handshake, but he was uncertain as to why she projected such feelings. Kristen, now Susan, had received fair treatment and a partial pardon from the president for her help in bringing many of those within Samuel Tillman's devious organization to justice. Yes, it was true that she now resided in a maximum-security federal prison, but that was much better than an uglier alternative.

Nevertheless, he had to play it cool in front of the warden who knew nothing of the real story, so he replied simply, "Thank you, Susan. Now, I have some information for you that will change your life in a positive way."

Not wanting to disrespect the warden, Susan was careful with her response. She could have said that almost anything would change her life for the positive in relation to her current situation, but that would not be wise.

Instead she kept cool while asking, "And what would that be, Agent Bishop?"

With the predatory guard having inched closer to his shoulder, Heath felt somewhat encumbered by her presence.

Turning toward her with a glance of disdain, then looking beyond to the warden, he asked pleasantly, "Excuse me, Warden, but would it be possible for me to continue this conversation with Susan more privately?"

"What do you have in mind?"

"Well, nothing extreme. This should only take a moment, and I'm just asking for a little space to communicate so that our conversation can't be overheard."

Under normal circumstances, granting such a request would have been unthinkable. There was never an instance when a visitor would be left alone with an inmate for any reason, as visitations could only take place in a securely monitored location with armed guards at the ready. However, this was an extremely unusual case. Since indisputable evidence and documentation had been provided to clear Ms. Greer of any wrongdoing, she no longer posed the same security threat that she would have in the past.

With a positive nod, the warden called the guard back to her side and motioned toward the lawn area within the track oval while stating, "How about right over there?"

Agent Bishop returned his own nod of approval, and then with an arm gesture said, "Shall we take a short walk, Susan?"

Before moving, Susan sought approval from the warden and, upon receiving it, walked with Heath toward the lawn where they came to a halt roughly twenty seconds later.

Turning to face him, Susan asked softly, "So what the hell is going on?"

Heath glanced casually over his shoulder and surmised that because the warden was now speaking privately with her two guards, they were probably being enlightened as to why the visiting agent and the inmate were given such latitude.

He then turned his gaze toward Susan and softly replied, "For the sake of appearances, you need to behave as if you are relieved and overjoyed when I hand you a letter. You can shed a few tears for authenticity if you want, but when I reach out to shake your hand, accept it enthusiastically. Got it?"

"All right, I got it. Now what's up?"

"You're getting out of here tomorrow morning."

After leaning away briefly to check his eyes for possible deceit, Susan squared herself and asked, "Are you serious, or are you just playing some sort of twisted game with me?"

"I'm serious."

She once again checked his eyes, as she had heard that an individual's eyes were rumored to be the gateway to their soul.

Believing that Heath was genuine, she replied, "All right then, give me the letter."

With that he pulled an envelope from the breast pocket of his suit and stated, "The warden has already read this letter, and the governor in Topeka confirmed with her while I was in her office that he had also received a copy from the attorney general. It states that there is forensic DNA evidence clearing you of committing the murders that the federal prison system believed you were guilty of. This is solid and irrefutable proof that you are innocent, so it's a done deal. You will be out in less than twenty-four hours."

Realizing that there had to be something more to it, Susan asked, "And what is the price for my release?"

"That will be explained once you're out of here, but for now, read and act relieved."

Susan did as she was told, glancing at the letter as if she was appearing to read it thoroughly and acted relieved as she placed a hand over her open mouth. Then when Heath reached out a hand, she gladly accepted it and shook it vigorously.

During the past few seconds, the warden and her two guards had been watching closely from a distance of about fifty feet, and they had no cause to believe that the reaction of inmate Greer was anything less than genuine. In perhaps the only instance since the inmate had arrived more than two-and-a-half years earlier, the warden and the guards were at a distinct disadvantage. They had no concept as to how well Susan could play a role, or how many times in the past she had been called upon to act out a more challenging part.

As Susan turned toward them and held up the letter, the warden placed an index finger to her lips as a signal to be quiet while also motioning that she and Agent Bishop should return to her side.

When they arrived, the warden maintained a reserved and stoic posture for appearances' sake, but quietly offered, "So congratulations are in order for you, Ms. Greer."

"Thank you, ma'am, I'm very happy to receive this news."

"I'm sure that you are. Now if I may ask a favor, could you please keep quiet about your good fortune? News of your pending release will undoubtedly agitate some of the other inmates, and that could lead to problems in your cellblock that neither one of us need."

"Yes, ma'am. I understand, and I won't tell a soul."

3

Freedoms Air

SLEEP WAS DIFFICULT for Susan that night. In fact, her restless tossing and turning mixed with bouts of staring at the ceiling was reminiscent of her first few nights at Ellsworth. Those actions were understandable then, as she was in new and troublesome surroundings with no idea of what might happen to her. Would she be seen as a weak target and therefore be beaten by other inmates whenever they pleased, or would she have absolutely no recourse if similar action was taken against her by the guards? Those justifiable concerns were now in the past, and luckily nothing serious ever unfolded, but her similar restless actions in the present time made sense for other reasons.

Susan contemplated the reality that it could be her last night as a prisoner, while at the same time trying in vain to not get her hopes up. She constantly had to remind herself of one specific problem. In spite of the claim made by Heath, she would not be out of prison until she was actually through the front gate. For that matter Susan would not feel completely free of constraint, self-imposed or otherwise, until she had left the state of Kansas in her wake. Of course, none of that would happen if the entire scenario put forth by Heath was just some elaborate ruse to mess with her head. To that end, a singular question kept gnawing at her throughout the long night. Would Heath be coming back for her?

For Susan, the morning brought forth a different passage of time than the usual, as she did not engage in any level of exercise. In direct opposition to the previous days, weeks, and months, she just sat silently on her bunk while waiting for a life-altering event to unfold.

Then a short time later, as with every other day, Susan ate breakfast and mingled with a few select inmates in the common area. Those routine actions helped take her mind off Heath temporarily, but the thought of him soon crept back into her head.

In response she returned to her cell, and as more time slipped past, Susan began to fume. During her quiet contemplation, a realization came over her that in conjunction with the current torment of waiting for Heath to return, she was still pissed off at him for his past action. She would have been fine if her incarceration, with the warranted protection of a solid, fabricated cover, was in any other location outside of Kansas, but for some reason he had decided to place her in Ellsworth. Therefore, when or if time ever permitted, she would have a serious discussion with Heath about his lack of judgement. As for the present time, her anger was centered more on the fact that he may have been playing some sort of sick joke on her with a claim of pending release.

With nothing else to do, Susan banged out a few sets of pushups and crunches before beginning to stretch for her upcoming run. Each passing moment made her feel as if this would be just another day in the life of her captivity. She realized the need to burn off some energy to get her mind right again and hoped that a faster and longer run than usual would do the trick. Unfortunately, her time to be outside, no matter what she might do for the female guards as appeasement, was still more than an hour away.

Then while Susan was in full stretch on the cell floor with her chin to her knee and the fingers of both hands laced around the sole of one foot, it happened. The approach of footsteps could be heard with a noticeable heaviness to them, and they were not those of the other inmates. Susan sharpened her focus on the sound and recognized that, although in nearly synchronized cadence, there was more than one guard approaching.

A few seconds later the footsteps stopped outside her open door, and she heard one of the guards say, "Inmate Greer. Stand and prepare to exit your cell."

Her disposition suddenly changed as she felt a surge of hope and anticipation, but Susan had to calm herself and play dumb for the time being. Standing instantly and then looking toward them, she recognized the two guards as women whom she had come to know more personally than others. Although neither expressed visible signs of being aware that she was being released, they may have known. Perhaps the warden had kept the matter closely guarded as she implied the previous day, or she may have informed this pair of guards while also ordering them to maintain silence until the inmate was safely away from the cellblock. The accuracy of either scenario was of no real consequence to Susan, as long as she would be getting out.

While trusting her instinct that the former was more likely, and not wanting to cause a scene by revealing what was happening, Susan asked, "What's going on?"

With a wave of instruction to exit the cell, the lead guard replied, "The warden wants to see you in her office."

"Have I done something wrong?"

"That's for the warden to decide. Now move along."

Susan could feel the excitement welling up inside her. Perhaps this supposed release was actually going to transpire. Being summoned to the office of the warden was nearly unheard of, and the only time that she had been in those confines was the day after her incarceration began. That meeting was not friendly, as it was solely about two things: explaining the rules of the facility and how punishment would be handed out for disobeying them.

Keeping her head low, Susan showed no outward emotion as the two guards walked her through the various security checkpoints within the prison. Then she maintained that same submissive demeanor as the three of them entered the office of the warden.

The warden looked up from the tablet screen on her desk, dismissed the guards with her customary wave of the hand, and said, "Good morning, Ms. Greer, please sit down."

"Yes, ma'am."

The warden began before Susan could get into the chair by stating, "As we were both informed of yesterday, some new information came to light that has impacted you in a most positive way. Agent Bishop, on behalf of the attorney general of the United States, presented me with documentation that verified through DNA sampling that you are innocent of the crimes for which you were wrongly convicted. In addition, I have received instructions from the office of the attorney general to process you for immediate release. Copies of those documents were also submitted to the governor's office in Topeka, and we have both corroborated the authenticity of them with the higher authority in Washington, D.C. All of the administrative paperwork has been taken care of, so I'm pleased to announce that you will be free of this facility within the hour."

While exhibiting a measure of giddiness and relief, Susan replied, "That's wonderful news, ma'am. Thank you very much."

"You're welcome, Ms. Greer, but don't thank me. Thank those who discovered the truth, as I had nothing to do with it. Now I believe Agent Bishop has something to say to you."

Susan had not known that Heath was in the office, as her escorted steps, directly from the door to the warden's desk, did not allow for her to look around the room.

Moving forward to a position next to Susan, Heath reached out his hand and said, "Ms. Greer, on behalf of the attorney general and the United States government, I sincerely apologize to you for a wrongful conviction. We are sorry that you spent any time in prison, and although we can't give you those years back, we can and would like to help you get back into the normal stream of society. That effort will include expunging your record of any wrongdoing and assisting you with future employment opportunities. I am here on behalf of the attorney general to expedite your immediate release and transport you to wherever you desire in the United States. Once there, you will receive a financial stipend as compensation for the error of our judicial system, and we will provide you with an apartment at no cost to you for six months so that you can earn and save additional money."

Susan finally felt as though she could exhale, as her release was indeed going to occur.

Turning to the warden, she asked, "What do I need to do before getting out of here?"

"Is there anything in your cell that you want to take with you?"

Not wanting to risk being duped back into her cell for any reason, she directly replied, "Ma'am, I don't need a single thing from inside that cell. I just want to get out of here and move on with my life."

"You have no pictures or personal items?"

"There is nothing that I can't live without, ma'am."

"Well if that's the case, then let's get you processed."

"Thank you, ma'am, I appreciate that."

Within the hour Susan was processed out and dressed in the rather ordinary clothes that she had been given for her transfer from the secretive Washington, D.C., facility to Ellsworth Federal Penitentiary. Then she and Agent Bishop walked freely through the front gate and headed for his rental car. Unlike the previous day, there was a cloudless sky above with no wind. Perhaps that was a good omen for the future, but then again having faith in such things had little meaning to her. Rarely did the atmospheric conditions of the day have any relevance on the good or bad outcomes that took place during the ensuing hours.

With the window next to her wide open, Susan was driven away from the facility. The fresh and, more importantly, free air felt wonderful on her face as the side mirror showed the buildings of her past few years of entrapment fading into the distance.

Silence between them ensued, but after a few minutes Heath finally broke it by asking, "Would you like to stop for some real food?"

Gruffly, she replied, "No thanks, I'm not hungry. Let's just put some distance between us and Ellsworth as soon as possible."

"All right, I'll just head for the airport then."

"Please do, and the sooner we get airborne the better."

Another moment of silence followed before Heath said, "So now that those prison walls are in the past, the cover identity of Susan

Greer is no longer necessary. For the time being, you can be Kristen Royce again."

"Good! I hated that name of Susan Greer. But why can I only be Kristen for the time being?"

Sensing obvious hostility in each response, Heath replied, "Because you will never again be safe or thought of positively as Kristen Royce. Therefore, another identity will need to be fabricated for you. But in the meantime, do we have a problem?"

After a deep sigh, she eased her defensive tone a bit and stated, "No. Not really. But there is something I would like to talk about later."

Although she said no, he could tell that the opposite was true. But based on what she had been through in recent years, there was reason for her to be somewhat distrusting.

Attempting to further ease the tension, Heath said, "So, Kristen. You changed your hair. It looks nice."

The innocent peace offering was well received, and Kristen relaxed her defensive posture a bit more while replying, "Thanks. At first, I cut it short out of necessity, but now I like it."

"You cut it out of necessity?"

"Sure. In those early days I didn't know how things would be in the cellblock or the yard. Would I become a victim of one or more of the other inmates, or would I be left alone? I thought that having hair halfway down my back could be used against me if I were to get into a fight, so I asked to have the prison barber cut it short. After a little while I realized how much easier it was to have my hair short, with the lack of quality shampoo and conditioner, so I kept it just a couple of inches long even after the threat of danger had passed."

With a nod Heath replied, "Well I guess that makes sense for both reasons."

Moments later they pulled into a small parking lot near the private jet that would soon whisk them away.

Before exiting the car, Kristen showed her desire to continue easing the tension by stating, "So that was a great cover story you gave the warden, not only about why I was sent to prison in the first place, but also that DNA testing had now proved me innocent of those supposed crimes. And then that speech in her office on behalf of the attorney general was really a nice finishing touch. I don't think she will ever have a clue as to what I had actually been guilty of, or what lies in front of me."

"Well she, or anyone else, will certainly never learn anything about the latter. As for the former, the story of your supposed crimes and eventual innocence is tight enough that she will never suspect any portion of it was fabricated for your safety. We put together all the correct documentation for your cover both when you were going in and now for your release, so you are good to go. In fact, it was all done so neatly that even the governor in Topeka has bought into the story."

With an enthusiastic nod, Kristen then asked, "All right, so where are we headed? And more importantly, what exactly is in store for me?"

"Well...for the time being where we are headed is not important. As for what's in store for you, let's get on the plane first. I'll explain it to you then."

4

Preflight Check

ONCE ABOARD THE small private jet with the door secured behind them, Heath pointed to a seat for Kristen before taking another that faced her directly. Then he began to detail, although somewhat incompletely, the purpose of why she had been released. Of course, during his explanation he neglected to inform her that the president was ultimately the one who wanted the plan to be carried out. It was, after all, the most closely guarded need-to-know aspect of the operation, and Kristen did not need to know. However, what he did tell her over the next several minutes was direct.

Kristen was faced with two options, which in all simplicity came down to either the carrot or the stick. The first of those, or the carrot, would be to work closely with and report only to Heath throughout the duration of the assignment. There were multiple terms within that relationship, some of which were clearly defined while others were not. Within the former of those categories, there would be a mandatory condition that she be implanted with multiple tracking devices before anything else could be done.

Heath explained that those devices, when activated, could be used to identify her exact location at all times. Although that could be viewed as a means of distrusting her sincerity in following through with the mission, he hoped that Kristen would view it in the light for which such a precaution was intended. Should she ever be caught and held captive by any law enforcement agency or unfriendly element during the mission, then the devices would be instrumental in assisting Heath with her whereabouts for an intervening extraction.

Kristen was informed that if she willingly agreed to the procedure and was to then carry out the stipulations of the plan, she would be rewarded by receiving a full and complete pardon for her previous acts. To solidify that declaration, Heath promised that his claim would be fulfilled at the conclusion of the assignment. In the meantime, she would be able to live in comfort with a reasonable amount of freedom to do whatever she desired.

The second option, or the stick, was less inviting because it would involve her continued incarceration for the duration of her original twenty-year sentence. Included within that choice would be a newly fabricated identity and conviction record, with placement in a different federal maximum-security facility than the one she had just been released from. Then to make that option less appealing, Heath informed Kristen that its location was in the more northern latitude of the United States. As a result, the typical winter weather for the region would be far less conducive for running or other forms of outdoor exercise.

Heath concluded the offer of her two possible futures by informing Kristen that she could take a few minutes to weigh the pros and cons of each option. The choice would be hers to make, and he would respect whatever she determined to be the wisest course. But he also made it perfectly clear to Kristen that there would be no opportunity for her to alter the decree. Whatever choice she made in the coming minutes would be binding.

Kristen took a moment, appearing to consider her options while she gazed out the window, but her mind had been made up almost instantly. She would choose option number one for the most obvious of reasons—in that it provided the opportunity for freedom in far less time than returning to federal prison—but there was an underlying factor that went beyond that. By selecting that option, she would also be able to spend a great deal of time with Heath until the mission was completed, and her thought was that they could perhaps rekindle the budding relationship they shared in Washington, D.C., before the events of the time brought forth a nearly out of control spiral. However-er, in spite of those reasons, she needed to mask her joy and make it appear as if some sort of concession would be required for her services.

Shifting her gaze back toward Heath, Kristen said, "All right. I accept the challenge of the first option and will do all that I can to see it through. However, I do have one condition."

"And what would that be?"

"Although I appreciate the cover and criminal narrative that you created for me while I was in Ellsworth, you are already aware that I couldn't stand the name you gave me. So, I want to be able to choose whatever names I will have for aliases in the future."

Heath was surprised, as he had expected a demand that could be more difficult to accommodate. After all, her disdain for the false prison identity seemed to him a trivial point in the grand scheme of things. But if all she wanted was the latitude to select her future names, then he would be an idiot to deny her the right.

With a subtle nod he replied, "All right, Kristen. That seems fair. So, you select the names of your numerous future identities, and if a background vetting doesn't turn up any issues with those choices, then we will build you an appropriate cover for each."

"Thank you, Heath. Now, what's next?"

As she had now verbally agreed to the prerequisite implant procedure of option one, Heath used a hushed tone to outline certain mission parameters. The identities of the four sanctioned targets were clearly defined, along with an unyielding directive that there would be no latitude for any alteration to a secondary target. Unfortunately, he could not provide any information as to the when and where each of the attempts would occur. In the current moment, it was simply impossible to determine either of those two factors.

Then, in understanding that the first of many challenging aspects had been conquered with relative ease, Heath moved toward and opened the door to the flight deck.

Leaning forward slightly, he then said, "All right, it's time for the implants."

Seconds later, a woman with shoulder stripes that identified her as the copilot emerged from the flight deck. She looked to be in her late forties, and although short in stature, she projected a commanding physical presence with a sturdy, thick frame, a strong jaw, and piercing eyes.

Offering a faint smile toward Kristen, she pointed at the long couch on one side of the fuselage and instructed, "Please remove your shirt and lie down so that we may begin."

After a quick glance toward Heath, she fixed her gaze on the mysterious woman and tempted fate by asking, "Why do I need to remove my shirt and lie down?"

"Because. I don't want to remove it for you after you have been sedated."

"Sedated?"

"Yes. Although this procedure will be rather quick, it can be quite painful both during and immediately afterward. Therefore, full sedation is recommended."

With a quizzical look Kristen asked, "Can be quite painful, or will be quite painful?"

"Good question, as I misspoke. Truthfully speaking, this will be quite painful."

"That sounds as if you might have firsthand knowledge of the experience."

"I do indeed. And believe me, you will want to be sedated."

"Well, can we use a local instead of putting me under completely?"

"I asked that same question years ago when I was about to receive this type of implant, but it was explained to me that the injection for each local could be more painful than the actual placing of the tracking devices."

"Well that doesn't sound good!"

"I know it doesn't. But you should know that I didn't believe the technician then, so I, like you, asked for a local. She did as I requested, but not long after she started the procedure, I altered my position and begged her for complete sedation."

"You must be joking? It couldn't have been that bad."

Now with a sterner look upon her face, the copilot asked, "Do I look like I'm joking?"

It only took an instant to reply with, "Well…no, actually. You don't."

"Good. Now look. There is no need for you to worry. I have done this procedure before, and each time the patient expressed relief afterward for having been sedated. You will sleep for about four hours, and then feel some pain for a few days as your body heals and adjusts to each implant. As for my part, once you are unconscious, I can do the procedure in a matter of minutes and then get back to my duties on the flight deck."

Unable to win her subsequent stare down of will with the copilot, Kristen turned to look at Heath while asking, "And this is an absolute must before we can move forward?"

His nonverbal answer came by way of a positive nod, which was instantly followed by the voice of the mysterious woman asking, "So, then, are you left- or right-hand dominant?"

"What?"

"It's a simple question. Are you left- or right-hand dominant?"

"I'm right-handed."

Based upon previous encounters with Kristen before the incarceration, Heath could confirm for the copilot that the reply was truthful. Then when his recruit again glanced toward him, he gave a reassuring smile while motioning toward the couch.

As she then rose to comply and removed her shirt as requested, he added, "Since Kristen is to be erased from existence, I think I will call you Phoenix until you can come up with something more to your liking."

5

Discomforting Fog

AS A RESULT of the potent sedative that had been administered just prior to the implant procedure, Kristen, or Phoenix as Heath now called her, slept for the entirety of the flight from Ellsworth, Kansas. Even now, more than an hour after landing, she was just beginning to stir, and what brought her back to consciousness more than any other factor was the pain and discomfort that the procedure had caused.

As she attempted to roll over and rise from her horizontal position, a sharper and more localized pain was felt in two specific areas of her body. The resulting audible scream was loud enough to inform Heath that his recruit had awakened.

In response, Heath looked up from the stack of four files he was reading through and said, "Phoenix. I'm glad to see that you're finally coming around. You were out for nearly five hours. I think our friend from the flight deck must have given you a little more sedative than was needed. Perhaps she has a soft spot for you."

Slowly and gently shifting to a seated position that favored her right side, the still groggy patient noticed that her belt, along with the button and fly of her pants, was undone. But in opposition of that unsettling fact, her shirt was back on. Those alterations from her memory of just before the procedure were discomforting as she looked through the cabin windows beyond Heath.

Then she asked, "Why are you calling me Phoenix?" and after another glance through a window on her side of the plane, she added, "Is that where we are?"

Humored by the second of her questions, Heath replied, "No. We are not in Phoenix or anywhere near it. Don't you remember the moment before the procedure? I said that I would call you Phoenix on a temporary basis until you came up with something better."

She gave it a couple seconds of thought and replied, "Yes, I do remember that."

"That's good. The fog in your head must be starting to clear."

"All right, so I remember, but I still don't know why you want to call me Phoenix."

"Well there are a few definitions of Phoenix, but one specifically comes to mind given the current setting. You see, in this instance, the most fitting definition implies that you are a fabulous bird reborn from the ashes of a previous life."

As Phoenix struggled to fully understand what had taken place, Heath handed her a bottle of water while asking her how she felt beyond the lingering grogginess. She gently attempted to distribute her weight evenly as she sat more upright on the couch, but the visible grimace on her face revealed there was considerable discomfort as she did so. Then Heath informed her that the copilot who performed the procedure had stated everything had gone as expected with no complications. He added that, as previously expressed, the associated pain for Phoenix would fade throughout the coming hours and days.

The mention of her persistent pain made Phoenix instinctively reach for and gently rub the second area of discomfort with her left hand, and that discomfort was suddenly magnified as she came to the realization of where the two implants must have been placed. She remembered that the sedative had been injected into her arm at the inner portion of her elbow, and with that she had no problem. But now she came to understand why it was necessary for the removal of her shirt. Something had obviously been done to the outer portion of her right breast near the armpit for the insertion of the implant, and logic dictated that the intense throbbing in her left butt cheek was due to a second incision. Phoenix felt a slight wave of embarrassment at the thought of those regions of her body being exposed during the procedure, and she was angry at Heath and the copilot for not informing her of what would transpire before the process began.

She asked curtly, "So did you watch while that woman performed the procedure?"

Heath realized that she was in defensive mode again, so with caution he replied, "No, I didn't. I was with the pilot on the flight deck while the copilot tended to you, and we had the cabin door closed."

"So, you didn't see my completely naked ass or chest while I was sedated?"

"No, Phoenix. But even if I was present for the procedure, you were never completely naked. According to the report she gave me when it was all over, the copilot loosened your belt and pants after I went to the flight deck. Then she implanted the tracking device deep into your left butt cheek. After that, she pulled your pants back up and moved to the second location. First, she needed to roll you to the left and unhook your bra so that she could access the outer portion of your right breast. Then she put the implant in, refastened your bra, and put your shirt back on for you."

"And you expect me to believe all of that?"

"Yes, I do, but you can ask her if you like when she and the pilot return. When I left the cabin, the sedative was taking hold and you were leaning to one side, about to go into a deep slumber. At that time, you were still in your bra with your pants up."

"That's the truth?"

"Yes, it is, so please don't get all freaked out. Now, throughout the upcoming months and beyond, we must trust each other over much larger issues than what has just transpired if we are going to successfully work together. So please, get a grip!"

Phoenix remembered that in the past, when he was unknowingly being lured into her intended trap, Heath had always been a gentleman, so his explanation of treating her modesty with respect in the present seemed plausible. He was probably telling the truth, and even if he were not, he would have only caught a glimpse of what she might offer him later, anyway.

For the sake of understanding what was now in her body, questions needed to be addressed. First, how large were the implanted tracking devices? Second, how deep under the skin were they? And third, what was the life expectancy of those devices?

Upon hearing the questions, Heath had quick and direct answers to them. The identical implants were slightly larger than an extra eraser head that one would slip onto the end of a pencil, each was about an inch-and-a-half under the surface of the skin, and they had an expected lifespan of five years before becoming less than reliable. He then informed Phoenix of the answer to a question she had not asked, and she learned that the tracking devices would not be revealed by a metal detector sweep or be visible on any airport security scan or X-ray.

A short time later, the flight crew returned from eating to prepare for their outbound flight, and Phoenix, for the sake of appearing to care one way or the other, asked the copilot if she could confirm what Heath had told her about the procedure. Without hesitation, she mimicked the description while also stating that three stitches were required to properly close each incision. Although they were currently covered with antibacterial ointment and small bandages, her suggestion was to purchase some Neosporin. Then, when in private, some of the salve should be applied to each location several times throughout the coming days to avoid possible infection and lessen the scarring.

That sage advice from one who had been through the ordeal was willingly accepted by Phoenix, which in turn generated a deeper reflection of what had been discussed moments before the procedure. She now understood without question as to why the copilot insisted that her patient be fully sedated. The thought of having a needle inserted deep into her ass and one of her breasts to provide the local anesthetics, followed by the cutting for insertion of the two devices while she was still conscious…it would have been more painful than she originally believed.

6

Lasting Impression

WHILE EXITING THE small jet and strolling across the tarmac with Heath, Phoenix looked around to see if any of the nearby terrain or landmarks might be familiar. Unfortunately, none were. Tall mountains with a slight dusting of snow at the peaks could be seen in one direction, and since the late-afternoon sun had already moved behind them, she correctly surmised they were to the west. Additional rugged terrain of several less-dominating hills rose in nearly every other direction, which proved their location was almost completely ringed in by higher ground.

Heath and Phoenix had still been aboard the plane when the engines of the small jet started, and now that they had walked roughly halfway toward a building on the edge of the tarmac, she could clearly hear their volume increase as the plane began to taxi.

After turning for a quick glance, Phoenix asked, "So where are they going?"

"We don't need them anymore, so they are headed east."

"All right, so that would imply we are somewhere in the west."

With a hint of sarcasm, Heath replied, "That's good, Phoenix. Using deductive reasoning based on information that has been provided is a skill that some people never develop. I knew from our earlier time together that you possessed that ability, and when we further enhance that skill, it will prove to be most useful for your future."

"Thanks...I think. And by the way, please don't call me Phoenix anymore."

After silently moving through and exiting the building, Heath continued toward a plain-looking four-door sedan with a rear cargo hatch in the adjacent parking lot.

Then while opening the hatch to place his suitcase and briefcase inside, he said, "All right, so what would you like your new name to be?"

"I would like to use Madison Sinclare if possible. I think that it has a bit more elegance than Susan Greer ever did, and it rolls off the tongue."

After Heath closed the hatch and they both were seated inside the vehicle, he turned to her and said, "You're right. That name does have a ring of style to it without being over the top. All right, Madison, I'll vet the name to check for any negative background, and if it doesn't raise a red flag, then it's yours."

"Thank you."

"You're welcome. Now we have a few errands to run, so unless you have an objection, I would like to take care of them before we stop for some food?"

"Sure, that's no problem. But will you tell me something first?"

While starting the car he replied, "What's on your mind?"

"Well, you told me on the plane that we weren't in Phoenix. The current temperature and the nearby mountains with a little snow on them would seem to prove that, but you haven't told me where we are."

"We are in Carson City, Nevada."

"Carson City? Why did we come here?"

Heath explained that this location was where they would establish a home base during the undetermined length of the mission. The airport in Carson City had been selected as the drop-off site because, unlike the nearby Reno-Tahoe International Airport to the north, there were no commercial flights going into or out of the facility. In addition, single or double prop engine aircraft, along with varied types of small corporate jets, came and went from the airfield with regularity. Part of that reality was due to wealthy individuals with their own planes who lived in the area or at nearby Lake Tahoe, while another aspect was based on the small population center being the Nevada state capital. Whether Madison was aware of that fact or not from her schooling was unimportant, but Heath was quick to point out that many people who were not familiar with the region or had never ventured to the western United States assumed that the mega playground and globally known glitzy city of Las Vegas was the legislative center of Nevada as opposed to Carson City. However, based on the actual truth, and because the state was significantly larger in square miles than any in the east, the governor and other representatives of the state government structure used the Carson City Airport to fly in from or out to various statewide locations such as Elko in the northeast corner or Las Vegas in the southern tip.

Each of those factors combined to make this specific airport perfect for what Heath and his operative needed. As hoped, their arrival had been stealthy—in that hardly anyone took notice of two people climbing out of a small jet, who then headed for the parking lot.

As they exited the airport by turning onto East College Parkway, Heath asked, "So now that you know where we are, what else have you noticed or been able to put together since we were preparing to leave Ellsworth?"

"You mean other than the throbbing pain associated with my implants?"

"Well yes, as it could be important for you to push beyond thoughts of pain while in the field. However, my question does relate to those implants, so think back. Was something said, done, or even asked of you that could have provided you with some insight?"

There was a moment of silence before she replied, "Well, I remember that the copilot asked me if I was left- or right-handed before she put me out."

"Yes, and?"

More silence ensued as Heath drove west toward the more populated area of the region.

Then Madison suddenly blurted out, "And afterward, when she was informing me of how to avoid possible infection, she pointed toward the location of her implants."

"That's correct. Now go on."

"What do you mean, go on? That's all she did before moving into the cockpit."

"Come on, Madison, think. Where did she point exactly?"

"Well, she pointed to the same places that my implants are. First, she pointed to her ass, and then at the outer portion of her breast."

"Be more specific."

Madison thought for a moment before saying, "All right. She pointed toward the right side of her ass, and then her left breast."

"That's correct. Now build on that memory. If you put that information together with how she originally asked the question of if you were left- or right-hand dominant, what does it tell you?"

There was another brief silence before a questioning reply of, "That she is left-handed?"

"Yes! Not only did she use her left hand to point at each location as opposed to you using your right, but her question of your dominant hand began with the left instead of the right. Therefore, there is a solid possibility that the copilot is left-handed."

"All right, I guess that could make sense. But why does that matter?"

"It may not matter at all, but then again, deductive reasoning is a valuable tool in the field. Now think about why she needed to know if you were left- or right-hand dominant."

"I don't know. Maybe it had something to do with where she put the implants."

"You're on the right track, so go with it. Touch each location of your incisions with your dominant right hand and think about why such placement might be important."

Madison complied with the unusual request, and a few seconds later said, "Well, I can reach both without too much difficulty, but it will be easier to put on the Neosporin and change the dressings with my left hand."

"Exactly, and that is why your tracking devices, as opposed to those of the copilot, were implanted where they are."

"What do you mean?"

"It's quite simple, really. Research over the years has determined that only the rarest of women, no matter how strongly motivated, would ever attempt to carve out a deeply implanted foreign object from either their breast or their butt cheek. Even though a bandage could be changed with relative ease, if the higher skill-level task of removing the object were to be attempted, it certainly would not be done by using their less-dominant hand."

Heath drove on through an elongated silence, as Madison was contemplating what had been presented to her.

Then she broke the silence with, "All right, so you make a good point about a woman not wanting to remove a foreign object from those locations. But what would happen if I had someone else remove the implants for me?"

"You would die within minutes, or perhaps seconds."

"What?"

"You heard me."

"I would die within minutes?"

"Yes. There are multiple safeguards built in that prevent anyone from attempting to remove the implants from a host body."

"Well, that sounds frightening. Just how many of these safeguards are there?"

"More than you think, and it would be foolish for me to reveal the entire list. However, to satisfy your curiosity, I can provide you with a few examples."

While Madison paid close attention, Heath explained that each implant was coded and linked specifically to the DNA pattern of the respective host. Should an implant no longer be completely surrounded by either flesh or muscle tissue from the host without it first being deactivated, it would release a fast-acting and fatal nerve toxin into the bloodstream. That is one reason why each implant is placed where the off- or non-dominant hand of the host would need to be used for attempted surgical removal. There just would not be enough time to create a large enough incision and successfully pluck it from the body before the toxin is released.

Heath continued by stating that if such a challenge of dexterity were overcome via a lightning-fast procedure performed by someone else, the implant would destabilize when fully exposed to oxygen in the room. Such an occurrence would cause an explosion with enough force to kill everything within a twenty-foot radius. The design speci-fications also took temperature into account as a deterrent against at-tempted cryogenic freezing of either the localized region of the body or the device. If the external surface of the activated implant varied by more than ten degrees Celsius from normal human body tem-perature, then a similar explosion would occur. That particular safe-guard had turned out to be most useful throughout the years in cases when an operative died in the field. What Madison learned, in simple terms, was that an implant could not be removed without being de-activated first, or the built-in safeguards would kill those who tried.

In closing, Heath added that, to his knowledge, no implant had ever been deactivated before the life expectancy of the device expired.

Madison was astonished at how calmly and clinically Heath had gone about describing the situation, while at the same time stunned by the severity of the few safeguards he mentioned.

Regardless of those thoughts, she felt the need to press with, "So will you please explain how the exploding body of a dead operative can be most useful?"

Heath hesitated before warning, "Sure, but you may not like what you hear."

"Try me!"

"All right since you insist. Destabilization of an implant elim-inates the ability for an enemy captor to parade the body of an op-erative through the streets unless it is done within a few hours after death. Because the temperature of a lifeless body will drop, a time-release explosion becomes inevitable. Such instances in the past have been tracked via GPS, and unfortunately, some were less than impactful as the bodies had only been left to rot where they lay. But there is also proof that some explosions occurred inside a facility where enemy personnel may have been killed. In those cases, the operative carried out a final act of patriotism."

"Wow! And I thought we were supposed to be the good guys. But using a dead operative as a delayed-reaction bomb is really extreme and...well...dark, don't you think?"

"Yes, I do. But sometimes our various agencies must use extreme measures to even the field with those who play dirty. Personally, I don't agree with the use of such tactics because civilians could inadvertently become collateral damage. However, I can see the reasoning behind creating an unsuspected weapon, as an enemy who killed the operative would never return the body to us, anyway."

"Well, I suppose that makes sense in a twisted way. But it's still dark."

"That's a fair assessment, and you now have added motivation to make sure your implants don't destabilize. But you shouldn't worry about it too much; the parameters of your mission will be far different and less dangerous than many of those who have been killed in the field. You will be the one targeting select individuals, and none of those four sanctioned assignments will involve the use of espionage against a foreign power."

After a long moment of contemplative silence, Madison said, "Well, I suppose there is some level of comfort in that. But at the same time, it's disturbing to know the designers of the device are using such drastic measures to keep someone like me in line."

"I know it's difficult, but please don't think of it that way. The implants are to help me extract you if something goes wrong, not to keep you in line. Besides, I have been assured by others, such as the copilot, that in time you won't even remember they are there."

"Well, that may or may not be true. I haven't had them long enough to dispute or confirm such a claim. But I can tell you I know they are in there now, and I imagine that even after my surgical scars have faded, the implants will leave a lasting impression."

7

Carson City, Nevada

WITH MADISON PONDERING the general scope of what she elected to label as a lasting impression, Heath pulled into the small parking lot of what would be the first of many errands for the evening. Taking the keys with him as she stayed in the car, he entered the post office where he had rented a box for receiving mail. As expected, there was an envelope inside the box that contained two debit cards and information related to a new bank account. Although Madison would never be made aware of it, funding for the account had been established by a Seattle-based business associate of the president. After removing one card and looking over the list of stipulations, Heath folded the envelope in half and slid it into the inside breast pocket of his suit. Returning to the car, he then drove to a nearby bank with an ATM so that he could withdraw the maximum daily allowable amount of cash.

Their third stop was just a few miles away at a Walmart, and Madison was surprised that Heath had put such importance on the location over that of getting something to eat.

Turning to face her after parking, he said, "All right, now let's get busy."

"What do you mean? What do we need to do here?"

"Well, I thought this would be a good place to pick up several items that you obviously need. In case you were unaware of it, everything that you once owned from your days of living in D.C. was seized and either sold, donated, or thrown out. And don't forget that by your own choice of free will, whatever you may have collected during your stay in Ellsworth was left behind this morning. Therefore, because you currently possess nothing other than what you are wearing, we are here to get you some new clothes and other personal items."

As it turned out, those initial purchases from Walmart would be limited to immediate essentials, and based on where they had been acquired, the clothing options were far from high-end. However, Madison understood that having some new items, such as a pair of jeans, a few T-shirts, some warm comfortable sweats, tennis shoes, and undergarments, as well as some basic toiletries, was what she needed. Although a wider range of items would be required soon, she was glad to have what was provided while also accepting the current posture of Heath. While moving through the various aisles, he quietly explained to her that they would make a few return visits to this and other stores in the coming days and weeks, but he wanted to remain as anonymous as possible. To that end, Madison learned of two tactics that would be employed to help accomplish the intended goal, and both of those went beyond what was routinely practiced by many in modern American society.

First, in order to avoid any unwanted attention, their haul of goods would be kept to a moderate level as they moved through the store and waited in line for a checkout register. And second, the payment for their purchases, made more reasonable by using the first tactic, would be in cash. Heath pointed out that using currency as opposed to credit or debit cards when plausible would create a level of anonymity, and he also believed that it would raise no suspicion as long as the amount wasn't too substantial. Then he added that although the latter may not always be true, learning to use cash more frequently would serve as a prudent practice for their future.

Afterward, they ate dinner at a recognizable national chain known for having a wide variety of cuisine to choose from, and although informed that the food was probably not the best to be found in Carson City, Madison felt that it was far better than what she had been accustomed to at Ellsworth. Once again Heath paid in cash while also leaving a modest tip, and he hoped that Madison would comprehend he was reinforcing the lesson that had recently been discussed. That lesson was simple. If one wanted to remain somewhat covert in their movements, then the best method for accomplishing that goal was to never become lazy while attempting to cover their tracks. Minimize any paper trail whenever possible and become less memorable to any serving staff by never leaving them a tip that was either too large or too small.

Lastly, they went to a grocery store to pick up some food and drinks for their apartment, which would sustain them for several days. Then with their most immediate staples secured, Heath drove them a few miles to an apartment complex where they unloaded his personal belongings and all of their recently purchased items from the car.

Entering a second-floor apartment, Heath said, "Welcome to your new home, Madison."

She took a moment to look around the living room, and although none of the furniture was in great shape, Madison conceded that it was livable. Then she moved to the kitchen area and, after opening a few cupboards, realized that stocking them had not yet been a priority for Heath. Moving on, she went through the door to a bedroom and could see an open door in the corner to the bathroom. Although not expressing it verbally, to her the apartment felt to be roughly the same size as the one she lived in while in Washington. That apartment had been nicely appointed, and she was quite fond of it while residing there, but it also held a most negative memory attached to the last day of her residence. It was where she, while clearly conflicted by the orders from her superiors, had attempted to kill Heath before subsequently being taken into custody.

Shaking those thoughts from her mind, Madison returned to the living room and asked playfully, "Only one bedroom, Heath? It's not that I mind sharing with you, but do you think the two of us will be all right in there? I mean, you know…is the bed comfortable?"

In skirting the question, Heath explained that he did not know if the bed was comfortable because he had not made use of it yet. As part of the staging for the upcoming mission, he had signed a six-month lease for the furnished apartment and paid a security deposit and rent through the first of the year. Then he had rented the P.O. Box for receiving mail, which would help to authenticate their presence. Although each had been accomplished two days before venturing to Ellsworth for his meeting with the warden, he had not stayed in town long enough to sleep.

Heath added that the apartment would serve their purpose as a base of operations whenever they were in Carson City, and would help to maintain their cover story of being an unmarried couple who moved into the area from Arizona for new jobs. Most of their belongings were supposedly in storage, and as they did not want to move any of the larger items until they found a home, a furnished unit was required.

Showing a bit of a wry smile, Madison responded, "Well, you have been laying some groundwork and seemingly have everything figured out. And I suppose for the sake of the mission that what you just told me would be believable and make sense to those on the outside. But Heath, it conveniently avoids answering my basic question."

"I told you. I don't know if the bed is comfortable."

"Yes, Heath. I understand that, but will we be sharing it?"

"Oh…no, Madison, we won't be sharing the bed. I will sleep out here on the couch."

His reply was not exactly what she was hoping for, and Madison needed to hide her inner disappointment, but things could change. Soon after, while rubbing her left butt cheek, she remarked that it had been an eventful day and she would therefore be calling it a night.

The following morning, Madison rose to the nearly silent sound of Heath's footsteps as he entered the room as well as the smell of fresh coffee in close proximity. Sleep had come easy during the previous several hours, as she had enjoyed the comfort of a large bed with a decent mattress for the first time since the last night in her Washington, D.C., apartment nearly three years prior. When she had been nudged from her slumber by Heath, she did not stir. Instead, Madison listened as he placed the large cup of brew on her nightstand while also waiting for the possible touch of his hand. A response to such an advance would have been positive, and there was plenty of room for Heath to join her if he had wanted to during the night or in the present moment. But alas, she remained alone. True to his claim, Heath had made use of the couch and slept in the living room, and now the quiet click of the door as he retreated signaled that he would not alter their current status.

For Madison, a few questions had been answered clearly, in that the bed was indeed comfortable and certainly large enough for them to share. But one question remained: Would Heath ever take advantage of a presented opportunity?

After splashing water on her face and slipping on some clothes, Madison emerged from the bedroom with her cup in hand and said, "Good morning. Thanks for the coffee."

Heath lifted his gaze from the stack of files that he had been studying and returned the kindness while adding, "You're welcome. It's from a little place about a block from here if you ever need more. Now, did you sleep well?"

Noticing the files spread out on the table, Madison theorized they were probably the same ones he was looking at when she awoke from the implant procedure.

Then while stretching both arms as best as she could without aggravating the incision on the side of her breast, she replied, "Yes, I did. Now what are those?"

With a wave of his hand toward them, he said, "These are files on each of the four targets, and I'm expecting to receive additional intelligence in the future."

Moving closer, Madison stated, "So I should start studying them as well, right?"

"Absolutely, we both need to know all that we can about each of the four mission targets and their tendencies. Unfortunately, we don't know when I will receive word of where you can make an attempt on them, or in what order those four opportunities will be presented. But in the meantime, we can become as fully prepared as possible, both mentally and physically, for each chance. Then as a team we can strike."

"So, we can begin my physical training then?"

"Not just yet. Starting this morning, we have other concerns to deal with before we can even think about that aspect of getting you ready."

"Like what?"

Heath leaned back away from the files and went into detail about what needed to be done. The first matter at hand would be to discuss whatever names Madison wanted to take on for her various future aliases, as Heath would need to vet each of them to determine if any red flags could prevent their use. He stressed the importance of starting with that so the necessary document preparation could begin as soon as possible. Once the selections had been cleared, they could work on developing suitable disguises for each passport photo, which would be checked at various customs offices. After that would be the research phase into what type of woman each target may have vulnerability for, as Madison could use that information in the event a comparable look would be required as bait. However, in each instance, the image would need to be different from the passport identity that she would use for entry into wherever they may be going.

8

Winter Education

THROUGHOUT THE NEXT handful of weeks, Heath and Madison maintained a busy schedule as they tended to various logistical matters. Their efforts included learning every possible detail from the intelligence sent to him regarding each of the four targets, along with the when and where of each future venture outside of the United States.

As Heath learned of her chosen aliases clearing the vetting process, visits were made to multiple locations in Carson City and Reno so that he and Madison could select clothing and other necessary provisions for each disguise. Included within that task were costume shops where Heath purchased different cuts of fake beards and mustaches that could be glued in place, and four separate stores where Madison could buy a range of different color and different length wigs. One reason she gave to the salesclerks for the purchases at each location was an unpleasant confession that an upcoming cancer treatment would cause the loss of her hair, while another tale spoke of a desire to spice things up in the bedroom.

With those important aspects taken care of, visits were then made to various locations where passport photos could be taken in the disguises. Soon after, Heath sent the sets of photos and the accompanying paperwork for each fictitious identity to a government lab where the counterfeit documentation could be completed.

In conjunction with that ongoing process, Madison had resumed a daily physical-fitness routine. With her pain in the region of each incision long since gone and the healing of her body complete, she began with simple stretching to go along with pushups and crunches. Soon, her daily exercise program expanded to include short runs, and Madison was amazed by how quickly the form and pace that she so easily demonstrated at Ellsworth returned. As she then strove for continued improvement on an oval that was not surrounded by barbed wire fencing and guard towers, Heath was pleased to join her on numerous December occasions at the Carson High School track.

With the calendar then turning to the year 2031, Madison took it upon herself to move things forward by inquiring as to when the training Heath had mentioned would begin. In response, he explained to her that in some regard the process had been ongoing for several weeks, as not all of what she would need to know would be based simply on physical abilities. It was true that certain physical aspects were an undeniable portion of what would be forthcoming in her training, but there were other skills for her to hone. Putting together various clues to help better comprehend the magnitude of one's surroundings, along with recognizing certain traits or tendencies of those in close proximity, was an important tool on covert assignments. To that end, Heath offered praise to Madison as he emphasized that while shopping, she had been doing so unconsciously since soon after they arrived in Carson City. Using the purchasing of her wigs as a prime example, Heath stated that Madison had skillfully read the demeanor of the salesclerk in each of those instances to determine which fable would be best received.

Heath continued by revealing to Madison that there would be more training of a similar nature to come, and throughout that training he wanted her to be aware of how other people reacted to her presence. His plan was to incorporate scenarios that would bring everyday citizens into the training program, as both of them could benefit from those unsuspecting individuals who would be targets of their scrutiny and possible persuasion.

In changing gears, Heath then mentioned that another factor in how Madison could be properly prepared was based on her diet, as good nutrition coupled with her exercise regime would help to minimize lethargy during key moments of the mission. With regard to the required level of focus, she would also need to learn how to maintain it and still function efficiently while under the influence of alcohol. Heath stressed that, going into each phase of the mission, she must understand and know within herself that getting close to a target could include drinking with them. If that were to occur, Madison must have the ability to pounce and seize a potential moment of created weakness. Therefore, even though the intake would be done in moderation, for practicality's sake, some of her physical training would be rehearsed after having a few drinks.

Continuing with the aspect of her physical abilities, Heath expressed no concern regarding getting Madison in shape for learning the techniques of self-defense and hand-to-hand combat. The exercise element and drive for both cardio health and extreme flexibility was already strongly present within her, which would make the upcoming physical training considerably easier. However, the challenge that Heath put forth to Madison, if one were to exist at all, was how her body would adapt to the training at higher elevations. He knew from her file that she had been posted in Europe as an ensign in the navy, and that during those years she had access to the steep, mountainous terrain in portions of the continent. But he also knew that the majority of her life had been spent in locations much closer to sea level, such as Eastern Kansas, South Central Texas, and Washington, D.C., when she served as a lieutenant at the Pentagon. Beyond those years of history, her most recent stay in Ellsworth also needed to be factored into the equation.

Heath informed Madison that Carson City, Nevada, was located at more than forty-six hundred feet of elevation, and although she had adjusted well to the thinner air after the first week or two, she could show signs of fatigue as they moved forward with more intense activity. It was a factor Heath intended to be mindful of, but he understood that any physical superiority over an intended target could be amplified by training at higher elevations than where they were currently running. Therefore, when weather permitted, he intended to include multiple training sessions at over sixty-two hundred feet on the nearby beaches of Lake Tahoe. Then when feasible, they could also use the higher elevations of meadows and hiking trails in the mountains that surrounded it.

When finally addressing her question of when the physical aspects of such training would commence, Heath eased the anxious spirit of Madison. He conceded that with many of the logistical aspects now properly in order, the time had come. They would jointly begin a most difficult regiment the following morning.

Hearing the news, Madison instantly flashed back in time. She remembered having received some training in self-defense and hand-to-hand combat at the beginning of her naval career, but unfortunately that was years into the past. She had no problem with admitting to herself, and Heath, that most of what had been learned then was, if not forgotten, very rusty. In turn, those thoughts triggered the distasteful memory of how she had been forced to simply accept the occasional leering eyes of wanting from a few superior officers while posted in Europe and at the Pentagon. How nice it would have been, in spite of her limited defensive skills of the time, to keep those various men and women with bad intent at bay via self-defense moves but doing so would have brought forth disciplinary action against her. Therefore, as a countermeasure, she had always relied on her wits so that she would never be caught in a situation that she could not easily escape.

Returning to the present, Madison eagerly took on the challenge of soaking up all the training and wisdom that Heath shared. As the winter months of January and February rolled past into March, the skills that had deteriorated over the years, and others that were never previously known, became an everyday aspect of her life. Heath had established a pattern of nearly endless lessons in the art of hand-to-hand combat while in diverse types of terrain, weather conditions, or cumbersome layered clothing, and in so doing had taken it to extreme levels. Some of his instructional sessions took on the challenging aspects of sparring while standing in bright, reflective light that hindered clear vision as rays of sun glistened off hard-packed snow or ice. Still others were given while barefoot in the loose sand and imperfect footing of vacant beaches as blizzard conditions swirled about them.

As an additional teaching tool, Heath also introduced Madison to cross-country skiing. Although it was obvious at times that his technique had become rusty through years of neglect, he had remembered how to ski from the days of his youth in the area. As they both struggled to master the delicate art, Heath conveyed to Madison that such a peaceful retreat was an excellent cardiovascular exercise while also demanding both proper body alignment and balance control.

While splitting their time between the mountains of Lake Tahoe and the valley of Carson City for their combined training, Heath continued to instruct and prepare Madison in a variety of ways with each passing day. Throughout the process, he always provided positive reinforcement that training under such conditions would make Madison far beyond lethal, and it would pay dividends when engaging one of her targets in more benign circumstances. Then as they relaxed in their apartment one evening in the closing days of March, Heath completed the last of her training by instructing Madison on what would need to be done once each of her targets was either subdued or vulnerable.

As he once again reminded Madison that each of the deaths should be made to appear as accidental, Heath introduced her to the first of two chemical components that could be used to aid in the process. He presented a ring that was intended to be worn on the index finger of her left hand, and showed Madison how to twist the dark stone counterclockwise and then shift it in such a way as to expose a tiny needle hidden within the underside of the band. Once exposed, that needle would be pressed against the neck of her victim somewhere near either ear, with a resulting discomfort of the prick being similar to that of a bee sting. A powerful nerve toxin housed inside the ring would then quickly enter the bloodstream of the recipient and render them unconscious within thirty seconds. The size and stature of the victim was a variable in how long their unconscious state would last, but Madison could count on having close to twenty minutes to work with. As Heath demonstrated how to reverse the process so the needle would be safely housed back inside the band, he stated that any trace elements of the toxin would become undetectable in the bloodstream after about eighteen hours. As a result, any medical personnel examining the body would need to work fast in order to discover it.

Heath expressed that the best-case scenario would be to use the ring, and then complete the sanction by staging what would be an untimely, yet accidental, death. However, if that could not be easily managed, there would be a backup at her disposal. Should the need arise, Madison would be equipped with a separate compact syringe that contained a high and lethal dose of pentobarbital. She would need to inject the contents of the syringe into the victim while they were already unconscious, and by doing so, the brain functions would slow and death via respiratory arrest would occur within minutes.

As with the many other lessons she received throughout the previous few months, Madison paid close attention to the instructions given. However, in this instance she asked Heath to go over the entire procedure again. She understood that none of the aspects of dangling her bait and getting close to the target in a private setting would mean much of anything if she could not perform this most vital facet of each sanctioned kill correctly.

When both were satisfied that she was well versed in the process, Madison stated, "All right, so I can do this. Now what's next?"

Presenting a pair of small stud earrings, Heath said, "These are to be worn while you are out in the field. There is a micro transmitter in each that will allow me to hear what is going on while you are attempting to carry out each sanctioned kill, and they give you a method as well of signaling that you are in distress should that occur. They will be quite effective unless you are in a crowded and bustling setting like a ballpark or a train station, but unlike your implants, they do have a limited range."

Nodding with understanding, Madison asked, "All right, is there anything else?"

"Well…no. This was the final portion of what I could train you to do. Certain aspects of the skill set required, such as the power of seduction, were present within you before we began the physical training. That ability, coupled with the talent to slip easily into various character roles, is part of why I selected you as the operative for this lengthy mission in the first place. As you have now added a lethal physical proficiency and a keen awareness to your surroundings, you are, in my opinion, ready to take on this assignment. In fact, if you had possessed your current level of skill three years ago in your apartment, then you would have been successful in killing me. However, should there be any aspect of our recent training that you are uncomfortable with, now would be the time to mention it. So, do you have any questions?"

Madison knew that Heath had been receiving occasional intelligence reports since their arrival in November regarding the targets and their intended movements. Just like him, she had studied them thoroughly in order to be fully prepared. However, what she did not know was that Heath had also used that same old-fashioned form of snail mail to maintain sporadic contact with President Harwell through Mrs. Dawson. The handwritten notes of just a few words he received from Washington informed Heath of not only the sustained intent to move forward with the plan, but the most recent included the cryptic code phrases he asked the president to provide so that each family would know who the message of death had come from. Understanding how vital that was, Heath had all four of them laminated.

As for his own notes through Mrs. Dawson to the president, Madison was also unaware that Heath had in recent days sent a concise message of just six words.

That message read: *Fully prepared with opportunity one presented.*

While sliding the ring off her finger and handing it back to Heath, Madison replied, "Well, thank you. It's good to know you believe I possess the skills to attempt the sanctions. Now for the record, I am sorry about the incident in my old apartment. If you don't already know this, Heath, I was conflicted then about following through with the order from above because I was falling in love with you. But my hesitation turned out to be a good thing, as you were able to thwart my attempt and easily subdue me. Otherwise we, with help from others, would never have been able to bring down the organization or spend this time together."

"I appreciate your apology, Madison, and the confession of the feelings that you had for me then. Perhaps when the mission has been completed, we can discuss them further. But for now, is there anything about the mission status that is unclear to you?"

"There's only one thing. When do we move on the first target?"

Pushing one of the files across the table, Heath replied, "We leave in four days. It will take time to get in position, and we need to complete the sanction in less than two weeks."

Looking at the photo of her prey, Madison smiled and said, "All right, I will be ready. Now is there anything else that needs to be done before we leave?"

"Yes, there is. Tomorrow morning, we must take care of an errand after securing a safe-deposit box at the bank. We will need it to hide files and any of our identity documents that will not be used for the first sanction. After that, there will be one last bit of shopping to do."

"All right, so what are we shopping for?"

"We both need some summer clothing and bathing suits."

SANCTION ONE

9

Reposition Cloak

AFTER MONTHS OF training and waiting for an opportunity, Heath and Madison were finally faced with the prospect of attempting the first of their four sanctioned kills. Of course, in order to do so, they would first need to position themselves properly on the global map. In understanding there would be multiple legs of travel to both reach and then return from their intended destination, Heath was cautious with the planning of their movements. He had spent much time during the previous few days arranging the booking of multiple flights, hotels, and even a boat rental, using some of their false identities to do so. The intent was to leave little or no trail that could be easily traced back to him or Madison, so beyond their false American passports for entry into Canada, he informed Madison they would each be fortified with three additional Canadian identities.

At five in the morning on Wednesday, April second, they left the apartment in Carson City and drove north for little more than thirty minutes to the Reno-Tahoe International Airport. With the first stop on their intended journey being within the United States, they were able to travel as Heath and Madison for a direct flight to Spokane, Washington. Once there, Heath rented a car by using an Arizona driver's license. The fictitious American identity was the same one that had been utilized when he rented their apartment, and as far as the counter agent at the airport was concerned, it was authentic. Heath selected a make and model of a four-door sedan that was similar to what they had been using for the past several months, as he wanted the car to blend in as nothing unusual nor flashy.

Their subsequent drive first took them east on Interstate 90 to Coeur d'Alene in northern Idaho, and then farther north along Highway 95 in the narrow panhandle section of the state through Sandpoint and Bonners Ferry toward the Canadian border. Throughout a portion of that two-hour stint, Heath and Madison had a chance to go over some of the mission specifics, such as where she could successfully eliminate the first target on the list. Then when the navigation system in the sedan informed them that the border was twenty miles out, Heath began looking for a wide enough place to safely pull over. The time had come for both of them to alter their looks enough so that each would closely resemble their fabricated American passport photos. As Heath had no wigs to alter the natural black color of his hair, he glued a goatee of similar shade in place and put on a well-worn baseball cap while Madison slipped on a wig of long, straight blond hair to go with tinted reading glasses.

Stopped at the crossing while the Canadian border agent checked the two passports, both Heath and Madison expressed a relaxed and happy mood. In an effort to assist with their cover story, Madison had placed a book from AAA that highlighted the Canadian provinces of British Columbia and Alberta on her leg nearest the center console.

When the woman in uniform inquired as to whether their visit was for business or pleasure, Heath responded with, "It's for pleasure. We are headed to the Banff area for some sightseeing, spring skiing, and maybe a little hiking if the weather cooperates."

"That sounds nice. So how long will you be staying?"

"We could be there as long as two weeks, but our plans are open-ended."

As Heath concluded his answer, the computer investigation on the passports had come through as all clear. Their ruse of two adults that were supposedly vacationing to a beautiful national park area was certainly believable enough for the woman checking them, and as no red flags came up on the passport scan, there was no reason to suspect otherwise. Had that scenario been their true intent, the drive to Banff would have taken three or four hours depending on traffic and road conditions.

Passing the documents back over to Heath, the border agent said pleasantly, "Welcome to Canada, folks. Enjoy your stay with us."

Heath took the passports and replied, "Thank you, miss, have a nice day."

Less than an hour later, they rolled into the large town of Cranbrook, which was on the way toward Banff. However, instead of continuing on as they claimed, a suitable location was found in order to once again alter their appearance before heading to the regional airport. Madison changed into a wig of neck-length red hair that was slightly curled, and Heath removed the goatee and baseball cap in favor of a full black-haired beard and mustache. Now using the first of their Canadian passports to match, they checked in for an upcoming short flight over the mountains to Calgary. Then after arriving in Calgary during the late evening, they each collected their two carry-on bags of luggage and moved easily through the airport to hail a cab. A few minutes later, Heath and Madison checked into the first of their hotels.

Once in the room Heath stated, "All right, it's been a long day, but everything went smoothly. Let's eat and get some sleep. We have another early day tomorrow."

The following morning, while each maintained the same look as the flight over from Cranbrook, Heath hired a different cab company for the short return to the airport. Then they caught an eastbound flight to Toronto and followed the same process of two cab companies being employed for another night in an airport hotel. However, when they returned to the Toronto Airport on Friday, April fourth for their subsequent flight south, a change in their appearance had been made that went unnoticed by others. Madison had donned a third wig of straight black hair that was cut just below the shoulders, while Heath had lost the full black beard and mustache in favor of a bushy black mustache and wire-rimmed reading glasses. After a quick inspection of their passports at the ticket counter, they boarded a southbound flight routed over the east coast of the United States and the waters of the Caribbean Sea to San Juan, Puerto Rico.

For Madison it would be her first trip to the region, and she thought the same was true for Heath. What she did not know was that he had flown to San Juan once before on Air Force One with President Harwell, who was offering his full support to a proposed vision. That trip in late May 2028 had been organized to help the president finalize a contract that would have the U.S.-held territories of St. Croix, St. John, and St. Thomas join with Puerto Rico in combined statehood. By pure coincidence, his speech and meetings that day with the territorial governors took place just a few days after Madison began her stint at Ellsworth under the name of Susan Greer.

As for the present moment, Heath was glad that just like the previous trip, passage through United States customs would be avoided. In the first instance he had flown directly from Washington, D.C., to San Juan, so even if he had not been protecting the president, no international boundaries had been crossed. However, this flight from Toronto, Canada, was in direct opposition of that fact, so on the surface it would appear to be different. But since neither he nor Madison intended to leave the San Juan airport for a venture into Puerto Rico or any other island portion of the recently formed state, they were directed to a holding area with many other unimpeded passengers. Those numerous travelers, as with Heath and Madison, were bound for one or more of several different Caribbean island nations.

After ninety minutes a call for their flight could be heard over the intercom, so Heath and Madison boarded a twin-engine prop plane with roughly thirty other passengers. They were destined for the small airstrip on Beef Island at the eastern tip of Tortola, and once there, officials of the British Virgin Islands would handle any matters related to customs.

10

Road Town

AS THEIR FLIGHT banked left for final approach into the airstrip, Madison maintained a steady gaze through her window. Throughout the past several minutes there had been a beautiful sight to behold, as a nearly uncountable number of small boats sailed or motored on the surface of clear light-blue waters that surrounded the various British Virgin Islands. Then to her surprise, the shrinking distance between the plane and that intoxicating blue water suggested that their landing could become a wet one. However, any concern that a plane flying at less than one hundred feet of altitude may have caused was immediately put to rest as the closely grouped shoreline, roadway, and then the landing strip came into view beneath her.

Exiting the plane into the warm afternoon sunshine and gentle breezes that the region is known for, Madison turned to Heath and asked, "Where has this been all my life?"

With a smile he returned, "No kidding! I think we've both been missing something."

After standing in a quick-moving line behind half a dozen other excited vacationers, their passports were given a token glance and stamped for entry. They were through customs, and their subsequent transportation aboard a loaded shuttle van to the largest population center on the main island of Tortola was easily secured. Madison learned as they climbed into the van that based on its proximity to nearby St. John and St. Thomas, the American dollar was used as the currency of choice throughout the British Virgin Islands. Their ensuing trip along portions of the coast toward Road Town was at times exhilarating due to the speed with which many narrow corners were taken, but the journey to where Heath had arranged for the two of them to stay was completed without incident.

Once checked into their modest room, Madison pulled the curtains closed before removing her wig to reveal her natural look of shortly cut brown hair. Then she changed clothes as Heath tended to the removal of his false mustache. Feeling less encumbered, they pulled out a map of the area and a file containing pertinent information from local websites that Heath had printed out at the Carson City library.

After jointly studying what lay in front of them for a few minutes, Heath said, "All right, so do we both have our bearings?"

"I think so."

"Then should we get started?"

"I'm ready if you are."

"All right, so let's walk around a portion of the town for a few minutes to get a sense of landmarks and routes for escape in case we need them. If we act as though we are shopping and searching for a nice place to get a cold drink, we should be able to blend in."

"Sounds good, but what about the charter place?"

"Well…we already have the theoretical itinerary for his Sunday charter. But it wouldn't hurt to verify our information by visiting the facility. We can ride over there in a cab after we take our walk, and then while posing as potential future customers we can inquire about what types of packages are offered for sailboats with a crew. I doubt they would give up any names of their clients, as for legal reasons they will probably be required to protect them. But, maybe they will provide us with a specific itinerary of crewed charters if we ask for it."

With a course of action established, Heath and Madison set about their quest to gain more insight by exploring some of the surrounding area. In the process they learned that leaving from their hotel could be accomplished without needing to pass through the lobby, which would in turn ease their ability to go unnoticed no matter what disguise was in use. There were also a few choices for escape routes if needed, with each leading to locations where numerous cabs or shuttles could be hired.

While those discoveries were being quietly discussed and logged into memory as they walked along the main street, Madison also utilized some of the observational skills that Heath had helped her further develop. She recognized just how relaxed many of the people they encountered were, as each person seemed to be lost in their own little world of vacation bliss. Therefore, noticing what she and Heath might be up to throughout the next several days would probably be of no concern to anyone. In addition, Madison recognized that very few of the women she observed were carrying purses or seemed worried about what their hair or makeup looked like. Noting that a few of them had something around their waist that was akin to an old fanny pack, she thought locating one for her use might be just what was needed.

While further pondering the notion, Madison came to realize that her small black purse with a long thin strap, intended to be a necessary component during the kill, was now in question. Although the summer clothing Madison purchased for the trip seemed adequate and appeared to fit in nicely, when opposed to what she had recently spotted, the purse could become a liability when the time came. As she continued to walk with the seemingly useless article slung over her shoulder and riding just above her hip, Madison suddenly grasped the fact that a separate issue also existed. The fashionable accessory, more apropos for a different setting, coupled with her minimal amount of sun exposure in recent months, loudly screamed out an annoying depiction. Not only was she unmistakably a tourist, but it was obvious that she was also one who had just arrived. Disgruntled that each aspect of the current reality could cultivate unwanted recognition, Madison decided that she would address both issues with haste.

After nudging Heath toward and into a place with an open patio deck that looked lively, Madison quickly scanned the room. There were lots of patrons in the establishment but based on the time of day there were also several empty tables. Then, in locating the correct mix of what she was searching for, Madison headed for a certain table and sat down.

Heath joined her and seconds later asked, "So would you like something to eat?"

"Not really. But I think a cold beer would be nice."

"That sounds good to me as well. I'll see what I can do."

Before he could rise and head for the bar, Madison had turned toward the young woman seated at the adjacent table.

Smiling at her, she inquired, "Excuse me. I'm sorry to interrupt, but that is a cute little bag you have there. Do you mind me asking where you got it?"

Turning from her group conversation, the young lady responded, "Not at all. I found it at a place about three blocks down the street."

"It's really cute. And a fabric bag like that with a zipper seems more practical than a purse in a place like this. It just clips around your waist, right?"

"Yes, it does. In fact, right after I bought it, I put my purse away in my luggage."

Then while pointing with her finger, Madison asked, "And the place you found it is that way?"

"That's right. You can't miss it."

"Well thank you very much. I'll go check it out."

Heath had listened to the entire exchange, and as he then left the table in quest of two beers, he smiled. Madison obviously had something in mind with regard to the use of a little bag such as the one the young lady possessed, and her technique to learn how one could be acquired was effective without causing undue suspicion.

After their short, thirst-quenching stop, it was time to press on. Madison rose and, with a courteous wave, thanked the young lady for the information. Then moments later she and Heath had located the identified shop, purchased the smallest version of the many sizes of bags available, and stepped out onto the sidewalk again. Soon after, they hailed an empty passing cab for a ride to the nearby charter facility where their target would begin his sailing adventure in less than forty-eight hours.

Throughout the ensuing hour-long tour of the facility, Heath and Madison were able to either confirm their knowledge of what the target would be doing in the next several days or add to it. Included within the former was the itinerary example put forth by office personnel that matched up identically with the theoretical one Heath already possessed. The young man behind the counter proudly boasted that any charter cruise aboard one of their sailing vessels, no matter for what duration of time, would undoubtedly become an adventure to be remembered. Then he added that if such a trip were to include a veteran crew of captain and chef, the experience would be first class.

In sensing that the positive body language of his inquiring guests suggested a potential future booking, the young man continued by presenting a large, detailed map of the region. With enthusiasm, he then set about randomly pointing out each of the nightly anchorages that could be used when booking a charter with a crew.

Madison waited for him to take a breath and then asked innocently, "Is there any particular order to the various locations, or does the captain just wing it?"

In response, the representative said, "That's a good question, miss. A crewed charter will follow a predetermined route when it comes to the nightly anchorages, which in turn will allow our guests time to plan ahead for various daily or evening activities."

"And what types of activities are those?"

"Well, snorkeling for one. It's a big draw in this area, so guests will be able to enjoy that experience every day if they wish. There is also the opportunity to dive on the wreck of the RMS Rhone or other sites, as we can outfit your charter with scuba gear and tanks."

"All of that sounds great, but what about shore excursions? Are those possible, or would everything be based on sailing and other water activities?"

"That's another good question, and you will not be required to either stay on the boat or be involved in water activities. There will be an opportunity every day to enjoy a range of great experiences ashore on the various islands, and the crew will recommend that our guests take full advantage of each one."

"Well that's good. A friend of mine back home in Chicago told me she went to a couple of places that we might enjoy. One is called Pusser's Landing at Soper's Hole, and the other is the Peter Island Resort. Can we visit those places if we want to?"

Now pointing at specific locations on the map, the young man explained that she could most certainly visit her listed locations. Not only were they two of the many stops scheduled for Sunday departure charters, but he inadvertently simplified the logistics of her upcoming task by spelling things out for her in detail. He provided the day and time during the seven-night sail that each would be visited, while also speaking of when other shore excursions that shouldn't be missed, such as Foxy's on Yost Van Dyke along with The Baths and the Bitter End on Virgin Gorda, would be offered.

At that point, Heath and Madison had been told everything they needed to hear and then some, and the new information would be most useful. Although the young man continued with his thorough explanation of what the remaining days would bring forth, it went largely unheard by his audience. When he finally concluded, they gave him a joint nod of approval and stated that they appreciated his time and liked the idea of possibly booking such a charter for the following year.

Then, with the contact information for the charter company representative and a few different itinerary sheets in her hand, Madison smiled as Heath asked, "And these crewed charters of yours get booked up on a regular basis?"

That was when he and Madison received an unlikely scrap of information, as the young man replied without caution, "Oh, yes, sir. There are two such charters out right now, and we have four gentlemen from the Seattle, Washington, area coming in tomorrow afternoon for another crewed charter. On Sunday morning, they will set sail in that catamaran right over there."

Looking in the direction of where he was pointing, they could each clearly see a name across the stern of the large catamaran. Then after both Heath and Madison shook the man's hand with an offer of thanks, they departed and remained silent until they returned to the main street where they could once again blend in with those around them.

Walking at his side after exiting the cab, Madison turned to Heath and said, "Well...we learned more than I thought we would. I never expected to get the name of his boat."

"I agree. That was a fortuitous surprise. Even though we already had an itinerary, now we have confirmation of each date and the timeframes narrowed down. It amazes me sometimes what people will reveal if you just let them ramble."

Later that evening in the hotel room, they finalized the plans for what Madison intended to do. She explained that she wanted to start things off with a brief encounter on Sunday at the Foxy's place that was mentioned. In her assessment, the target should be made aware of her existence at that time, but not be granted the opportunity to turn the random-chance visual of her into a lengthy conversation. She would dangle the bait when appropriate, but not make any solid eye contact with him beyond a casual observance.

The next step would be to set the hook the following midday at Soper's Hole Marina. Her target would be on land for ninety minutes to enjoy the atmosphere of Pusser's Landing, which would give her plenty of time to be both noticed and approached. Madison would begin a conversation at that time and then plant a notion in his head that could not be ignored. After fabricating a story as to why she would be available, she planned to have him ask to see her again. All he needed to do was discover that they would both be available for a less time-constrained rendezvous of drinks and dancing on Tuesday evening at the Peter Island Resort, and that is when she would strike.

11

Dangled Bait

AFTER MADISON SPELLED out her plan of attack to Heath, there were still a few logistical challenges to address. However, one concern that dealt with her ability to dangle the first offering of bait late Sunday afternoon could be easily overcome if another essential task were completed beforehand.

For her jaunt to and from the island of Yost Van Dyke, Madison would purchase a roundtrip ticket for a small ferryboat that provided service for locals and tourists between Cane Garden Bay on Tortola and the pier a few hundred yards from Foxy's in Great Harbour. That was the easy part. However, in order for Madison to catch that ferry, she would need to get to the north shore of Tortola first. Luckily, that could be accomplished with a little help.

On Saturday afternoon, while Madison did what she could to establish a base tan on her pale torso, Heath ventured back to the airport and rented a beat-up old car for their use in the coming few days. Then before noon on Sunday, he drove Madison from Road Town over the narrow streets of Mount Sage to the ferry departure point. Once there, she was motored to the island of Yost Van Dyke with plenty of time to spare.

After her arrival, Madison walked in the opposite direction from Foxy's along a dirt road that, if taken far enough, would lead up and over the western peninsula of Great Harbour toward the lesser-used anchorage site of White Bay. Beyond creating more time to work on her tan, her stroll to a point just short of the crest was done for two reasons. First, Madison would be able to view the entirety of the main anchorage site and the entrance to it from higher ground. Therefore, she could, in theory, more easily identify when the sailboat of her target was closing in to set anchor. At such a time, the second reason for ascending the dirt road would come into play. In returning along the road toward the beach and eventually Foxy's, Madison might be seen by someone who happened to look in her general direction. That possibility, even if she were only viewed by a single patron on the beach or at the bar, could lend credence to the cover story she intended to establish.

A few hours passed, and during that span there were a handful of sailboats that slipped either into or out of the oval-shaped bay. Then Madison saw a large catamaran entering, with the recognizable logo of the charter company that her target had hired emblazoned upon each hull. As it drew closer, she could see there were four young men moving about on deck, with a somewhat older man at the helm and a woman with blond hair on the bow. Beginning a slow move to her left and down the dirt road, Madison crouched and watched the boat as it turned into the prevailing breeze before the woman let loose a heavy anchor. The name of the craft was now clearly in her view, as the man at the helm added stability by setting a second anchor off the stern. Now firmly set for the night on the near side of the bay to her position, this was most definitely the catamaran that Madison had been waiting for.

The four young men on board and the presumed captain began their preparations to disembark, which would entail the use of a motorized inflatable raft to go ashore. Madison continued her observation of the happenings but did not move from her position. Her plan was to wait until after the group made landfall and then arrived at Foxy's before initiating a move to join them.

After depositing his clients on the beach and walking them toward Foxy's, the man piloting the inflatable raft surprised Madison by turning around to initiate a solo return to the catamaran. Although the move was unexpected, she realized that it could provide her with some extra time to set the stage while also adding one more set of eyes that might witness her descent along the dirt road. Pulling the garment loose from around the clipped waistband of her recently purchased little bag, Madison slipped her bright yellow tank top back on over her bikini before standing from her hidden crouch. Then she began a casual walk down the road toward the beach.

Ten minutes later, with her sandals now in her hand, Madison walked across the final stretch of beach to approach Foxy's. As she hoped, she could see that the four young men seated at a table in the sand on the near side of the establishment noticed her approach. The lads were less than subtle in hiding their collective interest, as the two with their backs toward her both spun to view what the two facing her were gawking at. Then, in an awkward attempt to remain cool, those young men quickly turned away when they realized that the object of their focus had caught them in the act.

Madison had predetermined that she would walk past them in a close-enough proximity so that one of them in particular would be given a chance to further inspect her as she headed for the bar.

Then while doing so, she gave a return glance with a smile to only that member of the group and said, "Hello."

The young man visibly perked up and smiled while mimicking her single-word gesture, but Madison did not break stride. Now unable to view their reaction directly as she moved on, she instinctively knew that her backside and well-toned legs were being judged by the collective. Of course, that was exactly what Madison intended, at least from one of them, and why she had worn a pair of snug shorts to lessen the mystery of what lay beneath.

Throughout the next hour, Madison relaxed at the bar and slowly sipped on a couple of drinks without paying too much attention to the table of the four young men. She noticed on occasion from the corner of her eye that the target had continued to show interest in her, but she made sure to minimize what could be misconstrued by him as direct eye contact. Much like many other patrons at the outdoor beach bar, Madison instead looked around and gazed at the diverse range of artifacts that hung from the rafters. She spoke a few words with other patrons if they engaged her, and during one such encounter, she seized the opportunity to point toward the far hillside and the dirt roadway leading up it. Then a moment later, she noticed that her target and his friends were pointing toward and discussing the same location.

Soon after their recognition of her supposed origin, Madison left the bar and headed off down the beach. In the process she did not pass close by the table of her target as was done when arriving, so there was no opportunity for him to attempt further contact. In her view, the intent of her visit had already been successful, so there was no need to linger and risk overkill. She had engaged the target in an innocent way without prolonged exposure and dangled some bait for him to think about in the process. Based on his initial reaction to her presence, Madison knew that the man was intrigued by what he had seen of her. As a bonus, he now also believed that she may have come from a sailboat anchored over the hill in a separate location to that of his in Great Harbour.

After disappearing from the view of Foxy's when she reached a small cluster of buildings and gift shops near the pier, Madison ducked inside one of them and waited patiently. Shortly after, the man who piloted the inflatable raft returned to retrieve her target and his friends for what, according to the charter itinerary, would be dinner aboard the catamaran.

When the ferry from Cane Garden Bay arrived a few minutes later, Madison waited until the boarding process for the return had already begun before she removed her bright yellow tank top and emerged from her hiding place. Then with it tightly balled up in her hand so that it could not be seen from afar as an identifying beacon, she moved within a group of roughly ten other passengers down the pier and into the hold of the boat. Having used the collective mass as suitable cover, and then in keeping low during the rapid boarding process, Madison felt confident that her target and his friends had not seen her.

As the ferry pulled away from the dock and headed toward open water, Madison peered through a small window from below deck. Although the motorized vessel passed within close range of the catamaran, there was no indication from any of those sitting down to dinner in the cockpit that they were aware of her location.

The ensuing return to Cane Garden Bay was quick, and based on the warmth in the ferry's interior cabin, Madison waited until they completed the crossing before putting her tank top back on. Soon after, Heath spotted the bright yellow beacon and picked her up.

As they began their journey along the series of narrow streets back to Road Town and their hotel, Heath asked, "So, were you able to make contact with him?"

"Yes, I was. But didn't you hear me?"

"No. I think your earring bug may have been out of range, or maybe the hill next to your location blocked a direct line of sight for the signal. So, what happened?"

"Well…I made visual contact and said hello. He took the bait and kept an eye on me as predicted. I'm in his head now, so he will definitely recognize me at Soper's Hole."

12

Setting the Hook

HAVING SUCCESSFULLY ACHIEVED her desired goal during the first random-chance encounter with her target, Madison could now move forward in creating the second. Fortunately, the plan of Monday morning leading up to her encounter involved less logistical concerns, as there was no need for Madison to catch a ferry to a separate island. Instead, Heath drove her along the twisting Sir Francis Drake's Highway to near the most western tip of Tortola and then across a short bridge to the adjacent Frenchman's Cay. Their coastal drive had been slightly longer than that of the previous day over Mount Sage to Cane Garden Bay, however it was decidedly easier due to a lack of navigational left and right turns onto various streets that the former required.

Nestled between the main island of Tortola and the Cay was the small, sheltered bay of Soper's Hole. Along with a ferry service to St. John or St. Thomas in the recently formed state of Puerto Rico, the bay maintained a full-scale marina and companies that chartered boats for day use or longer durations. There were also many shops and a few places to eat or drink, and it was in one such establishment that, according to the itinerary sheet, Madison could make contact with her target again.

With plenty of time to spare, Heath parked the car at a location on Frenchman's Cay that gave them a good view of the marina. Then as they waited patiently for a specific sailboat to enter Soper's Hole, he gave her the ring, a syringe, and a small, laminated object.

After Madison then peeled off her shorts and T-shirt, slipped on the ring, and put the syringe and laminated item into the fabric bag before clipping it around her waist, Heath asked, "Are you ready?"

"Yes, I'm all set. I have the syringe for the second injection in the event he doesn't want to meet after today, but I hope for both of our sake that I won't have to kill him here."

"I agree! This would not be the best place."

Then, after reaching across to gently grasp her arm, Heath explained that Madison should most definitely not kill the target at this location unless there was no other choice. Aside from the fact that it would be nearly impossible to make his death appear accidental, there could be any number of witnesses. Her anonymity, and the means of escape, would be put in serious jeopardy if she made her move here, so he asked that Madison take that into consideration before acting on impulse. But then Heath stated that if she felt with absolute certainty that it must be done without waiting for Tuesday as planned, Madison should give the emergency signal and carry out the sanction.

She nodded and asked, "And where will you be if you hear the emergency signal?"

"Make your way as fast as you can to the bridge, and I will pick you up there. If I'm not at the bridge when you get there, I will be soon. But don't stop to wait for me. Keep running across the bridge and then to the right until I catch up with you. Got it?"

"Yes, I understand. First the signal, then kill him and run like hell."

Silence then ensued as they both watched the catamaran of her target pull alongside the dock. A moment later four men disembarked and headed for the most well-known bar in the marina. Madison waited a moment or two, then after a few deep, calming breaths, she opened the car door and exited. Facing the window for the benefit that its reflection offered, she adjusted her bathing suit top to slightly enhance what was held within. Nodding at Heath who had watched her throughout the quick process, she then headed off on her quest.

While wearing nothing but her maroon bikini, a pair of sandals, and the little bag clipped around her waist, Madison strode confidently into Pusser's Landing and made her way through other customers toward the bar. While doing so, she smiled directly at one of the men who looked her over as she walked past. Then Madison climbed onto a stool nearby where he and his companions could still view her from head to toe.

Although many patrons in the establishment were dressed in bathing suits or shorts, her attire was a bit unusual in that she had failed to cover up her torso with a T-shirt or something else. She showed no interest in that a few women in her peripheral vision indicated displeasure with her existence, as Madison knew that their feelings toward her were probably based on envy. She could proudly boast of a body that those women likely never possessed, and if they did, it had been lost long ago. In either case, Madison would not be made to feel guilty about the hard work she had put in to achieve and maintain her present seductive form.

When a bartender approached and asked what he could get for her, Madison responded with, "I would love a Blackbeard Ale if you have one."

"All right, miss, one Blackbeard. Would you like a menu as well?"

"Oh…yes, I would. Thank you."

Within seconds both items were delivered with a smile, and Madison took a generous quenching pull from the bottle. Then, knowing that her target was watching her every move, Madison rose slightly off the stool and bent over the bar to reach for an additional cocktail napkin. For those several seconds, as she intentionally fumbled to retrieve just one from the stack, certain curves of her body were accentuated for the benefit of what she liked to refer to as memory reinforcement. The inviting curves Madison presented amplified the indignation of a few women in her proximity, but instead of caring about their issues, she was focused on how her target would react to the prolonged view. Taking another pull from her bottle of Blackbeard Ale, Madison then used the cocktail napkin as a convenient means to dab away droplets of water in her cleavage that had fallen from the bottle. As anticipated, the dangled bait yielded an almost immediate result.

One of the men at the nearest table made a whispered suggestion, and Madison smiled inwardly as the group then collectively encouraged her target to advance. Pretending not to have overheard, she glanced at the menu as if contemplating what to order. His courage to face the challenge presented would take another minute or so before emerging, but then it happened.

From a respectful distance of about six feet, her target asked, "Excuse me, miss, but you look familiar. Didn't I see you at Foxy's yesterday?"

Turning her body to face him, and then smiling as if pleased by his looks, Madison replied, "Well…it's possible. I was at Foxy's for a little while yesterday."

"I thought so. You were wearing a bright yellow tank top and you said hello to me."

Behaving for an instant as if she had to think about it while he moved closer, Madison broadened her smile while reaching out to gently touch his arm.

Then she said, "Yes. Now I remember. It was when I first arrived, and you were at a table with a few other guys."

"That's right. I was with my friends, and we had a great time. Did you enjoy the place?"

"Yes, I did. But unfortunately, I couldn't stay longer. I had to get back to my boat."

"So, you're on a boat like us. How do you like it?"

The fabricated tale Madison then wove for the man included an explanation of how she stayed at a hotel in Road Town for one night before spending the next three on a sailboat. They had just returned the boat to the charter company here in Soper's Hole, and although the adventure was fun, it was rather cramped with five people aboard. Therefore, she was looking forward to the next three nights at the Peter Island Resort, as it would give her a little more space and private time.

Her target asked, "You said there were five of you?"

"That's right."

"But you were alone yesterday, and again right now."

"That's true."

"So, if you don't mind me asking, who are you here with?"

Madison continued the fable of her cover by clarifying how she had come to the area, and what it entailed. Her boss back in Akron, Ohio, was coming to the British Virgin Islands on vacation with her husband, fourteen-year-old daughter, and her daughter's best friend. Their family business had done very well in recent times, so as a show of appreciation for five faithful years as her executive assistant, her boss offered the free trip with them as a reward. It was a gracious offer to be sure, and one that could not be refused. With the exception of a few personal expenses such as in their current setting, the entire trip—including roundtrip airfare from Cleveland, the boat charter they had been on, and her upcoming lodging at the Peter Island Resort—would be paid for.

Of course, that generosity came with a price, which on the sailboat meant very little time for privacy. Therefore, she talked with her boss after they anchored at White Bay the previous afternoon and was then able to break away for a visit to Foxy's. As for the moment at hand, the family would be shopping for at least a few hours before the group would make their way to Road Town and the ferry ride over to Peter Island later in the afternoon.

Madison could tell by the look in his eye that her target believed her story to be true, so she felt that it was time to reel him in a little more.

Inviting him to sit, Madison asked, "So what's the story with you and your friends?"

Climbing onto the stool beside her, he replied, "We're old friends from back in school, and we get together every year for a vacation. Usually it involves tropical beaches, but we thought it would be fun to add in some sailing."

"And where is home for you?"

"We all live fairly close to Seattle."

"I've heard that's a beautiful area."

"It can be, but it also rains too much and it's cold for the majority of the year."

Their joint-interview process about random subjects continued for a few minutes before her target offered to buy another round of drinks. Madison said she would accept, but only after she knew what his name was.

In an instant he replied, "Oh…of course. I'm sorry about that. My name is Cameron, and you are?"

Reaching out a hand, Madison replied, "I'm Brooke. It's nice to meet you, Cameron."

As the conversation lengthened, Madison continued her subtle seduction of Cameron by making sure to incorporate tools such as soft laughter combined with the gentle touch of her hand on his arm or leg when appropriate.

Meanwhile, the three friends of Cameron realized, as he continued to sit with her, that headway was being made. She was a hot woman who looked great in her bikini, and they hated to pull him away from her. Unfortunately, the time was fast approaching when they would all need to return to their catamaran.

One of them reluctantly approached and said, "Hey, Cameron, sorry to interrupt, man. But in a few minutes, we have to head back to the boat."

Turning to face his friend, then looking back toward Madison, and then back to his friend again, he replied, "All right. Just give me a few minutes and I'll meet you at the boat."

With a nod of acknowledgement, the young man departed with the other two in his wake, and when they were out of earshot Madison said, "It's a shame you have to leave, Cameron. I would really like to keep talking with you."

"I like talking with you as well, Brooke." Then after pulling a phone from his pocket, he added, "Can we exchange information so I can call or text you?"

Facing him directly, Madison spread her arms to once again highlight her form and show that in her present dress there was no place to hide such a device.

Then she said, "That would be great, Cameron, but I don't have a phone in my bikini or even in my luggage. I left it back in Akron because I wanted to get away from it and other forms of tech for a few days."

"Oh…well that's a shame. How about if you give me your number, and I can call you after you get back to Akron?"

Wanting to push him forward, Madison replied with a suggestion of, "I like that idea, Cameron, but maybe we can think of a way to see each other again here in the islands before then."

He pondered the thought for a moment, and then it suddenly hit him.

With enthusiasm Cameron said, "Hey, you said you were going to be staying at the Peter Island Resort for a few days."

"Yes. We are."

"Well…our boat is going to be anchored nearby tomorrow night. So maybe we can meet for dinner or something."

"That sounds great, Cameron, but where?"

"Our captain mentioned a place called Deadman's Beach Bar & Grill on the grounds of the Peter Island Resort. Let's plan on meeting there."

"Hey, I read about that place on their website before leaving Akron. Supposedly the place has a band every night, so we could do some dancing too."

"Great. So, let's do it. I mean why not, right?"

"Are you serious, Cameron?"

"Sure. We can relax to some music and drinks without feeling any pressure that one of us would need to leave in a hurry."

"You really mean this? You're not just kidding around with me?"

"Of course, I mean it, Brooke. I can be there at say…seven. And I hope that you will be, too."

"All right, Cameron, you convinced me. It's a date, and I'll see you at this Deadman's place at seven tomorrow evening."

As Cameron stood and reached out a hand, Madison cupped his face with both hands and smiled.

Then she gave him a little peck on the lips and said, "I think you're a nice guy, Cameron. Please don't be a jerk by standing me up."

Smiling from having received both acceptance of the offer and the unexpected peck, he replied, "Don't worry, Brooke. I will be there." Then after he paid for their round of drinks, he added, "Hey, you never gave me your number."

"Well if you show up tomorrow night, then I'll know that you really want it."

Madison then waved goodbye as Cameron jogged down the dock toward his awaiting catamaran. Turning back to face the bar, she enjoyed the rest of her Blackbeard Ale over the next several minutes before preparing to depart. When she was sure that his boat had sailed, Madison rose from the barstool, paid what she owed for the first beer, and walked out of Pusser's Landing feeling satisfied.

Back at the car, Heath greeted her with, "The entire conversation came through loud and clear, so we know the earring mic does work at close range. You did excellent work, Madison, and I especially like the way you baited him into asking you for a date."

"Thanks, but I was worried for a minute. If he hadn't figured out the opportunity on his own and acted, I was going to initiate the idea of meeting tomorrow evening. But now that Cameron has made his advance, there's no way that he won't show up. I could see it in his eyes after I gave him a little peck. He believes that the evening could involve something more than drinks and dancing."

13

Reeling Him In

WEARING THE SAME disguises that were used for entry into the British Virgin Islands on Friday, Heath and Madison checked out of their hotel in Road Town on Tuesday morning and returned the rental car to the airport. That was immediately followed by a cab ride for a short distance back in the direction of Road Town, where they were dropped off at a small upstart charter company in Fat Hogs Bay.

Although the two previous opportunities for Madison to create a chance encounter with Cameron had been arranged in short order, the location of what would be their third and final meeting had been selected by Heath and Madison before ever leaving Carson City. As a result, Heath had arranged for an overnight boat rental while also booking the various flights and hotel stays that were required for the current mission. Then to solidify the need for a one-night charter on such short notice, Heath informed the representative of the facility that it was intended to be a birthday present. The charter company learned from his further explanation that the girlfriend of their most recent customer had promised to create a lasting memory by way of an onboard experience to never be forgotten.

As they jointly strode toward the charter facility while carrying their luggage and a bag of food for the overnight, the man behind the counter gazed through the window and clearly understood what pleasures his customer would supposedly be enjoying. For the benefit of their ruse, Madison had donned her wig of straight black hair cut just below the shoulders and was wearing snug walking shorts and a crop top that revealed her flat, bare midriff. A strap of maroon fabric that fastened at the back of her neck indicated that she wore a bikini underneath, which, when revealed, would probably make her hourglass figure even more difficult to ignore. Meanwhile, Heath presented a relaxed and happy demeanor in his simple disguise of a black bushy mustache with wire-rimmed reading glasses.

The representative greeted them and gave Heath a quick instructional session of how to operate the single-cabin motorboat after finalizing the paperwork and cash settlement. He stated that the boat must be returned by eleven the following day, and Heath replied that they would be back long before then. They had a morning flight back to San Juan at ten, and he asked that a cab be available for the short ride to the airport ninety minutes prior.

After pulling away from the dock with a wave of thanks, Madison carefully removed her crop top while still in visual range of the man who helped them aboard. Then, standing behind Heath, she put her arms around his waist as he piloted the craft out to open water.

Ten minutes later, Heath and Madison, now far from view of the charter facility, began their final preparations leading up to the first sanctioned kill. Madison would lure Cameron into a seduction of death when the time came, and the only question of doubt that remained for Heath was if the young man would keep his promise to meet with her. Madison did not share that same measure of nagging uncertainty though, as based upon the encounter at Soper's Hole the previous afternoon, she knew that Cameron had been unknowingly drawn into her devious trap.

As she voiced her belief of that fact to Heath, he reminded her, "You need to be careful of overconfidence, Madison. Please keep in mind from previous experience that the assumption of a kill is not the same as carrying it out."

While nodding she replied, "You're right. Unlike that night, I need to keep my focus."

With their boat nearing the middle of the Sir Francis Drake Channel, and with no other motor or sailboats in the vicinity, Heath slowed their craft to idle. Comprehending his signal without words,

Madison pulled the wig loose and headed forward into the cabin. As Heath then tended to the removal of his mustache, she hung the wig on a hook and retrieved a few articles of clothing from within one of her bags. Moments later she emerged in the outfit she would wear for the upcoming evening.

In the final days before leaving Carson City for their current location, Madison had realized that although Heath had stated they would need bathing suits for the mission, more than one type would be required. Different cuts and styles of bathing suits were designed for various reasons, and therefore she wanted to be prepared. Her skimpy maroon bikini had but one function, that of optimum exposure and thus seduction via accentuation. To that end, the suit had worked perfectly. But Madison also realized that she would need a more functional style for use during the night of the kill, as beyond the strenuous movements of her body that would be required throughout, projecting a certain image was just as important.

As the establishment of Deadman's Beach Bar & Grill was in a relaxed setting, it was fair to expect that many patrons would be dressed in casual clothing of either swimsuits or shorts and T-shirts during the day. However, it was also located on the grounds of a high-end and pricy spa resort, so evening attire could be slightly more stylish while still adhering to comfort. Therefore, Madison chose to wear a light-blue, form-fitting one-piece bathing suit under a dark-blue patterned wrap in the form of a knee-length skirt that was knotted around her waist. Enhanced by small earrings, a simple necklace, and sandals to go with the little fabric bag, she could play the part without appearing to be ostentatious.

Pulling into the small marina section of the resort at five o'clock, Heath dropped Madison off at the pier and quickly retreated. She would have plenty of time to get into position for her date with Cameron, while Heath would wait in the boat at a location well over a mile from shore until hearing the signal from her to head for the rendezvous point.

After casually strolling around various parts of the grounds, and then sitting near the pool to kill some time, Madison made her way alongside a few guests of the resort on the path toward the bar. In the process, she noticed a group of four young men on the path more than one hundred yards in front of her, and she recognized that one of them was Cameron. Although pleased at the sight of him, it was unfortunate that he had brought along his entourage.

Noting that their collective presence could create an obstacle, Madison entered the establishment at six forty-five and made her way toward the bar to ponder a solution.

A moment later she heard the voice of Cameron say from behind her, "Hello, Brooke. It's nice to see you again. I'm glad you decided to show up."

Turning with a smile while also playing dumb to the presence of his friends, Madison replied, "Well, hello, Cameron. It's nice to see you again as well. But you really shouldn't be surprised that I'm here. After all, I told you that I would be."

After stating how lovely she looked, Cameron asked if he could take a seat next to her and added, "Can I get you a drink, Brooke?"

Madison replied, "Yes, please. That would be great."

Much like the previous afternoon, they sat on a couple of bar-stools and began a lengthy conversation. Reconnecting instantly, the two of them appeared to be having a good time, and although she once again gave out flirtatious signals of touching as they enjoyed the evening, Madison was cautious to not seem overly eager. As planned, she also drank her beers slowly and avoided the risk of overindulgence by dancing on numerous occasions with Cameron to the sound of a nearby steel drum band.

Meanwhile, the three young men who shadowed Cameron were sitting at a table no more than thirty feet away, but they maintained that respectful distance and gave him room to operate while they tried their luck with various other women. Still, the entourage was a factor that would need to be dealt with eventually. Therefore, Madison continued to view their collective actions through occasional glances as the evening progressed.

She knew that an opportunity would eventually present itself if she just waited for it, and soon her patience was rewarded when Cameron said, "Will you please excuse me for a few minutes, Brooke? I need to use the restroom."

"Of course, Cameron, it's nice of you to ask. But when nature calls, nature calls. Please, take your time."

"Thank you. I'll be back soon."

Madison watched him move around the corner of the building and out of sight. Then she quickly seized the opportune moment to further set the stage for her kill.

Moving with haste toward the table where his three friends were seated, she surprised them by asking, "So are you having a good time, gentlemen?"

One of them stood instantly while replying, "Yes. We are, thank you. This is a great place, and I'm glad the captain of our charter recommended it."

"I agree. It's a beautiful spot. And I'm glad that all of you can have fun without Cameron at your side. Now, we are all adults, so I'm going to be straightforward with you. Is that all right?"

"Well…yes, of course. It's Brooke, right? What's on your mind?"

"That's right, I'm Brooke. Now in case you haven't noticed, Cameron is beginning to believe he will get lucky with me tonight. I'm certainly aware of his thoughts, and not necessarily opposed to that possibility. But the two of us may feel somewhat encumbered in trying to pursue the impulse if all of you are nearby. So, if we should decide to take a romantic walk on the beach, it would be easier for us if the three of you just went back to your boat?"

After a glance toward each of his companions, the one that was standing said, "All right, Brooke. We can do that, but what will Cameron think when you return and we are gone?"

"Perhaps he will think you are all good friends who were giving him room to operate."

Taken slightly aback by her knowledge of a timeless code that existed between single male friends, his response was cautious while also attempting not to offend.

"Well…I suppose that's true. But wouldn't that be presumptuous thinking on our part?"

With a smile, Madison replied, "You are sweet to think in terms of my reputation. It's the sign of a true gentleman. However, as I said initially, we are all adults here."

"Thank you, Brooke. And yes, you're correct. We are all adults."

"So, we have an agreement then? You will leave without him?"

"Sure. We can do that for you and Cameron. Just tell us how you want to handle it?"

"Well…I think it would be good if you told Cameron you were leaving before we go on our walk. That way there would be no surprise for him when we return. Then if we should mutually decide to hook up, I would expect him to be a gentleman and buy me breakfast. So, if you don't see him in an hour or so, then don't expect to see him until morning."

14

Death Seduction

WITH A COOPERATIVE understanding reached, Madison thanked the three young men before quickly making her way back to the bar. A moment later Cameron joined her, and the events of their evening continued without missing a beat. Fifteen minutes passed and the crowd in the bar was visibly beginning to thin. Then the young man who stood while she addressed him tapped Cameron on the shoulder.

Smiling, he said, "Excuse me, Cameron, miss. The three of us are going to call it a night and get back to the boat. Send a text when you are getting close on the beach near the boat, and one of us or the captain will come over in the dinghy to pick you up."

"Oh…well, all right, but it may be a few hours."

While nodding with comprehension, he then shifted his glance toward Madison and said, "Sorry about the interruption, miss."

She smiled at the gesture and replied as if they were speaking for the first time. "It's Brooke, and there's no need to apologize."

Cameron was clueless as to the accord that had been struck between his friend and Madison a short time earlier, which was their collective intent. Then after watching them move off along the path, Cameron once again turned toward Madison to become lost in whatever she wanted to discuss. She let another fifteen minutes pass so the distance covered by the entourage and other departing guests would be lengthy, and then suggested a private walk in the opposite direction. With a nearly full moon occasionally peeking out from behind the considerable amount of cloud cover, she thought a stroll would be romantic.

With the bar more than one hundred yards to their rear, Madison then reached for and gently took hold of Cameron's left hand. They continued walking that way until reaching the end of the beach, and then took the wide, elevated footpath that led them over a rocky point toward a smaller, more secluded beach. Stopping briefly at the curve on the point, Madison smiled and leaned her head in closer to his. Cameron responded in the way she knew he would by kissing her softly. A few seconds later, he wrapped his arms around her waist, as she had suggestively turned her body and pressed into him.

They kissed for a moment longer before Madison said, "Why don't we walk to the far end of this next beach? I think we might have a little more privacy there."

With an enthusiastic nod Cameron replied, "That sounds like a good idea."

She smiled and gently pushed away from his grasp while simultaneously reaching for his left hand again to lead him along. Cameron was unaware of it, but Madison knew at that moment she had him. He would die soon, and it seemed fitting to her that the last place Cameron would enjoy a drink with a woman was at a place called Deadman's Grill. Now the only question that remained regarding that outcome was if he would be happy or not when it happened.

Moments later they reached the end of the beach and the spot Madison had preselected to complete the sanctioned kill. Releasing the sandals from her free hand, she once again looked into his eyes. Suggesting they sit in the sand roughly ten feet from the waterline, Madison took the lead and did so before he could protest. Cameron followed suit by tossing his flip-flops aside and plopping down next to her. Then as they talked for a moment, she covertly scanned the perimeter for signs of other people who might be in the area.

Satisfied they were alone, Madison leaned into him once again for another lingering kiss before moving around in front of him. Lifting her wrap slightly so it would not get caught beneath her, she was now kneeling between Cameron and the water's edge. She then slowly and seductively slid both bathing suit straps from her shoulders and off the arms to fully expose her breasts.

In a soft and inviting tone she said, "If you like, Cameron, we can take this further and make the most of this romantic setting. All I ask in moving forward is that you treat me respectfully without rushing. Take your time, and don't be troubled by a belief that I'm looking for some type of long-term commitment beyond breakfast in the morning."

With his eyes widened by the sight of what she had revealed, Cameron forced himself to look up and away from her chest before answering.

Then while once again making eye contact with her, he replied, "I would love to buy you breakfast in the morning, Brooke. But between now and then, I will follow your lead."

Madison smiled at the thoughtful response, even though his words were probably not completely sincere. Time could have eventually told her if he were a man of his word, but she would never know.

As she began leaning in from a distance to kiss him, she offered the compliment of, "I'm glad to know that you are willing to be such a gentleman."

Then having subsequently scooted forward to a position between his legs, Madison remained on her knees as they once again embraced. As Cameron's right hand soon moved up from her waist so that his fingertips could explore the firm contour of her left breast and nipple, she thought of how pleasant the next several hours could have been. Nearly four years had passed since she had been with a man, which translated into a time shortly before she even met Heath. Although she had nearly gone to bed with Heath during the night of her attempt to kill him, no opportunity had presented itself since that time. In fact, no person other than the occasional female prison guard at Ellsworth had touched Madison in the way she was currently being touched.

As for the present time, Cameron would not be the worst of men to have sex with. He was fairly attractive, and not so many years her junior that she would forever regret the decision for doing it. Beyond that, he had flashed aspects of an agreeable personality that at times was both intelligent and funny. If Madison had allowed herself to go through with what he understandably reasoned would occur, she may have been surprised by the outcome. Cameron could be a man who demonstrated an ability to care that the vacation conquest of a random woman should be treated with some measure of respect. However, those thoughts of wanting and optimism were soon replaced by the memory of why she was in his arms to begin with, as hesitation on her part now could allow this target to escape vulnerability.

Realizing that the time to act was now as opposed to later, Madison seized the moment. Feeling his hand now firmly upon her left breast, she broke off their kiss and rose up slightly while still kneeling to position his hand directly in front of his face. The obvious invitation did not go unrecognized, as Cameron then began to kiss both her breasts and nipples.

Resting both elbows on his shoulders with her hands stretched out beyond, Madison said, "Yes. That feels nice. Now just take your time, we are in no hurry."

There was no verbal response from Cameron, but then again, she did not really expect one. As he then began to kiss and use his tongue with intensified vigor, Madison used her right hand to rotate the dark stone on the ring of her left index finger counterclockwise. Following the instruction provided by Heath, she then shifted the setting that housed the stone to expose and flip open the tiny needle attached to the band's underside. Slowly folding the lower portion of her right arm toward his head, she ran her fingers through his hair while producing gentle moans of supposed foreplay pleasure. Then after moving her open left palm toward his neck, Madison struck her unsuspecting prey an instant later by pressing down hard with her index finger. As expected, the needle, not much bigger than one on the end of a lancet, easily penetrated his skin just behind and below the left ear to release its powerful nerve toxin.

Cameron instantly jerked his head a little to the side and back as his mouth broke away from her breast.

Then with obvious irritation, he exclaimed, "Ouch! What the hell was that?"

With a puzzled look on her face, Madison replied, "What's the matter?"

"It felt like something big just stung me on the back of my neck."

While hoping that he did not realize she was responsible, Madison smiled and replied, "Really? Well, are you all right? I mean... would you like me to kiss it and make it feel better, or does it hurt so much that you need to stop?"

Cameron recognized the slightly patronizing tone in her question, and that her perception of his manhood could be in question if he gave an answer that minimized his toughness.

Therefore, he replied, "Oh it hurts a little, but I'm sure it's nothing serious. I was just a bit startled."

"Well that's good to know. Because I would rather you think about me right now instead of something that may have stung you."

To that Cameron leaned back in to kiss her, and as Madison met his lips with hers, she thought to herself that the man deserved some credit. Here he was about to lose all motor function and consciousness within the next twenty seconds or so, and yet he still had the determination to continue foreplay into what he believed was inevitable. As that kiss then lingered over the next several seconds, Madison could feel the strength of his lips and arms suddenly diminish. With the nerve toxin quickly taking hold, it then became difficult for Cameron to breathe.

A few seconds later, he labored to ask, "Brooke, what did you do?"

Before his eyes rolled upward and he fell backward like a ragdoll to lay fully flat upon the sand, she replied, "Only what must be done."

For Madison, the first move was to push the ring setting of the stone back into the proper location with caution. In so doing, the needle retracted and was no longer exposed. She then increased her margin of safety by rotating the stone clockwise to its former position so the housing could not inadvertently be shifted again. Now satisfied that she would not accidentally jab herself, Madison moved quickly to a hovering position over Cameron. She gently slapped his face several times to check for the possibility of partial consciousness and was soon convinced that he was out. Scanning her surroundings again to see if there were any curious onlookers, she then pulled the two straps of her bathing suit back up over her shoulders and went to work. Unzipping the fabric bag around her waist and then the smaller pocket within, Madison took off the ring and placed it inside. Then she removed the laminated piece of paper that was consistent with the thickness of a standard business card by using only a tiny corner of her wrap. After zipping the interior pocket closed again with her free hand so the ring would not fall out, she looked at the card that was smaller than the printed wisdom offered in a fortune cookie.

The durable and laminated piece of paper revealed a coded message in bold type, stating only the letters and numbers of: *Staircase696*.

Madison, nor Heath for that matter, had any idea as to the cryptic meaning of the code. They only knew that it was imperative to plant the message somewhere on the body of her victim where it could not be missed.

With no land mass between them to obstruct the signal, Heath had been listening the entire evening by way of the microphone in her earring. He started the timer on his watch seconds after hearing Cameron ask Madison what she had done to him, with the understanding that if she moved fast there would be no need for the second injection.

Madison began by vigorously rubbing both sides of the coded paper on the sand while tightly pinching only the smallest portion possible of a corner with her wrap. She was wiping away the possibility of any fingerprints or other elements of DNA that her skin or the bag may have left upon it, and she cleansed the entire paper by releasing it and taking hold of a corner on the opposite end before repeating the process. Once that was done thoroughly, and while still pinching it only with the fabric of her wrap, she gently pushed the coded message deep into the left front pocket of Cameron's shorts. Then she removed his phone from the right pocket and pushed it into her swimsuit at the small of her back before removing his shirt.

Still hovering over her victim, Madison looked in all directions again to see if anyone might be able to witness what she would do next. The count in her head told her that nearly ninety seconds had already passed, but plenty of time remained. Assured that all was safe to proceed, she grabbed Cameron by both of his ankles and quietly pulled him across ten feet of sand into the water. Once there, she rolled him over to a face-down orientation before returning to the beach to smooth away the drag marks in the sand.

Beyond that of listening in, Heath had also tracked her movements via her implants to the end of the secluded beach. With the running lights off and the moon obscured by clouds, he would now move the boat into the recovery position under a cloak of near darkness.

Before returning to the water, Madison zipped the larger compartment of her fabric bag closed, twisted her wrap up into a belt-like piece of fabric, ran it through a loop in each sandal, and tied it around her waist. Then she waded into the water and pushed Cameron's head downward with one hand and held onto a wrist with the other as she began to quietly swim them away from shore. By that time, more than two minutes had passed since the nerve toxin was injected into Cameron, but he would drown long before it came close to wearing off. However, if for some reason he gave any indication of coming around, Madison knew that she could easily subdue him with the use of her recently acquired hand-to-hand combat skills.

Not being the best swimmer in the world, it took nearly fifteen minutes to move roughly one hundred yards using only her legs for propulsion. She knew the toxin would soon lose its effectiveness, if it had not already, but there had been no sign of awakening by Cameron. Madison carefully checked each of his wrists and his neck for a pulse while still holding his head down, and with no hint of one at any location, she then reached under the body to feel for any possible sign of life. His chest was cold and still with no movement from either breathing or heart activity, so an important question had been answered. There would be no need for any extreme measure of self-defense or the second lethal injection, as Madison knew for certain that based on her efforts to deprive him of oxygen for roughly fifteen minutes, Cameron was dead.

Back on the boat, Heath realized that the useful life of the toxin since its injection had now expired, so in keeping with the plan, he clicked his flashlight on and off three times during a fifteen-second interval. He would repeat that process for Madison every two minutes to guide her toward the boat while he used the tracking devices to monitor her progress.

Although she did not know it, the first of the signals from Heath was missed by Madison while she was checking for a pulse. But when she noticed the second set of flashing, she gently pushed Cameron's body away toward the nearby embankment of rocks that jetted out from the beach in a nearly parallel line to her course. Then turning her orientation to the left, she began a lengthier swim toward open water. Throughout the next fifteen minutes, a few minor course corrections were required by Madison, but with each passing sequence of flashing lights she drew closer and closer to her goal. When she could finally distinguish the dark silhouette of the small boat from no more than fifty yards away, she swam with added intensity to close the gap.

Heath shut the engine off before reaching down to grasp both of her wrists, and after Madison removed Cameron's phone from within the back of her bathing suit to let it sink to the bottom of the ocean, he pulled her up over the side of the boat with ease. As she then unclipped the strap of her fabric bag and untied the belt-like wrap so both could fall, Heath moved to get her a large towel.

As he turned back toward her, she said, "Wait just a second."

Following instruction, he held the towel at arm's length until she was ready. To his surprise, Madison slid the straps of her one-piece suit off her shoulders and peeled the dripping wet fabric all the way down to her ankles.

Then when stepping out of it, she reached for the towel and said, "Thank you."

Standing in astonishment, Heath replied, "You're welcome, but you could have given me some warning before you stripped down completely."

"I suppose. But I've been in the water for thirty minutes or more, so I'm cold and tired. My wet swimsuit was just going to make matters worse in this night air, so I wanted to take it off as soon as possible. And really, Heath, a few years ago you saw me in nothing but my panties and bra. Add to that the times during the past few days when you saw me in that same state of undress as I changed clothes in front of you, or when I was in my maroon bikini, and there couldn't be much left for your imagination to conjure up."

Heath thought about it for a moment, and then he replied, "All right, Madison. I see your point and understand why you wanted to get out of your wet bathing suit. You surprise me though, because what you just did is a long way from being concerned that I hovered over your implant procedure on the plane."

Now completely wrapped in a towel and seated in the forward passenger seat, Madison shook her head in disbelief and then looked over at Heath.

"Well…that's true. But at that point I hadn't spent any time with you in a few years. I was still trying to get a grip on all that was happening to me during those first few hours of freedom. Besides, I was pissed at you for sending me to prison in Kansas of all places. But now that we have been living and working together for several months, what's a little necessary nudity among friends?"

Heath realized that Madison was venting a little, and it was with good reason. Based on the adrenaline high caused by the actions of her first kill, and in now coming down from it, she was probably experiencing some level of shock. But then again, she could have also been facing a fear of doubt while in the water that she might not make it safely to the rendezvous point. Regardless of the cause, Heath knew enough to remain quiet until she calmed down.

Eventually he started the engine and set a slow course back toward Tortola. Until first light, Heath would not be able to identify exactly where they needed to go to return the boat at Fat Hogs Bay, but at least for the time being they were getting closer by heading in the general direction.

Sensing that enough time had passed for her to regain her composure, Heath eventually asked, "All right. So first off, how are you doing? Is everything all right?"

"You mean with the mission status?"

"Well…yes. But first, how are you?"

"I'll be all right, and I'm sorry I got weird like that. It's just that there has been a lot to process in the last few hours."

"I understand. Now if you need to say anything more, then out here on the open water would be the best place to do it until we get safely back to Carson City. If not, then please give me a mission update."

"All right, Heath, I get it. For the moment there's nothing more to add regarding my comfort level, so I'll give you a mission update. Cameron is dead and the coded message has been planted deep into a front pocket of his shorts. I have no doubts about either of those facts. As for the body, I pushed it toward the rock outcropping so it wouldn't float back to the beach. With luck, it may not be discovered until the middle of the day tomorrow."

"All of that is good to hear, and I offer my compliments to you on the excellent work. Now please tell me, do you think he died happy?"

Shaking her head in disbelief once again, Madison replied, "Well…I suppose the answer to that question would be based upon personal interpretation. I mean…you heard everything that was happening between us. Therefore, you probably already know that I bared my breasts for Cameron so that he would become, as you would say, more vulnerable. At the moment that I injected him with the toxin, he had one of them in his mouth, and afterward he was still focused enough as a man with desire to kiss me until just seconds before he lost motor function. So, I don't know, Heath. I guess you could say he was happy."

15

Escape Timing

HEATH HAD DRIVEN the boat—with its running lights turned off for about thirty minutes—at a slow speed to keep the sound of their engines as quiet as possible. Then when comfortable that they were closer to Tortola than Peter Island, he brought the throttle back to neutral and turned the key to off. With the boat just bobbing about somewhere in the Sir Francis Drake Channel for the remainder of the night, Heath and Madison were both able to separately get some sleep in the cabin while the other stood watch at the helm. Either of them could pilot the small craft to a safer position in a hurry if necessary, however, the need to do so seemed highly unlikely. As a general practice, no charter boats moved around in the channel at night, but Heath wanted to act with caution. There was always the off chance of some cargo vessel coming through at night as it went about delivering supplies to the various island marinas, so he didn't want to taint the success of what Madison had accomplished by being run over and sunk in the darkness.

Madison had slept first after putting some dry sweats on, and after the events of the evening and the long swim, she did so soundly. It was only by the grasp of Heath's hand on her ankle that she woke from a deep slumber. She then took the watch on deck, and as the soft pink-and-orange shades of sunrise faded away to the strengthening rays of the rising sun, Madison moved into the cabin and woke Heath in a similar fashion.

Noticing that they were in full daylight, he said, "Wow. I slept longer than planned. Have you seen any other boats around yet?"

"No. Everything is fine. It's all clear."

"That's good, and thanks for taking the watch. Now, we don't have a lot of extra time, so we should get organized."

"I agree. Let me get my things from last night into the sun so they can dry quicker, and then I can get ready for the marina and the flight."

Heath followed her out of the cabin to get a bearing on their location as opposed to Fat Hogs Bay, and then he started the engine. Madison checked to see if her bathing suit and wrap had dried at all throughout the night, but as there was minimal change from when she took them off, she draped them over the top of the windshield to accelerate the process.

Heading back into the cabin, she soon emerged wearing the same wig that she had on the previous day at the charter facility, but the comfortable clothing she selected for the flight was less revealing. Heath then took his turn of getting the mustache of his disguise into place, and then each of them packed what remained of their gear. As they began a slow motor toward Fat Hogs Bay, Heath kept an eye on the time while Madison thoroughly inspected the boat to ensure nothing had been left behind. Then, after waiting as long as possible before they were in close visual range of the marina, Madison removed her now only damp garments from the windshield, tucked them into a side pocket of a carry-on bag, and took a position of snuggling up to Heath.

As they pulled close to the dock at eight fifteen, there were a few employees of the charter facility standing at the ready. Heath gently nudged Madison away from his position so he could appear to have added concentration on the task of coming in smoothly. Then after offloading and completing the checkout procedure in the office, Heath gave the man who had rented them the boat a two-hundred-dollar tip.

The man smiled and said, "Thank you, sir. I hope that we can do business again."

"I would like that as well. My girlfriend and I had a really good time out there, and I will recommend your company to some of my friends. But for now, I would like to ask a favor."

"And what is that, sir?"

"Could we please keep this entire transaction private? If that is agreeable, then as far as you are concerned, I was never here. My wife back in Winnipeg just wouldn't understand."

Looking over at Madison as she stood near the cab that had just arrived, he nodded and replied, "I understand completely, sir. You and the young lady were never here."

The two men shook hands as a form of an unwritten pact before Heath headed for the cab. He knew there was a strong possibility that the owner of the charter company would not keep his vow of silence forever, but if the next four hours passed before he blabbed, there would be no issue. In fact, even if he did snitch before then, all he had for the sake of records or memory was a cash transaction and a belief that his secretive customer had come from Winnipeg.

A few minutes later, Heath and Madison arrived at the airport, where they encountered no trouble or delays when showing their Canadian passports at the ticket counter. Soon after, they boarded a ten o'clock plane bound for San Juan, Puerto Rico, and as their twelve thirty connecting flight was destined for Toronto, American customs would once again be avoided.

When the twin-engine prop was roughly halfway through its short flight, the three friends of Cameron were beginning to worry about where he was. To them, it seemed obvious that he had spent the night with Brooke, and they conveyed that belief to the captain and chef of their charter. But even if he and Brooke had shared breakfast at some point in the morning, Cameron should have made contact via text soon after. There was also no sign of him on the beach near the boat, either with Brooke or alone, and he was not answering his phone.

Finally, at ten thirty the captain was beginning to show his frustration in that there was a schedule to keep, so he took his three other passengers ashore in the rubber dinghy and joined them in a search for the missing Cameron. It was nearly eleven before they set foot on the sprawling grounds of Peter Island Resort, so they decided their quest would be best served by splitting up. More ground could be covered in a hurry that way, as various places such as the upscale restaurant, pool area, beach hammocks, and even the lobby and front desk would need to be checked. If none of that yielded a positive result, a walk farther down the beach to Deadman's Grill would be required.

The captain said he would take the lobby and front desk while the others looked into the other various, possible locations. His theory was that, based on his acquaintance with many of the managers because of sending charter clients their way, he might be able to obtain some information that any of the other three men would be denied. Those working in the lobby area and at the front desk were questioned, but they could offer nothing tangible. Then as the captain turned to leave the desk, the phone rang and the young lady who fielded the call motioned for him to wait a minute. She spoke a quick word to her manager, who in turn waved for the captain to come over so they could speak in her office.

She had just received some information from a staff member at the opposite end of the resort that could shed some light on the mystery. After confirming that a Cameron was the focus of his search, she relayed that someone by that name had been located.

At eleven thirty, the body that had been found floating near a rocky outcropping some hundred yards from the beach was positively identified by the captain and his three charter guests as that of Cameron. Two young teenagers who were staying at the resort with their parents had spotted the man facedown in the water shortly before as they clambered over the rocks for no other reason than it was something to do. Returning to Deadman's Grill at a brisk run, they in turn notified the bartender who was preparing his workstation for the upcoming lunch crowd.

While all of that was taking place and the local authorities were being contacted, Heath and Madison had already completed the first of their flights for the day and were waiting patiently at the San Juan Airport for the second. They would begin boarding shortly for the flight to Toronto, with no thought of being deterred.

Seated comfortably onboard the large jet at twelve fifteen as other passengers made their last-minute adjustments before takeoff, Heath and Madison had no way of knowing that members of a British Virgin Islands' police unit had finally made it over to the Peter Island Resort from Tortola. The pair of officers began their investigation of the drowning as they had done in the past, with an understanding that the event was not uncommon. Sadly, more than a handful of tourists were lost to the same fate every year. Some of the deaths were caused by stupidity and reckless, unsafe behavior, while others could be contributed to the overindulgence of alcohol and a lack of a strong swimming ability.

As the initial questioning of Cameron's friends began, the officers realized that none of them could shed much light on what had happened. Beyond the victim going on a private romantic walk with a woman he had met, and then presumably going for a late-night swim, they did not know anything else. So as the jet bound for Toronto lifted into the sky, they could offer little more than her name and that she had a great body.

Several hours later, the jet landed on schedule at the Toronto Airport, and Heath and Madison moved through Canadian customs with no difficulty. As they had done on their way to the Caribbean, a nearby airport hotel was used for transitionary purposes. It was only after they checked in that each of them removed their current disguises and then enjoyed a nice, relaxing meal via room service. As the evening progressed, a further awareness of their success began to sink in, and they both breathed a little easier. The first of four sanctioned targets had been killed, and their escape from the Caribbean had been made without any difficulty.

16

The Aftermath

ON THURSDAY MORNING, the day after he had been found dead, Cameron's friends were still understandably in shock from the loss of their longtime buddy. Per a police mandate, the body had been moved to Road Town Wednesday afternoon for examination before it would eventually be released for a return to the United States. The captain of the catamaran had also been directed to return the three young men to their charter base on Tortola. Although the guests would be allowed to stay on the boat if they wished, the authorities wanted them to be easily accessible should further questioning be required.

Meanwhile, Heath and Madison, under the cloak of different identities and disguises than the ones they used in the Caribbean, returned to the Toronto Airport from the hotel via a cab. Flights to Calgary and onward to Cranbrook were the legs to be completed on this day, and after their arrival they would retrieve the rented sedan from Spokane before spending the night in a Cranbrook motel.

With the first of those flights long since airborne and headed west, the results of the autopsy on Cameron, as well as the contents of what was found on his body, were being discussed by the doctor with his friends and a pair of investigative officers. The doctor had been able to confirm, as was initially theorized, that the time of death occurred sometime between ten and eleven on Tuesday night. However, his further examination of the body revealed that there may have been foul play involved. He continued by clarifying to all present that although drowning was the ultimate cause of death, minute traces of a powerful nerve toxin were still present in the victim's bloodstream.

As for the artifacts and personal belongings, there were also a few abnormalities. His footwear and shirt were found next to each other on the beach, presumably where he had left them before taking a swim, but his phone was not included with those items. It seemed highly unlikely that he would have taken the time to remove his shirt before going into the water while at the same time forgetting to leave his phone on the beach. However, since his wallet was still in his back pocket, it was possible that Cameron had overlooked both items. But if that were the case, then why was the wallet still on the body while the phone could not be found? A good amount of cash was in the wallet along with his identification, bank cards, and an unopened condom. Therefore, if foul play was involved, it was safe to assume that robbery was not the motive. In addition, there was one other object found on his person, as a small, laminated piece of paper with a few letters and numbers was discovered in his left front pocket.

As Heath and Madison flew onward toward the Canadian Rockies, the authorities on Tortola were baffled. Based on the findings of the doctor, they began a more intense line of questioning. Unfortunately, their inquiries of those who had sailed with Cameron led to dead end after dead end. The young men all knew that the woman their friend spent time with on the night of his death was named Brooke, but none had ever heard any mention of her last name. They admitted that she had been rather insistent about the three of them leaving Deadman's Grill and the area so she and Cameron could have some private time together, but none of them felt that she had any intent of harming him. When asked for a description that went beyond Brooke having a great body, they all agreed she was Caucasian with short brown hair that was maybe two or three inches long, and she was about five foot six or so. They could not remember anything else significant about her because they had mainly seen her up close for only brief instances, but the consensus was that she had no visible tattoos. Beyond that, most of what they knew was based on Cameron talking about her while the four of them were on the catamaran. According to him, she had been part of a charter with a family, and they had since moved over to stay at the Peter Island Resort. That was why he was going to meet her at Deadman's Grill.

Although much of that information, when added together, could lead to something, no aspect other than actually seeing her at three separate bars could be confirmed. None of them had seen the sailboat she supposedly chartered, or any of those in her party. A check with the charter company at Soper's Hole where Brooke claimed the boat had been returned found no record of a group of five persons that fit the description given. They had not in recent memory, or perhaps ever, chartered one of their sailboats to a husband and wife with two teenage girls and an extra adult female. As for Peter Island Resort where Brooke stated her group would be staying for three nights, there was no record of such a party booking a reservation. It was true that some families were present, as the two boys who discovered the body could attest, but none matched what was being searched for.

Everyone agreed that interviewing Brooke would have been beneficial in answering some key questions, as it was reasonably presumed that she was the last person to see Cameron alive. Based on the information she supposedly provided that was now found to be untrue, and with the question of the nerve toxin unanswered, Brooke was, at least in theory, the most logical suspect in his death. However, in finding no forensic evidence of her presence, there was nothing tangible to condemn her. In the end there were no concrete leads to follow, as other than a physical body that had been seen a few times, the woman in question was seemingly nonexistent.

With nothing concrete to build a case upon, the authorities of the British Virgin Islands reluctantly released the body to the custody of the three young men. Beyond keeping it in cold storage until ready, and then assisting with the transfer of the body to the airport, any further arrangements for returning Cameron to the United States would be of no concern to the local authorities.

Having been informed of that decision and the parameters that it entailed, the three young men realized that the time had come for the most challenging of phone calls to be made. They would need help from Cameron's parents to expedite the process of getting him home but informing them that he had drowned on vacation was something none of his friends wanted to do.

Upon hearing the devastating news that their youngest child had died, the shock, anger, and despair that was felt by Cameron's parents resonated back through the thousands of miles to the Caribbean. The family friend who had drawn the short straw and had to inform them knew that he was not at fault as they screamed at him on the phone, but it was necessary to accept blame for the moment.

In the hours that followed, no expense was spared so that the body of Cameron and those accompanying him could get home as quickly as possible. Flights were arranged by his father for them to go through San Juan and United States customs before heading to Dallas and on to Seattle so that the body could be received late Friday night. Then, within the content of the final logistical call between them, Cameron's father made it abundantly clear to the family friend that he was being counted on to be responsible for watching over the body of his youngest son and his personal belongings.

During the morning of Friday, April eleventh, Heath and Madison drove south from Cranbrook back into Idaho with no issues. She was in the disguise of long, straight blond hair and tinted reading glasses that had been worn nine days earlier when they used this same border crossing into Canada, while Heath donned his fake black goatee. The United States customs agent asked only where they had been in Canada and for what purpose while the computer checked the validity of their American passports.

Roughly three hours later, after having found an appropriate spot to remove their disguises and assume the natural look of Heath and Madison, they arrived at the Spokane Airport to return the rental sedan. Then they boarded a direct flight to Reno, and by nightfall they were in their Carson City apartment.

As Madison enjoyed a long, hot shower, Heath sifted through the mail that had come while they were gone. Although most of it was useful in some regard to the three remaining sanctions, the contents of one large envelope caught his immediate attention.

She emerged to ask, "So, did you get anything important in the mail?"

Looking up, he replied, "You could say that. We now have solid intel on when and where we can attempt the next sanction."

"Well, I suppose that's good news, but we just got back here less than an hour ago. Are we going to have enough time to prepare?"

"Relax, Madison. The opportunity is in early June, so we have some time to work with. However, we will need more high-elevation training."

"Why? Where are we going?"

"Have you ever been to Peru?"

SANCTION TWO

17

Answers and Questions

ON THE MORNING of Saturday, April twelfth, both Heath and Madison began the day in leisurely fashion by sleeping in much later than their established norm. Their actions, or more accurately a lack of them, came about by way of a joint decision made the previous evening. Feeling a bit fatigued after very little sleep on the boat and during the long trip home through Canada from the British Virgin Islands, coupled with learning that the next phase of their mission would soon be taking them to Peru, it was agreed that some decompression time was in order. That decision included their intent to remain mostly passive for the entire weekend, but for Heath the few days set aside for relaxation would not be completely idle. Beyond his need to think through what obstacles might lay in front of them, there was one specific item that demanded his immediate attention.

Heath recognized that for several reasons, he and Madison would be able to prepare for their second sanctioned kill with relative ease when compared to the first. To begin with, their combined false identities and the accompanying sets of disguises could be used again, so waiting for the lab to fabricate multiple sets of documentation was of no concern. In addition, further hand-to-hand combat training for Madison was not required, because in his opinion she was fully versed. Along with those obvious advantages, there was also what he viewed as the most vital element that would aid in their future success. Although both had believed they were prepared for the first leg of their mission due to their focus on physical training and their grasp of various tendencies and weaknesses of the target, their combined skill set had not yet been tested in the field. They knew, going into the Caribbean paradise, that a dress rehearsal would not take place, so every aspect of how they intended to eliminate their target had to be performed with sound communication and attention to detail. But now with that sanctioned kill of Cameron both successfully and covertly completed, they had proven an ability to properly mesh and work as a team in a real-world scenario.

As Heath pondered those positives while skimming through the most recent intelligence report on their second target, he also realized that complacency in how one prepared could destroy the best of plans more quickly than any other unforeseen obstacle. Therefore, he guarded against that possibility by focusing on matters that could be different from the first sanction. Then a thought suddenly hit him, and although not hugely significant in the present moment, he would need to discuss it with Madison.

A short time later, the two of them refueled with some breakfast, which at the current hour actually resembled more of a brunch setting, but their time at the table provided Heath with an opportunity to address his most recent concern.

He first reiterated their common intent to forgo any high-elevation, physical training until Monday morning, but in the meantime, there was something that he needed to research by way of a computer at the library. Heath could not confirm his suspicion with certainty at the moment, but he expressed a belief that a few vaccinations might be required before they could enter Peru. If that was true, then they would need to decide which false identities and disguises would be most suitable for the long flight to Lima and passage through customs so the vaccination records would match. Once those were selected, a visit to a clinic for the necessary injections in either Carson City or Reno would be required.

Not knowing how long the waiting period for such a procedure would take, Heath asked, "So if we need to make those arrangements, which identity would you like to use?"

Madison replied, "Well…can I think about it and get back to you?"

"Sure. Now I'll head for the library, and you can let me know when I get back."

Soon after Heath was out the door, but on the way to the library, he stopped at the post office to mail Mrs. Dawson a small envelope that contained a handwritten coded message for President Harwell.

Short and concise, it read: *Past first with an eye on second.*

Moving on to the library, Heath soon learned that his suspicions were correct. Certain vaccinations would be required for entry into Peru, but depending on where one traveled within the country, the number of shots varied. Fortunately, he and Madison would not be required to receive more than a few, as their plans of pursuing their target would entail avoiding the jungles near sea level in favor of much higher mountainous terrain.

As for that target, Heath smiled at the thought of what had been learned of him. Many everyday citizens still believed that they could go about their lives with whatever level of anonymity they wished to preserve, but in the modern world it was nearly impossible to keep any aspect of one's own personal life private. That sometimes uncomfortable truth was based on several variables, including the seldom impeded-upon practices of Google searches or social media outlets, along with the constant monitoring of credit card purchases and the use of cell phone tracking. If those methods weren't enough to keep tabs on what a person did with their life, the invasion of privacy by those with power could be further magnified via use of the Patriot Act, which allows for certain cracks in the shield of personal liberties.

According to their latest intelligence report, the target had booked flights to Lima and then directly on to the high elevation city of Cuzco. Those specific dates, along with the when and where he would be staying throughout the week, were also provided. Following the flight to Cuzco, the target had reservations for two nights lodging in the little village of Pisac before venturing on for a three-night stay at Aguas Calientes in the shadow of Machu Picchu. Then his final two nights before returning to the United States would be in Cuzco, so the intent of his vacation plan was clear. He would, as with most others who visited Peru, spend much of his time exploring various locations high in the mountains where ruins of the once proud Incan civilization were most prominent.

To that end, perhaps no site was more globally recognized and photographed than Machu Picchu, and based on the amount of people from various parts of the globe who wished to explore the ancient city throughout each year, entry tickets with the name of the guest and the specific calendar dates of visitation needed to be purchased in advance. That rule also applied for access onto the trail within the grounds that led up the peak of Huayna Picchu standing directly beyond Machu Picchu. However, in the latter instance, there were specific entry windows of time and tighter restrictions as to how many people would be admitted each day. Accordingly, their target had purchased his two-day entry ticket for the grounds of Machu Picchu, along with an accompanying early morning ticket on the first day to the adjacent Huayna Picchu trail.

In learning of that intent, Heath theorized that if they could just figure out how, it would be fitting for their second sanctioned target to draw his last breath while trekking about the ruins. However, as he clicked on a website that told of how one went about visiting Machu Picchu, he quickly realized that the opportunity would not be easy. Attempting a kill on the grounds could be challenging, while also creating another potential obstacle.

Turning first to the opportunity, Heath believed that the trail beyond Machu Picchu with its limited daily admission could be useful as the best option because there would be fewer hikers who might become inadvertent witnesses. Although many tourists probably believed that checking each patron before entry was unnecessary, Heath understood that the method served a purpose. In the case of Huayna Picchu, the secondary checkpoint helped to ensure not only an accurate count of those on the trail, but also that the ticket had not been either purchased or stolen from someone with a different name. Then as he began to study a map that detailed the trail and viewed a hand-ful of video clips that showed just how difficult reaching the summit could be, his belief was solidified.

For Heath, the physical demands of the trail implied that some hikers would visit only the summit before their descent and exit. Although a certain percentage of those who summited would face the added endurance test of venturing on toward the Temple of the Moon, he believed that a substantial amount of those who entered would not, as it lay beyond and far below the summit. As a result, the already minimal number of hikers would be thinned further, and Madison could be aided in her quest by hiking the extra distance with her target to further sap his strength. Then, based on what Heath had discovered from the map, she could then lure him to an even more remote location on the return loop from the Temple of the Moon to make his demise appear to be of natural causes.

As for the potential obstacle, both Heath and Madison would need to present valid passports at the entrance gate to Machu Picchu, ensuring that each photo matched the name on the accompanying ticket. But if the kill were to take place where Heath thought it would be best, Madison would need to do so again at the second checkpoint to Huayna Picchu.

With continued research, Heath learned that there was yet an-other potential stumbling block, as they would be visiting the region during the leading edge of the busy season. That poor timing might not have an impact on tickets for Machu Picchu, but Huayna Picchu could be a different story. Therefore, in realizing that the tickets could already be sold out, or at least going fast, Heath needed to purchase tickets for the appropriate dates quickly.

Clicking onto another website that would allow him to buy tick-ets, Heath was relieved to discover that some were still available for the required date and time. Once again, it was logical to believe there was minimal time to waste before the remaining tickets would be gone, so paying for them in cash after arriving in Peru was no lon-ger an option.

After completing his research, printing out a few pages of maps and useful information, and then exiting the library, Heath mulled over the various answers and questions that the past few hours had brought forth. He and Madison would again be faced with a question, as a determination needed to be made as to whether or not she could remain in disguise for a few days while initiating contact with and then subduing her target. The likelihood of that seemed minimal given the circumstances of strenuous hiking in hot and potentially humid conditions, so another course of action would most probably be required.

Heath concluded during his drive back to the apartment that the most logical way to proceed would be via the use of the lab. In short order, new false identity documentation for Madison with her natural look could be fabricated, and that process should be initiated immediately.

Then, as a consequence of that requirement and other aspects just learned of, Heath realized and humbly accepted another glaring fact. It was obvious that he may have been incorrect in his initial assessment, as this second sanction would perhaps be more difficult to complete than the first.

18

Above Tahoe

NOT LONG AFTER Heath briefed Madison on what he learned at the library, they drove to a location where she could get some new passport photos taken. Although that look with her short brown hair would become part of a new false identity to be employed while in contact with her target, Madison told Heath before they departed that she had selected a logical appearance for the vaccinations and subsequent flight to Lima.

As with the flight and entry to the British Virgin Islands, she planned on wearing her wig of straight black hair cut just below the shoulders. She knew that it was comfortable to fly in, while the look that it created, combined with her deepening tan, would allow Madison to blend in more naturally at the two airports in Peru. Heath did not want to employ the same disguise that had been previously paired with her straight black hair, so he decided to compliment her look by selecting his black goatee and well-worn baseball cap. As for what would be done after the short connecting flight to Cuzco, Madison could change again to assume her newly created identity of a single woman on a solo exploratory adventure.

Apart from when they were receiving their vaccinations, those choices of disguise would not be worn for weeks; however, the important issue at hand was that a decision had been made quickly. According to what Heath had researched, the vaccinations should be received at least five weeks ahead of when they planned to arrive. Therefore, with their timing being tight, Heath placed a call to a local medical clinic in Carson City to arrange an appointment for the necessary injections at some point in the next few days before he acted on the new passport photos.

Later that afternoon, Madison filled out the paperwork for her new alias passport with photos in hand, but having selected the name for the document only hours prior, some scratch paper was used in the process so she could develop an easily repeatable signature.

In the meantime, Heath initiated the vetting process of her chosen name and prepared an envelope that would be sent off to the government lab. If all went well with no red flags, they would have her newly fabricated documents weeks before they were needed.

Two days later on Monday morning, their latest round of physical training began with an initial workout of fifteen minutes of stretching and then a three-mile run on the mostly level grass at nearby Mills Park. Heath was pleased that in spite of them not running for nearly two weeks, neither he nor Madison showed any fatigue. Although that was a good sign, he knew that the flat surface of either Mills Park or the oval track at Carson High School would not begin to tax their abilities like the varied terrain in the high elevations of Peru. It was imperative that for the next phase of their mission, the cardiovascular endurance of both he and Madison would need to be reinforced. Therefore, more strenuous exercise was required, and Heath wanted to escalate their daily regiment as soon as possible by using the nearby mountains to their fullest extent.

Heath had not lived in the Lake Tahoe area for many years, but certain memories from his younger days were permanently ingrained. As a result, he knew while they were training during January through March that the region was experiencing a lighter than normal winter. Although it was only mid-April, Heath recognized the good chance that large sections of south-facing hiking trails, which meandered through the mountains and along various ridges above lake level, could already be free from snow. Consequently, he planned on introducing Madison to some of those trails as a means to ensure that neither of them would suffer any symptoms of fatigue while in the Andes Mountain Range in South America.

On Monday, April twenty-first, Heath and Madison began a regiment of high-elevation training from Spooner Summit on Highway 50. By using that location on the Nevada side of the lake, portions of the Tahoe Rim Trail, and various offshoot trails from it heading both north and south, could be easily accessed. While many of their evenings were used for recovery as they discussed the how and where Madison would most easily create a chance meeting with her target, the four-days-a-week program of hiking every Monday, Tuesday, Thursday, and Friday brought forth immediate benefit. Then, in having explored the region thoroughly during the first three weeks of their conditioning, Heath altered the plan slightly by incorporating different Rim Trail access points along Highway 431 that offered higher elevation options. That roadway snaked its way over the mountains between Reno and Incline Village at the north shore of Lake Tahoe, and it was near the summit at the Tahoe Meadows Trailhead that their training continued.

Now using south-facing trails, which in some cases exceeded nine thousand feet of elevation, Madison demonstrated the ability to run at a fast clip while wearing a small weighted backpack to simulate what might be carried on the trail during the attempted sanction. As a result, she felt and expressed during the final week of those training sessions that she was more than ready for Peru.

In the final few days that followed before their various flights to Peru, Heath and Madison stuck to running on the lawn areas of Mills Park in Carson City to avoid the possibility of an ill-timed injury. Then as they packed their bags, every aspect of the upcoming mission was repeatedly discussed in great detail. Within her gear were two items that had not been used in the Caribbean. First was a pair of surgical gloves that she put in one compartment of her small fabric bag, as Madison had realized soon after completing the sanction of Cameron that it would be a wise added precaution. She had been able to use her wrap and the scrubbing of the beach sand to eliminate any fingerprints on the laminated coded message, but now she planned on using gloves as a more reliable option.

As for the second item, it had been purchased specifically for Peru and she had no intention of returning with it. The new cell phone would be necessary as part of her cover because it seemed unlikely that anyone would venture to Machu Picchu without possessing some means of recording their experience either by video or photographs. Therefore, she would use the phone for that intent only, but the plan called for her to destroy the object if she were successful in carrying out the sanction.

Just as before, they began the mission by flying from Reno to Spokane, but then the plans for moving into and through Canada were altered slightly. As a substitute for venturing onward to Cranbrook and taking a flight to Calgary on the same day, they rented a quaint motel room in Bonners Ferry, Idaho, for the night of June fourth. Then after putting on their chosen disguises early the next morning, the short drive to the border and beyond to Cranbrook where they caught flights to Calgary and onward to Toronto followed. Once there, Heath selected a different hotel than what had been used prior for the Caribbean trip.

That evening in Toronto, Heath asked, "So before we get to Cuzco, where we need to appear as separate travelers, is there anything that troubles you?"

"What do you mean?"

"Well…it will be difficult for us to communicate on a regular basis once we appear to be separate travelers."

"Yes. But we have covered that, and I completely understand it."

"So, then what is your plan if you sense that the target may not want to follow your lead? Do you have an approach other than seduction?"

"Oh…now I see your point. Yes, I do. I thought the role of another adventuresome soul that has some familiarity with the area could work in developing a common interest."

"And do you think that approach would work with him?"

"Probably, but I don't think it will come to that. My plan of seduction will lure him in."

"Are you that confident of your looks and sexual prowess?"

Madison did not know whether to be flattered or insulted by his latest question. On the one hand, Heath had noticed and commented that she looked good while possessing obvious sexual energy. But on the other hand, he was seemingly implying that she might be overly confident that the target would automatically want to sleep with her. In addition, why was he bringing up the subject at this late time as opposed to during the previous few weeks?

Nevertheless, she calmly replied, "I understand that seduction may not always work, but in this case it will. Based on what we have studied from his files, our target has a long record of being a womanizer. He may be slightly overweight and not as attractive as he thinks, but apparently the family money behind him has worked in his favor to lure many women."

"That is true, but is his record of having many women at his pleasure enough of a guarantee that he will chase you?"

"Well frankly, Heath, yes. I believe it is!"

Realizing that Madison was getting defensive, Heath said, "Now, please don't get me wrong. You obviously have the tools to lure almost any straight man, but you may not be his specific type and we can't alter your look with a disguise."

"I know that we can't alter my appearance with a wig or another disguise, but what I know of this target is that it won't matter because he isn't picky. All that is required for me to be his type is that I'm a female and I have a pulse, so if we need to discuss anything on the matter, it should be logistics as opposed to if he would want to have sex with me!"

Their subsequent afternoon flight to Lima the following day with a stopover in Miami did not arrive until the smallest hours of the morning, but as that was the recognized norm for many international flights, it could not be easily avoided. While waiting in line for customs with Heath, it became clear to Madison that her current look was a far cry from what some of the obvious tourists presented. As she theorized, her disguise in the wig of straight black hair, the choice of comfortable, non-flashy clothing, and her tan presented the appearance that she hoped to achieve. Madison did in fact resemble what could be construed by others as a local woman.

19

The Sacred Valley

BASED ON GETTING some decent sleep on their two lengthy flights to Lima from Toronto, Heath and Madison both felt fairly well rested. As a result, they decided not to use an airport hotel for what would be only a few hours before the flight to Cuzco and instead opted for alternating nap time in the terminal while the other maintained a watchful eye.

With the flight into the mountains on Saturday, June seventh then completed, and their luggage collected, they each ventured into an airport restroom to remove their respective disguises and clean up by splashing some cold water onto their faces. When they emerged, Heath visited a kiosk to exchange some Canadian dollars for the local Peruvian currency of Nuevo Sol, while Madison headed to a separate one in quest of information. She explained to the woman at the kiosk that she and her boyfriend already had their lodging requirements at various places taken care of, along with roundtrip train tickets from Ollantaytambo to Aguas Calientes and entry tickets to Machu Picchu once they were there. However, they needed some help with their transportation from Cuzco to Pisac, and then onward to the train station a few days later. In addition, they were also looking for a means of returning to Cuzco from Ollantaytambo at the end of their trip.

As Heath approached, the young woman was informing Madison that her questions were quite common and easy to address. There was an hourly shuttle bus to Pisac nearby, and a separate shuttle van that left from that village for a trek through the Sacred Valley toward

Ollantaytambo every morning. As for the return to Cuzco, several similar vans would be available for hire at the train station.

Offering their collective thanks, Heath and Madison then headed in the direction of the shuttle for the one-hour ride over the mountain to Pisac. As intended, they arrived a full day ahead of when their target would begin his stay. Departing from the bus, Heath headed toward the same hotel that had been booked by their target and checked in. Madison in turn headed for separate lodgings in order to maintain her cover as a woman traveling alone. Throughout the ensuing hours, they each scouted the village and perused the large, outdoor craft market within the main square. By way of a few casual passes, they confirmed that where she intended to create the necessary chance encounter would work nicely.

While dressed in walking shorts, hiking boots, and a bright-orange T-shirt with her pack slung over her shoulders, Madison made her first move the following afternoon. A short time earlier, from a well-hidden position, she had watched her target step off the shuttle bus and check into his hotel that faced the craft market. Then she observed his subsequent entrance into a little place called the Blue Llama Café on the adjacent corner. Unlike his hotel, that restaurant could boast of a second-floor balcony for public use where hot or cold beverages could be enjoyed while overlooking the main square. Based on that, it had become a popular spot for those staying in or visiting the village to do some relaxed people watching from on high. Madison had firsthand knowledge of that fact, as she had visited the balcony for a cold beer the previous evening.

After seeing her target take a seat on the long balcony among a handful of tourists, Madison worked her way back around a few buildings to emerge on the brick road that led down into the village from the twisting mountain trail that descended from the Pisac Ruins. Spilling out onto the main square to the left and almost directly underneath the Blue Llama balcony, she was able to catch the eye of her target as he scanned the area below. Then, with the appearance of having just completed a long hike, she dangled her bait for the predatory wolf while casually glancing at what a few of the local vendors had to offer.

With her back facing the balcony, Madison whispered, "Has he been checking me out?"

Heath was sitting at a curbside table about fifty feet farther away from the Blue Llama, enjoying a cold beer, and had easily heard the question come through from the transmitter in her stud earring. His return signal of confirmation to the question was simple and hardly noticeable to the casual observer, as he slowly removed his hat and set it on the table in front of him.

Seeing the signal clearly, Madison made a quick purchase of a trinket from an elderly woman at one of the stalls, and then before turning toward the balcony, she whispered, "All right. Then it's time for me to get this started."

Strolling in the direction of the Blue Llama, Madison glanced up toward the balcony and could see that her target was looking directly at her. She knew that it would happen but telling Heath through her earring that she had been correct in her prediction would not be beneficial. He was a smart enough man to realize it without being reminded.

Offering a faint smile of recognition toward the man who gazed upon her, Madison then entered the building and ventured upstairs to purchase a bottle of beer before walking out onto the balcony. Although there were a few options as to where she could sit, she chose a barstool at the railing that would be somewhat close to the young man who was once again looking in her direction. Then after flashing him and others in the proximity a friendly smile, she removed her pack and sat down before taking a long, quenching pull from the bottle.

The young man could not resist the unexpected temptation that had come his way, and after saying hello, he asked, "So how was your hike?"

Turning toward him, she replied with a smile. "Fantastic! It was a beautiful day to look at the various terraces and ruins up on the mountain, and then the views of the Sacred Valley and surrounding mountains from the trail coming down were an added bonus."

She was accurate in that it was a beautiful day. But Madison had not really been up on the mountain to see any of what she described, nor had she completed the hike down. Of course, none of that actually mattered as the intent of her comment had been achieved. In relation to her target, the ice had been broken. As a result, she could now begin to work him.

After introducing herself as Paige, Madison slowly sipped on her beer and then one more during the next thirty minutes while she and her target Trevor discussed what each intended to do during their respective visits to the mountains of Peru. Throughout that time, he freely and inadvertently confirmed everything that Madison already knew in regard to him being a solo traveler from the Seattle, Washington, area—along with the when and where he would be staying during the next several days. Then as she stated her intent of summiting Huayna Picchu early Wednesday morning, Trevor realized that such a coincidence in their respective plans provided him with an opportunity. Although they would arrive in Aguas Calientes on different days for a much-anticipated look at all that Machu Picchu had to offer, they each had tickets on the same day and for the same time frame to the mountain beyond.

As Madison eventually finished off the last swig of her second beer, Trevor asked her, "So then, Paige, since we are both going to be there at the same time, would you like to hike Huayna Picchu together on Wednesday?"

Setting the empty bottle on the table next to the first, she nodded positively while replying, "Sure, Trevor. That sounds like a good idea, so why not?"

"Great! And how about letting me buy you dinner tonight?"

There it was. The young man had first taken the bait, which led to the engagement of innocent conversation, and after finding common ground, he was now making the first of his advancing moves. Based upon his reputation, Madison knew that he would be after much more than dinner, and if he got his way, she would fall victim to his self-perceived charms. If that were the case, then there would most probably be no hiking together on Wednesday. He would move on without care in search of yet another woman to conquer, so Madison knew that she had to maintain his interest while also making him believe that she would eventually be his to have.

In response, she answered, "Well…that does sound like a nice offer, Trevor, but I need to get a shower and some rest. Besides, my bus to Ollantaytambo leaves early in the morning, so a late night wouldn't be a good idea."

Trevor wasn't used to a woman turning him down for an offer of dinner or anything else and had no clue as to why she would be so reluctant.

So as Madison stood and then lifted her pack to sling it over one shoulder, he pressed further by asking, "Are you sure, Paige? I'm only talking about dinner, and there's really no sense in both of us eating alone."

Moving a step closer to him, Madison once again smiled and replied, "You do have a point about eating alone, Trevor, and spending more time with you is tempting. But as I just said, I can't do it tonight. However, I will make a deal with you. If you want to meet me in Aguas Calientes on Tuesday after you check into your hotel, we can go to the mineral pools for a relaxing soak. Then after our summit hike on Wednesday, we can have drinks and dinner. How does that sound?"

Madison noticed that her suggestion instantly caught the attention of Trevor, so it was therefore no wonder that he eagerly replied, "Well, all right, Paige. You've got a deal."

Then with supposed knowledge of Aguas Calientes from a fictitious former visit, Madison proposed a specific time and place to meet that would be easy to locate.

A moment later, she took her empty bottles to the bar and moved through the Blue Llama to emerge onto the main square directly below Trevor. Heath was still sitting at a curbside table down the street and had listened to the entire conversation on the balcony.

As Madison approached his position before veering off beyond it toward her little hotel, she whispered, "Is he still watching where I'm going?"

The affirmative signal was once again subtle, as Heath slowly placed his hat back on top of his head.

The following morning as they waited for the shuttle to Ollantaytambo, Madison stood at least twenty feet away from Heath while making sure that other people were positioned around and between them. There were subtle signs of pleasant recognition between all of those who would soon be sharing a ride together, but there was never a hint that Madison and Heath knew each other.

Suddenly she heard, "Hey, Paige. Don't forget that we have a date tomorrow."

Turning to the right, she saw Trevor striding toward her for what could only be described as an unexpected visit. The man was demonstrating his arrogant side by thinking that it was somehow acceptable to publicly announce they had an upcoming date, and in any normal circumstance, she would have admonished him for doing so. However, her cover of being a woman who found his ego to be both charming and enticing needed to be maintained, so Madison smiled and stepped out of line so that others, including Heath, could move past to board the van.

Now facing him directly, Madison said, "Well, this is an unexpected pleasure, Trevor. You didn't need to come see me off."

Not recognizing that she had been paying him a compliment, sincere or otherwise, for his efforts and good manners, Trevor replied, "Well…I was just on my way to eat breakfast and I saw the van. So, I figured why not."

"Well thanks for taking the time."

"No problem, Paige. So, then I'll see you in Aguas Calientes?"

"Sure, Trevor. On the bridge just like we planned."

20

Aguas Calientes

KNOWN AS THE gateway to Machu Picchu, the town of Aguas Calientes straddles a river by the same name at its conflux point with the larger Rio Urubamba. Within, there are four main bridges that serve as a means of traversing the waterway as it tumbles downward from the canyon above, and Trevor had agreed to meet Madison on the span of the one that was farthest up the hill. She had selected that location well in advance for two reasons, as her research indicated that it was not only the closest of the four to the mineral pools, but it would also serve as a favorable vantage point for when he approached.

Having first secretly watched Trevor from afar as he exited the train station and then moved through the adjoining and crowded artisan marketplace, Madison knew that based on what she and Heath had felt, he would be both fatigued from the journey and anxious to check into the comfort of his high-end hotel. That belief in the former was well-founded, as after their arrival via a shuttle van, and then the subsequent train ride down from the Sacred Valley twenty-four hours earlier, she and Heath had been impacted slightly.

Both segments of that journey were completed under the guise of traveling separately, and due to what had transpired moments before departing from Pisac, the use of that strategy proved to be a wise precaution.

As for the latter of checking into his hotel, that would take Trevor some time. Having experienced attempting to move through the crowd in the marketplace with vendors on either side vying for attention, and in also recognizing from her reconnaissance that his high-end hotel was located farther away from their rendezvous point than her current location, Madison knew that she had plenty of time at her disposal as she began the uphill jaunt toward the bridge.

Nearly an hour later, Madison spotted Trevor as he walked uphill in the crowd toward the bridge span. Although he hadn't noticed her yet, Madison knew that could change in an instant. Therefore, she acted quickly. Using an open palm to both disguise the movements of her mouth as well as direct the low volume of her voice toward her earring, Madison turned away from his potential view and whispered, "I see him now. He's just about even with your location, so he should get to me in about another two minutes."

Standing near the edge of the closest bridge to her, Heath had Madison in sight as she delivered the message. Then after hearing what she whispered; he altered his gaze to locate Trevor among those who were moving about between the two bridges on the opposite side of the river.

A moment later, Heath watched as he drew closer to Madison, and then as she waved toward the target, he heard Madison say, "Over here, Trevor."

Trevor walked toward her, and as she gave him a slight welcoming hug, he responded by saying, "I'm glad you decided to show up, Paige."

Madison pretended to be glad that Trevor was once again at her side as they engaged in a few minutes of casual conversation, but she also noticed that there was an issue to correct. Although Trevor had brought along a towel from his hotel, he had no swim trunks to go along with it. He was under the impression that they would be skinny-dipping in the mineral pools, so he did not think there was any need for something to wear. The assumption of easily getting her into a naked state was yet another example of his arrogant way of thinking, but Madison took it all in stride. She admitted to having skinny-dipped on occasion previously, and then falsely stated that she would not necessarily be opposed to it in the present time. However, the pools they would visit were public and probably had some children present, so clothing would not be optional.

With that explained, Madison motioned in the direction of the footpath while adding, "Don't worry, Trevor. If you don't want to soak in those shorts, then we can probably find you a place to buy some swim trunks along the way."

A few minutes later, Trevor picked up a pair of trunks in a storefront and asked, "So, what do you think of these, Paige?"

In truth they were awful, and in a subtle way she let that be known by saying, "Well…I guess those will do in a pinch. But the good news is you don't need them for more than a couple of days."

Once at the mineral pools, they paid the small price of admission and headed for the changing rooms. When Madison came out of the ladies' room a few minutes later, Trevor was waiting for her in his newly purchased trunks, and his eyes instantly revealed extreme pleasure as she moved toward him. Madison was wearing her maroon bikini with a towel draped over one shoulder, and the look produced a similar reaction from Trevor to that of Cameron in the British Virgin Islands.

With a smile, Trevor said, "That's a really nice swimsuit, Paige. You look great."

Knowing the bikini had exposed more curves of her body, and that by wearing it Trevor would be pushed over the edge of persuasion even if he wasn't already there, Madison replied, "Well, I'm glad you like it. Now shall we get in the water?"

For the next two hours they soaked in various pools, and occasionally got out to cool down and relax in chairs. Madison studied Trevor for anything that might be of consequence moving forward, and throughout that time she discovered something that would be beneficial. She could also tell that on several occasions Trevor had undressed her in his mind, as there was no question that her bikini was revealing enough to conjure up carnal images. Of course, thoughts of that nature were exactly what she was hoping to achieve and using the excuse of needing to cool down at the poolside on occasion gave Madison a chance to further solidify his desire through the use of memory reinforcement.

After changing back into their street clothes and heading down the footpath toward town, Trevor suggested that they get a drink and something to eat. Madison accepted, as it was his second offer for dinner in three days, but also stated that she intended to make it an early night. Then she reminded him that they had made a deal back in Pisac, and the terms of that pact stipulated that this dinner was not even supposed to take place until after they had hiked through Machu Picchu and summited Huayna Picchu.

Nevertheless, they sat down for a drink, glanced at a menu, and enjoyed a meal together. Despite his insistence that they partake in another round of drinks, Madison stood by her word with no intention of being swayed. With their tickets slated for the early entry window to hike the sacred mountain of Huayna Picchu and beyond, she wanted to make sure that they could catch one of the first buses up to Machu Picchu.

As they finished their meal, Madison reached into her small pack and pulled out some money to pay for half the tab. Perhaps it was just the way Trevor normally behaved, or perhaps it was because Madison had put an abrupt ending to the evening, but whatever the case may have been, he did not refuse her offer. It had been made clear that he would need to wait for the following day to even have a hope of sleeping with her, and maybe such a delay, if one like it had ever been presented to him before, was how Trevor determined if he would pay for dinner. She did not really care if that were true or not, but in order to keep him in peak interest, Madison needed to appease him in some way. Therefore, she informed Trevor that if he could just wait until the following day, she would invoke no restrictions on their actions, or how late they stayed out that night.

Madison had worded her statement most deliberately, as it was calculated to imply that as a consenting adult in her early thirties, she no longer had any inhibitions. Then, as she explained what a friend of hers back in Canada had shared about her own mountaintop experience, Madison revealed to Trevor that without inhibitions, anything with regard to physical exploration could transpire somewhere up among the ruins.

21

Machu Picchu

MADISON STOOD ON the sidewalk near where the end of the line was forming and watched as the first bus full of passengers pulled away for the trip up the mountain to Machu Picchu. She and Trevor could have been on that bus if he had arrived on time, but as of the current moment, he was still unseen.

Meanwhile, Heath was seated on a bench roughly twenty yards away and, for anyone who bothered to take notice, was exhibiting body language of someone who was simply waiting patiently for other members of his party to arrive. Madison was fully prepared both physically and mentally to carry out this sanction, so Heath anticipated no complications within the process if the opportunity was there for her. The ring that was now on her left index finger would render the target unconscious, and then she would use the syringe filled with pentobarbital in her pack as the second element to finish the job. Designed to slow down brain function and induce respiratory arrest, the fatal chemical compound would cause the death of Trevor in just a few minutes.

However, those positive feelings of Madison's preparedness were now clouded by a disturbing thought, as Heath knew that if Trevor didn't show up, all of the well-planned movements of the day would be for nothing.

When he did finally arrive, Madison offered a smile of understanding and apparent forgiveness, but thought that his excuse of needing to get some coffee before meeting her was another example of his self-absorbed behavior. Trevor obviously did not think to bring a second cup of coffee for her, nor did he find it necessary to apologize for being late.

As they stepped into the end of the line and then began to shuffle forward with the flow, Heath waited for at least a dozen others to fall in behind them before he did the same. The plan called for riding up the mountain in the same bus as Madison and Trevor, but if the cut-off line were to fall between their position and his, it was not a major concern. At this time of the morning, there would be another bus departing just a few minutes behind them.

Human nature dictated that those who boarded the bus would take the first available seats from front to back, and this instance was no different. As it turned out, Madison and Trevor were able to sit in the fifth row, and Heath took his place four rows behind them.

The road leading from Aguas Calientes up the mountain to the entry point for Machu Picchu was more of an adventure than Madison had expected, but she behaved as if she had experienced it before. After following the bank of the Rio Urubamba for a short distance, the bus crossed over a bridge before beginning a steep climb. Madison had studied a map on a Machu Picchu website, and therefore knew that there would be multiple switchbacks before arriving at the entrance area. But what that map did not reveal was that each of those thirteen switchbacks and the road itself were tight and narrow. There were many other passengers on the bus who showed visible signs of discomfort with each turn as the bus climbed higher and higher, and Madison found it humorous that they believed leaning to one side at a narrow point could actually prevent a catastrophe. In looking over the edge along one of the straight stretches between the tight corners, she realized that if the bus went over, there was little chance for anyone to come out of it unscathed.

Once unloaded from the bus, most everyone hurried to the gate where they presented their tickets and identification for entry. There were many who simply wanted to take in the majesty and engineering complexity of the sacred ruins, so once they were inside, there was no specific pattern or hurried pace to their movements. But for others, a mad dash ensued to locations where opportunities for early morning photographs of a nearly empty facility could be had for a brief time. Lastly, there were those focused solely, at least for the present time, on nothing more than Huayna Picchu, so they headed in that direction.

Although Madison and Trevor had moved briskly through the grounds of Machu Picchu, it still took fifteen minutes to make their way over to where they needed to be. By the time they reached the trailhead for Huayna Picchu at the Warden's Hut entrance, there were at least twenty other hikers already standing in line. Logically, nearly all of them had been on the first bus, and they, along with Madison, Trevor, and what would become the balance from the early wave of the two hundred to be admitted, were anxious to get started.

When the gate opened a short time later, the line that had grown in length behind Madison and Trevor began to slowly progress forward. Each hiker presented their entry ticket and passport for identity verification, and then signed a ledger while adding the time of entry next to their name. For Madison and Trevor, it would be no different, but she had a plan to make sure that her identity as Paige would not be next to his on the ledger. At the point when there were only four people between Madison and the check-in counter, she pulled out her passport from her small backpack while also pretending to have somehow misplaced her entry ticket. As she unzipped one compartment after another, those in front of her were moving on through the checkpoint.

Not wanting to hold up the line, she turned toward Trevor and said loudly enough so that those in close proximity could hear, "I know I put my second ticket in here someplace. You go ahead and sign in, and I'll step aside so that a few people can pass me while I find it. Just wait for me out of everyone's way a few yards down the trail."

Madison had been around Trevor long enough during the previous few days to know that he was self-centered, and his actions prior to boarding the bus a short time before had done nothing but confirm her belief. It was because of that action, and others, that she knew he would move on through the entrance when offered. Therefore, what followed was of no surprise.

Nodding in agreement, Trevor stepped forward without delay, showed his passport and ticket, then signed the ledger and wrote in the time of entry beside it before striding down the trail. As he moved on and others followed, a woman that looked to be in her mid-forties who had been about five people behind the pair reached Madison. She paused briefly while leaning over to see if she could offer assistance and added that the young man should have helped in finding the ticket before moving on.

In pretending at that instant to have just located her ticket, Madison exclaimed, "Here it is. Thank goodness!"

Then as she stood tall and flashed a smile, the stranger next to her said, "Oh that is good to hear. It would have been such a shame for you to have lost it."

"Yes, indeed, especially after all the effort it took to get here. It was kind of you to stop and make sure that I was all right. Now please, you go ahead of me and check in."

22

Huayna Picchu and Beyond

WHEN SIGNING THE ledger after producing her passport and entry ticket, Madison took note of the fact that there were six names between hers and Trevor's. Although the ruse of supposedly misplacing her ticket may have appeared to be an unnecessary precaution to employ, in her mind the plan had worked to perfection. She knew that if all went well during the upcoming few hours, Trevor would be sapped of his strength, which could simplify her efforts to complete the sanctioned kill. Then if successful, he would of course fail to make an appearance at the Warden's Hut for a matching exit signature in the hours that followed. In that event, one could surmise that an investigation of sorts as to his location would be initiated. But while the authorities attempted to find him and contacted those whose names appeared directly above or below his on the ledger, Paige would not be among them. Since she would not be considered as someone who could have possibly been hiking with Trevor, Madison would be using that valuable extra time to evade and escape.

Seconds after wishing the woman she had spoken to a good day, Madison spotted Trevor waiting as instructed a short distance away. Then for good measure after reaching his side, she verbally expressed a small amount of self-loathing for having misplaced her ticket.

Their ensuing trek toward the summit of Huayna Picchu was stunning while bringing forth both challenging and exhilarating aspects. Although narrow in places while either winding along a cliff edge or in traversing the spine of rock that connected Machu Picchu to the adjacent mountain, both the uphill and downhill sections of the well-maintained trail remained moderate throughout the beginning portion. Then the nature of the trail changed drastically, as it suddenly presented a steep, uphill climb consisting of rock stairs that were not evenly spaced or with a consistent rise.

Moving forward, Madison and Trevor encountered short and tightly spaced switchback after switchback as the trail snaked its way upward, and it didn't take long for her to realize that what had been carved out of the vegetated and steep rocky terrain was more than any novice hiker should undertake. There were even numerous places where the prudent move was to lean forward and use the stairs or roots protruding from the mountainside as helpful handholds while ascending. During that demanding quest for higher ground, Trevor, along with multiple others who pushed for the summit, needed the occasional rest period when a wide spot in the trail allowed for it. Fortunately for Madison and Trevor, as well as those hikers in their proximity, they were among the leading edge of the first two hundred to be admitted onto the trail that day. As a result of being in that early wave, there were not yet any others descending who would be vying for available space.

Based on the amount of high-elevation training that she had done with Heath in recent weeks, Madison did not really need to stop moving forward. However, to once again maintain her cover of allowing Trevor to believe he was somehow superior, she behaved as if also in need of rest and even took a few extra seconds of time when he was ready to move on.

Nearing the summit, there were a few different level spots among the ancient ruins that were suitable for photo opportunities and additional rest, so Madison played the part by using her recently purchased cell phone to take a series of stills and some video. Then after the final test of crawling through a tight tunnel that had been cut through the rocks, the last few yards to the summit were within sight. All that remained was a short ladder to ascend, and once that was done, Madison and Trevor sat with those who had arrived before them upon a large assortment of boulders to breathe in the view.

A loop at the summit led to a short descent over ruins and some terraces that would then rejoin the trail they had ascended, but an alternate route would take them beyond and downward from the summit toward the Temple of the Moon. Madison persuaded Trevor that they should press on and live for the moment, as she reminded him that she had been unable to do any portion of this mountain during her supposed previous trip five years prior.

He conceded to her point and followed her initial lead, but the trail was treacherous in some places with narrow descents of rock stairs, and in one instance, a long wooden ladder. Both elements demanded focus, so it was easy to fathom that on occasion a hiking tourist could make a misstep that could lead to severe injury or worse.

Then there was one specific location along their path that Madison let her mind wander, as at that moment it would have been so easy to kill Trevor. In her thoughts, she cautiously inched forward as far as possible to stand beside him while gazing over the edge. Then all it would have taken was for her to give him an accidental nudge off into oblivion.

No one would ever know with certainty what raced through his mind during those last few harrowing seconds of life, but Madison entertained the possibilities out of morbid curiosity. Would Trevor have enough time, and possess the mental acuity, while screaming out under the relentless force of gravity to self-question how he had fallen prey to her treachery? Or would his heart simply explode due to the terrifying realization of his plight? But then on the other hand, if she were to inject him with the toxin from her ring before pushing him over, would it take over his body to the point of inducing some measure of an altered mental reality? If so, then would his plummet become a brief but pleasant hallucinogenic thrill?

Regardless of which scenario might be true, if any, the man would surely be dead several hundred feet below. Perhaps there would be faintly heard sounds of squawking birds that had been disturbed as his body bounced off the rock face and ricocheted through the overgrowth of tree branches and jungle, but the ever-present green foliage would cloak any visual trace of his final resting place. Horribly broken from the fall, his body would then be feasted upon by creatures of the jungle as a form of natural selection unless it was located within the next several hours.

Those thoughts of a gruesome end for Trevor were quite appealing to Madison, and it took her a few seconds to fight back the urge to go ahead with it. Yes, it was true that Trevor, as the egotistical, womanizing prick that he was, probably deserved such a fate, but in the end, it would serve no useful purpose to the mission. Heath had devised a wonderful plan that would allow for her to plant the coded message on Trevor while still making it appear as though he had died of natural causes, and Madison wanted to see that through.

After reaching the small cave structure of the Temple of the Moon, Madison and Trevor were then faced with the tough climb back out from it. According to the map that she had in her small pack, they had descended about fourteen hundred feet from the Huayna Picchu summit, but not all of that needed to be regained. There was no need to double back along the same trail for a return to the summit, only to face another descent along what they originally ascended. Instead, they continued on a long loop that eventually rejoined the original trail from the Warden's Hut toward the summit, and during that lengthy trek, they experienced alternating steep uphill and downhill sections of the trail that in some areas clung to just the tiniest ledge of rock wall.

At the merging of the trails, Madison and Trevor encountered more pedestrian traffic, as hikers from both the first and second entry wave were moving in opposite directions along the trail. Then after finally making their way back along familiar ground to a location that was closer to the exit at the Warden's Hut, Madison mentioned that it would be a good idea if they took a little detour. At first, Trevor balked at the idea. He was nearly spent from a level of physical exertion that went far beyond what he normally experienced while working out at his local gym or walking in the mountains around Seattle, but Madison remained persistent. According to the map, it would not take much time to reach the summit of Huchuy Picchu as opposed to Huayna Picchu because it was a much lower peak. Therefore, it would also not be overly taxing, and she pressed that they should do it while they were here.

Sensing that he was still not completely sold on the idea, Madison then falsely admitted to also being tired in order to make Trevor feel better about his own exhaustive state. As a final nudge to convince him, she reminded Trevor with a playful smile of the story about what her friend back in Canada had done. With that, she was finally able to coax him into taking the short detour with the thought of potential physical pleasure at the top.

Madison and Trevor reached the lower summit with relative ease, and as Heath believed would be true, there were no other hikers on the short trail of Huchuy Picchu.

After gazing upon the ruins of Machu Picchu for a moment, Madison reached for Trevor's hand and said, "Just in case someone else comes up here, why don't we find a place back in those trees for some privacy?"

With a suitable location found that would offer no possible sightline from the higher peak of Huayna Picchu or Machu Picchu below, Madison took off her pack and sat down. Trevor nodded in compliance when she motioned for him to sit down to the left of her, and as he briefly turned away to remove his own pack before doing so, she twisted the dark stone of her ring counterclockwise and gently folded her right hand over the left.

A few seconds later Trevor sat down, and Madison wasted little time before leaning in to offer him a quick kiss before saying, "Thanks for doing all the extra hiking with me."

After a few seconds and another, lengthier kiss, she eased back to hear Trevor arrogantly state, "Well…your kisses are a nice first reward, Paige."

Then he leaned in to initiate another, and it was during that lingering forwardness that Madison was able to slightly shift the stone setting of her ring in order to expose the tiny needle from within the band. The time to act was now, and she knew it.

When the kiss finally ended, she said, "I like how you kiss me, Trevor. Please do it again."

Trevor took that as a sign that Paige was willing to let him advance upon her and did as she asked by leaning in for another, more passionate kiss. As he moved closer with the intent of laying her back onto the ground, Madison moved her left hand to a position behind his neck that would imply she was taking him into her arms. Then before he could fully lay her back, she quickly jabbed the tiny needle into his neck behind the right ear and pushed him upward with a strong right arm so that she could roll away from his grasp.

Surprised by the pain and sudden resistance, Trevor rocked back to his seated position and slapped his right hand to the area of the injection while asking, "What the hell was that all about, Paige?"

Madison had completed her roll and had gotten to her feet in a flash before moving farther away from his possible reach. Then she shifted the stone setting again to retract the needle, and by twisting it clockwise into its original locked position, she completed the safety procedure of ensuring that the needle would remain secured. Trevor had noticed that she was fiddling with something on her hand but had not yet fully grasped the reality of what it implied.

As she then prepared herself for retaliation in a self-defensive crouch, Madison glared at Trevor and with an unpleasant tone asked, "What's the matter? Don't you like my idea of foreplay?"

Trevor was completely baffled. Paige had first hinted at, and then with her ensuing actions had seemed to confirm, that they would be having a physical encounter while at the top of this mountain. But now she had not only moved away from him after jabbing his neck with something, she was acting as if she was prepared to fight him off should he approach.

Looking at her with astonishment, Trevor finally noticed the ring on her left index finger, and it came as a surprise. He had no recollection of Paige wearing any type of ring when they first met and talked in Pisac, nor while they were together in Aguas Calientes. It was, after all, a common practice of his to look at the left hand of any woman that he met, as a ring on the third finger generally implied that she might not be available or open-minded to the utterance of a pickup line.

Still feeling the back of his neck, he suddenly put things together and asked, "Did you just do something to me with that ring, Paige?"

In once again appealing to his ego, Madison replied, "Yes, I did, Trevor. That's very perceptive of you. I just injected you with a dose of fast-acting nerve toxin."

As Trevor then attempted to get on his feet for a lunge at her, the first wave of dizziness from the toxin came over him and he knew something was wrong.

Rocking back into his seated position again before a second attempt at standing, he exclaimed, "You bitch! Why did you do that?"

Madison smiled and relaxed her defensive posture slightly before responding. She had been silently counting the seconds since jabbing him with the needle and rolling away, so she knew that Trevor would not be in possession of his faculties much longer.

"The reason for doing it is not for you to know, Trevor, but I will tell you this. In a few seconds, you will lose consciousness."

"And then what will you do to me?"

In mimicking the phrase she had uttered to Cameron on the beach in the British Virgin Islands, Madison replied, "Only what must be done."

23

Racing the Clock

ALTHOUGH UNABLE TO get himself fully upright, Trevor gathered what little strength he had left to achieve a kneeling position before making a lunge for Madison. His desperate effort fell woefully short of where she stood, but he did not give up. On his hands and knees, he tried to crawl for a few seconds before grasping at nothing but air with an outstretched hand.

In an act of inviting another attempted swipe at her leg from his ever-weakening arm, Madison toyed with him by stepping closer while she audibly counted out, "Twenty-five…twenty-six…twenty-seven…"

Trevor could see that she now stood almost within reach, but he had no strength left to draw upon.

Then just seconds later, he faintly uttered, "You bitch!" before his head slumped and he fell flat to the ground as the toxin overwhelmed his system.

Madison took no chances and waited several seconds before closing the remaining distance between them. Then while he lay flat on his stomach, she circled around behind him and quickly lifted one of his feet to fold it over the back of his opposite knee. With his legs now in a figure-four position, she used her other hand to grab and fold his second foot upward toward his buttocks. It was a simple defensive move that had been taught to her long before she ever met Heath, and if conscious, anyone on the receiving end of the folded-over legs would be highly susceptible to suggestion. However, in this instance, the figure four would serve as insurance to determine if Trevor were somehow just playing possum, as the pain associated with pushing forward on the second leg would quickly snap him out of it.

Once convinced that Trevor was indeed fully unconscious, Madison proceeded to unfold his legs and roll him over onto his back before untying and removing one of his hiking boots. Then after pulling off the thick sock underneath, she reached into the small fabric bag that was within her pack and removed the small syringe to be used for the second injection.

Madison had noticed the previous evening while they sat near the mineral baths that the middle and fourth toes on each of Trevor's feet were remarkably close together. In fact, there was a slight overlap to them from years of presumably being crammed into pointy shoes. She realized then that such a spot on his body would be perfect for what she needed to do and that it would most likely never be thought of as an injection site during an initial postmortem examination.

After spreading his toes, Madison injected the syringe full of pentobarbital into his soft, receiving flesh, and the drug was then quickly absorbed into his bloodstream to induce what would later be construed as death by respiratory arrest. There was no one in close proximity that could help him, and even if another hiker came along at this very moment, Madison knew it would be highly unlikely that Trevor could be saved. Any other hiker, or a group of them if that were the case, would first need to have the ability to overpower her. If they could accomplish that goal, they would then need to deduce what was wrong with Trevor and be able to do something about it quickly. She had serious doubts as to the first of those factors being accomplished, let alone as to the rescuing party having the knowledge and the readily available means to medically counteract the drug.

Within minutes, all of those thoughts became irrelevant, however, as Madison was getting no sign of a pulse from Trevor in either of his wrists or his neck. An additional check for any breathing from his nose or mouth then confirmed that he was already dead, so with care she pulled the two surgical gloves out of her small fabric bag and put them on before returning the empty syringe to its rightful place within. Then she grabbed a corner of the small, laminated coded message and pushed it deep into the left front pocket of his hiking shorts.

As was the case with Cameron, the message read: ***Staircase696***.

With the message now securely planted on Trevor, Madison straddled herself over his outstretched legs and pulled the thick sock back on. Then she slipped his boot back on and tied the lace in identical fashion to that of the opposite boot. Had she done so from an orientation that faced the toe of the boot and his body beyond as opposed to straddling his legs, the laces of each boot would have been tied in a different pattern. Although that fact may have gone unnoticed, Madison did not want to risk someone concluding that one boot could have been removed and then retied for some reason.

Before rolling Trevor back onto his stomach, Madison took his phone and glanced at her watch to see how much time she still had at her disposal. After policing the area to ensure that no trace of her existence was left behind, she swept away the majority of her boot prints with a fallen piece of shrubbery. Then she removed the memory cards from both his phone and hers, which would contain any photographic history of the day, before using Trevor's T-shirt to vigorously wipe away any fingerprints on both phones and flinging each as far as she could out over the distant jungle below. With faith that all was secure, Madison removed the surgical gloves and stuffed them back into her small fabric bag before starting off on her downhill trek to rejoin the main trail.

Covering the distance quickly before stopping twenty yards short of the merging point, Madison crouched down behind some thick bushes. Peering through a tiny opening, she listened for the sounds of any other approaching hikers, while also feeling comfortable that her choice of drab-colored clothing for the day would blend in with the foliage if anyone passed by. When satisfied that no one was in her proximity, she glanced at her watch again before moving from her camouflaged position to join the trail. Time would eventually become a challenge if she delayed, so she would need to move at a brisk, yet non-alarming, pace.

When she then closed to within one hundred yards of the exit point, Madison could see a group of six slow-moving people between her and the Warden's Hut. Quickening her pace, she caught up to the weary hikers just in time, and politely asked if she could check out before them.

As she signed the ledger and wrote in her departure time before making for the main entrance with a purposeful stride, Madison took a quick glance and noticed that at least one-fourth of those in the initial entry wave had not signed out yet. That was a good sign, as it would provide more time for her to evacuate the area before anyone thought something might have happened to Trevor. She reasoned that the authorities would surely wait until nearly everyone else in that initial group had exited, and hopefully at least half of the second wave, before they would show any concern as to the whereabouts of a potentially missing hiker.

Near the opposite end of the Machu Picchu grounds, Heath was sitting comfortably with a pair of field glasses pressed to his eyes. He had lost the signal from her earring transmitter when Madison and Trevor began their descent on the far side of Huayna Picchu toward the Temple of the Moon, and it had remained that way until recently. However, as they ascended toward the lower summit of Huchuy Picchu, a more direct line of transmission had been reestablished. As a result, Heath had heard the conversation between Madison and Trevor both before and during the subsequent death scuffle. Therefore, he knew that the sanction had been carried out and surmised that all was well with Madison. If that were true, then all that remained now was for her to make her way back into and through the Machu Picchu ruins to the main entrance, and based on what the tracking devices revealed, she would be coming into view over the distant rise shortly.

After spotting Madison with the field glasses, Heath continued to track her progress visually and waited until the appropriate moment to alter his location. Then as she neared the area to exit the ruins, he was closing in on that same point.

No one took notice outside the main gate as Heath set a bottle of water on the short rock wall less than one hundred yards from the line to board the buses, or that Madison had whispered "Thank you" as she picked it up while walking past a few seconds later.

There was still a short line for the departing buses, so they were both able to separately get seats on the next one out. Madison knew the bus had thirteen switchbacks to negotiate before ever getting down to the river, and while staring out the window, she planned to silently count them off as the bus took on each one. However, what she did not expect during the descent occurred just after the first hairpin turn, as another bus bringing more tourists up the mountain was suddenly directly in front of her face. It could not have been more than two feet away from her bus as it passed, and the thought of how close they were gave cause for concern. A few moments later it happened again, and Madison realized that there would probably be several more before the descent was completed. As the driver of the third moved past her window, the side mirror of his bus was so close to her that she wondered how it had not clipped the side mirror of the bus she was riding on. Once again, the thought of a bus cascading over the edge entered her mind, and it was not a pretty picture. She couldn't see a way for a bus to stop tumbling over and over until it reached the bottom, while she also theorized that during those first few rolls of the carriage, there would be screams of agony before all fell silent. Then it occurred to Madison that these bus drivers probably do passes like she had just witnessed countless times every day, and therefore they knew exactly when and where to do so in relative safety. To that end, they were actually better drivers than most of what she had seen back in the United States.

Safely back in Aguas Calientes, Heath and Madison exited from the bus. They had rented separate rooms within the same small hotel in the event that Trevor decided to follow her after the mineral pool excursion, and now they would venture separately toward their hotel with a plan to rally in her room.

While crossing one of the pedestrian bridges along the way, Madison stopped briefly to gaze upon the river. Then after a quick check to see that she was not being scrutinized by a random observer, she casually dropped the two memory cards that she had removed from the phones into the turbulent rapids below.

After arriving at the hotel and rallying with Heath, Madison took a shower to get cleaned up while he checked out of his room with nearly everything that they had brought with them and headed for the train station. What was left, along with her small pack in the room, was nothing more than a clean set of clothes, a hairbrush, and her train ticket.

The subsequent train ride went smoothly, as Madison enjoyed a seat on the side of their carriage that provided a nice view of the Rio Urubamba for several miles. Although they were in close proximity, they did not ride together, as Heath sat four rows behind on the opposite side of the aisle.

When they arrived in Ollantaytambo and disembarked, both headed toward the row of shuttle vans that would soon depart for Cuzco. Heath and Madison maintained their cover of traveling separately, but they made sure to be on the same van. The subsequent ride with nearly a dozen other passengers took them partway through the Sacred Valley, and then along a twisting road up over a mountain pass and high plateau before descending into the large city. That portion of the journey was not nearly as hair-raising as the bus ride down from Machu Picchu, but as the roadway was steeply inclined at various points, there were times when the added weight of passengers and luggage made for very slow progress.

A taxi ride to the Cuzco airport would follow from the central drop-off point near one of the town squares, but only after Heath and Madison took care of some personal business. Moving in opposite directions from the van, they were each able to locate restroom facilities for a quick and necessary change into their disguises for the flight to Lima and then onward to Toronto.

While in the stall, Madison removed the small syringe from her fabric bag and stepped on it forcefully to break it into several pieces. Then she carefully wrapped the needle in a wad of toilet paper and placed it, along with a few of the broken pieces, into the fingers of one surgical glove. After twisting and folding the excess of the glove over itself two times, she tied a knot in the wrist area of the glove. The object was now small enough that it could be flushed as though it were bodily waste, so Madison did so before placing the remaining pieces of the syringe into the other glove and flushing it down in a separate stall.

She met up with Heath again near the drop-off point, and although available time was growing short before their planned evening flight out of Cuzco, both felt confident the deadline for boarding could be met if no lengthy delays were incurred. Fortunately for them and a few other passengers, passing through the security checkpoint at the airport proved to be of little consequence. Therefore, they were able to board their flight without running through the terminal.

After the arrival in Lima, Heath and Madison knew that they had about four hours before they would need to board their post-midnight flight to Toronto. They were fortunate to have the extra time since a tremendous amount of attempted drug smuggling out of Peru was an everyday reality, and security for outbound international flights from Lima was stricter than what Madison had ever encountered. As her bags were thoroughly searched for contraband, Madison came to fully realize the importance of why Heath had instructed her to destroy and dispose of the syringe.

Finally, through all the security checkpoints, Heath and Madison used their remaining time wisely by having some food and drink at one of the airport bars. As she theorized that the most difficult aspects of their escape were now behind them, Heath was quick to point out that they were not safely back in Carson City yet. He understood that once their flight touched down in Toronto, both he and Madison would probably be faced with another intense round of inspection while moving through customs. That questioning and search through their belongings would have nothing to do with any perceived guilt in relation to what they had actually done while in Peru, but rather for the simple fact that their flight had come from Peru. Although the Canadian customs officials knew that security forces in Lima apprehended many drug smugglers before they boarded planes to various global locations, they were also aware that others slipped through unnoticed. Therefore, passengers on an inbound flight from Lima would probably be handled with more scrutiny than those from another of the Commonwealth of Nations or the United States.

As the clock at the bar revealed that it was half past one in the morning, they kept an eye on a broadcast of the local news. There was only thirty minutes remaining before boarding would commence, and they wanted to see if anything might be cause for concern. At one point, a few photographs of the Machu Picchu region appeared on the screen, but neither of them could fully comprehend what was being verbally conveyed by the reporter.

Madison asked the man nearest to them, "Excuse me, sir, do you speak English?"

The man had been watching the news broadcast as well, and when turning his gaze from it, he replied with a friendly smile, "Yes I do, miss. Can I help you with something?"

"Yes please. What did that man on the television say about Machu Picchu?"

"Oh…it was something that happens up there occasionally. Unfortunately, it probably won't be the last this busy season, as there tends to be a couple of them every year."

"So, what happened?"

"There was a missing hiker on the Huayna Picchu trail, so they sent out a search and rescue party. A body was eventually found just after dark with identification to match that of the missing hiker, but unfortunately, the man was already dead when they found him."

SANCTION THREE

24

The Waiting Game

BACK IN CARSON City, Heath and Madison were able to fully exhale. As he had predicted, customs in Toronto was difficult when compared to when they returned from the Caribbean. However, once they were through, the subsequent flights westward to Calgary and then Cranbrook, as well as the drive south across the border into Idaho and on toward Spokane, were all uneventful. Then the final legs of flying from Spokane into Reno and the short drive south to their apartment were a snap.

Before noon the following day, Heath informed Madison that he needed to run a few quick errands. Some groceries were required, as well as a visit to the post office to gather what mail may have been delivered to the box during their absence. However, what Heath failed to mention was that he had also prepared a note for the president while Madison was in the shower, which would be sent off to Mrs. Dawson when he collected the mail.

That note for the president contained only two words: *Halfway home.*

What neither Heath nor President Harwell realized when the note was sent and received was that several months would pass before any opportunity presented itself for an attempt on either of the two remaining targets.

During the early weeks of the waiting game, Heath received intelligence reports that suggested that neither target intended to travel in the near future, but that created no cause for immediate concern.

After all, there were still sixteen months beyond the approaching July fourth weekend before the optimum deadline of completion would be upon them.

In realizing that their period of no action created an opportunity, Heath wanted to use the time wisely. On the first of July, he and Madison moved into a new apartment complex about three miles from where they had been living. The initial six-month lease on the old place had expired at the end of April, and they had been renting on a month-to-month basis during the two months since. Therefore, it was already beyond the time to relocate in order to maintain their original cover story of renting until purchasing a suitable home. Heath knew a slim possibility existed that either of them could randomly run into the manager of their previous apartment somewhere in town, but even if they did, all they had to say was that things were going nicely in their new home.

Meanwhile, Madison had decided to improve upon her swimming skills. Although it never came into play while they were in Peru, she was dissatisfied with her level of fatigue after the lengthy swim in the Caribbean. So, in theorizing that either of the two future sanctions could possibly require some time in the water, it seemed a prudent course for her to become more capable in that area. Therefore, as the waiting game lingered on through July, August, and into September, Heath and Madison incorporated swimming into their high-elevation exercise program of hiking, running, and practicing her hand-to-hand combat skills.

By mid-September, Heath was beginning to get anxious about a lack of new information coming his way, so he contacted the surveillance teams gathering intelligence on the two remaining targets to request that they expand their efforts in an unusual way. He wanted to know in their next report if any phone or email contact had been made between members of the four families during the previous three months. He had no evidence to support his theory, but Heath was grasping for a reason as to why travel plans for the adult children in both remaining target families had come to a halt. Therefore, he was willing to take a shot in the dark that one or both of the families who had already lost their youngest child would have somehow warned the other two of pending trouble.

Then to help pass the time of waiting for either new updates or an actual call to action, Heath once again read through previous reports that outlined certain habits of each remaining target. As a result, he believed that one of them could possibly repeat a trip to a previous vacation spot in the upcoming months, and if so, then an attempt in that location would certainly merit consideration. But before proceeding with any plans, he would first need to discuss his thoughts on the matter as well as his theory of the families potentially warning each other with President Harwell.

A short note that read, *Face to face required soonest,* was sent to Mrs. Dawson.

Five days later, a response came back: *All clear for same place and time, 927.*

For Heath, there could be no misinterpretation of the instructions from above. In less than a week, he would be meeting with the president in the residence during the evening hours of September twenty-seventh.

25

The Residence

WHILE UNDER THE watchful eye of a secret service agent that he had once mentored, Heath knocked on the bedroom door of the president and entered when instructed to do so. After being greeted by a firm handshake and a smile, the scene became all too familiar as President Harwell motioned for Heath to sit down on one of the twin couches while moving toward the other.

Heath waited respectfully until the president was seated, and then said, "Thank you for seeing me, sir."

"It's no problem, Heath. You and your operative, whoever she is, have been doing excellent work up to this point. Although we both know that you can't forward my compliments to your colleague, at least be aware that they exist and are well deserved."

"Thank you, sir, that's kind of you."

"Think nothing of it, Heath. Now what's on your mind?"

Throughout the next few minutes, Heath expressed his thoughts on how the four families may have communicated with one another after the first two sanctioned kills, and as a result of that hypothesis, what might be required to move forward with the initial plan if they had. There was still ample time to work with, and Heath hoped that altering their course to a different strategy would not be required, but it could become necessary if neither of the two remaining targets ventured outside of the United States during the coming year.

President Harwell leaned forward to state, "You must believe this is a strong possibility, Heath, or you wouldn't be here to discuss alternatives."

"Well, sir. I have no evidence to support my theory yet, but it is possible. So yes, I do believe that it would be prudent to plan for such a contingency."

"That's one of the many reasons I selected you for this unusual assignment, Heath. You are always thinking ahead and planning for what might have been unforeseen."

"Thank you, Mr. President."

"So, if you are correct, how do you suggest we move forward?"

Heath outlined his thoughts that if neither of the remaining targets planned to travel anywhere before Christmas, then attempts on them should be made in Seattle soon after. He also expressed that he was not going to give up hope that they would leave the country for some reason and was looking into possibilities of where each might be likely to go. Based upon his early research, there was still no guarantee of anything regarding one target, but Heath believed that the other could possibly be heading to a location in Canada for some skiing prior to Christmas. If that were found to be true, then an attempt could be made while that target was north of Vancouver in the resort area of Whistler.

President Harwell was intrigued by the prospect and listened carefully as Heath listed some of the obvious advantages, such as the requirement of less strategic planning with only a rental car needed for the minimal travel. However, he also discussed a greater number of disadvantages for the potential opportunity that the president needed to consider. For one, if the target Heath spoke of followed her previous travel pattern, then the trip would not be made until mid-December. Beyond that factor, the location of the sanctioned kill could be a concern as Whistler not only sat within the boundaries of a friendly international neighbor, it also boasted of being an extremely popular vacation spot for skiing and other winter sports. Therefore, keeping tabs on the target within large crowds could be difficult, and identifying a secluded location at the correct moment to make the kill could be challenging. Heath also mentioned that other uncontrollable variables such as the weather existed, as poor road conditions from an early winter storm could impact the drive south toward Vancouver on what would essentially be the only logical escape route.

When Heath finished, the president nodded positively while expressing his understanding that the negatives appeared to outweigh the positives in this instance. But in truth, he was not all that thrilled with the prospect of having a sanction carried out in Canada if other options were possible. Of course, somewhere in the United States was even less appealing, but if it must be done that way, then so be it. However, if the Seattle area were to somehow enter the equation, then President Harwell conveyed that nothing should be done until after Christmas had passed. Therefore, he directed Heath to be prepared for such an action as of January first if no other opportunities on foreign soil presented themselves before then.

26

Altered Plans

JUST MOMENTS AFTER returning from wherever he had gone, Madison learned from Heath that although it would not take place until at least January first, they needed to plan for the possibility of carrying out the third sanction somewhere near Seattle. He freely admitted that there could be increased levels of risk associated with attempting the kill on United States soil, which included the real possibility of unfriendly witnesses helping investigators to quickly put together damning evidence against Madison. Then there was also the influential family of the target who would most assuredly use their power in the region to grease the wheels of justice so that they could uncover the truth as to what had happened to their youngest child. Both of those issues were significant problems that could spell doom for Madison, but for some reason, Heath still felt more at ease with the thought of Seattle as opposed to Whistler. Regardless of that fact, prudence dictated that plans be forged that would ensure success in either location.

Heath and Madison collectively brainstormed and, over the next few days and weeks, presented various ideas for open discussion that involved how she might attempt the kill in both the Seattle and Whistler contingencies. Some were feasible, while others seemed too risky. They had eliminated the thought of Madison posing as a room service attendant or a maid at a hotel in Whistler due to the overwhelming uncertainty as to when or even if a delivery of either food or something like fresh towels would be needed by their target. Therefore, an opportunity might not exist to inject the nerve toxin and complete the sanction by perhaps smothering their target with a pillow.

In continuing along a similar line, the idea of posing as either a bartender or food server somewhere in Seattle seemed futile, as beyond the obvious impossibility of knowing which establishment would need to be infiltrated for any attempt, a familiarity would exist among the staff that could hinder the effort. Throughout all their discussions, the associated challenges that continued to be uncovered at nearly every turn made for a frustrating experience, and Heath began to feel a measure of self-induced pressure. In the end, it was decided by both Heath and Madison that the most effective way to proceed, no matter where the sanction might need to occur, would be to once again initiate some random-chance encounter with the target.

As a result, Heath had stated, "I hoped for your sake that this particular sanction wouldn't require seduction. Unfortunately, it may be necessary."

Madison had replied with understanding, while adding, "The files of this target indicate that she has dated men and women in the past, which in the modern world is not all that surprising. Therefore, I'll do what I can to gain her interest in me and seduce her, but it could be difficult if she's currently in a phase where men are more to her liking."

"It's true that her current preference could be an issue, and hopefully close observation will shed some light, but if need be, are you willing to get physically intimate with her?"

"Well yes…but it wouldn't be my first choice. I would prefer to enjoy that activity with you when we can, Heath. But I was kissed and groped by some of the female guards at Ellsworth from time to time, and the photographs we have of our target show that she is much better looking than any of them. So, if I have to do it, then at least I won't feel as powerless or repulsed in the process."

For Heath it had been a comforting thought that Madison was willing to go the extra mile if need be for the sake of completing the sanction, but he was also glad to know that she preferred to not make a habit out of being with other women. His romantic feelings toward her were beginning to reemerge to the point of where they had been before Madison attempted to kill him, and although this certainly wasn't the time to act upon those stirrings, Heath could tell by her statement that at some point in the future the time could be right.

Then in early November, Heath received two updated intelligence reports that instantly relieved much of the pressure he was experiencing. The first dealt with his previous inquiry into whether any of the four families had communicated with each other during the most recent few months, and much to his relief, no evidence of that was found through either cell phone or email records. As for the second report, it addressed one of the two remaining targets. Her upcoming travel plans would solve a problem, as Heath now had a favorable alternative to either Seattle or Whistler for Madison to eliminate their lone female target.

Turning their focus to the newly presented information, Heath and Madison began to weigh the associated pros and cons. From a positive standpoint, their target would be leaving the confines of the United States and traveling to the distant land of New Zealand without involving Canada in any way. Her upcoming two-week trip was scheduled to begin on the Monday following Thanksgiving weekend, with three- or four-night stopovers already booked at multiple locations that included Queenstown and Wanaka. As a result, there could be any number of good opportunities for Madison to complete the sanction.

However, on the negative side beyond Heath and Madison now having only four weeks to put some sort of plan together, there was an additional obstacle. Unlike her solo ski trips to Canada in recent years, for this adventure to the southern hemisphere, their target would be accompanied by another young woman. Such plans could mean that their target was currently more interested in female companionship than male, or it could mean nothing of the sort. They could just be traveling as friends who were either in search of men or no other companionship at all, and if so, it would not bode well for

Madison. But if they were not opposed to external liaisons, then introducing Madison as a third party into the equation with the intent of seducing the target might not be perceived as any kind of threat. However, if the vacation was intended to be a romantic getaway for the two young women, then the presence of Madison could be viewed quite differently.

Of course, none of that conjecture could be addressed until after all four of them were in New Zealand, where Heath and Madison could begin a surveillance of the two young women. For Heath, the reasoning behind why the target would have another woman with her was not all that important other than it would dictate how Madison moved forward. In his eyes, all that really mattered was devising a method that would separate the target from her companion for a long-enough duration so that Madison could complete the sanction.

27

Vanished Tomorrow

THREE DAYS BEFORE their target was scheduled to depart from Seattle and make her way over the Pacific to Queenstown, New Zealand, via Los Angeles and Auckland, Heath and Madison began a move of their own. As with the previous two sanctions, they stuck to the plan of covering their tracks with three sets of disguises and false identity passports before traveling into Canada and then making their way south. However, in this instance, their initial flight from Reno on Friday, November twenty-eighth was bound for Seattle as opposed to Spokane, with the subsequent drive across the border from Idaho to Cranbrook substituted by a similar-length journey near the coast toward Vancouver.

Once those initial legs had been taken care of, Heath and Madison used the second of their fabricated identities to board an overnight Air Canada flight to Sydney, Australia. Then a few hours after their early morning arrival and clearance through customs, the third was employed for a three-hour flight east over the Tasman Sea to Queenstown on the South Island of New Zealand.

During the lengthiest middle portion of that process, an entire calendar day vanished into oblivion due to moving west across the International Date Line before their arrival in Sydney on Sunday the thirtieth. However, they had not experienced any form of time travel in the scientific sense, just a minor slippage of dates on the calendar that would be corrected when crossing back over the line while moving east. Their subsequent jaunt over to New Zealand from the east coast of Australia brought them to a beautiful island nation that could boast of being one of the first places on Earth to greet the dawn of every new calendar day, and as the plane flew over the Southern Alps and descended into Queenstown, Heath and Madison soaked in the fantastic views. They were now nineteen hours ahead of Pacific Time in the United States, but more importantly, they would have three days to do some reconnaissance in both Queenstown and Wanaka before their target would arrive.

The first order of business after clearing customs was for Heath to rent a car, and while he was taking care of that, Madison headed for an information kiosk in the terminal. After a few minutes of asking questions, she came away with a handful of useful brochures and maps to go along with a wealth of knowledge.

Satisfied with the interaction, Madison then located Heath and they made their way out to the car. Perhaps it was due to fatigue from all the hours of air travel, or it could have been that she just forgot for a moment where they were, but Madison instinctively headed for and opened the door on the right side of the vehicle.

In turn, Heath asked, "Oh…did you want to drive?"

Madison took a quick look inside the car before shaking her head from side to side as she uttered, "No thanks. I'll leave that to you."

Heath smiled at her response while loading their bags into the trunk, as Madison had clearly not remembered that the rules of the road in New Zealand were just one of many examples where the British colonial influence remained.

After climbing into the right side of the car to drive, Heath said, "You know, Madison, it's not too late to learn. Driving from the opposite side of the car and on the left side of the road is no big deal and knowing how to do it could prove useful at some point."

"Perhaps, but for now I have other more pressing considerations."

Throughout all of Monday and Tuesday, Heath and Madison surveyed everything they could in the area that included and surrounded both Queenstown and Wanaka. Within that process, they not only scouted various local attractions and places where their target and her companion might enjoy excitement, food, or nightlife, but also aspects of the hotels where they would be staying in both townships. The most recent intelligence report of their target, which arrived at the P.O. Box just prior to Thanksgiving, revealed no reservation for a car rental in Queenstown, so it was reasonable to assume that both women probably shared the same opinion as Madison with regard to the local driving protocols. If that were true, then their target and her companion would be at the mercy of shuttle and bus schedules, or taxis, for transportation from one location to another.

28

Queenstown Arrival

BEFORE LEAVING THE confines of their own hotel to take up positions of waiting, Heath had confirmed that the flight from Auckland on the northern island that carried their target and her companion was due to arrive on time. That news, coupled with the knowledge of the shuttle transport time, meant that they could accurately gauge the arrival from the airport to the hotel lobby.

As the Crowne Plaza Queenstown on Beach Street sat close to the shoreline of Lake Wakatipu, it was easy for Heath and Madison to watch for their prey from locations that were close by without raising suspicion. Not wanting to be seen together, he stood across the street on a dock area with a camera in hand as if he was interested in taking photographs of the lake and mountains beyond. Meanwhile, Madison was positioned about one hundred yards down the street from the lobby entrance near the door of a storefront that could be easily ducked into if need be.

When the airport shuttle dropped their target and companion off Wednesday afternoon, neither of the women looked around before entering the lobby. They appeared to be a bit haggard, and their actions were not all that strange considering they had traveled for many hours on three separate flights. Heath theorized that the two women simply wanted to get into their room as quickly as possible to drop off luggage and freshen up a little. Then in time, they would re-emerge to begin an exploration of what the town had to offer.

His assessment proved to be accurate some fifteen minutes later when they exited from the lobby and turned in the direction of where Madison was positioned, but not before they had unknowingly provided him with some meaningful information. Long before hitting the street again, both had ventured out onto one of the fourth-floor balconies to take in the view. They gave each other a celebratory high-five while doing so, but there had been no embrace or any other physical touching involved. Enough time was provided for Heath to behave as if he was taking photographs of the mountains beyond them, but in reality the camera was far enough away from his face so that he could count off their balcony position in relation to each end of the building. Within seconds, he not only had the exact location of which room they had been assigned, but also a hint of evidence to suggest that they were not romantically involved.

Madison had seen them appear on the fourth-floor balcony and high-five as well, but her angle from the same side of the street as the hotel did not allow her to ascertain exactly which room they were in. Then when they did emerge roughly ten minutes later to head in her direction, Madison ducked into the storefront to stay out of view.

Not long after they strolled by, oblivious to her presence, Madison spotted Heath trailing them from the opposite side of the street. He gave the appropriate hand signal to proceed with a tail from her side, so she fell in a short distance behind with a distant view of the two women.

The plan called for continued individual surveillance with the hope of learning more about the relationship between the two women, so throughout the latter stages of Wednesday, as well as most of Thursday and Friday, Heath and Madison each covertly observed their target and her companion as they engaged in a myriad of activities. Only then did they discuss their common consensus, which confirmed what Heath had initially believed could be true, as it became obvious over time that the trip for the two women to New Zealand was not intended to be a romantic getaway. Neither had shown signs of caring for each other in any way beyond friendship, while at the same time demonstrating that they appeared to have come on the two-week adventure with separate romantic motives. While the companion was clearly focused on some of the men in town, be they available or not, their target exhibited subtle signs that her quest was indeed that of meeting another woman.

Based on those observations, Madison believed that the time was right for her to create a chance encounter, so after witnessing the two young women venture into a pub early Friday afternoon, she acted upon the given opportunity with no hesitation.

Ducking into a public restroom, Madison removed her wig of long, straight blond hair, her tinted sunglasses, and her studded earrings before stuffing them all into a plastic bag that she carried within the small fabric bag around her waist. Then after reemerging, she headed in the direction of Heath to hand it off. Barely breaking stride as she moved toward and past him, Madison gave Heath a wink as he reached out for and took the plastic bag.

Now prepared to make her initial move, Madison moved closer to the door of the bar. She waited outside the establishment for a few minutes so that her target and the second woman could get settled, and then entered the English-style pub to see them sitting near a corner section of the bar. After observing their actions from behind for another moment, she advanced to sit reasonably close to them while taking note of what her target was drinking. Once seated in plain view of both women, Madison then asked the server for advice on some of the local beers. Without realizing he had done so, the man then helped her break the ice with the target as he outlined some of the available options.

Reaching for the line of taps, he said, "This is one of our popular summer beers. It's refreshing without being heavy, and in fact, this is what those two ladies are drinking."

Madison looked in their direction across the corner of the bar and listened, as they were pleased to offer an endorsement for what the bartender suggested.

In response, Madison smiled at the two of them before saying to the bartender, "Well, all right. I guess I'll try one of those, please."

After the beer was delivered, her target waited a moment for Madison to take a few sips, and then asked, "So, what do you think?"

Madison smiled again and replied, "You were right, and thank you. This is a nice beer."

The woman locked her eyes on Madison and said, "It's no problem. Glad to help."

With the ice broken in a pleasant way, Madison introduced herself as Nicole while knowing before they could offer a return introduction that her target and the companion were Alisha and Emily, respectively. Throughout the following half hour, the three women engaged in some lighthearted conversation, and Madison could sense that an immediate comfort between them had been established. She was pleased with how easily the initial contact with Alisha had gone, while also noticing that she had hardly looked in any other direction since they began talking. The same could not be said for Emily, however, as she did allow her attention to waver on several occasions. Then when the conversation shifted to what plans they all had while in New Zealand, Alisha inadvertently confirmed everything that Madison had already known from the most recent intelligence report.

As Emily continued to flirt with the bartender and give nearly every dark-haired man who entered the pub a good looking over, Madison realized that there could be an opportunity to get Alisha alone in the future if Heath was willing to participate. She would not be able to discuss her idea with him in the present moment but creating useful scenarios in the field was one of the lessons that Heath had stressed during her training. Therefore, Madison came up with a plausible story as to why she was visiting the South Island of New Zealand, and she did it quickly.

With Alisha attentively engaged, Madison explained that she and her brother had come to New Zealand at the request of their parents and grandparents. Sadly, one of the elder pair only had about six months to live, as she was stricken with a terminal illness that could not be corrected via medication or surgery. Upon hearing of her distressing fate, this imaginary grandmother had supposedly put forth a dying wish toward her loved ones. She wanted the multiple generations of her extended family to gather someplace exotic while she was still able to travel, instead of waiting to come together at her funeral. New Zealand happened to be one place that she always wanted to visit, so that was the site selected for said reunion. Although the family spoken of was spread far and wide, which would in turn make a trip to New Zealand an inconvenience for nearly everybody, the fictitious, ill grandmother had been insistent.

Madison continued by emphasizing that she and her brother had spoken about the trip and had then agreed to make the journey only if they would offer each other moral support. Dealing with their parents on a somewhat regular basis was one thing, but hanging out with the grandparents, aunts, uncles, and cousins for extended periods of time would be difficult. Neither wanted to create any unnecessary hurt feelings, but she and her brother wanted to do some things away from the crowd, and in some cases, perhaps even away from each other. They both recognized that some might think their actions would be selfish in nature, but both she and her brother saw it as a way to help maintain the sanity of everyone until gathering together for the big party in Christchurch.

With her pint glass then empty and the fabricated story of her presence in New Zealand told, Madison decided to take the next step. She looked at Alisha and Emily while stating that she would really like to spend more time with them, but unfortunately, she had agreed to meet up with her brother back at the hotel in a little while. Then before either woman had a chance to utter a response that might resemble a permanent goodbye, Madison looked directly into the eyes of Alisha and suggested that the four of them meet for a drink at their current location later in the evening.

Alisha locked onto Madison's eyes with her own and, while flipping her long black hair back over her shoulder, said, "That sounds like a great idea, Nicole. I would really like to continue our conversation."

Madison smiled at her and replied, "So would I, and I think that my brother Tyler would enjoy meeting Emily. Shall we say outside on the patio at around six?"

"Sure…that sounds perfect."

With that Madison stood, pulled out some cash to pay her tab, and exited the pub.

Heath had watched Madison enter the pub after he put her wig and other accessories into his backpack and was somewhat perturbed that he couldn't listen to all that was being said once she was inside. However, based on the amount of time that had passed since, he understood that she had probably not only initiated the chance encounter with her target, but was also making some headway. When he then saw her emerge from the pub and walk in his general direction, he had no clue as to what she had conjured up. Only her hand signal before veering away gave him some indication that all was well, but her second gesture was more telling. She needed to discuss something with him in a hurry, so he broke off his surveillance of the pub and headed toward their hotel.

29

Double Date

HEATH MADE HIS way back to the hotel about ten minutes after Madison had arrived, with his tardiness being attributed to waiting a moment before beginning his trek and then taking an elongated route through town. As he then gave Madison her plastic bag while listening to her explain what had transpired in the pub as well as her intent for the evening, Heath shook his head in disbelief.

Looking at her with questioning eyes, he said, "You want me to do what?"

"Go on a double date this evening and pose as my older brother Tyler."

"You have got to be kidding?"

"No, Heath, I'm not kidding. You will be our fourth so that Emily doesn't get bored while I build upon the seduction of Alisha that was initiated at the pub."

Madison described in more detail what she had told the women about why she and Heath, as Tyler, were in New Zealand, and what her long-term plan for the next few days could entail. If all went well, Emily would be attracted enough to Heath that he could occupy her in one location while Madison went about completing the sanctioned kill on Alisha somewhere else.

After a moment of thought, Heath said, "So just to be clear. I'm supposedly your brother Tyler, and you want me to cozy up to Emily for what could be a few days so that you can work Alisha."

"That's right."

"And how do you propose that I gain her interest for that long?"

"Well…it shouldn't be that difficult if you just use a little imagination and some of your charm. Emily is a young and somewhat attractive woman who looked over every dark-haired man that came within shouting distance while I was sitting with her and Alisha. Now, in looking back over the past few days, there were several other men around town with dark hair that she scoped out while we were observing them. She gives off the vibe of being lonely, and since you have dark hair, you are probably already her type without needing to do much more than breathing. In fact, from what I saw of her actions at the pub, she is searching for a tryst while far from home that will give her a fond memory throughout the coming years. Based on that and your good looks, you could probably get her into bed without too much effort."

Heath listened to the plan, and other than the aspect of bedding Emily, he had to admit that it could possibly work. But that would only be the case if Emily wanted to spend some time away from Alisha, so he still had doubts. After all, they had traveled nearly halfway around the world together for a vacation adventure, so why would they want to separate?

Seeking validation before agreeing to the double date in a few hours, Heath asked, "So you really believe that I can charm Emily enough to eventually give you time alone with Alisha?"

"Well, of course, Heath. That is if you don't act like a bore this evening. Show her you have some real interest beyond mere conversation throughout the next several days, and it could create the catalyst we need. Now the date for six tonight is already arranged and based on the excited response by Alisha when I suggested it, they will be there. But this will only work if you are willing to be a part of it, and if not, then let me know so that we can try to come up with a different angle."

Heath realized by her tone that Madison believed she was really on to something tangible, and that alone would be enough for him to act upon the groundwork she had already laid. With that in mind, he reluctantly agreed to go on what amounted to nothing more than a blind date for the sake of the mission.

The warm, early summer evening of drinks on the pub patio turned out to be a great success. Heath and Emily got along splendidly as they talked about a few subjects, while Madison continued to slowly work Alisha with flirtatious smiles, gestures, and the occasional brushing of the arm or a gentle pat on the hand. Heath noticed that her efforts were having an impact as the woman responded positively and continued to smile while she breathed in every essence of what Madison put forth. To him, it seemed as though Alisha could be killed on that very night if Madison wanted to pursue more intense physicality, but as nothing had been arranged as of yet to occupy Emily, that was not part of the plan.

From Madison's perspective, she believed, at least in the present moment, that Alisha could be manipulated into time away from her friend Emily via the suggestion of a romantic tryst. A most recent action of reaching under the table had seemed to confirm that theory, as Madison felt the touch and subsequent rub of the young woman's hand upon her upper thigh. Madison knew that her response to the exploratory gesture was critical, as Alisha could get the impression that she was being either dismissed or overly encouraged in the next few seconds. Therefore, the problem for Madison was that she could not behave as if nothing would ever happen between them, but at the same time she couldn't move too quickly by hopping into bed with Alisha on this first night. Killing her in either of their hotel rooms would only lead to the potential of Madison being caught for doing so, and that would serve no constructive purpose other than having the third sanction completed.

On the other hand, she had no intention of losing any future opportunities to eliminate Alisha in what would appear to be an accidental death by irrationally dismissing her. Neither option would suffice for the grand plan, so as always, Madison got a grip on the situation. She understood that what she wanted and needed to do was to carry out the sanction without being caught, but in order to do that, she had to make Alisha believe that they would hook up at some point in the coming days.

Before the evening of drinks and laughter was completed, Alisha glanced over at Emily to see if she could get any kind of sign from her in regards to Tyler. The response was that of a smile and a positive nod, as Emily had enjoyed his looks and company throughout the past few hours. As a result, Alisha asked their two latest acquaintances if they would like to get together again at some point in the next few days.

Having advance knowledge of where Alisha and Emily would be lodging throughout the length of their vacation, as well as any big-ticket items they had previously booked, provided Madison with an advantage that only Heath was in tune with. She was aware of the fact that the two ladies would be checking out of the Crowne Plaza Queenstown in the morning and heading over to Wanaka via a shuttle bus for the ensuing four nights. But based on a credit card reservation that had been made for Saturday, December sixth, she also knew that they would not be in Wanaka for the majority of the day. Instead, Alisha and Emily would have a day of splendor away from Queenstown before shifting over to Wanaka and checking into their hotel, as they had pre-booked an expensive Hopper flight over the Southern Alps to Milford Sound on the west shore. Then they, like countless thousands of other visiting tourists every year, would enjoy a scenic boat ride through the length of what could be compared to Yosemite Valley half filled with ocean water. At the current time of early summer in the southern hemisphere, there would be multiple waterfalls to admire as they tumbled down rock outcroppings or over the lip of sheer cliff walls into the sound below. Then after soaking in all that glorious nature, the return flight and a subsequent shuttle ride would bring them to Wanaka.

As a result of knowing the itinerary that awaited Alisha and Emily, Madison stated, "I think it would be great if we could get together again, because I for one have had a really nice evening. But, unfortunately, this will be our last night in Queenstown."

Heath followed the lead of Madison and echoed her sentiment of having an enjoyable evening before adding, "We will be heading over to Wanaka at some point tomorrow for the next several days. But maybe we could come back to Queenstown one evening and meet you two for dinner or something."

Madison, and Heath for that matter, already knew from her previous body language that Alisha was hooked. She just had to be reeled in.

Therefore, it was no surprise to either of them when she said, "Hey, that's great news. And you don't need to come back to Queenstown for dinner with us. Starting late tomorrow afternoon, we will also be in Wanaka for several days."

30

Wanaka

AFTER ALISHA AND Emily returned from their adventure to Milford Sound, they checked into their modest hotel overlooking Lake Wanaka and then walked a few blocks into the heart of the quaint, little town for a rendezvous. Madison and Heath were waiting for them as agreed on the balcony of a bar with a lake view and following welcoming hugs that would appear to be those of longtime friends, the four of them sat down to have a cold pint.

Discussions ensued about what had been seen throughout the day, and what each of them still wanted to do. Once again, based on information within her file, Madison knew that Alisha was fond of boating. Therefore, she mentioned that she wanted to go kayaking in the morning and was wondering if anyone wanted to join her.

Heath assisted her play by stating, "Sorry, Nicole. You know that's not really my thing, but maybe the ladies will join you."

Within an instant, Alisha said, "Well, I'm not very good at kayaking, as I've only done it a few times, but I'm in. What do you think, Emily? You want to try it?"

While shaking her head from side to side, Emily stated, "I'd rather not. And it's nothing personal, Nicole, I just don't enjoy being in the water very much unless it's a hot shower. Besides, I was thinking of trying to play a round of golf in New Zealand if possible, and since Alisha doesn't play, this could be the perfect opportunity for me."

Heath knew that the moment to seal the deal for Madison was in front of him, so he quickly asked, "So you're a golfer, Emily? So am I.

Maybe we should go play a civilized game on the links while Nicole and Alisha are splashing about in their kayaks."

Turning to face him, Emily responded, "Sure, Tyler, why not. I read there's a course here in town, so I don't see why we can't have a little fun of our own."

"Great. How do you feel about playing at say one o'clock? If that's good with you, we could meet at the clubhouse a little before that, and then after the round we could have some dinner."

With a smile toward him, Emily replied, "That sounds perfect, Tyler. It's a date."

Heath had not played golf in well over a decade, but that did not matter as he had no intention of showing up to meet Emily for a game.

Nevertheless, in response, Heath nodded and echoed, "It's a date."

Madison looked over at Alisha and said, "Well…I hope you brought a bathing suit, as it looks as though we have a date as well. Unfortunately, it will be much earlier in the day than what they have planned, so perhaps we should call it an early night."

Soon after the evening of what had been a busy day for all came to a close, and Madison smiled inwardly. Everything was all settled and perfect for attempting the sanction. She would get Alisha alone for hours out on the water in kayaks, while Heath had made Emily believe that they would be golfing in the afternoon before having dinner together.

The following morning, Madison met Alisha at the information kiosk on the beach, which was where nearly any type of activity for the surrounding area could be booked. There were a handful of options to choose from when it came to renting kayaks or other water toys for accessing the lake, but one company in Wanaka provided a service that set them apart. For an additional fee, the kayaks and those renting them would be loaded into a large shuttle van and driven by a representative of the company to one of several locations along the lengthy shoreline. A detailed map of Lake Wanaka was provided with visual instruction as to where other drop-off points were located, and the customer could decide where and when they wanted to be retrieved. All they needed to do when they were being dropped off was notify the driver of their intent.

Based upon scouting the area previously with Heath, Madison knew that the first option near Ruby Island to the southwest of town was too popular for what she required. It was not only a spot that many motorboats and other kayaks visited, but it was also a landmark that was photographed from shore with regularity as it sat in prime view from the nearby Rippon Vineyard & Winery. Therefore, she had already decided, and informed Heath, that she would opt to use the much safer second option farther down the road.

Consequently, Heath would do his part by following them at a safe distance in the rental car and by keeping tabs on their whereabouts throughout the morning via Madison's tracking implants. If all went well, she would then complete the sanction, and he would pick her up somewhere along a remote section of shoreline.

31

Glendhu Bay

WITH THE MAIN thrust of summer crowds not due to descend upon the Wanaka region until Christmas week, the shuttle from the kayak rental facility had only eight passengers, including Madison and Alisha. Of course, Madison would have preferred that there were less, but it was not one of those factors she could control. She knew that any of those in the shuttle with her, including the driver, could provide a description of her to the authorities later if need be. Therefore, Madison took the precaution of wearing large sunglasses and borrowing a plain baseball cap from Heath to cover the top of her head. It certainly was not the best disguise she had ever used, but it would at least offer some cover from those who might remember minute details about her hair and facial features. Then, as a means of being even less memorable at both the rental facility and aboard the shuttle, Madison maintained a quiet and low profile while she was in close proximity to anyone other than Alisha.

The first drop-off point near Ruby Island proved to be all that she could hope for, as the family of four and the two other passengers had selected that location for their particular kayaking adventure. As a result, Madison and Alisha rode alone with the driver when he pressed on several kilometers farther toward their drop-off point near the campgrounds in Glendhu Bay.

Once the two kayaks and associated gear had been positioned at the shoreline, Alisha began preparing herself to climb into the seated position. As she did so, Madison pulled the driver aside for a moment to whisper a few words. She requested that she and her friend be granted whatever time was available until the latest hour he could possibly pick them up, with a quick explanation that both of them wanted to enjoy an entire day away from the remainder of their families.

The young man nodded positively, and then moved toward the kayaks to see if he could offer the other woman some assistance with entering and steadying her craft. It became obvious to him that Alisha was not an expert based on how she was struggling to get seated without tipping over, but he soon had her situated before giving her kayak a gentle nudge away from shore. Madison, on the other hand, had gotten herself into her kayak with minimal effort, and smiled at the driver while using her paddle to push away from the beach. With both of his final two customers now safely afloat, he wished the pair a pleasant day on the lake without ever knowing it would be the last he saw of them.

Throughout the next few hours, Madison and Alisha enjoyed their time alone as they explored various inlets and reaches of Glendhu Bay. Some areas were sheltered with smooth water while others were less placid due to gusting winds, but Madison did not care which they encountered. She had lashed her life jacket and T-shirt to the bow of her kayak in order to get some sun, and upon seeing her in the maroon bikini top, Alisha had done the same. Then, in knowing they had several hours at their disposal, Madison suggested they venture farther into the western portion of the large bay.

They paddled a good distance along that course while taking in some fantastic views of the surrounding mountains and landscape, and Madison took note of two important factors. They were now completely out of sight from any portion of the campgrounds, and the water in the bay throughout the journey had been a dark enough shade of blue so that the bottom could not been seen once away from shore.

When they reached a section of the bay that was broader than others, Madison quickly scanned the area to see if any stray hiker or fisherman might be watching from any distant bluff. When satisfied that all was clear, she suggested that she and Alisha head for a tiny stretch of rocky beach that could be seen in one of the inlets to go for a swim.

Upon reaching the shore, Madison climbed out of her kayak and pulled about half of its length out of the water. Then she moved toward Alisha and helped to steady her kayak as she got out. Once that craft was also secured in a similar posture, Madison took off her beach shoes and unzipped her walking shorts. Then, while shifting her hips slightly from side to side, she pulled them down to reveal the bottom portion of her maroon bikini.

Alisha stared at the splendor of Madison's hourglass figure for a moment, and then said, "Wow! You really make that suit look great, Nicole."

"Thanks. The thought of wearing it gives me incentive to stay in shape."

"Well, if you don't mind me saying, the incentive has worked."

"I appreciate that, Alisha. Now, let's go for a swim."

A moment later, Alisha had also taken off her shoes and shorts to reveal the remaining portion of her one-piece suit, and then she grabbed hold of Madison's outstretched hand so that they could successfully negotiate the rough, pebbled surface below their feet. Stepping gingerly, they were soon waist-deep and feeling the chill of the water that had not yet been fully warmed by the summer sun. Wanting to avoid inching her way forward, Madison suddenly released the hand of Alisha and dove headlong into the water. After coming to the surface some twenty feet later, she turned and stroked her way back toward Alisha before ducking her head under once more. Then when able to stand about five feet directly in front of her, Madison did so while lifting her arms to smooth back her short brown hair as the water streamed down from it.

Alisha gawked again at the beautiful upper torso in front of her as the water dripping from Madison glistened in the sun.

No words were spoken as they gazed at each other for several seconds, and then Alisha said, "You know, Nicole. I have wanted to kiss you since not long after we first met."

Madison was quick with a smile and the reply of, "I've been thinking about that too, but I didn't want to kiss you in front of Emily. You know, in case she would be offended."

"That was nice of you, but Emily and I have been friends for a long time. She has seen me kiss other women before, so she wouldn't have been shocked. Besides, even if she did have a problem with it, she isn't here now."

With another smile, Madison fell backward into the water and stroked about fifteen feet away while replying, "Well…I can't argue with that, Alisha. But if you want to kiss me, then you need to swim out to me first." And as she then demonstrated that the water was not quite up to her shoulders, she added, "And look, we can still touch the bottom here."

Alisha took several eager, yet gentle, steps forward in anticipation of her prize, and when she got to Madison, they simultaneously leaned into one another and shared a delicate kiss. That first gentle, lingering taste was followed by another of more vigor, and before long Alisha closed her eyes and became totally lost in the passionate moment. Madison moved her hands above the shoulders of Alisha to gather up the now wet strands of her long black hair and broke off the kiss. As she then draped the hair over the front of Aisha's right shoulder to rest between them, Madison gently kissed the left side of Alisha's neck before refocusing her attention onto her mouth. With the subtle move completed, Madison then rested both of her arms on the shoulders of Alisha, gently brought her hands together, and twisted the dark stone of her ring counterclockwise. As the kissing continued, Madison slid the stone setting ever so slightly to expose the tiny needle within.

Then as Alisha thought of the extreme pleasures that she could possibly experience with Nicole during the next few hours and beyond, Madison carefully lowered her right arm to wrap it around the waist of Alisha. Once a firm hold of her torso had been established, Alisha followed suit with an exploratory move of her own by sliding her right hand up to feel the firm curvature of Madison's left breast. Madison paused for a few seconds to enjoy the sensation of another's touch, but then remembered that hesitation is what kept her from killing Heath three years prior. Instantly, she regained her focus, slowly folded her left arm so that the hand would be close to the back of Alisha's neck, and in one quick thrust jabbed the tiny needle into the vulnerable soft tissue behind and below the left ear.

Their lips parted quickly as Alisha reached with her free left hand for the area of sudden pain, and Madison pushed away from her victim so that those few seconds of confusion and disorientation could be put to good use. With her eyes locked on Alisha, who was no more than four feet away, Madison carefully readjusted the ring settings so that the needle would be retracted and secured. Then she lunged toward a bewildered Alisha, and by firmly covering her mouth with an open palm, temporarily muffled any attempted screams.

Alisha grabbed hold of Madison's wrist with both hands and pulled the hand away for an instant, but as a defensive measure, Madison coiled her legs underwater and thrust them hard into the midsection of Alisha before she could scream out for help. The jolt of both feet into her stomach and ribs made Alisha wince in pain, and after letting go of Madison's wrist, she struggled to move into shallower water where she could try to regain solid footing.

Madison moved quickly by reaching out for and grabbing hold of her victim's long hair. Then after wrapping a portion of it around her hand, she gave a firm pull that yanked Alisha backward and submerged her head for an instant. In response, Alisha thrashed away as she resurfaced for some air and swung an arm in the direction of Madison to strike her. There was no doubt that the woman in peril was putting forth a good effort, but with Madison having a firm grip on her hair from behind, it was difficult for Alisha to effectively fight back. She needed at least one hand to attempt freeing the grip on her hair if she were to have any hope of breaking loose from this woman who had suddenly gone insane, and as she was also standing nearly chest deep in the water, it was impossible to use her full range of motion with the other arm.

Nevertheless, Alisha continued to swing wildly with her dominant arm, but Madison easily deflected the majority of the efforts with self-defense methods. Then when Madison noticed that the fury was beginning to lessen, and a glazed look was beginning to appear in the eyes of Alisha, she knew that the battle would soon be over.

Looking her in the eye, Madison said, "Please don't fight this anymore, sweetheart. Just let the toxin take over."

She understood that the toxin would act faster and last longer on Alisha than either Cameron or Trevor because she was smaller in stature. Although Cameron had been in good shape and weighed somewhere between the two, Trevor was considerably larger. In fact, he had probably outweighed Alisha by about seventy-five pounds.

The body in her grasp fell nearly limp soon after, so before the eyes of Alisha could close for the final time, Madison began walking them into shallower water.

Now only waist-deep and wanting to give Alisha one last chance to speak, Madison said, "You don't have more than a few seconds, so say what you need to say quickly."

Looking over at Madison as extreme wooziness took hold, Alisha asked, "What have you done to me, Nicole?"

At that moment Madison did not have the heart to repeat the same witty phrase that she uttered to her two previous victims, so instead she offered a more nurturing response of, "That doesn't matter now, Alisha. Just go to sleep."

A few seconds later, Alisha could not fight the toxin any longer. Her eyes closed and then her head fell limply to the left. However, Madison did not take any chances, as Alisha could have been faking. In a quick movement, Madison drew back a hand and slapped Alisha hard across the face. There was no reaction at all, so she did it a second time and waited a few seconds before grabbing Alisha by the chin and shaking her head from side to side. There was still nothing. Alisha was most definitely unconscious.

Knowing that status would need to be altered, Madison acted quickly by walking Alisha closer to the shoreline before laying her down so that her head rested on dry land. She then moved to retrieve her small fabric bag that was lashed along with her life jacket and T-shirt on the front of her kayak. After unzipping the main compartment and one of the smaller ones within, she placed the ring inside before pulling out and putting on a pair of surgical gloves as she had done in Peru. After grabbing Alisha's shorts from the beach, Madison dunked them into the water before pulling them up over the limp and somewhat buoyant legs of her victim. Once they were zipped and buttoned, she pulled the laminated coded message from within that same unzipped compartment of her fabric bag and pushed it deep into the front left pocket of Alisha's shorts.

As with the other two sanctions before this, it read only: *Staircase696.*

The next step was to put Alisha's shoes back on and pull her about ten feet from shore so she could roll her over into a face-down orientation. Once that was accomplished, Madison glanced at her watch and began a countdown of minutes.

With those minutes clicking past, which were necessary to have Alisha die of what would be considered accidental drowning, Madison went about her other tasks. First, she guided her own kayak out as far as she could walk before giving it a gentle push into the open bay, and then she returned to shore to get dressed in her shorts, T-shirt, and beach shoes before clipping the small fabric bag around her waist. She put one end of both kayak paddles into the hold of Alisha's craft, and with the body still in a face-down orientation, she tied the bowline around both of Alisha's ankles. Then as the final step, Madison pushed the kayak from shore and began a swim out into the open bay while pulling the craft and the trailing, lifeless body behind her.

32

After the Kill

WHILE SWIMMING FARTHER away from shore, Madison had checked often to see that Alisha remained face-down in the water. As a result, she was confident that the body had never rolled over a single time to provide even a whiff of fresh air into the oxygen-starved heart and lungs. Madison had discarded one of the paddles from within the kayak roughly five minutes into the swim, while keeping an eye on her own kayak as the wind in the bay took it farther away from her. Then she flung the other paddle aside a few minutes later and was now preparing to get rid of the second kayak.

Madison inched toward the body of Alisha so that she could untie the bowline from her ankles, but before doing so, she would first check for any possible breathing, a heartbeat, or a pulse. She realized that the occurrence of any life sign would be most doubtful, as Alisha was assuredly drowned after being helplessly unconscious while face-down in the water for nearly fifteen minutes. Even so, Madison was prepared to act quickly if her most recent target was somehow still alive. Fortunately, there was no need for her to act in self-defense, as no life signs could be found.

Satisfied that her latest victim was dead and that the two kayaks and their paddles would now be properly dispersed, Madison freed the bowline from Alisha's ankles, and after pulling the phone free from within the lashed down T-shirt, she capsized the kayak to minimize the drift. Then she let Alisha's phone sink to the bottom of the bay and began swimming again while pulling the body of her victim along by the shoulder strap of her one-piece suit. After covering another one hundred yards or so, she set the body free and began a more vigorous pace toward a distant, bluff-lined shore.

Heath had been monitoring the location of Madison from near the bay via her tracking implants and had listened to the sounds of their brief catfight not long before. According to their plan, she would complete the sanction and set the body adrift somewhere in the large bay before swimming toward a shoreline area that was dominated by bluffs where he would be prepared to receive her. There were a few dirt roads leading off the main roadway that could get him within reasonably close proximity to those various bluffs, and as her position closed in on the shore, he would select which of those would be best for her extraction.

Fifteen minutes later, Madison completed her swim to shore and began climbing up through a rift in the bluff. Her chosen path was less steep than a vertical ascent, and after reaching the top with little trouble, she could see Heath approaching from a distance in the rental car. She took her T-shirt off to wring it out the best she could while beginning to jog toward Heath. Then when she and the car converged, Madison removed her walking shorts for the same purpose. Now clad in nothing more than her maroon bikini and the fabric bag, she welcomed a towel from Heath as she jumped into the car and removed the surgical gloves. He drove along the dirt road slowly so as not to stir up a large dust trail, and then once back at the main roadway, Heath turned left in the direction of the Glendhu Bay campgrounds and the town of Wanaka that lay well beyond. Throughout portions of that fifteen-minute drive, Madison held her clothing out the window for additional drying, and by the time they passed the Rippon Winery and the adjacent stables, she was able to at least put her T-shirt back on.

Just before entering the central township of Wanaka, Heath turned right onto Cardrona Valley Road as opposed to venturing straight ahead toward Highway 6. That change in course would take them higher into the mountains and through a pass before descending on the opposite side via a twisting route to reach their intended destination, but it would also cut off several miles and precious time from the more benign valley and canyon path of Highway 6 through Cromwell. As they moved farther up the valley, the name of the route changed to Crown Range Road, but before reaching the summit of the range, Heath turned left again onto a road that led up to a winter ski field.

The parking area had a few other vehicles that belonged to hikers, but he was able to locate a remote spot so that Madison could get out of the car and hide between two open doors to change from her wet bikini into comfortable dry clothing for the upcoming flight away from New Zealand. Then with Heath and Madison in disguise to match the passport identities used for entry into the country, they headed back toward Crown Range Road.

Before turning onto the road, Heath looked at his watch and said, "I'm supposed to meet Emily at the golf course in a few minutes, and she will be upset that I stood her up."

Madison looked over and replied, "I agree. Her feelings will be hurt when she realizes that you're not coming because no woman ever wants to be stood up."

"That may be true, but in this instance, I'm not the one to blame for making her feelings a casualty of the mission."

As they crested the summit a few minutes later, an amazing view opened up in front of them. The entire southern half of Lake Wakatipu and the mountain ranges on both sides of it could be seen, but Heath could only take in the splendor for a few seconds before beginning a steep descent with a handful of switchbacks. Down at the mountain base, the road joined up again with Highway 6, and from there it was an easy jaunt into Frankton and the adjacent Queenstown Airport.

By the time Heath and Madison pulled into the airport, Emily was starting to wonder where her date was, as Tyler was now almost thirty minutes late for their agreed upon meeting time at the Wanaka Golf Club. It appeared as though he had decided to stand her up for some reason, and unfortunately for Emily, Tyler, like many other men in her life, had demonstrated that he cared more about his own needs as opposed to spending time with her. In knowing that her friend Alisha was also off kayaking with Nicole for the day and would not be available until the evening hours, it was obvious that her afternoon would be spent in solitude. However, she was not going to allow the actions of Tyler to spoil what she intended to do in the first place, so Emily rented some clubs and began a round of golf.

Meanwhile at the Queenstown Airport, Heath dropped Madison off at the terminal before returning the rental car so that she could begin the process of finding them a flight out of New Zealand. When he got back to her side a short time later, negotiations were under way for two separate seats on a flight to Melbourne, Australia, that was departing in two hours. It was not exactly where they needed to be for their flight back to Vancouver, but the city in the south of Australia would at least serve the purpose of getting them far away from Wanaka and the body of Alisha.

Shortly before that moment, a group of four hikers who were exploring the bluff areas along the circumference of Glendhu Bay noticed what appeared to be an overturned kayak out in the bay. Further visual inspection of the area led to the discovery of another similar craft in the distance, what could have been a double-bladed paddle, and then, much to their dismay, what looked like a body.

The security checkpoint at the Queenstown Airport was light when compared to those in the United States, so Heath and Madison moved through with ease and boarded their flight. By the time Emily completed her round of golf and enjoyed a cold drink in the clubhouse with an older couple she had joined up with for the back nine, Heath and Madison were beyond the Tasman Sea and over the southeastern portion of Australia. Then as time progressed toward when Emily and Tyler were supposed to once again meet up with Alisha and Nicole, the plane landed in Melbourne.

33

Recovery

ONE OF THE hikers who had spotted the floating debris reached for her phone and placed a call to the police in Wanaka, while another searched for a safe means of descending to the water below. Although on the far side of the bay from where Madison had ascended, he soon found and then used a similar rift in the bluffs to make his way downward. Then, after reaching the narrow, rocky shoreline a few minutes later, he yelled up at his companions for directional assistance. The other male and female in the group pointed him toward the body and motioned for left or right course corrections as he swam farther away from shore. But even with their help, it was several minutes before he was close enough to see the lifeless, floating body on his own.

Rolling the body over after reaching it, the man knew instantly that the woman was beyond help. If her pale face and blue lips were not enough evidence, then the lack of a pulse or a hint of breathing proved that she was dead. Regardless of that fact, the man slapped her gently on the face and shook her to see if she would respond, but there was nothing. He could not do anything for the woman except try to get her back to shore, and he would need to do that quickly before he met with the same fate of drowning in the cold water. Grabbing hold of one wrist to drag her along, he began a sidestroke swim back toward his fellow hikers while one of them began a descent from the bluff.

Not long after the body of Alisha had been brought up on shore, a police boat from Wanaka arrived. Moments later, an ambulance and a police vehicle made their way along one of the dirt roads to where the other two hikers were located, and the questioning began. Nobody in the group of hikers knew who the woman was, but it seemed logical based on what she was wearing that she had been using one of the two kayaks they had seen.

Both men on the police boat had seen another kayak on their way into the far reaches of the bay and confirmed that the hikers had probably reached a correct assessment. But as their immediate concern was reaching the found body, they had wasted no time in searching for another. That process would commence immediately, as another boat was summoned to join the recovery process, but in the meantime, a decision had to be made. Would it be best to place the drowned victim in their boat while the search progressed, to struggle to carry it up the bluff to the awaiting ambulance, or to meet the ambulance back at the campgrounds for an easier and more humane transfer of the body? For practicality purposes, the third option was selected, and the transfer was completed in less than an hour from when the call for help came in.

Immediately afterward, the police boat, the second craft, and then a third that had recently arrived began searching Glendhu Bay in a grid-like pattern to see what could be located. Throughout the process, both kayaks and their double paddles were recovered, but a second body was never found.

With no reason to believe that any drama had unfolded out on the lake, Emily had finished her beverage in the clubhouse and had returned to the hotel to shower and change for the evening. Her original intent, based on what he had said the previous evening, was to have dinner with Tyler after their round of golf, but that was no longer an option. Therefore, Emily decided to head for a bar that had a view of the lake, and if anyone other than Tyler showed up to join her, it would be a bonus.

Not long after she arrived and got a drink, Emily saw the shuttle from the kayak rental company roll past and then pull into a nearby parking area. As she watched to see if Alisha and Nicole would then be moving in her direction, she heard a few other patrons discussing that specific adventure company and something they had heard rumor of. Apparently, the police boat for the town was seen with two kayaks in it as it returned to the dock, and a female tourist who had drowned in Glendhu Bay was in the hospital morgue.

As Emily listened to the gossiping drinkers' ongoing chat, she learned that they had no idea who the woman was. However, they had heard from a friend who worked in the hospital that she had been dead for a couple of hours before the body was recovered.

Meanwhile, customs in Melbourne, Australia, for Heath and Madison had proved to be no issue, especially as they were posing as separate Canadian citizens coming in from New Zealand. With that behind them, they then began a quest in short order to secure a required connection. Although their lengthy flight over the breadth of the Pacific to Vancouver would not be until the following midday, it was departing from Sydney as opposed to their current location. Therefore, Heath and Madison separately purchased tickets onto one of the many commuter flights that went back and forth between the two large cities.

34

Frightening Realization

AT FIRST, EMILY put off the story of a drowned tourist as nothing more than some idle bar gossip, but as she had not yet seen any sign of Alisha or Nicole returning from their kayaking adventure, curiosity began to get the best of her. When she could no longer fight the urge to know if the story was truth or fiction, she left her half-empty cocktail on the patio table and ventured across the street to speak with a representative of the company.

After identifying herself as a friend of the pair of women who had rented kayaks that morning, Emily learned that apart from Alisha and Nicole, all of their clients for the day had been retrieved and returned safely. With no easy way to break the news, the man explained that there had been an accident, and the local constables had the kayaks and gear in their possession as evidence while they investigated what had happened. He further expressed that he would be happy to walk her over to the station a few blocks away if she desired, so off they went.

Once at the police station, Emily explained her relationship to who she thought could possibly be the drowning victim. She was a longtime friend of one of the two women who did not return, and for identification purposes, she requested the opportunity to view the body in the morgue. That request was granted, and upon seeing the body of Alisha just a few minutes later, Emily gasped at learning that her longtime friend was dead.

Unfortunately for Emily, that would not be the end of the story. Based on information they had already received from the coroner, the police had some questions for her. The cause of death had been confirmed as drowning, however, there were a few aspects of her demise that led the authorities to believe she may have been assisted in that process. There was some bruising to her hands and forearms from what could have been a struggle with another individual, which seemed logical when combined with some minor bleeding on her scalp in an area where a large clump of her hair had been pulled with significant force. In addition, there were also some marks and minor abrasions around both ankles, which could have been caused by a small amount of rope burn.

When asked to provide some information as to her own whereabouts during the time in question, Emily stated that she had slept in after her friend left to go kayaking with Nicole. Then she showered and had gone into town to do a little shopping and get a bite to eat before heading out to the golf course. There was no one who could possibly corroborate her claim of the morning hours except her server or a couple of store clerks, but fortunately, she was able to present a few receipts with time stamps that cleared her of being in Glendhu Bay when the drowning occurred. As for the afternoon hours, she had played the front nine alone since her date failed to show up but was joined by an older couple for the completion of the round.

One of the constables taking note of the receipts heard what she said and clarified by asking, "You had a date to play golf and he didn't show?"

"That's right."

"And have you heard anything from that person since?"

"No. But I really don't want to hear from him, especially now that Alisha is dead."

The constable looked over at his superior, who in turn gave him a nod to proceed. His next few questions would be delicate, but they needed to be asked.

Turning his gaze back toward Emily, he inquired, "Miss, how long did you know this man who didn't show up for your golf date?"

"Not long. We met him and his sister Nicole in Queenstown a few days ago, and it's Emily, by the way."

"Very well, Emily. And please forgive me for asking these questions, but your answers may help us to determine what happened."

"I understand. Anything I can do to help."

"Thank you. So, you and Alisha met this man and his sister Nicole after you arrived in New Zealand?"

"That's right. Tyler and Nicole are here for a family reunion of sorts, and the four of us have been spending some time together."

"I see. But then why were you having time apart? I mean, why were you and this Tyler going to play golf as opposed to kayaking?"

"Because Nicole wanted to go kayaking and asked if any of us were interested in joining her. Tyler said that it wasn't his thing and maybe us ladies would join her. Alisha was eager to do it, but I expressed my intent to avoid the water before I mentioned a desire to play some golf while in New Zealand. He offered to join me while they were out on the water."

"So, then it was Tyler's idea to meet you?"

"That's right. I think we both knew that Alisha and Nicole wanted some time alone since they seemed to be drawn to each other, and to be honest, I wouldn't have minded spending some time alone with Tyler. Since we both shared an interest in golf, it seemed like a good way to make everyone happy."

"I see. So, you all collectively agreed to split into pairs for the afternoon and evening."

"That's right. Then we would get together again at some point later this evening after dinner. Of course, all of that is irrelevant now because my good friend Alisha has drowned."

With that the constable offered another glance toward his superior, who in turn motioned with his hand that it was time to ease off.

Then he took the lead himself by moving closer to Emily and asking, "So do you know where Tyler and Nicole were staying here in Wanaka? Or their last name and where they are from?"

Emily thought for a moment before stating, "Actually, no. I don't know any of that. All I really know is that they are due to meet with other family members in Christchurch for a reunion in a couple of days."

The senior constable nodded positively with comprehension, and then stated, "Well, Emily, we will continue our search for this Nicole woman. But it's possible that her body will never be found in Glendhu Bay or anywhere else in the lake."

With a puzzled look in her eye, Emily asked, "Why not?"

That was when she faced the most difficult question of all, as he asked, "Has it occurred to you that Tyler could have been meant as nothing more than a diversion for you? Perhaps his role was to keep you occupied so that Nicole could do harm to Alisha."

A few brief seconds of contemplative thought were followed by extreme shock as the alarming realization of what the man expressed began to sink in. The more Emily thought about it, the more his claim made sense. Beyond a few sketchy details, absolutely nothing was known about either Nicole or Tyler. Sure, Emily could provide the authorities with a decent physical description of both, but she had not taken a photograph of either with her phone. Unfortunately, even if Alisha had with hers, since the constables hadn't mentioned anything about it, she had to assume that it had not been recovered with her other belongings. As Emily focused more intently on several events throughout the past few days, including how both couples had coincidentally been heading to Wanaka on the same day, it suddenly hit her. She and Alisha had been played by the two strangers from God knows where, and because of it, Alisha was now dead.

After shaking her head from side to side in a moment of self-loathing, Emily then looked at the senior constable and said, "There isn't any family reunion in Christchurch, is there?"

Relieved that she had already moved beyond the initial denial stage, he replied, "No, Emily, I don't think so."

By the time Emily had come to that conclusion, Heath and Madison had already landed in Sydney. With a room in an airport hotel subsequently secured for the night, they each got some much-needed rest and a more comfortable setting to once again alter their disguises before boarding their midday flight to Vancouver.

35

Altered Perspectives

THE SOUTHBOUND DRIVE from Vancouver, Canada, toward Seattle had been dark and dreary with the constant threat of rain, which was a radical shift from the early summer conditions of New Zealand that Heath and Madison experienced while in the southern hemisphere. Although the rain never developed into a torrential downpour, there was always enough of a drizzle to dictate that the windshield wipers could never be turned off. In essence, it was a most typical early winter day in that particular region of the Pacific Northwest.

The flight east across the International Date Line had meant that Heath and Madison picked up the calendar day they had previously lost when traveling west toward Sydney, and as a result, their lengthy flight landed in Vancouver on Monday, December eighth at an hour that was actually earlier than when it had departed on the same day.

Once clear of Canadian customs and then across the American border into Washington, they stopped in Bellingham to remove their respective disguises. That was now a few hours into the past, and both Heath and Madison felt more at ease with the most difficult aspect of their journey behind them. Then when rolling past the freeway exit for the University of Washington, the weather took a positive turn as the cloudy skies over Seattle parted to allow the low-angled winter sun to shine through. Shortly thereafter, the downtown skyline was only visible to them via the rearview mirror as Boeing Field came into view on the right side of Interstate 5.

Nothing had been verbalized by either Heath or Madison in regard to passing the university or in laying eyes upon the Boeing facility, but Heath flashed back to the last time he had visited both. That Saturday, slightly more than five years prior, in mid-November of 2026 had begun in peaceful fashion, but it most certainly did not end that way. As a consequence, Heath would never forget that day, for he had been the lead agent on President Harwell's protective detail and the one to inform him that a horrific act of terrorism had just been committed on American soil. Then just seconds later, he had also given the order to evacuate the area before whisking the president away from Husky Stadium to the more secure confines of Air Force One parked at Boeing Field.

That day triggered a series of events that would put the nation as it was known in an altered state of reality for the next few years, and Heath now sat next to someone who at that time had been a willing participant in the insurrection.

However, those dark days were now well into the past, and Madison had proved without any doubt that she had become someone Heath could both work with and trust. Therefore, he viewed the current day in Seattle with an altered perspective to that of the past. Not only was the country intact again after having navigated through those fracturing times, and President Harwell was safe from that previous threat to his legacy, but the mission intended to eliminate the most current perceived threat to the president was now three quarters complete.

In the meantime, Madison had been doing some quiet reflecting of her own throughout the past thirty minutes, and because of it, she also developed an altered perspective to what she had just viewed. Before the most recent of days when driving north toward Canada from the Seattle-Tacoma Airport, Madison had never visited the region. She knew from speaking with each of her first two sanctioned targets that they were from the surrounding suburbs, but that had been the extent of any connection she had with the city. Then during the drive to Vancouver, she had noticed freeway exit signs that identified

more precisely where those suburbs were located, and she had reflected momentarily upon her memory of each man.

Cameron was a nice guy and a seemingly kindhearted soul in
his mid to late twenties who probably would have been successful in
life. It was even quite possible that based upon his behavior, he would
have made some woman in his future into a happy spouse. In that regard, eliminating him from existence for the sake of the overall mission, although completely necessary, was unfortunate.

Trevor, on the other hand, had proven time and time again to be
a jerk that tended to view the world in a most self-centered way. Although born the same year as Cameron, he had not reached the same
level of adult maturity. In her eyes, Trevor saw those in his life, be they
brief encounters or otherwise, as inferiors who were only there to
serve as a means of pleasing or satisfying his needs. Although killing
him, from a logistics standpoint, had been challenging, the act itself
could probably be viewed by some as a favor to humanity.

Throughout that trek along Interstate 5, Madison had also noticed an exit for a suburb where her third sanction lived, but at the
time had given it minimal thought. However, the same could not be
said on this day, as over a brief span of time in New Zealand, she
had gotten to know something about Alisha. Therefore, when Heath
had driven past the exit for Highway 520 and Alisha's hometown of
Bellevue a short time ago, Madison could not help but feel some remorse. In her eyes, Alisha was a beautiful and intelligent young woman who had been just beginning to explore all that the world could
offer, but because Madison had snuffed her life out for the sake of the
mission, she would never get a chance to realize her potential.

Meanwhile, in Bellevue to the east of Lake Washington, the
Walker family was still in a state of shock. It had not yet been thir-
ty-six hours since they had received the news about Alisha from Emily, with many of those sleepless hours spent either crying in anguish
or attempting to work out all the necessary details for a trip that no
one should ever have to take. Now with those logistical hurdles taken
care of, the family patriarch gave his grieving wife a reassuring hug

before departing for the airport. Within a few hours, he would board the first of his flights to New Zealand for the purpose of retrieving the body of their daughter Alisha.

Twenty minutes after that tearful parting, Heath and Madison returned the rental car to the Seattle-Tacoma Airport that they had used for their most recent venture into Canada. As he finalized the paperwork with the attendant, she unloaded their bags from the trunk. Then they made their way into the terminal, checked their bags, and headed for the security checkpoint.

Roughly an hour later, while seated near the gate for their upcoming Alaska Airlines flight to Reno, Madison took the opportunity to fight off the boredom. As airport terminals were typically one of the best places for people watching, she practiced her observational skills by focusing on a wide range of travelers and their pace of movement.

While continuing to scan what was in her visual periphery, Madison noticed one man passing by whose clothing and look appeared to be somewhat off. That was not to say that he exhibited a vibe of being a security threat, just that the relaxed and comfortable look of his jeans, T-shirt, and tennis shoes were offset by a very well-tailored and expensive looking sports coat. In addition, the items that he intended to have as carry-on bags seemed to be mismatched. Over his left shoulder was a well-worn backpack that was not completely full, while a high-end, expensive leather computer bag was gripped tightly in his opposite hand. Madison continued to scrutinize the man as he moved toward the closest bar and noticed that he exhibited a fixated stare on his drawn and saddened face, which suggested both deep, troubling thoughts and a lack of sleep in recent days. What Madison did not realize as the man disappeared into the bar was that he would soon be on his way to New Zealand via Los Angeles to retrieve the dead body of his youngest child.

As Derrick Walker then sat down to throw back a preflight double, he had no idea that he had just strolled within fifty feet of the woman who had killed his daughter.

36

The Winter Lull

AFTER THEIR LATE-NIGHT return to Carson City from Seattle on December eighth, Heath and Madison learned that they would have plenty of time to relax throughout the holiday season and beyond. According to the intelligence report that was waiting for Heath in the P.O. Box, their final target could possibly be traveling abroad in April, but not before then.

Of course, Heath found the time shortly after reading that first report to both secretly write and mail a note to Mrs. Dawson for the president.

Brief and concise like all the others, it read: *Eagerly waiting to score from third.*

With little else to do from mid-December through early February of 2032, Heath and Madison remained in top form by running substantial miles in various places throughout town and by embracing a daily calisthenics habit. Then whenever the weather conditions were favorable, they ventured up to Lake Tahoe for some higher elevation hand-to-hand combat sparring or cross-country skiing.

One event that didn't involve physical training of some sort was that of switching apartment complexes again during the lengthy winter lull. Both Heath and Madison had decided in early January that since the initial lease of six months had just expired, another move was required for the sake of their cover. Therefore, on February first, a second shift across town took place.

The prep work of searching for a suitable, yet still affordable, apartment, coupled with the actual relocation and acclimation into their new surroundings, had become a necessary distraction for both Heath and Madison. A few weeks prior to when that process began, both came to realize that Heath should no longer be relegated to the couch in the living room. After all, they had now shared a room and in some cases the same bed on numerous occasions while at hotels during their transit either to or from the site of a completed sanction. Therefore, it seemed reasonable that for comfort's sake, the large bed in the apartment should be shared while they waited to attempt the final sanction. Although sound in theory, the idea was flawed in that Heath and Madison had on a few occasions been dangerously close to doing more than just sleeping through the cold winter nights.

After settling into their new place, a discussion had ensued about the dangers of their mutual desire for physical intimacy. It was decided then that waiting for a more appropriate time to follow through on those feelings would be better for the mission status, so as a result, Heath resumed the nightly practice of sleeping on the couch.

Then with Valentine's Day looming, Heath received an updated intelligence report that revealed a few important factors about their final target. First, it could now be confirmed that he would be traveling abroad in late April for what appeared to be a lengthy golfing vacation in Scotland. Aside from the typical monthly purchases that had been monitored for the previous year and a half, one of his credit cards had recently been used to book hotel stays for five nights in Glasgow and an identical duration in the smaller city of Dundee before moving on to Edinburgh for the final few nights of the trip. In addition, a separate card was used to reserve tee times for three players at multiple golf courses along both the west and east coast that coincided with the dates of each hotel reservation.

Although the news was good in that it provided a where and a when for an attempt upon the last of the four sanctioned targets, the second aspect of those credit card reservations revealed a potential difficulty for completing it. Further digging had revealed that the two older brothers of their target, and each of their wives, would be joining him for a total of fifteen days. It was possible that with tee times for three, the two wives would not be playing, but entertaining such a presumption was not only unjustified in the modern world, it was in this case irrelevant. Heath did not care who the target would be playing golf with, as chances were that Madison would have much better odds of eliminating him at some place other than the links.

The second aspect of the latest report dealt with levels of communication between any of the four families, and Heath was happy to learn that even after the most recent sanction of two months prior, there had still been no contact made between any of them via the use of email, text, or phone. Because of that most favorable news, Heath contacted his surveillance teams and informed them that monitoring each family for communication purposes was no longer required. Instead, he wanted them to focus solely on the actions of the one remaining family.

In returning to the intent of their target to play several rounds of golf, Heath understood that Scotland was the birthplace of the game, and that many a golf enthusiast had the desire to play over there if given the opportunity to do so. With that in mind, Heath believed that although no specific strategy for Madison had been discussed yet, the apparent golfing passion of their target could prevent a window of opportunity for her.

Having tried his hand at the game on a few occasions during his distant past, Heath was still familiar with some of the sports-associated lingo. Even though he never really was what one could consider a serious golfer, he saw this new development as a teaching opportunity for Madison. He believed that in case it might be needed, it would not hurt for her to become educated in how to talk a good game of golf, even if one could not be played.

37

Presidents' Weekend

THE HOLIDAY SEASON at the close of 2031 had not been one filled with joy for the Walker family. As one could certainly understand, they were not in a festive mood after learning that their youngest child Alisha had drowned while vacationing in New Zealand just a few weeks prior to Christmas. That tragic news from her traveling companion Emily had come to them in the very early morning hours of December seventh, and as a result, Alisha's mother and father had been focusing on getting the body of their daughter home to Bellevue before any other consideration.

After her call of dreadful news, Alisha's father Derrick had flown to the South Island of New Zealand where he met up with the distraught Emily before speaking with the local police authorities about his daughter. She had been kind enough to pack all of Alisha's clothes and other personal belongings after being informed that Mr. Walker would soon be on his way to Wanaka, but had respected the dead by not touching or even viewing any of the items that were found either on her person or with the kayak. Emily believed that task should be reserved for Alisha's father, and upon hearing that she had made that decision, Derrick Walker was appreciative. Now with her own luggage in a state of near readiness, Emily planned on cutting her trip short and returning to Seattle with Mr. Walker at the appropriate time.

The senior police constable who met them at the morgue informed Mr. Walker that as a matter of protocol, certain tests had been done on the body of his daughter soon after she was brought in. From those tests, a toxicology report revealed trace chemical elements of a nerve toxin in her bloodstream. The information came as a complete surprise to Derrick Walker, as to his knowledge, Alisha had never been one to be involved with drugs of any kind. Nevertheless, he continued to listen as the coroner and the constable spelled out what little they did know about her untimely death.

Once they finished, he began with the obvious question of, "But why would Alisha have nerve toxin in her body?"

Without pause the constable replied, "That's what we want to know, Mr. Walker, and this young lady with you has stated that your daughter never did any drugs other than alcohol. Now do you have any reason to suspect otherwise?"

"No, actually…I don't." And then after motioning toward Emily, he added, "And this woman has known my Alisha for many years, so I believe her statement."

A moment later, Derrick Walker was able to view the body, and afterward he was given the opportunity to privately go through the personal effects that Alisha had with her when she drowned. Within those few items, there was a small, laminated object that had been retrieved from the front left pocket of her shorts, but in his current state of despair the combination of bold letters and numbers upon it that read *Staircase696* didn't register as anything important. However, in a time of greater clarity, they would. As for the present moment, all he wanted to do was kiss his daughter on the forehead and begin the process of returning her to where she could be put to rest.

Once that progression of required red tape had been waded through and the body was flown back to Seattle, the collective interest of the Walker family had then turned to the funeral services that followed. While also doing what they could to move an investigation of Alisha's death forward with the authorities in New Zealand, they basically shut down with regard to any of the social engagements and holiday parties that were usually a mainstay during the month of December. As a consequence, to that most understandable posture, Mr.

and Mrs. Walker had allowed all communication with most others to cease.

Then during the mid-February holiday weekend of Presidents' Day, Alisha's oldest sibling Lauren decided that it was time to start sifting through some of the accumulated unopened mail that her parents had pushed aside in their grief. After all, it had been two months since the services for her little sister, and as the weather for the entirety of Northwest Washington was forecast to be horrible for the next few days, why not put the time to good use by accomplishing something that needed to be done.

Within that stack of correspondence and the ever-present junk mail, Lauren came across several of the standard Christmas letters that many families, like her own, would send out to various acquaintances that they seldom see or communicate with. It was most unfortunate, although wholly understandable by those who knew the family well, that the Walker letter that had been prepared for mailing before Alisha died was never sent out.

Regardless of that fact, there were two of the incoming letters that caught the attention of Lauren beyond all the others, for unlike the large stack of typically boastful holiday greetings, these two did not include only the positive accolades of what their family had accomplished throughout the past year.

The first such letter came from the Eldridge family, and although it did speak of positives in their life, the overall tenor of their message to friends was that of tragedy. Sadly, their youngest child Trevor, who still had been a few years short of being thirty years old, had died of respiratory arrest while he was on a strenuous hiking vacation in the Machu Picchu region of Peru during June of 2031. Lauren had not seen the man whom the letter spoke of in perhaps four or five years, but remembered from that last encounter that he was not the easiest guy to spend any time with. Nevertheless, learning that Trevor had met with an early death was not a positive update, and she would let her parents know that they were not alone in their grief of losing a child.

The second letter was discovered roughly thirty minutes later, and the contents within hit even closer to home. She did not really know the Jenkins family very well, as she had only met them on a few occasions in years past, but the news of tragedy in their Christmas letter was eerily close to what had happened in her own family. They had also lost their youngest child to an early demise in April of 2031, but unlike Trevor Eldridge, Cameron Jenkins had drowned while on a sailing vacation in the British Virgin Islands. Although neither of the two deaths could equal the pain she felt at having lost her only sister, Lauren felt sympathy for the other two families because of the tragic happenings that had fallen upon them.

She cautiously presented the letters to her parents, who in turn expressed their grief in learning that four people they had known from many years ago were also experiencing the difficulty of coping with losing a child.

Lauren then risked the possible agitation of her mother's still frail condition by stating, "I know that we will all miss Alisha for as long as we live, and I also feel sad for the Eldridge and the Jenkins families because of their respective losses, but doesn't it seem a strange coincidence that the youngest child of three different families would all die within the same year while on vacation in foreign lands?"

As her mother's head then slumped down and into her open palms as a reaction to the question, Lauren instantly knew that she should have never broached the subject. The strange coincidence she spoke of was probably nothing more than her own unchecked imagination running wild, as in truth, each was surely just a random occurrence. Therefore, all she accomplished by introducing the thought of it being more than that was to make her mother start sobbing over the loss of Alisha once again.

Derrick Walker shot Lauren a look of displeasure as he moved to comfort his wife, and in response she moved to the opposite side of her mother and offered a heartfelt apology.

Later that evening Derrick entered his study, closed the door, and after sitting at his desk, he removed a small item from one of the drawers. He had first seen the object in Wanaka, New Zealand, when he was given Alisha's personal effects, but it was not until some point during the long flight home from Auckland that he realized the meaning behind it.

Based on what she had told him when he arrived in Wanaka, Derrick knew that Emily had not seen the object. Then upon recognizing the magnitude of what it implied, he was actually relieved that she had not. It became one less thing that he would be forced to lie about if Emily sought clarification, and at that moment on the flight, he came to a stark realization. He vowed to himself that neither his wife nor his other two children would ever learn of the laminated paper with *Staircase696* boldly printed on it.

Now as he stared at the coded message for perhaps the twentieth time since hiding it in his desk two months prior, Derrick Walker was mortified by the memory of what it brought forth. But based upon what his eldest daughter had inadvertently uncovered, it was quite possible that two other men whom he knew from many years ago were in possession of a similar laminated object. The message hidden within the code was clear, and he understood the implication behind it very well. He realized by the how and where Alisha was killed that another member of his family could be next if he didn't act with restraint, and he was terrified by the belief that more harm could come to his family if he were to ever speak publicly of something that Jordan Harwell had done in his past.

38

Reflective Thoughts

THROUGHOUT THE REMAINDER of February, the entirety of March, and the early stages of April, two topics of extreme magnitude continued to weigh on the mind of Derrick Walker. First, his wife remained in an overall hazy funk in response to the death of their youngest daughter in early December. In fact, she had recently demonstrated more signs of slipping into an even deeper depression as opposed to working her way beyond the tragedy. As a result, some form of medication beyond that of sleeping pills was being considered.

Secondly, while hoping that by his continued silence no further repercussions against another member of his family would occur, Derrick could not shake an uneasy feeling within. Something in his gut told him that this whole ordeal was not yet over, and if something that he was unaware of had not already happened to the youngest member of a specific fourth family, then perhaps it would in the near future.

To magnify his concerns over the latter, his oldest daughter Lauren occasionally tried to corner him for a frank discussion about her continued belief that there might be something more to the three deaths than mere coincidence. Derrick knew that his stance must have been frustrating for Lauren. In spite of her raising the issue only when there was no possibility of her mother hearing what she attempted to examine, and always maintaining a respectful approach in the process, he provided no indication of knowing something that could clarify the issue while also seeming sympathetic to her query. Regardless of that, Derrick knew that he would eventually need to put a stop to her questions. There was simply too much at stake if she continued probing and was then careless about what might be uncovered.

Meanwhile, Heath and Madison were in the final week of preparations for their upcoming departure to Scotland. Per the usual, they had studied the file of their target thoroughly and paid close attention to certain details, but as this was the final sanction to be executed in order for Madison to gain her ultimate freedom, she magnified her level of focus.

Within those preparations came another extensive set of lessons, as through reading up on the subject and absorbing all that Heath could teach her about the vocabulary of the game, Madison became fully versed in golf terms and how they should be used within a conversation while speaking with an avid player. They even went so far as to visit a practice putting green a few times, in the event that she decided to create her first chance encounter with the target at one of the abundantly numerous courses in Scotland.

As for when they were outside the apartment, one matter that demanded attention before flying over the Atlantic was that of altering her wardrobe. Unlike what had been worn while in the British Virgin Islands, Peru, and New Zealand, Madison realized that she wouldn't be able to entice her latest target with either her revealing maroon bikini or her walking shorts and T-shirt. She understood that the typically damp and cold spring weather conditions of Scotland would require some much warmer clothing that provided more complete covering of her body and had taken care of that issue while shopping at various stores during the previous few weeks.

Throughout that process, there was further reflection as to what would be best to wear while she was in her chosen disguise. In recent weeks, Madison's scrutiny of the file taught her that the target Preston was more frequently drawn to redheaded women as opposed to those with another hair color. Although that certainly did not mean he would completely ignore other opportunities, she planned on making her effort to create the initial chance encounter and subsequent seduction a little easier by modifying her appearance into what he most frequently sought. With that in mind, she knew that certain items just would not be practical while wearing a redheaded wig with soft curls that was cut just below shoulder-length. As a result, Madison had paid greater attention to what was pulled from the racks and tried on.

When the date of departure was finally upon them, Madison was fully prepared and anxious to get it over with. She and Heath began their latest journey on Thursday the fifteenth of April by repeating the first few legs that had been used for the trip to New Zealand. They flew from Reno to Seattle, and then rented a car for the drive north to the border and eventually Vancouver. But because slight alterations were always a factor in what Heath planned, they stopped in Bellingham just short of the border to change into one disguise, and then spent the night in a cheap motel after crossing the border. Then during the late morning of April sixteenth, Heath and Madison once again altered their appearance before driving to the airport and catching their early evening flight to Glasgow.

Throughout a portion of that drive toward the border, Madison reflected upon how she felt leading into and after each of the sanctions. At first, she was not fully confident that she could successfully kill four total strangers and was fearfully nervous throughout the entire ordeal with Cameron in the Caribbean. But based upon completing that first sanction and gaining confidence from it, she then moved on to Trevor with little apprehension about using the lethal second injection to finish him off. Madison remembered what had been said to her afterward, and admitted to herself that Heath had been correct. At that time, she did feel a little too much pleasure in the results of Peru, and therefore, she had perhaps lost a bit of her soul in the process. However, that shortcoming was soon corrected and then reversed at a later time, as a drastic shift in her outlook took place after the third sanction. Madison had felt a significant level of remorse at having to eliminate Alisha, and in moving forward from that time, she came to realize that if not for the requirement placed upon her to complete a fourth sanction, she would have been done with killing. Unfortunately for Madison, at that point she was too near the end of the mission to throw all her efforts away for the sake of her emerging morality.

SANCTION FOUR

39

Glasgow, Scotland

WHEN ADDING THE eight hours forward time change to the duration of the flight from Vancouver, Heath and Madison did not touch down in Glasgow until the midmorning hours of Saturday the seventeenth. Once they were clear of customs with luggage in tow, they picked up a rental car and headed for their hotel.

While in route, Heath asked, "So what fictitious name have you selected for this final leg of the mission?"

"I was thinking of Danielle. It has some flair without being too memorable."

Heath thought about it for a few seconds and replied, "I agree. Danielle it is."

They checked into their hotel a full two days before their target Preston and his older family members would arrive in Glasgow, which in turn gave Heath and Madison plenty of time to scout out locations for her to potentially initiate a chance encounter. However, it was known going in that once they arrived, Preston and two of the others would be playing golf on most of the days. Therefore, his planned schedule instantly narrowed the windows of opportunity for when he could be approached, while it also made the potential staging of an accidental death even more difficult.

Throughout the afternoon and evening of Monday, April nineteenth, while Preston and his family members were adjusting to their jet lag, the surveillance of them began. But within those first few hours of scrutiny, neither Heath nor Madison could imagine that someone in the Seattle area had put some pieces together with regard to the three previous kills.

Using a variety of looks and outfits that were augmented by her wigs of either long, straight blond hair or the more manageable shoulder-length black hair, Madison was able to loosely tail and observe Preston for portions of that afternoon and evening as well as much of Tuesday. From that, she learned that it would also be possible to venture out at times while sporting her natural look of short brown hair and a concealing hat, as she had not seen the young man ever show the slightest interest in any of the many women he encountered with a similar hairstyle.

Heath had also done his fair share of surveillance, but unfortunately throughout all of their collective efforts, neither saw any real opportunity for Madison to initiate contact with Preston, as he was always at the side of his two older brothers and their wives.

Then on Wednesday morning, the three men headed off to the southwest of Glasgow in order to play the first of eight intended rounds of golf, so Heath and Madison followed them all the way over to Troon. Unfortunately, they could do little but watch Preston's rental car from a distance as they waited for the trio to complete their round on the old course.

As the remainder of Wednesday and then the entirety of Thursday passed, the observation of Preston and those at his side continued throughout most of the non-golfing hours. However, for both Heath and Madison, there was a building frustration that came from those efforts, and they subsequently arrived at the joint realization that nothing could be done regarding Preston while the group was still in Glasgow. After all, the men still had one more round of golf to play along the west coast on Friday, which would most probably be followed by one last group dinner and evening in the city before their planned transition to the east coast on Saturday.

With that in mind, Heath and Madison shifted their focus to Dundee in the hope that greater opportunities for a chance encounter would occur in the smaller city. Perhaps at some point during those ensuing multiple days and nights, the group might begin to tire of spending nearly every waking hour together, and if that were to be the case, then it could in turn provide Madison with the opening she needed to advance.

40

Contact at Dundee

WHILE PRESTON AND his siblings were playing golf on Friday, Heath and Madison pulled out of Glasgow earlier than originally planned and drove in a northeastwardly direction so that they could arrive in Dundee roughly a full day ahead of their target. As they drove through some magnificent countryside, they passed within sight of Stirling Castle before reaching the city of Perth and then beyond to their ultimate destination. The centuries-old structure was quite impressive as it sat on rocky crags that overlooked the plains below, and a brief conversation ensued as to the fierce battles that must have been fought on those grounds in years long past. Then once they arrived in Dundee and had checked into their hotel, Heath and Madison began scouting the immediate vicinity to become more familiar with their surroundings.

The following evening, they watched the Talbot family group exit their hotel about an hour after checking in to begin a stroll for what could be assumed as a search to enjoy some of the local nightlife. In her disguise of the redheaded wig and clothing that would not stand out as unusual or ostentatious, Madison then left Heath in her wake to begin a solo tail. While maintaining a cautious distance, she eventually saw them enter a pub, and after then closing the gap to the establishment, she could see through a window that the five souls were in the process of securing a table. Luck was on her side, in that after waiting for the two ladies to be seated, Preston then selected a chair that appeared as if it would provide him with a view of both the entry and the area of the bar.

With an understanding that she could initiate the process of a random encounter on her target's first night in Dundee as opposed to later, Madison waited a few more minutes for the entire group to order a round of drinks before moving toward the door and entering. Pausing for a moment after stepping inside, she casually scanned the room to discover that what she believed to be true a few moments earlier was accurate. Preston was in a position where he could easily see her. Madison made no lingering, direct eye contact with him, and as she continued her scan for several more seconds, it could be easily believed that she was just looking for a place to sit. Then acting as if nothing seemed to fit her need, Madison began a slow walk through the crowd toward the bar. Once there, she smiled at the woman behind the taps and ordered a pint.

Preston had watched her the entire time since just seconds after she entered, as the soft curls of her red hair had caught his immediate attention. For the next several minutes, he continued to look her way, and as she remained alone with her drink at the bar, he informed those in his family that he would return to them in a little while.

Pretending as if he did not already have a nearly full glass back at the family table, Preston moved to a position at the bar next to Madison and asked the barkeep for a fresh pint. As he waited for his drink, Madison turned toward Preston and offered a slight smile to give the impression that she would be open to some conversation. He took advantage of the silent invitation by returning the smile and saying hello, while also asking her if she minded him standing next to her.

Madison replied that it was kind of him to ask, while adding that even if she had the right to make him move elsewhere, she had no objection to his company. From there the ice was broken, so Madison and Preston began to converse while sipping from their respective glasses.

After a few minutes, he said, "By the way. My name is Preston."

In response, Madison said, "Well it's nice to meet you, Preston. I'm Danielle."

Feeling comfortable in each other's presence, they continued to talk and eventually ordered a second drink. But as they were roughly halfway through it, Madison stated the need for her to call it an early evening. Her reasoning included the explanation that she had waited a long time to play the championship course over at nearby Carnoustie, and she didn't want to feel much less than one hundred percent when she stood on the first tee early the next morning.

Upon hearing of her plans, Preston said, "Hey, I didn't realize that you play, Danielle. I'm a golfer too, and we have a scheduled time at Carnoustie on Monday."

"Oh really, well I suppose that's nice for both of us to be able to play it. But who is we?"

As he gestured slightly in their direction, he responded with, "That would be me and my two older brothers sitting at that table over there."

Madison knew that she had to at least look for the sake of a feigned interest, but she was not happy after doing so. All four of the people sitting at the table were looking directly at her and Preston, and when the two ladies in the group offered a slight wave, she had to reply in kind. However, Madison then quickly turned her attention back toward the bar and took another pull from her now nearly empty glass.

Before any of the four might possibly venture to the bar to ask if Preston and his new friend wanted to join them, Madison reiterated that she really must be going.

As she subsequently rose to make her way toward the exit, Preston asked, "Hey, Danielle. Before you leave, can I ask you a favor?"

While keeping her back to the family group, she answered, "Well I don't know, Preston. What's the favor?"

"Well…it's like this. My two brothers have been playing me really close so far on this trip. In fact, one of them almost beat me at Troon the other day. I could really use a little advantage over them for our round on Monday, so I was wondering if you wanted to meet me for another drink tomorrow evening and perhaps give me some advance insight about the Carnoustie greens?"

Reaching over to caress his arm, Madison replied, "Now that is a strange way to ask a woman if she wants to meet you for a drink, Preston, and I'll give you credit for originality. But I don't think it would be good for the intended spirit of the game if I were to provide you with an unfair advantage. However, if you want to meet me for a drink tomorrow evening while understanding that we won't be discussing anything about Carnoustie except for my score, then I accept."

41

Confidential Gathering

AFTER FINALLY DECIDING in late April that he needed to do something about the lingering doubt in his mind, Derrick Walker initiated contact with both Nelson Eldridge and Terrance Jenkins. In the course of each individual call, he first offered his sympathies for the loss his opposite had endured, while also confessing that he would have given them sooner but had not learned of their tragedy until well after the holidays.

In each case, an explanation then came back as to having placed the information within their yearly Christmas letter, at which time Derrick revealed that the letter they spoke of had unfortunately been put aside until mid-February.

That in turn created the questioning as to the value that Derrick had placed upon each relationship, since their letters were intended to be read upon receipt. However, Derrick countered that if the dreadful news within each letter was so important for him to know, then why hadn't he been informed the previous April or June, respectively.

Of course, Derrick Walker realized that he was guilty of the same lack of disclosure, and in knowing that it needed to be corrected, he informed each old acquaintance that he had also lost his youngest child just a few weeks before Christmas.

With a clearer understanding given of why he had pushed their letters aside, and with calmer heads on both ends of the line then prevailing, Derrick was then careful with his approach toward each man as he pressed on. He discovered through gentle prodding that in both instances a small, laminated object had been found among the personal effects of the dead. It was within a pocket of their shorts, and at that point, Derrick admitted that the same was true for Alisha. Without asking exactly what the object conveyed, he then suggested that a secretive face-to-face meeting between them be arranged as soon as possible to discuss what could be done moving forward.

Both Nelson and Terrance pushed back a little initially, as neither wanted to risk any further reprisals by discussing the matter publicly. However, after Derrick offered each a persuasive stance that the topic at hand would only be privately debated among the three of them, a time and place was agreed upon.

On the afternoon of Monday, April twenty-sixth, Derrick Walker drove his car into a shopping mall parking lot and headed for a distant and nearly empty corner of it. Waiting for him there were two other vehicles with a few empty parking spaces in between, and as he filled a portion of that gap with his own vehicle, a man emerged from each and climbed into his four-door sedan.

Although there had never been any sort of falling out among the old college friends, for various reasons there simply hadn't been any face-to-face contact between them in several years, other than the occasional party where each man and their family had been invited by a random acquaintance. In fact, this may have been the first instance that no one other than the three of them were together since they, along with Blake Talbot, had formulated their collective pact with Jordan Harwell as he began his climb to political greatness.

Glancing at each man while he gave a subtle nod, Derrick Walker said, "Thank you for meeting me, gentlemen. It's been a long time."

From the back seat, Nelson Eldridge replied, "Yes it has, Derrick, perhaps too long."

Then Terrance Jenkins in the front seat added, "Indeed."

During the next several minutes, the three men discussed what had happened throughout the previous year. They began by first disclosing their receipt of and then presenting their coded message of

Staircase696, while also agreeing that what had been planted on the dead body of their youngest child could only have been sent by Jordan Harwell. The man had obviously employed his extensive reach of power to make each of them painfully aware that they would be foolish to ever betray his trust in their everlasting silence. Each of the three impacted fathers admitted to having previously arrived at the decision to keep quiet for the remainder of their lives about what the current president had done in his past, but it wasn't until recently that any of them thought that it could be safe to discuss the recent events of his treachery with each other.

Turning toward them, Derrick Walker attempted to maintain a measured tone while speaking directly, in that he and they should be aware of what had brought this on. In the event that either of his companions had somehow suppressed the facts into non-memory, Derrick reminded Nelson and Terrance that the three of them, along with Blake and Jordan, had been having a really great time before the incident at Staircase Campground while celebrating their collective completion of grad school back in June of 1996. But based upon the now three-and-a-half decades of personal reflection since, he believed that each man should have also realized that in having too much fun they had all, with the exception of Jordan Harwell, committed a horrific criminal act while suffering from a monumental lapse in both their individual and collective judgement. Derrick stated that they never should have done the things they had done to that young woman, and Jordan was the only one of them in that moment who was enough of a man to realize that what was going to transpire was ethically and morally wrong. He continued by adding that Jordan did his best to stop all three of them and Blake from advancing, while having absolutely nothing to do with repeatedly violating the woman. Nor did he agree, when she was nearly dead from the ordeal, to bind her with weights and sink her to the depths of the nearby lake.

Upon concluding his walk down the darkest of memory lanes, Derrick asked the two men whose heads were now bowed in shame, "So can you both agree with my assessment of that long-ago night?"

In unison, both men nodded and replied, "Agreed, Jordan had nothing to do with it."

"That's right. Now I'm not saying that the man is a saint—as a matter of fact, we all know that he is far from it. Jordan has done several despicable things within the business world during his power climb that screwed a lot of people, including each of us, out of potential opportunities that he then took full advantage of. We couldn't do anything about his actions then, nor can we alter what happened now, as it was impressed upon us that his extortion was just part of the price we had to pay. We all agreed that in exchange for his continued silence as to our misgivings, the final payment from us would be to remain silent about his less than ethical behavior until after his political career had ended. If we did so, then we could each live a peaceful and comfortable life with ample opportunities to benefit from. Now, would you both also agree with that?"

Again, the response was unified. "Agreed."

"That's good. So, I have not been anywhere close to those campgrounds and lake, or for that matter have not even ventured to the southeast corner of Olympic National Park since that time. Now based upon having nothing ever come from the events of 696 at Staircase more than thirty-five years ago, I think it's safe to assume that as long as we keep our mouths shut, then we will remain in the clear in that regard. Do you agree?"

Once again, there was a duet of, "Agreed."

"All right, then. And since Jordan has recently raised the ante of this high-stakes game so that our silence continues beyond the time of his political career, I for one have no interest in pushing the game forward even if I wanted to take him on. I'm telling you both right now, there is just no way that my wife could endure the prospect of losing another child. Now with that said, do either one of you want to keep playing?"

Shaking his head in the negative, Nelson replied, "I know that I don't."

Then Terrance added with similar conviction, "Neither do I."

In realizing that he had both men in a regretful and penitent state of mind, Derrick Walker brought up an associated topic by stating his belief that all three of them should collectively do something if they had any sense of humanity left within them. Although he understood that it would be impossible to counteract what had already been done, or to take on the powerful reach of Jordan Harwell, if they were searching for a way to partially correct a horrific wrong from their youthful past, there was a way. It was imperative that they use the knowledge gained by the deaths of their own children to help their old associate Blake Talbot avoid the pain they had each already endured. However, in order to do that, it was necessary to warn him that his youngest child could be next.

42

Warning Cry

WITH A UNANIMOUS decision reached by the three men, Terrance Jenkins placed a call to Blake Talbot and put the phone on speaker.

After hearing the voice from his past, the man receiving the call offered, "Well. This is a pleasant surprise. It's been a long time, and it's good to hear your voice, Terry. And before you say anything, I would like to once again offer my sympathies with regard to Cameron. We were devastated to learn via your Christmas letter that he was no longer with us."

Terrance Jenkins appreciated the sentiment, while at the same time wondering why Blake or his wife hadn't called at some point during the holidays after receiving the news to offer their thoughts verbally instead of just sending a return sympathy card.

Regardless of that fact, he replied, "Thanks, Blake. I appreciate that, and it's good to hear your voice as well."

After another moment of pleasant, yet hollow, chatter between the two, Terrance informed Blake as to why he had called. He wanted to find out if everything was all right with him, and if anything unusual had transpired with his family during the past few months. In response, the man listed a few things that would probably become a portion of their next year's Christmas letter, but they offered nothing tangible. However, when he finally got to the news of what his three sons were currently doing, Terrance became concerned. Blake mentioned that they, along with the wives of his elder two, were in Scotland for a golfing and sightseeing vacation.

Based upon what had happened to his own son Cameron, as well as Trevor Eldridge and Alisha Walker, Terrance knew that he needed to interrupt and get to the point quickly. With each of the three dying a mysterious death while they were abroad, he feared that the same fate could be awaiting Blake's youngest son Preston.

Cutting off the prattle that was streaming over the speaker, Terrance said, "Listen, Blake, that's all good news, and I'm sure there's more to tell, but I'm here with Derrick Walker and Nelson Eldridge at the moment. Now, there's just no easy way to say this, but…"

"Hey, Nelson is with you? Could you please forward my sympathies to him with regard to Trevor? It was just horrible news about him as well."

After a deep, calming sigh, there was the reply of, "Sure, Blake, no problem. Now please, could you just listen to me for a minute? We all think this is really important."

A brief pause was followed by, "All right, Terry, what's on your mind?"

Terrance explained that Alisha Walker, Derrick's youngest, had also died during the past year, and before he could be interrupted again, he stated to Blake that he would pass on the upcoming offered sympathies when he had the chance. Then he continued by informing Blake that he, Nelson, and Derrick had jointly agreed to call and offer him a warning. Their information in singular form would have been fragmented at best, but by getting together during the previous hour and disclosing what each man knew of the events surrounding their own child's death, some pieces of the puzzle could now be put together.

Of course, none of the information he was about to offer had become public knowledge, but Terrance did reveal that a trace amount of nerve toxin had been found in Cameron's bloodstream after he drowned. Although nothing of the sort was discovered with regard to the second death that could imply similar foul play, Nelson had stated that even though his son did not generally take proper care of his health, no one in the family or those close to them could ever fully accept the thought of Trevor dying due to respiratory failure at such a young age. Those two deaths had taken place nearly a year into the past, with the circumstances and personal beliefs associated with them never revealed in the respective Christmas letters of either family. Therefore, because no connection between them seemed to even remotely exist, it was not until a few months after a third suspicious death occurred among the children of their families that a question arose.

In closing, Terrance added, "So, Blake. What you need to know now is that in similar fashion to when my son Cameron was in the Caribbean, Alisha Walker was more recently drowned while she was vacationing in New Zealand, and we all think there's a connection."

Blake Talbot waited a few seconds before responding, as based upon the tone with which it had been delivered a moment prior, he understood the less than subtle verbal message that Terry sent. He was a man who did not like to be interrupted. However, there was a part of Blake that wanted to correct his old college buddy by suggesting that what he meant to say was that Alisha had drowned as opposed to having been drowned, but the larger part of him realized this was not the proper time.

Instead, when he then felt that it was safe to comment, Blake replied, "Well, I'm sorry to hear that, Terry. From what I remember, she was a nice young woman, and it is indeed terrible news for Derrick and the rest of the Walker clan that she is gone. But at the risk of sounding insensitive, why do you believe the two drownings are somehow connected? I mean…couldn't they just be a tragic coincidence?"

Derrick Walker took the opportunity to speak up by answering, "Well, on the surface it might appear that way, Blake, but traces of the same nerve toxin found in Cameron were also present in the bloodstream of my Alisha. Now, none of us have any solid proof of this, but we are betting that there may have been an undiscovered chemical component that led to the demise of Trevor when he was in Peru. Therefore, the belief among us is that all three of our kids were targeted for a specific purpose, and it is with that in mind that we have called to warn you. We honestly believe that, based upon each of our youngest having met with a supposed accidental death, your son Preston could be in danger as well."

Now realizing that he was on speaker with the threesome, Blake thought about what had been presented for a moment, and then replied, "Well, all right, gentlemen. Now I can see why all of you would think that the deaths might be somehow connected, even if the part involving Trevor is somewhat tenuous. And believe me, I do appreciate your concern. But I just don't see how that all fits in with me or my family."

Terrance had known for years that his old roommate was not always the easiest to convince of anything, therefore, he added a final piece of evidence that was sure to sway him. He told Blake that all three of them were currently in possession of an identical, small, laminated coded message that had been left on each of the bodies at the time of death. That message not only proved to them that the victims had been intentionally targeted, but it also identified who was ultimately behind the order to kill them.

Then after lowering his voice to a whisper as if someone other than those in the car might overhear, Terrance said, "Blake, that message reads **Staircase696**, and it's obvious to all of us that our old friend Jordan is the one who sent it."

After hearing the latest information, which would have convinced him of their stance much sooner if presented, Blake Talbot moved the phone away from his ear and stared at it in disbelief. He knew what the letters and numbers meant instantly and was attempting to absorb the implications of that message while somehow remaining calm.

Then while moving the phone back toward his mouth, he gulped deeply and, with his voice cracking, replied, "But if that is true, then Preston can be gotten to anywhere."

"That's right, Blake. So, do you know where he is right now?"

"Yes. Well, no. I mean…not exactly. I know that he and the others are in Scotland, but I would need to check their itinerary to see which course they are playing today."

Looking at his watch quickly, Terry reminded Blake that Scotland was eight hours ahead of the time in Seattle. As a result, his adult children were probably already enjoying some nightlife.

Then before ending the call so that Blake could try to reach his son with a warning cry, Terry informed him of what was known about Cameron before Derrick did the same about Alisha. Apparently, both had become the fallen prey of a woman, and the friends who traveled with each all confirmed remembering her as being around five foot six or so, good-looking, and physically fit with short brown hair. Unfortunately, anything else that might have been known about her, such as where she came from, was probably fictitious, as the woman had used the name of Brooke while in the British Virgin Islands, and Nicole in New Zealand.

43

The Last Supper

WHILE THAT EARLY afternoon call on the west coast of America was transpiring, the three Talbot brothers had completed their round of golf at Carnoustie several hours earlier. However, instead of then relaxing over a typical after the round pint at a local pub, they had driven the short distance back to their hotel in Dundee so that they could all get cleaned up in anticipation of enjoying a night on the town.

The two elder brothers had then ventured out with their wives in a foursome, while showing no concern that the younger Preston would not be joining them. Their evening began with a pint at a little pub called Tickety Boo's in the heart of town, which was then followed by a stroll of several blocks to enjoy a meal at an establishment with a pleasant view of the bridge that spanned the Firth of Tay.

As for Preston, he followed a separate planned agenda for the evening that would not make him feel as though he continued to be the nightly, cumbersome fifth wheel with his brothers and their wives. Instead, he had completed his primping ritual and went off to meet Danielle for a third date that consisted of drinks and dinner.

Madison had prepared for the evening by putting on the same disguise that had been used for the initial encounter with Preston two days prior and once again the following evening for drinks at another pub. That look of softly curled red hair cut just below the shoulders had been complemented on each of the two nights with clothing that was far different from what had been worn during any of the other three sanctions, with a plan to do the same again for this third consecutive evening. Sporting comfortable jeans and low-heeled boots on each occasion as opposed to shorts or the maroon bikini, Madison could continue to blend in well with other women who were present in most establishments. As an added bonus, the heeled boots could also serve as a means of inflicting intense pain to the groin area of Preston if need be.

With regard to the upper portion of her torso, for the initial chance encounter she had worn a thick pullover sweater before shifting to a thinner, formfitting turtleneck golf shirt with an open sweater vest for their second meeting. Now for the third date, Madison further accentuated the curve of her breasts by wearing a snug, button-up long-sleeve blouse that was tucked into her jeans, while leaving the top three buttons invitingly undone for enticement purposes. Then for added warmth, she slipped on a looser-fitting, middle-weight zip-up jacket over it.

Her premise for those particular selections on this third encounter was both simple and twofold, as once inside a pub for drink and food, she could easily remove the jacket so that Preston could not help but take notice of her form. In addition, as neither clothing article would need to be pulled over her head for removal, there was little chance that her wig would accidentally shift if she were to eventually undress in front of him.

As with each of the other three sanctioned kills, Madison kept the accessories simple by wearing nothing more than the studded earrings and the ring on her left index finger. But there was one minor alteration. She had reverted to the small black purse that had originally been thought of as being useful for the Caribbean before discovering the clip-on fabric bag.

Madison and Preston thoroughly enjoyed their evening at the latest pub for drinks and dinner, and then while in the midst of listening to the festive sounds of a local band at another, they shared their first kiss. Several more ensued before it was mutually decided to escalate their newfound affection to a level that wouldn't be appropriate within the pub, so they ventured outside to begin an often-paused stroll through town.

As their kissing became ever more frequent and lengthier, Madison said, "I'm getting a little cold. Maybe we should go inside someplace where it's warmer. Is your hotel close by?"

Preston replied, "Well…yes it is, Danielle." Then with a subtle gesture of his hand, he added, "It's just a couple of blocks that way."

Of course, Madison already knew that to be true, and thus the timing of her inquiry was well-timed. A few minutes later, they entered his hotel and headed upstairs for additional comfort in moving forward with their intended carnal pleasures.

Meanwhile, with the hour approaching nine thirty, Preston's sibling foursome had nearly completed their most recent round of drinks and were preparing to call it a night. Then not more than fifteen minutes later as they began a lengthier stroll back to the same hotel, one of their phones rang. After pulling his phone from a jacket pocket, the eldest Talbot brother noticed that the caller was his father. However, in knowing that taking a call from anyone during their evening out would have been disconcerting to his wife, he did not answer it. A few seconds later, a gentle chime informed him that a voicemail had been left, but before he could pull the phone back out again to listen, the phone of his younger brother rang. The same caller was attempting to reach another one of his sons, and as doing so in such rapid succession was unusual behavior for their father, it implied that he must have an immediate need to talk with one or both of them. As a result, the middle Talbot son answered the call.

After several seconds, he slowed his gait to listen and then replied, "No, Dad. Preston isn't with us right now. He felt as though he was a fifth wheel all the time when we went out, so he was nice enough to go do his own thing tonight while the four of us had drinks and dinner."

After listening to another statement, he then stopped his forward motion, and while demonstrating a rather typical American behavior, he turned on the speaker as if all those in his proximity would be interested in what was said by both parties.

With his phone now held out in front of him at waist level so all could hear, he asked, "Are you sure about this, Dad?"

Through the speaker all four of them then heard the reply of, "Yes I am. I can't tell you the specifics of why, but I just need you to protect Preston. He could be in danger."

Looking at his brother and the two ladies who had now formed a circle around the phone, the middle Talbot son then said, "Well... have you tried to call him, Dad?"

"Of course I tried to call him! What a stupid question. I did that several times and got no answer, which is why I then called your older brother and now you. So you say that Preston isn't with you, fine. But you need to locate him and stay at his side until you hear otherwise from me. Is that clear?"

After a quick glance around the family circle, he said, "All right, Dad. We all understand what you are saying, but we don't even know where Preston is right now. I mean, he could be at any one of fifty pubs or restaurants with a woman he met."

"A woman he met? I thought you said he went off to do his own thing!"

"Well, yes, but it was to have a dinner date with a woman he met a few nights ago."

There was a dramatic pause before Blake Talbot replied, "Now listen to me carefully, because this is important. That woman he is with could be the one he needs protection from, especially since he just recently met her. So you have to find him quickly and make sure that he is safe. Understand?"

"All right, Dad, we'll get on it right away. But just so you know, it could take us a while to find him."

"Understood, now get moving and call me when you know something."

With that, the call ended, and the Talbot foursome took a moment to think about where Preston might be. Splitting up to search multiple pubs or restaurants in various directions seemed like the best course of action, as it would cover the most ground in the quickest fashion, but then again that strategy could yield absolutely nothing while also wasting time. It was then suggested that while three of them followed such a course, the fourth could contact the police to help with the search. Unfortunately, they would not be able to provide the police with any reason to believe there was cause for concern other than the word of a frantic caller from the United States.

Finally, one of the ladies said, "We need to think about where a woman would want to go if she intended to corner and then harm someone. I mean…she wouldn't just do it in a public place like some pub, would she? Wouldn't it be better to do it someplace extremely…"

After a few seconds of the deafening pause, the other woman in the group finished the thought by uttering, "Someplace private, like in a hotel room."

44

Death by Redhead

BY THE TIME that discussion was taking place, Madison and Preston were in his hotel room and were moving forward with the exploration of each other's body. Although still vertical and fully clothed from the waist down except for their footwear, each seemed willing to eventually change that status. Preston had pulled off his sweater and shirt, while Madison had untucked and completely unbuttoned her long-sleeve blouse.

She knew that this location was not the best place to carry out the sanction, and that it would be impossible to stage the death as accidental, but it was the best alternative. The hotel room Madison shared with Heath could not be used because both of their fingerprints and DNA samples would be all over the place. Therefore, once the body of Preston had been discovered, an investigative team would have them both pegged in no time. Madison also knew that she was running out of time, and she did not want to fall back to the last resort of trying to kill Preston in either the daylight hours or in Edinburgh a few days from now. As a result, her thought was that much like when she had seduced and killed Cameron roughly a year before, Madison would offer Preston the distraction of her naked breasts as a way to then inject him with the nerve toxin.

As for Preston's family members, they were beginning to move in the direction of their hotel. However, that had come with some debate. It was possible that if the woman had wanted to trap Preston by using a hotel room, then chances were good that she would have taken him to wherever she was staying. But since no one had any clue as to what hotel that might be, they were left with the only logical choice of trying Preston's room in the hope that they would be there. Of course, even that led to another question, as after bringing up the premise that Preston and his date could be in either of their hotel rooms, the two women in the group were steadfast against either one of their husbands rushing into the room of their younger brother to disturb him. If their father were somehow wrong about this entire scenario, then it would be highly inappropriate for either of them to interrupt while Preston was involved in intimate relations. To further emphasize their point, each of the two wives stated that no woman would want to have the brothers or friends of the man she was making love to burst into the room while she was in a compromised position.

Meanwhile, Madison had slipped her unbuttoned blouse down from her shoulders, and when reaching behind to unfasten her bra, she said to Preston, "How about pouring each of us a little drink before we continue?"

Preston smiled and turned toward the minibar after watching Madison drape her blouse and bra over the same chair that her jacket and purse occupied. Then as he mixed them each a drink, she twisted the dark stone of her ring counterclockwise and shifted it to expose the tiny needle in the underside of the band. When he then came toward her a few seconds later with a drink in each hand, she did not take one and instead carefully placed both of her forearms gently upon his shoulders. Then without hesitation, she leaned in to kiss him and pressed the length of her left index finger into the back of his neck just below the left ear.

Both of his arms had been at his side during that brief instant, and while holding a glass in each hand, Preston was unable to grab Madison before she could quickly step back. With an astonished look on his face, he calmly turned away for a few seconds so that he could take the glasses back over to the minibar.

After then feeling at the injection site on his neck, he turned back toward her and asked, "What the hell was that, Danielle?"

Madison had used those few precious seconds when she could not be seen to once again shift the settings of her ring so that the needle would be safely housed. However, instead of then taking up a self-defense stance like she had done with Trevor in Peru, Madison stood tall and composed while silently counting off the seconds.

She then gave an emphatic shoulder shrug, which caused her breasts to jostle a bit, and as Preston's eyes then locked onto the enticing view, Madison took another precious second before replying, "What do you mean?"

"Oh, come on, Danielle. You stuck me in the neck with something."

"Now why would I do that?"

Refocusing on her face, he said defiantly, "I don't know, but you did!"

Just a few seconds later, Preston began to feel the first wave of dizziness, and he needed to reach for a corner post of the bed so that he would not fall.

The count of seconds was now nearly twenty, and as Madison held her ground passively, she motioned with a hand toward her chest and said, "Preston. I think you should just focus on these for the next few seconds. It will be a pleasant memory as you fade away."

In suddenly realizing that he was losing all bodily control, Preston attempted to look Madison in the eye while asking, "As I fade away? What is happening to me, Danielle?"

As he then slumped to his knees while still holding the corner bedpost, she replied, "You are going to die in the next few minutes, Preston, and as there is nothing you can do about it, I just thought you might want to have a nice view before you black out."

"But what did you do to me?"

The silent count was now at twenty-eight, so while cautiously stepping a bit closer to him, Madison raised her arms with her palms turned skyward and replied, "Only what must be done, Preston. Only what must be done."

As Preston then fell flat on his face a few seconds later, Madison continued the silent count in her head until reaching nearly a minute. Then she pounced onto his back and twisted one of his arms into a position that would have caused great pain and a verbal reaction from someone who was either conscious or playing possum. As there was no such reaction, she knew that the toxin had done its job.

Moving quickly, she grabbed her purse and retrieved a pair of surgical gloves from within. Once they had been put on, she pulled out the syringe of pentobarbital and moved back toward Preston. After rolling him over, Madison straddled his chest and ribcage area while firmly setting a knee upon his outstretched and supposedly dominant right hand.

It was only an educated guess that Preston was right-handed, and certainly not fully guaranteed, but her belief was well-founded based upon how he had mentioned either hooking his golf ball to the left or slicing it to the right on a few occasions while playing throughout the past several days. Heath had taught her those golfing terms before they had begun this final leg of the mission, but it was only through reading up on the subject that Madison had learned how to properly apply each one of them. Only a player using right-handed clubs would say hooking to the left or slicing to the right.

Regardless of whether or not her belief was accurate, Madison had used the skill of deductive reasoning in the field as Heath had taught her before the mission began. In this instance, she had at least theoretically determined the dominant hand of her victim. In accordance, she was now hindering its use from any possible resistance.

A few seconds later, she injected the entire content of the syringe into a vein along the inner portion of his right elbow. Although knowing that the lethal amount of the drug she had put into Preston would slow his brain function and subsequently cause respiratory failure, Madison wanted to speed up the process by using both of her hands to cover his mouth and pinch his nose closed. Roughly three minutes later, she loosened her grip and began checking his vital signs. Unlike Trevor in Peru, Preston had no shirt on. Therefore, after finding no hint of a pulse in either wrist or the neck, it became easier for Madison to check for a heartbeat or any potential breathing.

Once convinced that Preston was dead, Madison reached into her purse again to pull out the small laminated message of *Staircase696*. Then after shoving it deep down into the front left pocket of the golf slacks that Preston had worn for the evening, she rose to her feet and stood over him for a moment before preparing to leave the scene.

45

The Chase

HEATH HAD HEARD everything that went on in the hotel room between Madison and her final target Preston. As a result, he knew that although her kill would probably never be viewed by the authorities as an accidental death, she had at least completed the fourth sanction and would be coming toward him in a few minutes for extraction. Unfortunately, what Heath heard next as he anxiously waited for that moment was not only unexpected, but far less pleasing.

While still wearing the surgical gloves, Madison had put her bra back on and took care of what needed to be done within the hotel room. She thought of the few places where she could have possibly left fingerprints, such as the chair where she had placed her possessions and rubbed them clean. But in reality, she had been very careful to not touch anything with her bare hands other than the body of Preston. Once confident that all was good to proceed, Madison slipped her blouse over both shoulders and pulled her heeled boots on. Then she grabbed her jacket and purse along with Preston's rental car keys and headed for the door with the intent of buttoning up her blouse as she moved toward the three flights of stairs.

As she gently swung the door open to exit, Madison glanced back over her shoulder for one last look at her final sanction before entering the hallway. But as she then began to quickly turn away from the door after quietly pulling it closed behind her, she bumped forcefully into something.

Looking startled as the man she ran into lightly grasped both of her shoulders, Madison said, "Oh, excuse me, sir, I didn't see you standing there."

Without releasing her, he replied, "That's no problem, miss. But if I may ask, aren't you the young lady who was having dinner with my brother tonight?"

Madison recognized the man from several days of surveillance as being one of Preston's older brothers, and although she did not know which one of them he was, that was irrelevant. She knew that he had at least caught a glimpse of her on both the first and second evenings at the pubs, but he should not have been standing in front of her at this most inopportune moment. Regardless of this random event, his presence did bring forth a simple, yet all important, question. Just how long had he been outside the door to Preston's room?

With an understanding of their joint recognition of each other, Madison knew that lying to the man would serve no purpose.

Therefore, in response, she said, "Well, yes. I did have dinner with Preston tonight."

After glancing down toward her bra, which was exposed via her completely unbuttoned blouse, he asked, "And then the two of you decided to come back here?"

"Yes, we did."

"And now you are coming out of his hotel room alone?"

Doing what she could with one hand clutching the strap of her purse and a set of keys that were hidden beneath her jacket, Madison attempted to close her blouse somewhat with her free hand while replying, "Well, that is obvious now, isn't it? But Preston and I have had our fun, so to speak. And since he is now sleeping soundly and I have an early morning, I thought I would just be on my way."

Now looking at her fist that held her blouse together, the man nodded and said, "Oh…I see. And why are you wearing surgical gloves?"

Madison knew that it would be difficult to provide an explanation that could possibly be believed, but she offered a feeble attempt by stating, "Oh, these? Well...this may sound odd. But it had to do with a fantasy that Preston wanted to play out. I'm sure that he will tell you all about it later if you ask him."

The man knew she was lying, because even if that outlandish suggestion had been true, why would she still have the gloves on if they had finished having what she referred to as their fun together? Therefore, he tightened his grip upon her shoulders and turned Madison slightly while attempting to press her against the door as he started to kick it several times.

Calling out loudly, he said, "Hey, Preston. Are you all right in there? Come on, man, wake up and come to the door."

With his attention partially diverted from her, Madison broke free from his grasp with a few swift moves. After dropping her jacket, purse, and the keys, she raised her arms up to the inside of his and then forcefully flung them outward. Before he could fully recover from the sudden resistance to his grasp, she thrust the butt of her palm into his nose and then used the few seconds of shock that followed as he stepped back to kick him hard in the groin. With him then doubled over in pain from the direct hit, Madison wasted no time in landing another solid kick to his chin.

As the man flew backward into a horizontal position on the floor, Madison had to fight back what would have been her instinctive reaction. She did not eliminate the immediate threat by killing the man, but instead reached for the keys along with her jacket and purse before running down the hall away from him. In spite of being the lone witness who could place her at the scene of her latest kill, the life of the man had been spared for one simple reason. Heath had made it crystal clear from the very beginning that there was to be no collateral damage during the entirety of the mission, and that rule was most especially true if the secondary victim just happened to be another member of the target's family.

As Madison then neared the end of the hall with her wide-open blouse behaving as if it were a miniature cape, a woman turned the corner. She had been following her husband up the three flights of stairs, but after slipping out of a shoe and nearly falling, she had slowed the pace of her ascent. Now roughly fifteen feet in front of Madison, the woman could plainly see her husband in the distance as he still lay flat on the hallway floor. With little time to act even if she was trained in how to do so, she did her best to stop the fleeing Madison. While well intended, that was not the best idea. With one quick grasp by Madison and a sweep of the legs, she was easily brushed aside.

Directly across the hall from Preston's room, an elderly man opened his door to see what all the commotion was about. He saw a man with a bloody nose writhing in pain on the floor in front of him, and at the end of the hallway there was a woman attempting to gather herself and stand up.

She looked in his direction, and while pointing at the man near him, she yelled, "Sir. Please check to see if my husband is all right, and then call for the police right away."

Without waiting for any reply, she then took off as best as she could after Madison but was unable to close the gap between them while they both descended the stairs. Along the way, Madison was able to incorrectly button up a portion of her blouse, and as she began to move quickly and quietly through the lobby, the woman trailing her emerged from the stairwell.

Spotting the other married Talbot couple in the lobby, she pointed at Madison and shouted, "I think that's her. Don't let her get away!" Then while passing the front desk, she paused briefly to emphatically add, "Please call the police. We need help."

Madison bolted from the hotel front, but she did not move toward Heath's car. He was proud of her for that action because she was demonstrating her grasp of another one of his lessons. Although simple by definition, the essential rule for an operative in the field could be difficult to adhere to while under pressure. Never compromise an asset by leading an adversary to them while attempting to evade and avoid capture.

Based on that first move when exiting the hotel, Heath thought that Madison would try to evade the family members of Preston and the soon to be involved police by getting lost in the town somehow. Then when provided with a safe opportunity, she would whisper into her stud earring where she was located for extraction. However, instead of doing that, what she did next came as a complete shock. Madison ran toward Preston's rental car and started it up in an attempt to make her getaway. Although perhaps worth a try in a different circumstance, this was foolhardy. She was not familiar with the local roadway patterns, and beyond that, Madison had no experience with driving on the left side of the road.

Then Heath noticed two of Preston's family members hailing a taxi that had just dropped off a fare, and seconds later, the taxi began pursuing the car that Madison had stolen. Being unfamiliar with the driving regulations and habits of Scotland, that chase did not last long as Madison quickly created a traffic accident not more than a kilometer from the hotel.

While nearly unconscious from the collision, Madison was then pulled free from the car and subdued by the angry brother of Preston. Based on the combined factors of her two scuffles in the hallway, running down three flights of stairs while attempting to get away, and then being pulled from the car and tossed about after the impact force of the traffic accident, Madison's redheaded wig had shifted loose from its original position.

As she lay face-down after being placed into the position of an all too familiar figure four, Madison regained full consciousness and said aloud, "This may be the end."

Not realizing that she was speaking only so that Heath could know of her predicament, the man who now forced his weight down upon her back replied, "I think you're right."

Meanwhile, back at the hotel, the woman who had attempted to halt the escape of Madison had come back to the front desk after having briefly run outside, and she proceeded to explain about the altercation that took place in the fourth floor hallway. She stated that her chase of the woman had begun after seeing her husband lying prone on the floor, and that there was reason to be concerned over the health of both her husband and younger brother-in-law. In turn, those at the desk contacted the police and the front desk manager ventured upstairs with the woman to check on the men in question.

By that time, her husband had reasonably recovered from the forceful kick to his groin, but any thought that he may have entertained about being intimate with his wife would now be put aside for another night. Regardless of that, he was genuinely concerned about Preston. In spite of his nearly continuous pounding on the door from either a flat or a more recently seated position, there had still been no verbal reply from inside Preston's room.

Wasting no time, the manager used his passkey to enter the room with the woman a stride behind, and they instantly saw a younger man flat on the floor who was naked above the waist.

Having had some minor medical training in the past, the woman then rushed to the body of her brother-in-law and dropped to her knees so she could check for vital signs. After then finding nothing to indicate that Preston was alive, she immediately began CPR and requested that an ambulance also be called.

As for Madison, the police arrived at the accident within a few minutes after CPR had begun on Preston. At that time, they had no way of tying her to what had happened in the hotel room and did not know that the young man she left behind would soon be declared as dead. But based upon witness accounts, they would be able to question Madison about her reckless driving and the accident it caused. In addition, there was the claim by the man who had hastily removed and subdued her that the car she was driving had been stolen from his brother. Therefore, in an attempt to safely sort everything out, the police handcuffed Madison and placed her in their car for safekeeping while the people in the vehicle she had struck, as well as Heath from a greater distance, remained baffled by the recent events.

46

Captured

WITHIN THE NEXT thirty minutes, the officers present at both crime scenes had conferred with their opposites, and as a result, the woman in their custody at the accident site was taken to the nearest police station for further questioning. Clearly not the redheaded woman that she pretended to be, the reasoning behind why an altered look to her natural appearance was necessary would be one of their first inquiries.

As for those in the Talbot family, one of them would need to place a most disheartening phone call. Having completed the necessary reports and interviews with the local authorities about all that had transpired during the previous few hours, the collective of four returned to the confines of one couple's hotel room. The eldest Talbot brother was flat on the bed with his golf slacks removed by his wife, and there was a bag of crushed ice perched upon the boxer shorts that covered his still aching groin. There was another bag set gently over much of his nose and chin, so he was currently in no position or frame of mind to speak with his father. In response, his younger brother unsteadily poured himself a drink from the minibar, and then prepared to take on the task himself.

Once sufficiently braced for the upcoming conversation, he tapped his father's name on his phone, and a few seconds later said, "Hello, Dad?"

As the next moment of explanation ticked past, loud, inconsolable screaming from the opposite end of the line could then be heard by those in the room even without the benefit of speaker mode. As a result of what had been conveyed, the man was understandably horrified about learning that his youngest child was dead, and he took little solace in then hearing that the woman responsible for the dreadful act was now in custody. What mattered most to Blake Talbot in the present moment was that his other two sons had been too late in their attempt to locate the now confirmed threat.

Meanwhile, the further questioning of Madison had begun in earnest, and Heath listened intently after parking two blocks from the police station. Fortunately, they had not yet begun to process Madison for her upcoming internment, so she was still in possession of her studded earrings and the ring on her left index finger. However, Heath understood the reality that she would not have them for long.

According to what the investigators had revealed to Madison, Heath realized that the proverbial shit had hit the fan. They had her dead to rights with the now empty syringe of pentobarbital that was found within her purse, as well as an eyewitness account of her exiting the room of a man just moments before he was pronounced as dead. Surely the eventual results of a toxicology report would verify that Preston had been injected with a lethal dose of that drug moments before his demise, and matching those test results with the traces still in the syringe would spell doom for Madison.

A few minutes later, Madison was moved to a different room where her fingerprints could be taken for testing, so Heath listened as the results were then discussed. It had not taken the computer database more than a few minutes to spit out a fingerprint match, and there was no surprise for Heath by what was learned.

Nothing had shown up for Madison in any type of civilian, military, or criminal database under her birth identity of Kristen Royce, as all records, including her military service, from those prior years had been completely wiped from existence. She also registered no hits under her current name of Madison Sinclare or any of her Canadian passport identities in the multiple cooperative international databases. In effect, that was a testament to either how careful she had been to leave no trace behind during each of the three previous sanctions, or to the carelessness of those investigating in each instance. However, her prints did come up as a match to one Susan Greer from the federal penitentiary system of the United States.

Subsequent digging into that match led to the discovery that this Susan Greer person had been previously incarcerated in the state of Kansas for the murder of three individuals, but had been released roughly eighteen months prior to the current date, as DNA testing and evidence had proved that she was not the guilty party. Nevertheless, the authorities in Scotland now had a name for the mystery woman in their custody, and as all the collected evidence pointed to her being guilty of this murder, she would be charged accordingly.

The last verbal banter that Heath heard before contact was lost occurred shortly before midnight when a female officer escorting Madison into another room said, "All right, Ms. Greer. Strip down to your undergarments and remove all jewelry."

To which she sighed deeply and replied, "Well, that's plain enough language for me to understand that there is nothing more to be said."

Heath comprehended her double meaning. Madison knew that her ability to maintain the one-way verbal communication with him would be gone, and that she was now forced to once again accept the ordinary moniker of Susan Greer that she so despised.

Regarding her stud earrings, there was no concern, as Heath knew that they would never be suspected by the authorities as being anything more than decorative. However, he also understood that Madison would need to be incredibly careful while removing her ring and placing it into the bag of personal belongings before they took her away. He hoped that she recognized that fact, as it would only add to her troubles if her captors discovered what was housed within the band.

After hearing what he surmised to be the sound of a box lid closing over her belongings, Heath realized there was little he could do for Madison at the current time. Attempting to break her out of jail singlehandedly in the near future would be foolhardy at best, so he understood that his best course of action would be to stealthily make his way back to the United States and attempt to seek help from President Harwell.

47

Solo Return

HEATH AND MADISON had planned on departing for Vancouver from Glasgow at some point soon after the fourth sanction had been completed, but now based upon her current status as being that of a captured killer, he would need to significantly alter those plans. Therefore, Heath returned to their hotel room, packed their respective belongings, and then after a short nap and a shower, he quietly checked out before five o'clock.

Driving south from Dundee across the lengthy bridge that spanned the Firth of Tay, Heath eventually made his way to the Edinburgh Airport in the early morning hours of Tuesday, April twenty-seventh. Along the way, he stopped to alter his look with a disguise and pulled out a Canadian passport to match that appearance.

His reasoning for the altered look, identity, and city for the flight was simple. Heath realized that even though she had no identification with her at the time of the sanction, the authorities might dig deep enough into how Madison, who they knew only as Susan, had come to be in Scotland in the first place. If they were to do that, then it could in turn lead to discovering what identity she had used for entry and if anyone was traveling with her. Fortunately, Heath had nearly all of her belongings with him, including each of her Canadian passports and the one from the United States, so it was a long shot that they would be able to connect her to him. Nevertheless, Heath had decided that beyond Edinburgh, he would also use a different airport in Canada on the opposite side of the Atlantic.

After conferring with the company representative and fabricating a reason as to why the rental car was being returned in Edinburgh as opposed to its point of origin in Glasgow, Heath paid the required extra charge in cash and headed inside the terminal. Then, in realizing that there could be a handful of options throughout the day, he put his name on the standby list for any available flight to Toronto.

Once safely in Toronto that same evening and clear of customs, Heath needed to stay in a nearby hotel for the night. Then early the following morning, he added his name to the standby list for a flight west to Vancouver, where he could pick up the rental car they had driven north from Seattle. Not long after that arrival, he changed to a different disguise before driving across the border into Washington and subsequently returning the car to its rightful place. The duration of time while waiting for an available standby seat on each of the two flights, as well as the drive that followed, had been taxing, but there was still one more leg of the journey to complete before he could attempt to make contact with the president.

Heath once again placed his name on standby for a much shorter flight to Reno, and after finally returning to the Carson City apartment at close to midnight on the twenty-eighth, he wasted little time preparing and mailing off a note to Mrs. Dawson before getting some sleep.

Significantly more detailed than any previous message for the president, it read: *Run scored successfully before player captured. Manager is safe in home dugout but requires meeting soonest.*

Heath knew it would be at least a few days before any reply would come, and he hoped that the president could fit him into his demanding schedule at some point in the near future.

Six days later on Tuesday, May fourth, he received a return note that read: *Glad you are safe, same place and time on 519.*

As with the prior correspondence he had received from the president while waiting for an opportunity at the third sanction, Heath understood the cryptic meaning about the numbers within. It was good news that he would be able to meet with President Harwell privately in the residence on Wednesday, the nineteenth of May, but that also meant that Madison would spend another fifteen days from the present moment in captivity until a discussion involving the possibility of negotiating for her release could even begin.

Heath realized that it would be a waste of energy to fret about that pending timeline, because altering it was beyond his control. Besides, Madison was a big girl who had already spent two and a half years of her life in a federal penitentiary. Therefore, she would be able to take care of herself and cope with her surroundings in the short term.

With that in mind, Heath stopped worrying about how Madison was coping with her internment and turned his focus elsewhere. He knew that, based upon the successful completion of the fourth and final sanction, Jordan Harwell would at least listen to his desire to rectify the current problem when they met face-to-face. Therefore, he began his mental work on the aspect of developing a reasonable plan for her extraction, as well as how he would broach the subject with the president in regard to the safe return of their operative.

48

Dual Convergence

WHILE HEATH HAD been waiting for a reply from President Harwell, the two elder Talbot brothers and their wives had flown back to Seattle from Glasgow on Monday, May third as originally planned. Obviously, the last six days while they were in Scotland were vastly different than what any of them had envisioned, and the portion of the trip that would have included four nights in Edinburgh at a hotel with a view of the massive castle was scrubbed. But after a few visits to an American consulate and after all of the associated legal red tape was waded through, they were able to bring the body of Preston home in the cargo hold of their specific flight.

There were instances during that long flight when each of the four wept either individually or as a collective, but their tears were for a reason that went beyond the pain of Preston's death. In a case of something none of them ever remotely considered, a woman they did not know had taken the first-class seat next to them. While that by itself was not unusual, her presence in the seat that had originally been reserved for Preston was a bit unnerving. It certainly wasn't the fault of that unknowing customer who had sought the available upgrade, nor could the airline be blamed for their business practice of not letting the expensive seat go unused, but it did serve as a constant reminder that, for the masses, his death would be of no real consequence.

Fortunately, that would be far less obvious back in Seattle, as many friends and associates had then turned out to pay their respects at the funeral service and reception on Saturday, May fifteenth. Within those gathered, one man took a private moment to slip Blake Talbot a scrap of paper.

Four days later, with that scrap of paper in hand, and without any way of knowing that Heath would be conversing with President Harwell at nearly the same instant, Blake drove away from his home for a clandestine meeting at the secretive location that was printed on the paper.

Once again, Heath stood in the upstairs residence portion of the White House at the agreed upon date and time and entered the bedroom of the president when instructed to do so. He was prepared with a conceptual plan to extract Madison from Scotland, while also knowing that he must be mindful of how he presented it to President Harwell if he hoped to have the necessary backing.

After shaking his hand enthusiastically, the president motioned toward one of the twin couches and said, "Have a seat, Heath."

Following the instruction, Heath moved toward the couch and said, "Thank you, sir."

Once both men were comfortably seated, President Harwell asked, "So, Heath. I'm aware from your most recent note that the fourth sanction has been completed. That is indeed good news, but can you brief me on what happened afterward?"

While Heath began to apprise the president of the events leading up to the current status of their operative, Blake Talbot pulled into a shopping mall parking lot and proceeded to one specific and nearly vacant corner of it. Once there, he got out of his car and opened the front passenger door of Derrick Walker's larger sedan.

Within seconds, two hands reached from the back seat and gently grabbed his left shoulder as Blake heard both Nelson Eldridge and Terrance Jenkins offer their condolences for the loss of Preston. Derrick Walker followed suit from beside him while reaching out with a welcoming hand, and when Blake then shook the hand of his old acquaintance, he knew that each of the three men in the car could understand his grief. Of course, what had most unfortunately changed since they collectively spoke on the phone just a few weeks prior was that now he could also understand theirs.

After releasing the hand of Derrick, who had given him the scrap of paper four days prior, Blake reached up to pat each of the two hands on his shoulder before the conversation between the four of them began. Within the body of that discussion, Blake thanked his three old acquaintances for their efforts in warning him about the danger to Preston, as well as for showing up for the service and reception. In response, each stated the commonly used phrase of those events being nicely done, along with a wish that they had collectively figured things out sooner to prevent the need for them.

In moving forward, it was agreed by all that Jordan Harwell had more than proved his point. As a result, each of the men vowed to never reveal to anyone what the current president was guilty of, or to inform their wives or family members who had seen the *Staircase696* coded message what the meaning was behind it. Keeping all that information as a closely guarded secret among their tightly knit fraternity of four until beyond the moment of each man's final breath on Earth was the best way to ensure the future safety of their respective families.

At roughly that same moment, Heath was completing his briefing with the president about Scotland, and he closed with, "Mr. President. If you will allow me, sir, I believe that with your help, there is a way to get our operative out of prison and safely back into the United States."

President Harwell raised an eyebrow in response to the statement, and after a brief pause, he replied, "Well, Heath. Although I'm not opposed to looking into that possibility, before we move forward on that path, there may be certain considerations to explore. From what you have told me, your operative is probably not in some rinky-dink holding cell. Therefore, breaking her out of wherever she is may be rather difficult. But based on you stating that there is a way, I can only surmise that you have already put some thought into it."

Although pleased to hear that the president was willing to look into helping him, Heath had also taken note of something else. The president had referred to Madison, who he did not know by name, as "your operative" as opposed to "their operative." That distinction, which created instant disassociation from the president, along with his mention of considerations, implied that the man wanted to keep his distance in the process. Therefore, Heath realized that he could be faced with a larger challenge and would continue to refine his method of extracting Madison from the Scottish prison in the event that the president would be unable to aid him in the endeavor.

In not wanting to leave things as they currently lay, and to perhaps bring the president closer to his way of thinking, Heath replied, "Sir. You need to be aware that I have no intention of breaking her out of prison. If my plan works, then she will walk out freely with me at her side."

49

Interred

BY THE TIME each of those two meetings were simultaneously transpiring, Madison had been interred for the crimes of murder, assault on two individuals, attempted theft of a vehicle, and reckless driving. Of course, the latter two crimes were fairly insignificant in the grand scheme of things, as both had occurred after the first two more serious felonies took place. Arriving at that mindset was due largely to the fact that the family of innocent American tourists who had rented the car had purchased the maximum amount of additional insurance coverage, so the cost of all repairs for the damage caused after it was stolen was fully covered. As a result, the party involved in the accident who now had a replacement vehicle had no desire to press any charges against someone who was already in jail for murder and assault.

After the initial hearing where evidence of the pentobarbital was presented and several people willingly testified against her, Madison remained in custody and was then transferred from Dundee to HMP Glenochil under heavy guard. As a result, that prison just to the east of Stirling had become her new home for the time leading up to, and most probably well beyond, her pending trial.

Unlike her time at Ellsworth in Kansas, inmate Greer quickly learned that she would not be in a private cell with enough floor space to do daily stretching and calisthenics. In sharp contrast to that perceived level of luxury, Madison had been assigned to a slightly larger cell that would be shared with three other women. Beyond that surprising, yet much more common, approach to global prison confinement, she came to realize that the overall conditions of the facility were also not nearly as comfortable as those she had become accustomed to during her former incarceration.

After being escorted to and then stepping into her shared cell, Madison was greeted with a mixed reaction. On the one hand, the three women within were not pleased with the thought of their already tightly spaced area being occupied by a fourth person. But on the other hand, they did find it intriguing that their new cellmate was from across the pond.

As Madison placed her blanket and thin pillow on the lone empty bunk, a woman that would now be one of her roommates said hello and asked, "So what's your name?"

Madison had gone by a handful of names that she enjoyed since the time of her release some eighteen months prior, but unfortunately none of them could be used in this instance. Instead, she would have to revert to the one she despised.

Therefore, she turned toward the woman who had addressed her, and while trying not to choke on her words, she replied, "It's Greer. Susan Greer."

In an instant another one of the women asked, "You don't snore do you, Greer?"

Shifting her gaze in the direction of the voice, Madison replied, "No. At least I don't think so."

"Well that's good. I don't like it when other people snore in here."

Based on that brief exchange, Madison learned who the alpha female was within the group of three. It was pertinent information to have this quickly, and she surmised that the pecking order of the other two would probably become obvious within the next few minutes. As for mounting a challenge to those positions of self-important status, Madison had no desire to do so at the present time.

The following morning, after listening to the alpha occasionally snore throughout the night, Madison got her first look at the exercise yard not long after breakfast. Marching outside with her three cellmates and numerous other inmates, she instantly recognized that the area was significantly smaller than what she had hoped, while also having no running track to help her stay fit.

Knowing that she needed to remain at least partially submissive while learning the ropes of what could and could not be done, Madison felt it was prudent to remain with her cellmates as they began to walk around portions of the yard.

A short time later, she was given a chance to prove that she would not be just another patsy, as a nearby inmate asked, "Hey, new girl. Is this your first time in?"

Shaking her head in the negative, Madison replied, "No."

"It isn't? So then what were you in for the last time?"

Madison had decided during her restless first night that perhaps the best way to survive in this prison was to fully assume the role of Susan Greer. Of course, that meant she would also have to appear to the other inmates like she was guilty of what Heath had originally fabricated for her.

Therefore, without breaking stride, she replied, "I killed three people."

Her response gave the woman pause, but as she was another alpha who could not appear to be fazed, she pressed with, "And why are you here now?"

Madison halted her gait and turned to face the woman as she replied, "The same thing, but this time it was only one."

Of course, the oddity in combining the fabricated history of Susan Greer with the actual crime that had recently been committed was that the number of those slain was factual. Madison had indeed killed four people, with all those sanctioned events occurring in not much more than a year.

Back in the cell, Madison noticed a visible change in how her cellmates viewed her. Although the alpha maintained her status, she almost immediately seemed less harsh in how she communicated with the latest addition to their enclosure. Madison took that as a sign that the woman had grasped a simple strategic concept, which was a good move on her part. The alpha recognized that if she were to be less combative with this new Susan Greer inmate, then it could add strength to her own pack while also making her less vulnerable to attack from either within or from other leaders.

That stance was fine with Madison, and she played the role of soldier moving forward, as it made her life a little more comfortable while she hoped that Heath would devise a way to extract her. However, there was a problem. Under normal circumstances, she would be able to inform Heath of her location via whispering into her stud earrings, but unfortunately those had been taken from her. Therefore, Madison could not be sure that he knew where she was.

50

Follow-up Briefing

HEATH HAD ONLY been able to lay out the general concept of his plan nearly three weeks prior, but upon meeting with the president once again on the seventh of June, he could offer the man a clearer picture of the intricacies within. During those nineteen days since their last face-to-face meeting, Heath had refined several aspects of his plan and felt confident that it could be carried out successfully with help from the president. However, what he was not aware of going into their meeting was that during the same time frame, President Harwell had also put some thought into what he already knew of the plan. As a result, Heath was about to learn what the man had meant when he stated there would be considerations.

President Harwell was impressed by two important elements as Heath specified what his plan for the extraction of the operative would entail. First, he liked how meticulous his protectorate had been in the preparation of how his intended actions, and those of a few others, would develop and transpire. There was even a backup plan in development as an added precaution. As a result, the president now felt as though he knew much more about the plan than at any point previously.

Secondly, he was pleased with how the plan could, if successful, leave no significant tie to either him or the United States. That alone, as with the plan for the sanctioned kills, remained as something of paramount importance to Jordan Harwell. Of course, for that reason there was also great concern because the extreme risk involved could create the exact opposite effect. It was easy to see that many of the essential components of the envisioned design would need to fall correctly into place in order for the extraction to work, and at this time, that seemed unlikely. Nevertheless, as a result of Heath's proposal, the president gave it a few more minutes of due consideration before eventually siding with his previously reached decision.

The ensuing response of the president was unfortunately not what Heath was hoping for, as it was explained to him that it would be problematic, and perhaps even detrimental, for him to support any move forward at this time. Based on Heath's plan, the United States ambassadors to both Canada and Scotland might need to become involved if something were to go wrong, and if that happened, then each of their respective counterparts would most assuredly have something to say about what had been attempted. The president further expressed that any ensuing dialogue between those four ambassadors as to why the woman in question had been in Scotland to begin with, as well as why she committed those crimes while on Scottish soil, would become a fascinating listen for any spectator. Within the course of those discussions, the United States ambassadors would need to explain why the country they represented wanted the woman extradited from Scotland into Canada, along with the added intent of her eventual return to American soil. Then when reaching further into the realm of what-ifs, the president stated that if the covert extraction failed, the cooperation of both Canada and Scotland to create a secretive accord in exchange for certain favors would undoubtedly be required.

However, with all of that stated to Heath, the president still believed that the plan was a sound approach and one that could possibly be successful without any of the aforementioned diplomatic concerns. Therefore, based upon having a steadfast belief in the abilities of Heath to both devise and then orchestrate the intricacies of a plan to its conclusion, President Harwell expressed that he would do what he could to assist with the endeavor. But in order for Heath to gain that support, there would be a stipulation that must be agreed to at the present time.

That mandatory prerequisite dealt with the scheduling of the intended attempt, as it could not be done with the president's blessing until just after the upcoming 2032 November election. Heath was reminded that both of the party conventions would be taking place in July and August, and although the president was in a lame-duck position by having nearly completed his second term in office, there was a significant need for him to avoid any unnecessary negative press for the benefit of his particular party. Should any aspect of what Heath planned to do somehow go sideways and become public, then the subsequent negative press that would undoubtedly arise from it might ruin the credibility of Jordan Harwell and each of the two men who had served as his vice presidents.

In the event that it had been either unknown or forgotten by Heath as a result of his prolonged and still ongoing focus with regard to the four-sanction mission, the president reminded him that his party was already split nearly down the middle and in danger of losing the White House at the upcoming election because of it. He continued by adding that there were two strong candidates within the party who had been fighting it out over recent months, but no matter what any public opinion poll might imply, there was no serious advantage that one had over the other heading into the convention. To then make matters worse, the president stated that he already knew in his heart what many others rightfully suspected. Neither of those candidates would be willing to work together on a joint ticket that could easily defeat the opposition. Both former Vice President Sutherland and current Vice President Flynn had served one term each as Jordan Harwell's second-in-command, and neither wanted to serve in that capacity again while in the shadow of their opposite.

As for his part in the events of the coming months, the president stated that he had handpicked each of the two men to be his running mate at a time when it seemed like the correct thing to do. In the first instance, Sutherland had been a solid choice to help bring in a region of the country that would assure victory, but he had then become antagonistic toward his superior at a time when his unwavering support was needed most. For the second term, Flynn had been the right man to help hold off the former vice president who was mounting a combative charge of his own for the presidency.

Although Jordan Harwell respected each man for various reasons, and he wanted his party to maintain the White House for at least one more term, he expressed to Heath that he could not endorse either candidate to be his successor. Doing so would show undue favoritism while also admitting to a potential lack of proper judgement in previously selecting the other as his running mate. But what made the entire scenario both problematic and potentially detrimental, in relation to extracting the operative from Scotland, was that at this late time in the election cycle, he as the current president could not undermine the efforts of either man by suddenly being viewed by two of the United States' strongest allies, or the rest of the world for that matter, as a man who could not be trusted.

The president concluded his remarks about his stipulation, and Heath completely understood the president's explanation as to why it was put forth. On more than one occasion during the history of the United States, bizarre and sometimes unfathomable complexities in the never-ending political game of chess had been brought to the surface, and this would be just one more example of that construct. Unfortunately, that was a reality that would probably never change.

As to the message the president delivered about the need to shelter his party from the outside, Heath realized why it was so important to the man. But he also recognized that as a result of that protective stance, Madison would have to endure her current plight for nearly five more months. However, in spite of that discomforting thought, Heath knew that the best chance of extracting her would be to verbally agree to the president's demands.

Therefore, as he rose from the familiar couch, Heath respectfully stated, "All right, Mr. President, you have a deal. In exchange for your assistance, I will wait until early November to attempt a rescue."

51

September, Tuesday

EXACTLY ONE WEEK after his somewhat displeasing private meeting with the president, Heath had returned to Carson City on June fourteenth to take care of some business. His task at that time had been to collect everything that belonged to either him or Madison, and then place whatever he thought would not be needed until after the extraction in a storage locker. Once that had been taken care of, Heath terminated the rental of their apartment and forfeited the cash that was required for the remaining portion of the six-month lease that ran through the end of July. Then, with his status of being on special assignment for the president terminated, Heath returned to Washington, D.C., and once again took up his post as the president's primary protectorate.

Since that time, both political party conventions had taken place, with the chosen candidates then being identified and presented to the voting American public for their individual bias of either preference or scrutiny. In the case of President Harwell's party, after a bitter fight and a close vote, the delegates had selected current Vice President Damian Flynn as the man to lead them forward.

Then on a Tuesday morning in late September while Heath stood his post near the Oval Office, the president seized a brief instance when they were alone to ask, "So, Heath. It's been more than three months now. Do you still want to go through with it?"

"Excuse me, Mr. President?"

"You know what I mean. Yes or no?"

It was true. Heath did know exactly what the president was referring to, and his stance on the matter would not change whether it was three days, months, or years.

Therefore, without pause, he calmly replied, "Yes, sir. I do."

The president turned his head toward him and nodded with comprehension. Then before the moment of their solitude would be lost forever, he quickly scribbled something onto a piece of paper and motioned for Heath to approach the desk. With the still unread note clutched in his hand, Heath returned to his post just seconds before Mrs. Dawson entered the room with an update to the daily schedule. At that point, all that Heath could do was slowly and stealthily push the note into his front pocket and wait to be relieved from duty before reading it. Later in the day, Heath finally had the chance to do so, and as a result, he complied with the written instructions by knocking on the bedroom door of the president at precisely seven o'clock in the evening.

After being offered his usual place on the couch, Heath listened as President Harwell said, "So, I understand that you still wish to proceed with the extraction of your operative, and I want to thank you for being patient in waiting until the conditions to attempt it will be more favorable."

"Yes, sir. I would like to proceed because of what she has meant to both of us. Therefore, I believe it's important to get her out as soon as possible. However, I do understand why we must wait."

The president knew how much he personally owed the woman for her efforts in completing the four sanctions, but his previous suspicions of what she might mean to Heath had not been confirmed until the most recent of statements.

But now that he had such confirmation, the president leaned forward to look directly into Heath's eyes, and he asked, "So, then. When was it that you first discovered you were in love with her?"

Heath was surprised by the question, because of all the thousands of daily things that the President of the United States might be concerned with, the potential feelings of a protective agent certainly should not be near the top of the list.

Nevertheless, he owed the man a straight answer, so Heath replied, "Well, sir. To be honest, I think that I may have loved her from nearly the beginning. But unfortunately, those feelings needed to be pushed deep down inside after her attempt on my life. Then with her being locked up for a few years, my feelings for her seemed to fade away. It wasn't until after being in close quarters with her again for a prolonged period of time that they began to resurface and grow."

For the briefest moment, Jordan Harwell was not the president anymore, and it actually felt good to be relieved of the stress. In this instant, someone whom he had trusted with his life for nearly a decade was confiding in him as if he were a brother or a close friend. That man was obviously troubled by the circumstance, and the president wanted to help him resolve it if possible.

However, there was one detail that needed to be clarified first, so he asked, "You mean that our operative, the one you're in love with, is the same woman who tried to kill you nearly five years ago?"

"Yes, sir."

"So then you're saying that she not only recently completed the four kills I sanctioned, but that she is also the one who rolled over on the Tillman organization in January of 2028 to help you and I bring them all down?"

"That's correct, sir."

"Well, I'll be a son of a bitch!"

"Excuse me, sir?"

"Heath, I honestly had no idea that was the woman you claimed would be perfect for the job when we first discussed the four sanctions. Why didn't you tell me this before now?"

"It was a question of plausible deniability for you, sir. The less you knew, the better."

"Well, I can understand that precautionary measure, Heath, and as always I appreciate your efforts in that regard. But without question, this woman has earned my best return effort of freeing her. Now, the timetable of early November that we discussed a few months ago will have to be maintained, but other than that, just tell me what you need."

Heath realized that he may never be presented with a better opportunity than the present moment to broach a subject that he would not bother to discuss unless Madison had successfully completed the required four sanctions. But since she had accomplished the feat, it needed to be addressed.

Therefore, he stated, "Thank you, Mr. President. But before we get into what will be required for the pending extraction, there is one item that you can easily take care of at this time."

"All right, Heath, I'm listening."

"Yes, sir. I recognize that you were lenient with her because of the help she provided in bringing down the Tillman organization, but when I recruited our operative for the mission nearly two years ago, I made a promise to her."

After a pause, the president asked, "All right, Heath. What was that promise?"

"Sir, I promised her that if the task were completed successfully, she would be granted a full pardon for her previous wrongdoings. Now that she has done so, I would like to honor that commitment."

"She wants a full pardon?"

"It was my idea, sir. I felt that it would be deserved when considering what she must accomplish before receiving such a gift."

"I see. But why didn't you mention this to me before?"

"There was no point, sir, unless she successfully navigated the fourth sanction."

"But she didn't do so. She's currently in prison and needs our help to get out."

"Begging your pardon, sir, but she is now in prison because of completing the fourth sanction. Therefore, she has fulfilled the terms that were spelled out beforehand."

For several seconds, the president sat silently while pondering what had been said, and then with a nod of his head, he replied, "All right, Heath. I see your point and understand why it was necessary to put forth that measure of incentive. She can have the full pardon. You have my word on it. Now, let's get back to what you need from me for her extraction."

Heath went back over the main thrust of his plan for the president, while reiterating that from a personnel standpoint, the need was minimal. He even went so far as to mention that he had the perfect individuals in mind to assist with the endeavor. But more to the issue of how the president could make things easier for him, Heath stressed that diplomacy would be vital in obtaining what was needed.

In response, the president said, "All right, so if I can acquire the necessary documents through a secret diplomatic angle, can you and your support personnel be ready to proceed on the day after the election?"

"Yes, sir. The two members of my team and I will be ready."

"Good. Now all we have to do before then is figure out exactly where she is located, but I should be able to get that information without anyone being much the wiser."

Heath was relieved to learn of the president's newfound enthusiasm regarding the pending extraction, and that he had been empathetic when hearing just how important her safe return was. Those secrets of Madison's identity and grander role, as well as his feelings for her, were two topics that Heath was glad to have divulged to the president. However, there was one thing that Heath knew he must keep from the president in the event that the man's feelings of goodwill toward Madison ever changed. Jordan Harwell would never know that Madison had two implanted GPS tracking devices currently in her body, or that because of their existence, Heath already knew her exact location.

52

Countdown of Days

THROUGHOUT THE NEXT five weeks or so during his off-duty hours, Heath continued to refine his plan in several ways that could yield potential benefit. Within the earliest portion of those actions, he had covertly recruited and then secured the promise of future assistance for the endeavor from the two individuals that he felt would be perfect for the task. Then, to bring matters into an even sharper focus, he also included a quick roundtrip venture to Carson City so that he could retrieve some clothing items and the blond wig for Madison in the hope that her future extraction would be successful.

Therefore, when Heath reported for duty on Friday, the twenty-ninth of October while knowing that only five days remained until his plan for extraction would be put in motion, he believed that all of the necessary logistical issues were in order. In his thoughts, everything was ready to go with the exception of the plane that would be used, but that twin-engine corporate jet that was safely parked at a nearby airfield would be repositioned on the night of November second by the two members of his team, with Heath as their lone passenger. At that time, they would make for a non-commercial airfield in Maine before leaving American airspace via their second filed flight plan to St. John's at the most eastern edge of Canada. Then, when fully fueled, the jet would head east toward Scotland on the third and lose five hours in the time zone changes while in the process of flying over the north Atlantic.

Meanwhile, the president had done his part to aid Heath throughout the previous few weeks by covertly collecting on a pair of outstanding markers. First, he communicated a fictitious story to a high-ranking ministry official in the United Kingdom as to why he needed the man's assistance. Being that Britain was still the closest ally to the United States of any nation in the world, and as the man had been skillfully leveraged by the president's knowledge of an event that he preferred to keep secret, he was happy to oblige given a negative alternative. As a result, the required documentation that would expedite the transfer of a prisoner to the friendly Commonwealth Nation of Canada was processed and mailed to Mrs. Dawson at her home address, while a copy would arrive at HMP Glenochil on the third of November with instructions as to the when and where of that transfer.

As for the North American side of the equation, the second marker was collected from a Canadian official who would make it possible via further documentation for that prisoner to be brought into and then through Canada to an unidentified exterior location. However, there was a qualifying term to that temporary access that had to be adhered to in order to ensure that particular minister would feel safe from the threat of future prosecution. He declared that under no circumstances would that prisoner, or those who were bringing her in, be allowed to stay in Canada for longer than the required time to land and refuel before moving on. In addition, once they were through Canada and on to wherever they were going, those persons involved would not be allowed to ever return.

Finally, there was the aspect of what Heath and his team needed in the way of personal documents. Therefore, the same government lab that had been used for all his and Madison's Canadian passport identities was once again called upon. Along with alias names for each, Heath sent that lab recent photographs of himself and the two members of his team. Within a week, he received the fabricated sets of Canadian identification cards and badges that would help them pull off the caper.

As for the president's thoughts on the matter as the date of the election and thus the subsequent extraction attempt drew near, he had digested an undeniable intent within the terms set forth by the Canadian official. Through time, he had pondered the wisdom behind it, and he had come to the logical conclusion that a portion of that mandate could also be applicable for his own self-preservation. Therefore, when the president met with Heath again on that Friday evening prior to Halloween, he informed his protectorate of the two final and most exacting provisions as they moved forward.

Although preempted by the good news that full pardons for the identities of Susan Greer and Madison Sinclare had been taken care of by President Harwell, after receiving from the man copies of the official documents to that end, Heath learned that the most recent provisions the president spoke of would be life changing. Heath was informed that in exchange for those pardons and for the help with the extraction, the first requirement would be for him to resign from the secret service immediately after the inauguration of whoever won the upcoming election. In his opinion, Heath had been the most trusted of personal protectorates during his entire tenure as the chief executive, and the president didn't want to sit in retirement with the thought of Heath providing that noble service to anyone else as of late January 2033. Therefore, he expressed that although Heath had earned the right to be as near to the podium as possible when the transition of power took place, he would have to resign before the day was through.

As for her actions after the extraction, the president stated that he expected to hear nothing of the operative during the nearly three months until inauguration day. That in turn led to the second of his provisions. After Heath resigned on January twentieth, both he and the operative would be required to leave the United States by the first of February and never return. The president knew before stating them that his terms would come as a bombshell, but if willingly agreed to, then Heath could have the green light to move forward with his plan on the day after the election.

Although baffled by the stipulated terms, what Heath quickly realized was that he really had no alternative. It was certainly too late in
the planning process to move forward without first securing the two
sets of documents issued by Scotland and Canada from the home of
Mrs. Dawson later that evening. Nor would it do him any good to remain as a member of the secret service while knowing that he had left
Madison behind permanently. For that matter, what good would it do
him to live a life without her by his side?

Therefore, as he once again stood from the couch, Heath offered,
"Very well, Mr. President. I willingly accept your terms."

53

Reflection and Hope

ALTHOUGH IT HAD never been a big deal for Madison even when she was a child, for some reason those who shared in her current plight assumed that it would be since she was a yank. Therefore, a handful of inmates made it a point to inform her that it was Halloween day. As a result, Madison realized that it had been almost two full years since the date when Heath came to remove her from her protective cover at Ellsworth. That surprise extraction had occurred slightly more than a week after the midterm elections within the United States, so she knew that another election of even greater importance would be taking place within the coming few days. After briefly pondering the media circus that would accompany any given election in America, Madison took a few minutes to reflect upon the various events that had transpired in her life during the past two years.

Moving in reverse order, she began with thoughts of the six months she had been in this Scottish prison, which led to the self-awareness of how different the experience had been when compared to what she now grasped as a relatively comfortable existence in Ellsworth. Madison recognized that swapping locations at this very moment would be a welcome relief, even though the opposite facility was in Kansas.

As for the trial shortly after she began the current stint, there had been solid evidence against her and no way to defend herself against the guilt. Therefore, it was no surprise that a sentence of thirty years had been handed down. Although there had been many instances when Madison wished Heath had been by her side, that was the day that she needed him most to come rescue her. She missed him very much and wanted to hold him, but she knew there was little chance at this point that she would ever see him again. If there had been a way for Heath to learn of her location and get her out, then he would have done so by now.

Turning her retrospective attention to the length of the mission, Madison first thought of her most recent target. It was during her haste to complete the fourth sanction by killing Preston that she had become sloppy at the worst time and was captured. The weird twist in that regard was that by fulfilling the terms of her contract for supposed lasting freedom, she was now faced with a sentence that was ten years longer than what she had already begun to serve back in the United States.

Before Preston there had been Alisha, and the wonderful splendor of New Zealand. Madison had fond memories of the time she and Heath had while on the South Island as they set a trap for their third sanction in the best team effort of the four. She smiled when thinking back to shortly after safely returning from that segment of the mission, as they had on a few occasions nearly consummated their increasing love for each other with intense physical passion. On those few occasions, nothing would have stopped them from moving forward if not for their rationale to postpone the inevitable until after the final leg of the mission had been completed.

Trevor was next in the regression of time, as well as the logistical challenges of targeting him in Peru. He had been the one target that had provided her with the most satisfaction, as he was one of those men who perhaps should have been eliminated long before she did so. Of course, the cost of that second sanction had been Heath mentioning that because of enjoying the kill too much, she might have lost a little piece of her soul in the process. Admittedly so, it was probably true.

Finally, there was Cameron. Her first target within the parameters of the overall mission, and the one that made her feel the most nervous about her ability to carry out the assignment. Although she had previously employed the suggestion of sex as a method to manipulate certain men and women for information or privilege, that sanction was the first instance that she had used the lure of her body to actually kill someone.

Through all four of the sanctions, Madison had felt abundantly grateful for being able to spend all that time with Heath. As a result, she recognized her now deep and unquestioned love of the man who she nearly killed on a New Year's Eve long since passed. There were thoughts of how for roughly eighteen months, they had shared various apartments together in Carson City, as well as of all their high-elevation training at nearby Lake Tahoe. That in turn made Madison reflect on those first few days in Carson City when she was just beginning to learn what it meant to be free again.

It had all started on that day in November of 2030 when Heath had come to rescue her from Ellsworth before offering her a peculiar opportunity. That was followed by the bizarre events that took place in the private jet before taking off, as that tougher-than-nails female copilot had performed a procedure on her body that…

At that moment of recalling a clear and distant memory, Madison suddenly realized that perhaps there was a ray of hope for a way out of her most current predicament. As a slight smile came across her face at the thought of realizing that Heath did indeed know where she was, Madison had to also silently admit that what the copilot had said on that day turned out to be correct. She had indeed completely forgotten through the passage of time that she had two tracking implants, one buried deep into the side of her right breast and one in her left buttock.

54

November Surprise

BEFORE LEAVING CANADA, Heath and his team had learned of the election results in America. The vote had taken many hours to tabulate through Tuesday, the second, and into the morning hours of the third, but eventually a victor in the closely contested race could be identified. Beyond the confines of the United States, there were thousands of expats and millions of citizens from numerous countries in various areas of the world who had viewed whatever available news broadcast there was to learn of the outcome. Although some were pleased by the selection of the woman who would lead the United States into the future, the remnants of one family in southern Brazil could not share in that joy. With the defeat of Damian Flynn, any hope of restoring the power base that the Tillman organization once cherished had completely vanished into the wind.

Roughly twelve hours after the decree, a twin-engine Cessna Citation Latitude landed at the Perth Airport shortly before two o'clock on the morning of Thursday, November fourth. It had just completed a long flight of over twenty-one hundred miles from St. John's, Canada, and after refueling the tanks to their maximum level, the jet would be primed in anticipation of a westerly return once the transfer process was complete.

Slightly to the southwest at HMP Glenochil, Madison and her three cellmates were suddenly awakened at that same time when a bright flashlight beam shined in on them. The probing light swept from the head of one surprised inmate to another until finally fixating onto Madison. Then seconds later, the sound of the cell door unlocking and opening could be clearly heard.

Moving toward the upper bunk of her chosen inmate, the large guard wielding the intrusive flashlight barked, "Inmate Greer, you are being transferred to another cellblock. You now have one minute to collect all your personal belongings and bedding. As for the other three of you, stay in your racks."

The order came as a shock to Madison, but she was in no position to debate the reasoning behind the given instruction. She had learned through time that the guard had previously served as a member of the military police and, as such, was unforgiving to those who tested her authority. Therefore, Madison quickly hopped down from the top bunk, put on her prison-issued tennis shoes, and gathered a few items that she then rolled, along with her thin pillow, into the blanket.

Then, while standing tall with the blanket roll cradled across her forearms, she said to the guard, "I'm ready to go, ma'am."

The guard glanced at her watch, and with a positive nod, she replied, "Only forty-three seconds. That's good, Greer. Now let's go."

With that, Madison was escorted clear of her cellblock and into a waiting area by three officers. At that point, the blanket roll was taken from her as sets of wrist and ankle restraints with lengths of chain attached to a waist ring were put on her by one of the now five guards. That type of security measure was standard procedure for many prison facilities all over the world, and as a result, the restraints would severely limit the mobility of any prisoner who wished to suddenly lash out.

A moment later, Madison was handed something resembling a pillowcase that contained her clothes, ring, and the stud earrings. Then, apart from what had been prison issue after being processed into the facility, the contents from inside her blanket roll were added to it.

She was then loaded into the back of a van, and as it began to drive away, she asked, "Where are we going? I thought you said I was being transferred to another cellblock?"

There was no response from any of the three guards with her except that of a stern glare, and as the driver was sealed in a separate compartment, Madison had no choice but to just sit back and relax. At that early hour of the morning, there was hardly another car on the road, so in well under an hour the van had reached its destination and came to an abrupt halt. The driver exited the van, and a few seconds later, Madison could hear the faint and garbled sound of two voices conversing. She wasn't able to ascertain what their brief discussion entailed, or that the woman who had been waiting for the van to arrive was about to receive her.

As the rear doors then suddenly opened, one of her guards inside said, "All right, Greer. Move along now, it's time to go."

Madison once again followed the directive and gingerly stepped down from the van while a few bright lights shone directly in her face. Attempting to not stumble and fall as a result of the chains restraining her movements, Madison did not realize that her new surroundings were incredibly bleak. Then, in looking up after the lights were moved away from her face, she noticed that they were not at another prison facility. All that could be seen in the cold November darkness was a lone twin-engine jet plane and the van she had just arrived in.

Turning toward the lead guard, she asked, "What is this? You said that I was being transferred to another cellblock."

"That's right, Greer, and you are. But it won't be in Scotland. Now, you hear me well. If you ever do get out of prison, don't come back here. We don't want any terrorists in our country."

Before she could respond to the misguided allegation, Madison heard another female voice from the distance say, "All right. That's enough. Let's just get this over with. But before we take her, we need to make sure that she is clean. Has she been searched?"

Somehow the voice sounded vaguely familiar, but she could not quite place it. Then a few seconds later, she saw the woman approaching from out of the darkness. Her stocky build and the formidable set of her jaw was significantly more recognizable than the voice, and Madison knew from that first glance that the woman was the copilot who had implanted her tracking devices nearly two years prior. With that, she theorized that some type of ruse must be underway, so Madison remained in a submissive posture while waiting patiently for the act to play out.

One guard who held on tightly to Madison's left arm replied to whom she had been led to believe was a member of the Canadian Security Intelligence Service, or CSIS. "This inmate was taken directly from her bunk in the cell to a waiting area and put into these restraints for transfer. Trust me, she's clean."

"Fine, but that's not what I asked. So, let me try again. Has she been searched?"

In recognizing the authoritative presence of the woman approaching, the guard did not dare lie as she answered, "Well…no, ma'am, she hasn't."

"All right, then please do it now before I sign the documents for the receipt of the prisoner. I don't want any surprises if, in the event, she had been sleeping with some type of homemade blade when you pulled her from the cell."

With that, Madison was thoroughly patted down to ensure that she did not possess something harmful, but she did not mind as she was impressed by how the copilot had handled the situation. Had the woman just blindly accepted the word of the guards that their prisoner was clean, then it could have raised suspicion that she was not really who she claimed to be. However, in demanding a search before signing whatever needed to be signed, and in watching them closely after expressing a reasonable concern as to why it was required, she had demonstrated a professional comprehension of what would seem to be the appropriate procedure given the circumstances.

Through all of that, Madison was glad that the crudely fashioned blade she did have had been left in her cell at Glenochil. Since realizing a few days back that Heath must have known of her location during the past several months but had for some reason left her to rot, Madison contemplated suicide via the act of gouging out one of her implants to avoid spending the next three decades of her life in prison. As a result, she acquired the small blade from another inmate in exchange for added protection from a rival, but as there was little opportunity to do so without others being present, she had not yet begun the process of digging away at her left buttock to expose the device for detonation. Fortunately for them, and as it would now appear for her own sake, Madison had vowed after the fourth sanction that she was done with killing. She simply had no desire to take the life of one or more of the inmates along with her own during the explosion of the implant.

When the guards finished patting Madison down and reiterated to the awaiting fictitious CSIS agent that the prisoner was indeed clean of any weapons, the copilot then nodded with agreement and asked aloud, "All right, she's clean. Are we good to go?"

At that moment, Madison heard a more recognizable and welcoming voice boom out, "Yes. We are good to go. But our flight crew has informed me there could be some rough weather ahead, so sign the documents for the receipt of the prisoner and let's get her on the plane."

It took all that Madison had within her to maintain a level of poise and not break down into tears when she then saw Heath emerge from the darkness and walk toward her. For some reason beyond what she could currently fathom, he, like the copilot, was posing as some sort of prison official or agent. However, a fragment of why both were doing so became clear just seconds later.

Stopping within a few feet of Madison, Heath reached out to shake the hand of the lead guard while saying, "On behalf of the Canadian government, I would like to thank you and the Scottish authorities for apprehending and imprisoning this dangerous individual. Based upon her acts of terrorism against my country, we have been attempting to accomplish what you have done for quite some time. You have served Scotland well while providing a great service to both Canada and the Commonwealth as a whole."

The guard gave a slight nod of acknowledgement in appreciation of the comments that had been made by Heath. Then while in possession of the appropriately signed documents that permitted the transfer of inmate Greer to the team of CSIS agents, she prepared to hand over the prisoner. As the female Canadian agent, who those from Glenochil did not realize was also the copilot of the flight crew, latched on to the left arm of Madison, the lead guard allowed Heath to do the same on her side of the so-called terrorist.

A moment later Madison, while still bound in chains, had been guided up the few stairs of the hatch and into the plane. She was then taken to the aft of the interior where there were no windows and was presumed by those on the tarmac to be securely locked to a modified seat with restraining, strong bars. As the sound of the twin, idling engines then ramped up for a taxi to the runway, the shades for each of the windows were pulled down to conceal what was happening inside. Using that brief cover to her advantage, the copilot removed her dark blazer and blouse before quickly covering up again with a white shirt that had three stripes on each shoulder to signify her second-seat rank. Then, in knowing that due to the pilot's location she would be partially shielded from a viewing angle where she might be recognized, the copilot moved into the flight deck and took her seat before the plane could complete a ninety-degree turn to the left.

As they were the only aircraft to be moving anywhere on or near the airfield at the time, the jet was cleared for immediate takeoff by the tower as it rolled away from the van and prison guards. After slowing enough to once again pivot at the end of the runway without coming to a complete stop, the flight crew shoved the throttles forward so the jet could stream away into the night sky.

55

Flights of Deception

HAVING CLIMBED OUT of Perth, Scotland to then set a wester-ly course at the instructed altitude for the transatlantic flight, the twin-jetted Cessna Citation Latitude began cruising at the best pos-sible speed for optimum fuel conservation. Although there were only four souls onboard and the scarcest of added weight from either lug-gage or gear, those on the flight deck wanted to pad the buffer as best they could so that no unwanted problem would occur.

Madison had been unshackled by Heath within minutes after takeoff so that she could be more comfortable for both the lengthy flight and his forthcoming explanation of why he had not come for her sooner. Just seconds after her arms were freed, Madison wrapped them tightly around Heath and kissed him a few times. She realized how dark her life had become without him during the past several months and stated when taking a breath that she wanted him by her side from this time forward.

Heath echoed the sentiment while adding, "I'm sorry that you had to wait so long for extraction, but the delay was beyond my control."

Madison smiled and replied, "That doesn't matter now. You got me out."

During their ensuing discussion of what was planned for the additional flights beyond their current one, as well as what role she would need to play throughout, Heath informed Madison that she would be put back into the chains just before they landed in Canada. Although unfortunate, Madison understood the necessity of the move so that the Canadian customs agents could be fooled.

Within that accounting and reply, Heath noticed that Madison had picked up a bit of a Scottish brogue and commented that the lilt suited her in a way.

In response, she intensified her voice inflection and half-jokingly said, "Aye, and thank ye for the compliment, sir," before returning to her normal voice and adding, "I picked up the Scottish tongue by being immersed in the way the other women in prison spoke."

As the conversation continued, Madison learned that those at the top of the prison system hierarchy in Scotland had been provided with fictitious documentation identifying Susan Greer as one who had escaped justice for acts of terrorism against Canada. In addition, the American government wanted her as an example of correcting a wrong. They were embarrassed for having previously released her via evidence that exonerated Susan Greer from other crimes without knowing that they were holding one of those who had been part of the November 2026 insurrection against the United States.

That in turn led to the discussion of how Madison had been captured in the first place. While Heath thought it was great that she did not compromise him as an asset by running toward him when she exited the hotel, there was a question that begged for an answer.

To that end, he inquired, "Why did you decide to drive away from the scene in the car Preston had rented as opposed to evading your pursuers on foot?"

"I thought if I took the car, there would be less chance of his family members catching up to me during the chase. Things just didn't work out like I hoped."

"But you had no experience at driving on the left side of the road?"

"True. And that lack of knowledge ended up costing me almost immediately."

There was a part of Heath that wanted to say he had tried to teach her the skill of driving on the left while they were in New Zealand, but he thought it would be best left unsaid. Madison was an intelligent enough person to realize that was true without being reminded of it.

As for those flying the plane, the copilot continued to monitor their fuel consumption rate every thirty minutes against how many miles of travel still remained in front of them. With every passing hour, she and her superior pilot felt as though they would be all right with the intended plan, but there may not be much more than two hundred miles of fuel to spare. During the previous flight east from St. John's, Canada, the jet had easily covered the distance required without refueling, as it was more than five hundred miles less than the twenty-seven-hundred mile fuel range of the craft. However, the theory that the same would be true for their return was invalid, as the plane continued to be faced with the ever-present jet stream headwind.

Then with about five hundred miles to go, and fuel for close to eight, the jet encountered an increase in the wind resistance it had already been facing. Unfortunately, the flight crew could not alter their route, as neither Iceland nor Greenland was a viable option. The first was now more distant to the rear than the intended eastern reaches of Canada, while the southern tip of the second, although perhaps safe to land upon, could offer no means of refueling. Therefore, the only option afforded to them was continuing forward in the hope that the now stronger headwind would not completely eat away at what remained of their minimal fuel buffer.

As the time clicked past, both Heath and Madison had been getting some sleep and were unaware of the issue. But as they could do nothing to alter the situation, those in the cockpit remained focused on their task as opposed to creating unnecessary concern by informing their passengers. Eventually, a few faint lights from St. John's could be seen in the distance as dawn began to break in the east behind the aircraft, and the flight crew realized that they would be fine as long as the controller in the tower didn't place them into a lengthy holding pattern for some reason.

Before long, they were cleared for their initial approach, so the copilot got on the intercom and stated, "We will be landing in a few minutes."

With that, Heath moved toward Madison and said, "Sorry, we need to get these shackles back on you. But I promise that they will be taken off again after we leave St. John's."

As the pilot then descended through two thousand feet a few minutes later, he asked his copilot, "Just out of curiosity, how much did we have left?"

The copilot did not conceal the truth as she replied, "Well...we weren't flying on vapor yet if that's what you're asking. But I would calculate that we only had about thirty minutes of fuel left before the engines would have flamed out."

The ensuing customs check by the Canadian officials that had come on board went smoothly, as they believed the authenticity of the credentials that Heath and the flight crew presented that showed they were CSIS agents. In the process, they also observed that Madison, known to them as the prisoner Susan Greer who had been extradited from Scotland, was securely restrained. Then, with the necessary clearance to proceed, the plane was fully refueled for the next intended leg of the westward journey.

Now in full daylight, they took to the air once again, and the flight crew felt much more at ease with what lay in front of them. Although the span of miles from St. John's to Winnipeg was just short of the length that they had already flown, at least the vast majority of the distance would be over land with plenty of alternative landing sites available if needed.

Meanwhile, Madison had once again been unshackled by Heath, and she remained in marginal comfort while either chatting or sleeping throughout the length of their second deceptive flight. Then, when on the initial approach into Winnipeg, he chained her again for the sake of completing the ruse.

As he locked the fifth restraint, Heath said, "This is the last time that I must do this, Madison. Soon you will take on a much more fitting role."

Although not liking the feeling of being restrained again, Madison replied, "I understand."

With the plane then on the ground and rolling toward a side terminal, the copilot broke the protocol of remaining seated until the plane came to a complete halt. Instead, she used that moment of probable safety to enter the main cabin and swap out her flight crew shirt for the blouse and blazer she had worn while on the ground in Perth.

Heath took that moment to say, "All right, Madison, here's what's going to happen."

As she listened closely to what would be in store, Heath explained that he and the copilot were going to escort her across the tarmac to an awaiting van under the guise of transporting their prisoner to the local prison. Should any security personnel stop them along the way, their identification badges as CSIS agents would be enough to get them through because any members of airport security, if encountered, would be unaware of two important things. First, the documentation he carried called for no one to leave the plane, as it was being refueled before venturing on to a location outside of Canada. But more importantly, he had arranged through a cash payment to have the van parked nearby for their needs. As a result, once in the van, the three of them would head for a place where Madison could shower and get changed into the clothes and disguise that would be necessary for the third leg of the trip. While that was transpiring, the pilot would have the plane refueled as he handed in a flight plan to the United States.

Madison understood that the time for her to play another role was fast approaching, and she was glad to have the opportunity to alter her present appearance. Throughout the recent stint in prison, her hair had grown out considerably from the two-inch-long cut she had maintained during the previous four and a half years, and although she planned on allowing that to continue until it reached nearly the length of her final days as Kristen Royce, it was not currently in the best condition for her to pose as someone of professional status.

Therefore, when they did arrive at the location that Heath spoke of where she could shower, Madison wasted little time in peeling off the prison garb that she had been issued before heading toward the bathroom in nothing more than her bra and panties. Fortunately, beyond the shampoo, soap, and towels in the safe house, Heath had brought along a few basic toiletry items, a set of undergarments, some clothes and low heels, and the long, blond-haired wig from her belongings in Carson City.

Not much more than an hour later, the three of them returned to the airport with their respective American passports in hand and made their way toward the plane that would carry them southward. Once aboard, the copilot changed into her flight deck uniform and joined the pilot in the cockpit as Heath and Madison got comfortable in the main cabin. Moments later, they lifted off for a shorter flight to Casper, Wyoming, and as dusk closed in on them, they touched down.

Posing as the wealthy owners of the Cessna who had been on a business trip to Winnipeg, Heath and Madison presented their American passports to the gate agent in Casper and identified the male and female with them who were carrying what little luggage there was as their personal flight crew. Once the four passports were stamped and the group was granted entry into the United States, Heath continued to play the part of being their boss by instructing them to wait near the door as he arranged shuttle transport to a local hotel. Once that was done, the copilot continued to easily carry the suitcase that contained all the chains Madison had been wearing as they headed for the elongated van.

A short time later, two rooms—one for the males and one for the females—were paid for in cash before they collectively headed off to dinner.

Then before turning off the light for some much-needed sleep after a very long and successful day, the copilot asked Madison, "So, at any time during your captivity, did you ever consider it?"

Not knowing what may have been implied by the question, she responded with a puzzled look, "Did I ever consider what?"

"Oh, come on! This isn't some sort of bullshit agency psychological evaluation. It's just us. Now tell me, did you ever consider exposing one of the implants to end your life?"

Until that moment, Madison had not been one hundred percent convinced that the so-called reality of an implant exploding under certain conditions was factual, but now she was. She also understood that the female agent asking her had the same devices inside of her. Accordingly, she deserved an honest answer.

Therefore, Madison replied, "Oh, that. Yes, I did."

56

Safe at Home

THE FOLLOWING MORNING, the flight crew headed back to the Cessna jet as instructed by Heath so that they could prepare for a venture east toward Washington, D.C., where their part in the mission of extraction would end. Per what had been intended from the beginning, the multiple flights from Scotland to eastern and then central Canada before heading south into the United States had gone off without a hitch. For each of those three legs, the pilot had used two fictitious identities of Canadian and American origin that Heath had provided to file the flight plans, and in that regard, the upcoming final leg under his real name would create the disconnect that was needed. When coupled with the nearly eighteen-hour gap between the arrival and departure for their one-night stay in Wyoming, the domestic flight from Casper to near the nation's capital on Friday, November fifth would probably not raise any level of suspicion unless someone really looked into it. Only the tail number registration of the craft would implicate the plane as being linked to international involvement between Washington, D.C., and central Scotland.

As for Heath and Madison, they would not remain with the plane. In breaking from the original plan of flying east, Heath believed it would be best for them to head west on a lengthy road trip. The benefit in that recent alteration was twofold. Beyond avoiding the possibility of a negative element waiting for their arrival in Washington, D.C., Heath would be able to explain to Madison while they had several hours alone just exactly what had been mandated for both of them as a condition to get her out of Scotland. In addition, once they were safe at home in Carson City as opposed to Washington, D.C., she would be able to wait out the next eleven weeks of the laying low period in open spaces, instead of being forced into a means of reclusive hiding.

With a rental car secured from the airport and the Cessna having just lifted off, Heath and Madison began the lengthy drive west across portions of Wyoming, Utah, and Nevada. Shortly after getting onto Highway 220, which would take them to 287 and eventually the junction of Interstate 80, Madison pulled the blond wig from her head and released the pins that had been holding the increased length of her natural hair in place. Then, after putting it in the backpack of her belongings that Heath had brought to her, she began another quiet reflection while enjoying the scenery.

With the fourth sanction successfully completed, Madison rightfully believed that she had met the conditions that had been negotiated for her early release from federal prison. Therefore, she would be free of those past bonds, and thanks to Heath riding in on a steed and rescuing her yet again, she was also liberated from what would have been a lengthier sentence in a Scottish prison. As a result, she could now get on with living what remained of her life as an uninhibited woman on terms that she and no one else would dictate. To that end, the most important of those terms included the immediate plan of marrying Heath once they were back in Nevada.

At the present time, Madison was unaware that Heath had sacrificed the remainder of his intended agency career in order to retrieve her, nor did she know that he would be required to report back to Washington, D.C., for duty in short order, as the special assignment of him monitoring her efforts was now completed.

However, that ignorance, along with the blissful thoughts of how she would live moving forward, was changed quickly as Heath said, "So, now that we will be alone on the road for the next two days, there are a few things that we need to discuss."

Shifting her position so that she could look at him more directly, Madison replied, "Well that's good. I mean…I didn't expect that we would just sit here in silence for hours on end. So, what do you want to talk about?"

As Heath began a detailed account of what they would face, he made sure to conveniently leave out every aspect of President Harwell's involvement. Upon hearing of the requirement for Heath to resign before long, Madison expressed her feelings of regret for him that it would be so. While appreciative of the thought, Heath was fine with the inevitable, as he had freely chosen that he would resign from the secret service within hours after the newly elected president was sworn in. However, in the meantime, he went on to explain to her that his oath of serving Jordan Harwell and the nation would remain intact by him faithfully performing his duty to the best of his ability until that time.

His statement of resolve informed Madison without question that Heath would be returning to wherever the president needed him to be during the upcoming eleven weeks. However, she theorized that most of that time would be spent in Washington, D.C., as there was little need for the man to travel and meet with the leaders of foreign nations anymore.

With that in mind, Madison asked, "And what happens to us throughout the next few months?"

"Unfortunately, we will be apart again for much of it."

"Well, I could figure that part out, Heath! But what am I supposed to do during that time?"

"Anything you want. We will rent you a place in Carson City for the short term, and after I resign, we will look for a new place together."

"Well…all right. But wouldn't it just be easier to find a place for both of us now so that another move is not necessary?"

At that time, Heath informed Madison of the other directive regarding her extraction, which would bring forth exhilaration for the opportunity and a fear of the unknown. Madison pondered the thought of leaving the United States forever, but after a moment of contemplation, she realized that as long as they were on the adventure together, things would probably work out well.

After several hours of driving through southern Wyoming and northern Utah, Heath and Madison arrived in West Wendover, Nevada, where he suggested they stop for the night.

When asked how much longer it would take to reach Carson City, Heath replied, "As long as we don't get any bad weather, about six hours, give or take."

With a hotel room secured, Madison was finally able to convince Heath that in her mind, no other distractions, nor the need to wait for the sake of the mission, existed any longer. They could both relax while sharing a bed for the umpteenth time, as they were free from all constraints.

Therefore, as she slipped out of the last of her clothes and climbed under the covers, she said to him, "Well…it's your move."

57

2033 A.D.

HEATH AND MADISON were married just hours after pulling into Carson City from West Wendover on the night of Saturday, November sixth, and even though they had been separated by a great distance for much of the time since, he had been able to visit her in their short-term rental place for nearly twenty-four hours during the first week of December. That all too quick rendezvous of passion was not much longer in duration than the hours they had experienced as Mr. and Mrs. Bishop within the same location in early November, as Heath was retrieved for duty in the morning on Monday the eighth.

As for the soon to be outgoing President Harwell, he had enjoyed his final Christmas as a resident of the White House while cooperatively doing his part to ensure that the transition of power to his successor, regardless of her party affiliation, went as smoothly as possible. He had taken the time to visit with and thank nearly all of the staff members within the mansion who would continue to work in their positions for the next president, as well as those who would be departing with him. There were some people out there who were saddened that his tenure was coming to a close, while others either felt relief or did not care one way or the other. But no matter how he was viewed during his time as the so-called leader of the free world, maybe simply as a person who they knew, that was in some regards irrelevant. Jordan Harwell believed that the office was grander than any one man or woman, and he realized that, even though he had perhaps used his power in some ways that he shouldn't have, it was time for him to take especially good care of those who had done the most for him.

Therefore, as a post-Christmas gift, Heath was able to enjoy three full days off for a holiday break during what would be his last month of duty. With transportation included in the deal, he used that time wisely by making his way toward Madison as quickly as possible during the closing hours of New Year's Eve. After being dropped off at the Carson City Airport by those who had helped him retrieve Madison from Scotland, he arrived at their place carrying a necessary trinket with a stone setting that didn't twist and shift into a potential weapon of death.

In the meantime, Madison had done what she had been asked to do during the previous eight weeks by using cash for every purchase of groceries or any other needs she might have. In doing so, she was able to maintain a low profile as well as minimize her traceable footprint. In addition, Madison made herself feel healthy again by running and exercising on a regular basis with intense enthusiasm in her effort. As a result, she had recaptured her solid physical form and stamina from the year prior that she wished to maintain.

Throughout that time, she had also ventured to the library on a few occasions to do some research on where they might wish to go at the end of January. She understood that beyond the locations of the British Virgin Islands, Peru, New Zealand, and Scotland, Canada was also not an option. Therefore, she focused on the possibility of someplace in the southern hemisphere.

After a long embrace in the doorway of their place, Heath and Madison stepped inside their temporary place and he presented her with a diamond engagement ring that, had there been time, he would have purchased previously.

Slipping it onto her obviously accepting finger, he asked, "So, it's nearly eleven o'clock. Is there anywhere that you would like to go this evening to celebrate the dawn of a new year?"

"Well, I suppose we could go have a quick drink, and if we find the right place, we could watch the west coast replay of the ball drop at Times Square on the television."

They had done the same thing to usher in 2032 at a pub not long after returning from the third sanction, but as Madison had been laying low for eight weeks, Heath thought that she deserved whatever she wanted. As a result, they walked a mere two blocks to the nearest watering hole and proceeded to watch the broadcast from Times Square in New York City, which signified the dawn of 2033, with a host of total strangers.

After the ball dropped and everyone in the establishment cheered and hugged or shook hands with the closest person to them, Heath asked, "So, would you like another drink?"

Madison smiled as she replied, "Not really. Why don't we just go to bed instead?"

Back in their own space, Heath undressed and climbed into bed, knowing by his internal clock that it was nearly half past three. Nevertheless, as Madison moved into the bathroom, he was not concerned with how much or how little sleep would be coming his way in the next few days.

She emerged after a moment in nothing more than her bra and panties, and while standing a few feet from the bed, she said, "I just bought these a few days ago. What do you think?"

Heath knew that it could not possibly be true, but he could not help having a little fun with her.

Therefore, in response, he said, "You look great in those, but before you come any closer, just give us a little spin so that I know you don't have a knife tucked into the back of your bra."

Nearly three weeks later, Heath took a final ride in the presidential limousine with President Harwell. They were driven from the White House to Capitol Hill, and then the millions of spectators viewing the action via the broadcasts of numerous channels watched as Heath exited and performed one last visual sweep of the area before opening the opposite side door. Jordan Harwell paid the man homage by shaking his hand in gratitude as he stepped out of the vehicle, and then he waved to those citizens within distant visual range before both men entered the building.

A short time later, the procession of political dignitaries, including Jordan Harwell, began taking their assigned seats among those who were already in position for the transition of power, and Heath matched the pace of the president from a respectful, yet dutiful, distance. Among those present were his most recent Vice President Damian Flynn, who had been a whisper away from being the one that would be sworn in to replace the outgoing chief executive, as well as the man who would become the new vice president in a matter of minutes. Heath had not had much contact with the former, as a completely different set of agents were on his detail. As for the latter, in reality, Heath knew little of him or the woman who would replace President Harwell at noon eastern time. His role as a secret service agent was one that paid no attention to political affiliation, but even if he did, Heath had been too busy in recent months to have learned much of anything about which candidate stood for what issues.

Finally, the recently elected leader of the country entered the arena and, in what seemed to be only a few minutes, was sworn in as the new President of the United States. Heath watched as the peaceful transition of power took place with all due respect given to those both exiting and entering. Even former Vice President Flynn remained cordial during the process, although Heath realized that inside, the man must have been asking, "What if?"

Then, after the inauguration ceremony was completed and he subsequently returned to the home office for what would likely have been some new assignment, Heath fulfilled his part of the bargain with the now former President Harwell by resigning to the surprise of nearly everyone in the office. His director, who knew that Heath had been the favorite of Jordan Harwell and had thus been requested for special assignment on numerous occasions, asked if he wanted to reconsider. But much to the director's dismay, the answer was no. Within the next few hours, Heath was processed out of the secret service, and based upon how he had served, he was offered transportation to wherever he wanted to go when ready.

The following morning, while stepping onto a more posh corporate jet than what he had had access to throughout the previous few years, someone asked him, "Where to, Bishop?"

Behaving as if he really didn't have a preference at the time, Heath shrugged and replied, "How about Lake Tahoe? I used to live there."

58

Bon Voyage

ON THE MORNING of January twenty-fourth, 2033, just four days after completing his two full terms as President of the United States, Jordan Harwell sat peacefully in the study of his home that overlooked a portion of the Puget Sound and the Olympic Mountain Range beyond. In what was presumed to be his final flight aboard Air Force One, he and the now former first lady had been brought west from Washington, D.C., to the state of Washington soon after his successor had taken the oath of office.

As he relished in the thought of his attention no longer needing to be tugged in multiple directions on a constant basis, a call from a member of the secret service detail at the front gate interrupted his solitude. Taking the call and acknowledging that the first of his two guests for the morning had arrived, Jordan Harwell understood that in a matter of minutes, he would be able to know if he could breathe easy for the rest of his days, or if an amplified form of persuasion might be required at some point in the future.

Soon, a gentle knock on the door informed him that the answer to his question would be forthcoming, as one of the agents on his post-presidential detail entered and announced, "Mr. President. There is a Mr. Derrick Walker here to see you, sir."

Without standing, he replied, "Yes. Thank you. Please send him in."

Jordan Harwell knew that no harm would come from the man, as long before getting anywhere close to his study, he had already been through a metal detector and an X-ray scan in the event that he had been carrying a weapon. In addition, he had been swept for electronic signatures that could locate a recording device.

The man from his youthful days of college and grad school entered the room and waited for the door to be closed before uttering, "Hello, Jordan. It's been a long time."

"Jordan? Don't you mean Mr. President, Derrick?"

"No, Jordan. You are no longer in office, so the title is misleading, unless spoken by someone who has or still works for you."

Jordan Harwell had to admit that Derrick Walker was not a man who bowed down easily.

Therefore, out of respect for their time together at the University of Washington, he replied, "All right, Derrick. I suppose that's fair. So, what brings you here?"

As that conversation was going on, the second of Jordan Harwell's guests for the morning had arrived and was going through the same security protocols as the former. Once cleared, he then sat in a waiting area where he could see the closed door to the distant study. As he looked around at some of the interior features of the stately home, what flashed through his mind was the last time he had been there. It had been roughly nine years prior when Jordan Harwell was just beginning to gain significant ground for his party's nomination to become the next president. As a result, his superiors had posted Agent Heath Bishop to the man's personal detail leading up to the convention. In the months that passed, a chemistry of comfort between the two emerged, so after Jordan Harwell became the party nominee and then eventually the president, Heath became a permanent member of his protective detail.

His pleasant thoughts of yesteryear were interrupted when one of the secret service agents at the nearby security checkpoint asked, "So, Bishop. What made you decide to resign?"

Looking up, he truthfully replied, "Well…I feel as though I have helped to protect a great man for the past nine years, and even took two bullets in the process. It's just time for someone else to have the glory."

"So you were on his detail for the entire time?"

"Yes, I was, and I first met him in this very room when he was one of three men from the party who might emerge as the candidate."

"No kidding? Well...the service is going to miss you."

"Thanks. In some ways, I will miss it, too."

A moment later, the door to the study opened and Derrick Walker emerged to make his way toward where Heath was seated. With his head hung low, the man who Heath quickly surmised to be roughly the same age as the president made brief eye contact but did not say a word as he passed within ten feet. Neither man who had come to see the former president that morning had any idea as to who their opposite was, or why they were there in the house at nearly the same time, and they had both been instructed to adhere to the time of their appointment. The man who was now exiting the house was intentionally scheduled before Heath in the event that things did not go the way Jordan Harwell wanted, but as they had, the point now became moot.

Nevertheless, Derrick Walker was unaware that he had just passed the man who had been the mastermind of his youngest daughter's demise. Sadly, he had never bothered to ask Emily when in New Zealand, or at any time afterward, about the man who she had been spending time with while Alisha was being seduced by that Nicole person. As a result, he had no physical description that could make him believe Heath was that man. He certainly did not need additional insult to his injury, but Derrick Walker had now at separate times been within close proximity to all three of those who had turned the life of his family upside down.

Only a moment before exiting the study, Derrick Walker had given Jordan Harwell a simple, yet most humbling, message. He had been sent as the representative of the other three men to inform their former schoolmate that he had won the battle. They clearly understood the message that had been sent by the former president, and in return for the promise of leaving their families alone, they vowed to never utter a word of what they knew about his past dealings.

In response, Jordan Harwell had stated that those terms were agreeable to him and extended a hand toward his guest, but Derrick Walker had shaken his head from side to side and refused to shake the hand of the man responsible for killing his daughter.

Then as he turned away, he said, "This will be the last you ever see of me or the other three."

After Derrick Walker left the house, the agent who had been speaking with Heath a moment before said, "We have been instructed that you do not need an escort to the study or an introduction. Just go on over and tap on the door."

Heath did as the man said, and when told to enter immediately, he said in his customary way, "Good morning, Mr. President. You wanted to see me, sir?"

Jordan Harwell smiled as he rose to shake the man's hand, and like those few secretive meetings in the White House residence, he replied, "Indeed I do, Heath. Please, sit down."

"Yes, sir, and thank you."

In recognizing that Heath had arrived with his usual punctuality, Jordan Harwell also realized that there would be no need to ask him if he would perform a final task. It was clear that Derrick Walker and all of the other fathers would be compliant.

With that, he turned his attention to the understanding that, in a matter of seconds, he would be experiencing the last meeting of vital importance in relation to his presidency. Throughout the years, his current visitor had proved his worth and loyalty a thousand times over by faithfully performing his duties as a steadfast protectorate, and in more recent times by taking on the assignment of overseeing the successful completion of four sanctioned kills. No matter what the case, Agent Heath Bishop could always be counted on. Now, in spite of calling in a few high-end markers to help that man with the covert release and stealthy return of Madison after her capture, the former president believed that he still owed him this one last favor for having saved his life from the two bullets of an assassin.

When both were seated comfortably, Jordan Harwell explained from behind his large oak desk that, as much as the earlier meetings to discuss the mission required use of the private residence as opposed to the Oval Office, this rendezvous needed to take place when he was no longer the president. Heath understood why that message had been conveyed and was happy to comply with the wishes of his former boss by conversing in their current surroundings.

Looking directly at his guest, Jordan Harwell asked, "So, Heath, I must know. Was there ever a time when you were able to decode the meaning of the message that I had you and Madison plant on each of the sanctioned victims?"

Heath knew that it was a test and that care must be taken in how he responded for the sake of his own future safety. Fortunately, he had not cracked the code, so even if he wanted to risk exposing what its true meaning was, he would not be able to. For Heath, it became a simple case of plausible deniability in reverse, because he had not put any serious effort into discovering what he did not need to know.

Therefore, he could truthfully respond, "No, sir, I didn't. I did eventually come to understand what the numbers may have represented based upon your notes back to me when I requested face-to-face meetings. For the first one, you wrote 927, which I took to mean just a few days from when I received the note. You were prepared to speak with me at that time, so it was logical for me to believe that grouping the month and day together was your intent. That method continued with the notes regarding our other meetings, and as a result, I recognized the pattern. I knew that 696 couldn't be a month and day but based on my belief in your established pattern of using the grouping of numbers, I surmised that it symbolized a month and year. Therefore, something about June of 1996 could have been one aspect of your coded message. But, as for the word of staircase that was next to the numbers, I have no idea, nor do I care what that might refer to. That was meant to be something that only your intended sanctioned families would understand, so I left it at that."

Jordan Harwell smiled across at Heath while nodding his head as the one nagging question throughout the entirety of the mission was addressed. He felt secure that Heath was telling the truth about not completely breaking the code and not caring to do so. Knowing the month and year of some random event meant nothing in the grand scheme of things, especially since Jordan knew that he was the one of the five men that was innocent through it all. Heath would never learn of what transpired, or the location among millions of possibilities.

With that peace of mind established, Jordan Harwell pulled a large envelope from the top drawer and set it down on the desk in front of Heath as he said, "That's all I needed to know, Heath, and thank you. But now I want to show you my appreciation for all that you have done, both in the line of duty and in functions that went beyond it. This should be enough to get the two of you started."

Without even opening the envelope, Heath surmised what was inside, and in reply, he said, "Sir, this is completely unnecessary. I don't expect anything from you for doing my duty, and you can count on me to keep my word without any kind of extra incentive to do so. As per the terms of our agreement for the safe return of Madison, she and I will leave the United States as promised within the next week and never return."

"I know that you will, Heath. You are a man of your word who has just spent many years living in a world of those who have no concept of how to keep theirs. You have passed more tests of loyalty to me than most people could ever imagine, so please understand that this is not intended to be a payoff that will ensure your silence. Instead, try to think of it as a tax-free, one-hundred-thousand farewell severance for actions above and beyond the call that will help you and Madison to establish a secretive new life together."

Heath stared blankly at the envelope for a few seconds, and then replied, "I don't know what to say, Mr. President. This is extremely generous of you."

"Not at all, Heath, you have more than earned it."

"Well…thank you, sir. We will try to put it to good use."

"I'm sure that you will. And do you have any idea where you will go?"

"Yes, Mr. President, I do. But in the interest of maintaining your plausible deniability, as well as the continued safety for both me and Madison, I believe that it is best if you don't know the answer to that question."

As Jordan Harwell rose again to shake the hand of his most trusted protectorate, he nodded with comprehension and said, "Well then, I guess this would be the time when we part ways. But I do have one small favor to ask before you go, Heath."

"Certainly, sir, what can I do for you?"

"Will you please call me Jordan as we say our goodbyes?"

Heath looked at who had been the most powerful man in the world for the previous eight years and noticed that there was a bit of a tear welling up in his eyes. He had to be experiencing a measure of fear of what lay in front of him during the upcoming days, weeks, months, and years, as many of those who once sought his attention and praise would no longer be around to vie for it.

While comprehending that the president had done him a tremendous favor by secretly orchestrating the release of Madison, as well as that he also thought enough of Heath to provide safe passage out of the country and a financial stipend, Heath would have done nearly anything asked of him to appease the president in their final minutes together. As it was, the request by the president would be most easy to accommodate. But in also sensing that something beyond being called Jordan was what the man craved at that moment, Heath once again showed his loyalty by relieving the pressure of his former boss in needing to ask for it himself.

Stepping forward slightly, Heath replied, "Absolutely, Jordan. I consider this a great honor to address you by your given name. But I have a return favor to ask."

"What's that, Heath?"

"As we say bon voyage, it would mean the world to me if you would accept a hug as well."

59

Curtain Call

WHEN HEATH RETURNED to Carson City from Seattle so that he and Madison could complete the last of the preparations to permanently depart from the United States, he realized that there would no longer be any need for concern over their collective safety. Upon reflection, Heath recognized that his current mindset represented a significant shift from that of his previous viewpoint. In the aftermath of her capture, the now former President Harwell had demonstrated through his so-called considerations that he would potentially want to leave Madison in prison to rot. Based solely upon that, Heath had entertained the possibility that, due to his firsthand knowledge of the intent and execution of four sanctioned kills, the man could even dispatch another operative to eliminate him.

That viewpoint was altered when the president then put forth an effort to help with her extraction and safe return to the United States, but Heath maintained a cautious stance. He understood that his boss may have done so only to prevent Madison from spilling her guts to her captors as she had done years prior with regard to the Tillman organization. Even though the president had no need for such concern, it was at that point Heath worried for her safety, more so than the time when she was interred in Scotland. After all, the president was still in power at that time and she was now in-country. However, silencing Madison would have been unnecessary, as she had never learned that the president was the one behind the entire operation. Nevertheless, he could have come after her in some way while Heath was back in Washington, D.C., protecting him from harm. Therefore, based on that ironic circumstance of Madison's vulnerability, Heath had hidden her in Carson City while asking her to lay low until after he resigned, and then they could make their escape.

All of that seemed rather misguided in the present, however, as Jordan, who Heath could now call him, had given them a substantial financial gift as a bon voyage to begin a new life together. Although the origin of the one hundred thousand dollars would never be revealed to Madison, as doing so would potentially expose who wanted the sanctions carried out, Heath believed that the money would provide an opportunity to explore portions of the globe without needing to plan out another sanction.

In keeping to their promise, Heath and Madison began what they considered to be a long overdue honeymoon on Sunday, January thirtieth while on a quest for what would soon be their permanent home somewhere in the southern hemisphere. Based on completing one of the sanctions in New Zealand, it could not be considered for the time being. But as the neighboring Australia had only been used for flights while transitioning both to and from New Zealand, it appealed as a serious contender. However, before making their way to Brisbane and the numerous points beyond, they decided to begin by traveling where most things were generally less expensive. Except for Peru, which could also create an unwanted problem equal to New Zealand, Heath and Madison began sightseeing their way through various regions of the South American continent. Then, at one point roughly ten days into that exploratory February, they ventured into the small coastal city of Praia Brava in southern Brazil for at least a two-night stay.

The following late morning, they were strolling through the large, central marketplace, and like hundreds of other folks, they were sampling some of the available food and craft items that they found to be intriguing. Heath and Madison were having a wonderful time and never thought that they might eventually encounter another serious care in the world.

Having entered from the opposite side, a young and attractive American woman of twenty was on her weekly walking expedition through the large, central marketplace with the elder female members of her family. After what had been about thirty minutes of meandering from one vendor to another, she spotted Heath from a distance of roughly fifty feet.

Turning to her mother, aunt, grandmother, and their longtime female family confidante, she said, "Wow. Now there's a man that I should get to know. Y'all might think that he is handsome, but I would go with hot!"

After shifting her gaze toward her daughter, Courtney Tillman replied, "Oh, come on now, Jennifer. We all realize that you are constantly on the lookout for a man. But with so many of them here at the marketplace, we don't know which one meets your fancy at this particular moment. Perhaps you could let us know which of these men you are talking about."

With a subtle nod in the general direction, Jennifer said softly, "That one right over there with the dark hair and light-blue button-up shirt next to the woven baskets."

Quickly locating the man, Courtney studied him for a few seconds and said, "Hmmm. Well I do have to admit, Jennifer, you're right. He is a good-looking man."

With a measure of subtlety, the other three ladies then joined the pair in a collective gaze, and something occurred to each of them. For some reason that they could not quite put their finger on, the man of Jennifer's fancy looked familiar.

Then a few seconds later, Ms. Holloway said, "I think I recognize that man. Where do we know him from?"

Victoria Tillman rarely forgot a face, which had been a useful tool for her and the needs of the Tillman Empire throughout the years when she and the family were creating and entertaining new business associates.

As a result of that skill, she solved the riddle by stating, "I'm afraid that we know him from a visit he once made to our home in Crockett."

Courtney then exclaimed, "What! Are you sure?"

"Yes. I remember it well. That is agent something or other who came to inform us that Domonique had been killed."

Courtney took another look and said, "You mean Agent Bishop?"

Victoria then grasped the shoulder of her daughter-in-law and said, "Yes, Courtney. That's his name, and thank you. Now, I wonder what he is doing here in Praia Brava, of all places."

Ms. Holloway interjected with, "Perhaps the larger question for us to investigate is why the woman with the long brown hair in the yellow blouse is so friendly with him?"

Releasing the shoulder of Courtney and leaning toward her longtime confidante, Victoria whispered, "Maybe she's his girlfriend or wife."

"I think the latter based on the rings, which is unfortunate. I remember her as being one of our former operatives that labored for our interests in Washington, D.C."

Victoria took a closer look at the woman in question, and while spotting the diamond ring and wedding band on her left hand, she replied, "I don't recognize her. Are you sure about that?"

"Oh yes. Samuel and I had detailed biographical files that included a few photographs of each of our numbered operatives and those who worked for them. That woman reported to number twenty-nine, and if I remember correctly, her name is Kristen."

"But if that's true, then why is she here?"

Ms. Holloway mimicked the gesture of leaning in toward her longtime friend and said, "I'm not sure that's the question we should be asking, Victoria. But the fact that she appears to be married to the man who brought down our organization could put our minds at ease while also answering the most important question of all."

"And what's that, Ms. Holloway?"

"I think Jennifer just accidentally stumbled upon the proof we needed to clear Beau of what we all hoped was not true. And in the process, we have also learned who the actual traitor was that brought down our organization."

About the Author

Within the course of his high school years, Kurt wrote articles for the school newspaper before embarking on his university experience as a journalism major. After eighteen months along that path, Kurt spent a semester backpacking through Europe on a few dollars a day just as many in his age group had done. The multiple cultures, history, art, and languages throughout the continent made a lasting impression on him, which fueled his desire to explore even more of what was out there. Kurt subsequently left university life behind him and began a few different careers that enabled him to live in and discover what various regions of the United States had to offer. Unable to escape the allure of his writing or storytelling, Kurt quickly began to develop journals of his adventures. Those scribblings provided him with an excellent foundation for future reference, and once he began writing them, he never stopped.